Praise for *T*

~ The movie in my head had all the
Do read this and g
~ Andrew Barrett paints vividly   _ …disturbing)
pictures with every keystroke.
~ An utterly absorbing story of what might be.
~ A strikingly good police procedural.
~ Andrew Barrett is a master who has earned a new lifelong fan!
~ Real life characters who are believable and interesting, great plot
and a read that easily compares with Jeffrey Deaver, Lee Child, James
Patterson, Patricia Cornwell and all the big names.
~ This is quite the most powerful and enthralling thriller that I have
read for some time.
~ A wonderfully clever entertaining read.
~ Good conveyance of the feeling of being hunted and not knowing
where was safe.
~ I challenge anyone reading this book to fail to become influenced
by the story and characters.
~ A cracking, well-paced political thriller which I literally couldn't put
down.
~ Truly chilling as it doesn't seem that far-fetched from reality.
~ One particular incident that happens to Eddie and his family was
quite literally heartbreaking. The chapters to do with it, I found to be
really raw in the way it had been written and quite often I would find
tears streaming down my face.
~ A truly amazing and well written book.
~ I absolutely loved the writing style - clever but straightforward.
~ I find myself often thinking about it and the storyline, haunting me
if you like. I'm sorry that it's behind me because I'd like to read it all
over again.

The Third Rule

CSI Eddie Collins Series: Book One.

By Andrew Barrett

Prologue

January

The next few minutes were the last normal minutes of Eddie Collins's life.

At ten-thirty on the evening of Thursday January 15th, he slammed the car door, and shivered the key into the ignition, glad his shift was over. As he drove away from the police station, icy gusts whipped overhead telephone wires and hurled sleet against the fogged windscreen.

He stopped shivering at the end of Bridge Street, and turned left towards the dual carriageway that would take him to his motorway junction. He checked the dashboard clock and expected to be home before eleven, cuddling up with Jilly by half past.

But Eddie was wrong.

As he picked up speed, the houses on the left became a dark grey blur, and he was about to relax and fill the car with some Pink Floyd when something caught his eye. In the orange hue of a street lamp, he glimpsed a woman sprinting along the snowy footpath. A man dressed in black chased her. One more glance, before the scene was behind him, showed Eddie that the woman was screaming.

He forgot about the music and tried to see them in his rear-view mirror. But they were just grey shadows among grey shadows, turning streetlight-orange every fifty yards or so.

As the road opened out into a dual carriageway, he approached a gap in the central reservation, and he approached a junction in his life, a choice: do nothing, or do something. He indicated, turned and drove back the way he'd come, white knuckles on the black steering wheel. The sleet came heavier and the sky darkened further. There was no other traffic in sight; the road and the situation were all his.

There they were up ahead to his right. A man chasing down a screaming woman. Eddie couldn't take his eyes away from the terror on her face. Her hair flowed behind her, yet there were wet curls of it flattened against her forehead as though frozen there. In her right hand she held a bag, and Eddie knew that's what the man wanted.

He slowed and turned in the road.

She glanced over her shoulder and the man pounced.

Now from behind her, Eddie saw them land in a heap on the freezing, wet footpath, and imagined her face grazing along the slushy tarmac. For a moment, they were a tangle of arms and legs, but from the tangle emerged the handbag, and the robber ripped it free.

He slammed on the brakes only yards away and her crumpled shape turned white in the headlamps. The coldness and the sleet stabbed Eddie as he leapt from the car, ignoring the audible alarm sounding, *door ajar, door ajar* – and ran towards the woman. She lay in a heap on the wet pavement, her clothes soaked, her skin pale and wrinkled like that of a corpse pulled from a lake.

She tried to stand, and the light caught the pain in her eyes and the wet snotty face; it caught the string of saliva whipping from her mouth.

A million thoughts ripped through Eddie's mind: he was going to be late home if he didn't hurry, and Jilly would be worried about him. And then he wondered about his car, door open, engine running, and an awkward conversation with the insurance company coming his way. "How could you be so stupid, Eddie?" Jilly would shout, and he could say nothing in his defence because it *was* stupid. How many people would interfere with a street robbery these days?

As he helped the poor woman stand, only one of those thoughts caught his attention: *get her in the car and get her out of here.*

But that wouldn't be an end to it.

Eddie guided her into the front seat. He climbed into the wet driver's seat, closed his own door, and set off after the madman.

The woman cried. From the grazes along her right cheek, tiny spheres of blood grew and dribbled down her wet face. Her hair hung in black strands across her shoulders, and steam rose from her trembling fingers.

In between shivering sobs, she said something; might have been *thank you, kind sir*; or, *why didn't you get here earlier, asshole*; or it might have been, *shouldn't you call the police?* He didn't know. All he knew was that he was gaining rapidly on the man in black.

Eddie stamped on the brake, told the injured woman to stay there – actually shouted it at her – and then leapt from the car again. His feet patted through the glossy wetness on the pavement and ran through the orange streetlight, mottled with falling sleet, chasing down the man who had chased down the woman. His trousers were shiny and wet, and the wind ripped into his legs as though he were wearing nothing but a pair of shorts. His hair was a mass of freezing water that drained the heat from his head, and dripped inside his collar. His ears ached, his cheeks were numb, and the cold air rasping into his lungs felt like he was smoking an industrial blowtorch.

He shouted to the figure, but the figure kept running. Eddie was gaining when the man ran down a shallow grass embankment covered in patches of snow, before slipping on his arse, sliding towards a low wooden fence that gave out onto some industrial units under construction. He kept hold of the bag, though.

Eddie's feet now pattered through freezing grass and slipped on the mud at the top of the embankment. Still there were no other cars around. No one to help.

The man turned, knowing he was trapped. He looked around, head flicking from side to side, and saw that he had two options: hop over the fence and become stuck in a building site quagmire, or run along the fence-line until he came to the motorway. Eddie closed the distance down, and shouted, "Hand it back, arsehole!"

The man stood his ground.

Eddie edged down the slippery embankment, and the man turned out to be a skinny rake of a kid probably only twenty years old.

Eddie felt uneasy. The kid should be shouting his submission by now, he should be scampering up the embankment trying to formulate some kind of deal: *Hey, mister, give the lady her bag back, and we'll call it quits, okay?* Or, *I'll leave the bag here and walk slowly away, you don't follow, and then everyone's happy.* It didn't happen.

At first Eddie thought there was fear in the kid's eyes. But it wasn't fear; it was laughter. The skinny rake of a kid was laughing at him.

Why would he laugh? He was cornered. *He would only laugh,* Eddie thought, *if he had the upper hand.* Why did he think he had the upper hand?

And then Eddie's world shattered.

May

Of the whole affair, the *London Tribune* said:

If proof were needed that the Offensive Weapons Amendment Act 2007 was little more than a toothless tiger, the events of Friday morning in Victoria Underground Station thundered it home with irreverent bluntness.

At first people thought it was a terrorist attack. Bystanders were shot down in a hail of fire not from some inhuman terrorist, but from one of their own. Terence Bowman was a stockbroker of repute...

...and he was a man going places. At least he was, until the doctors had told him he would be wasting his deposit if he booked a winter holiday this year.

Just enough time had elapsed for him to accept that he was going to die, when a stranger approached him. That stranger was a big man with broad muscular shoulders, a man who didn't really have a neck to speak of, just a head and then a body. The stranger had a proposition for him.

Terence took eight days to agree to that proposition.

And this was the result. Friday morning, rush hour in the capital, standing room only in the claustrophobic station where the bustle of people and their smell was overwhelming. Terence Bowman was still a man going places, though today he would be going to hell, the direct route.

He stood on the platform awaiting the 07:32, palms sticky, forehead a clammy mess, and a mild tremor radiating through his body from the heart outwards. Terence filled his lungs with the sour air and wiped tears from his cheeks.

Inside his holdall, in the place usually reserved for his sandwich box, was a killing machine: Glock 18C semi-automatic pistol.

It was time to make his family's future secure, the stranger had said.

Before he knew it, his hand curled around the Glock, and because of the next two and a half minutes, Terence Bowman's name would become infamous as the event that felled a government.

He could hear the approach of the train.

Terence dropped the holdall and pulled the trigger. He held it tightly and turned around quickly, almost majestically as though in a waltz.

For him, the world grew calm and quiet. He squinted as flecks of warm flesh spattered his face. The silent screams of those fleeing were the accompaniment to the Glock's rhythm, and the waltz grew quicker.

In reality, the noise was enormous; pandemonium reigned as a red mist showered those a little further away.

The last of the rounds left the muzzle. Shell cases tinkled onto the floor. A ripple of heat from the gun wafted into the air. Terence stepped off the platform into the path of the 07:32.

...police are baffled by the killings. Twenty-three people died in the massacre. It brings the total of gun-deaths in the UK to 228 this year, eighteen per cent up on last year.

It is time for Labour to move over and give the opposition leader, Sterling Young, and his shadow Justice Secretary, Roger King the chance they have so vehemently sought. Gun crime is the most feared crime in Great Britain, and it will take a new administration with radical policies to tackle it.

The Yorkshire Echo.

Great British Independence Party victorious
"We're getting out of Europe," says PM Sterling Young

By Michael Lyndon

IN A wave of euphoria usually reserved for rock and film stars, Prime Minister Sterling Young was driven through London yesterday and took up residency in Downing Street.

A spokesperson for the party said: "Sterling's first job is to extricate UK from the claws of European servitude. This country has long needed to be its own master again, and G-BIP has set in place the necessary elements to bring about that new freedom."

He went on to say: "And then the real work can begin: that of fighting crime. And who better to lead that fight than the newly installed Justice Secretary, Sir George Deacon who recently replaced the late Roger King."

Roger King MP was murdered outside his Kensington home three weeks before the general election. Some sceptics still ponder the so-called sympathy vote caused by him being shot dead in front of his family.

"If you want to kill serious crime, you have to kill serious criminals."
Sir George Deacon

Chapter One

Friday 29th May

When he came to, the brandy bottle lay next to him. His cheek was wet with liquor, the crushed cigarettes were a murky brown colour floating on the small pool next to his face. Eddie closed his eyes tight. Anything to stop the tears.

You're a drunken twat.

Words spoken by Jilly weeks ago – months ago. The scar on his left leg ached.

Yes, he was in a bad state, but his problem was infinity; his problem was time running along the x-axis versus stress running along the y-axis. But there never seemed to be time without stress. Stress was a constant.

Only the end of time could stop it all. But what use would sobriety be to him then? Who cared if the guy in the coffin was pissed or not?

* * *

It was after nine on Friday morning and Eddie, stinking of brandypuke and piss, sank into a cool bath, cigarette dangling from his mouth. This was Eddie's existence: going to work, coming home, and getting slaughtered.

Actually, that was a rather simplistic résumé. "Home" was about five miles from this yellow-stained bathtub. He looked around the grey room, at the mould in the corner by the window, at the torn linoleum that always seemed to squelch underfoot, and listened to the cistern's overflow dripping water into a bed of moss in the yard around the back. This flat over a carpet shop in Wakefield city centre was just a stopgap. It was ninety quid a week and it was somewhere to get pissed and ignore the x-axis.

Yes, Jilly was five miles away, and their son, Sammy, would have spent last term at school sharing disaster stories with other kids whose folks had split up. Eddie smiled at the thought of his boy. Another couple of sleeps and they could spend the day together, pretending none of this had ever happened, pretending to be a real father and son.

He had never felt so alone. "Have you told me I'm wonderful today, Sammy?" Eddie's voice echoed.

Sammy's eyes would roll upward and he would tut before saying, 'Daddy, you're wonderful'. They would laugh and roll around on the floor tickling each other.

His smile spilled off the side of his face as thoughts turned to Jilly. She was a wonderful woman, a superb mother and actually quite an artisan in the bedroom. Another tiny smile ruptured Eddie's lips and then vanished as though it was an absurdity it ever having been there. She was a bitch too. It wasn't her fault, though. It was his.

The next part of the résumé, the going to work part, was reasonably accurate. He was a CSI for West Yorkshire Police. It was a civilian role, a good job that was sometimes exciting and sometimes so infuriating he would reach for the job paper – and then put it back. He couldn't do anything else. Didn't really want to either.

The only truly accurate piece of the résumé was the getting slaughtered part. He did it on a regular basis. He liked to be regular, did Eddie. Though last night's effort was a little more extreme a slaughtering than normal.

A knock came at the door, forcing Eddie back into his own private existence. The bath water was cold. "Bollocks!"

The knock came again.

He climbed from the tub, winced at the pain coming from the scar on his leg, slung a towel around his waist, and squelched across the lino and out into the lounge again, heading for the door. "Who's there?" The smell of puke lingered large and loud.

"Me."

Eddie turned the key and went to the kitchen. "Cuppa?"

"Phew! Jesus, Eddie." Ros stepped in and dropped a parcel on Eddie's crumpled sofa. "You are disgusting."

"Yeah, sorry." He grabbed the kettle. "Heavy night."

"Really?" Ros grimaced. "Oh God. Now I can smell piss."

"Yeah, sorry. Like I said—"

"I know, I know." She stepped into the kitchen, and cringed at the greasy hob hiding beneath frying pans, at the crusty plates in the sink and stickiness on the floor. "You have to sort your life out."

Eddie nodded solemnly and sprinkled coffee in two mismatched mugs.

"Don't patronise me when I'm trying to lecture you."

How come the stress levels always curved upwards against the y-axis whenever there was a female around?

"You'd better do something radical, Eddie, or else grow wings and a halo."

He shrugged, and sat on the sofa. "I'm sick of it." He raised his eyebrows, tried to smile, "I want to be back with Sammy…"

She paused before saying, "I sounded like Jilly just then, didn't I?" She perched on the edge of her seat, elbows on knees. "I'm sorry, I didn't—"

"You coming over tonight?" Eddie changed the subject as easily as turning the page of a newspaper.

"Is Mick?"

Eddie shrugged.

"He is, isn't he?"

"No. I don't know. Maybe. Yes. He'll be here at six."

Ros giggled, sipped the coffee. "Count me in."

"Thought you didn't like him."

"But I *do* like you. He's an alky and you need all the protection you can get."

"Protection? From what?"

"He's a bad influence. He's on his own and he wants to see you on your own too, so you can be on your own together." She reclined in the seat. "He's jealous of you."

"Who, Mick? Naw."

"He messed up his own life, Eddie; and all he can see in you is another sap like him. And what's worse than going through life as a sap? Going through life as a sap on your own. He's happy to see you wreck any chance of getting back with Jilly."

"He's not smart enough to think like that."

Ros shook her head, "Your only hope of getting together again rests with you quitting the booze. I've seen how she looks at you when she smells alcohol on your breath. Her eyes turn to hatred."

Eddie stared at the curtains.

"I'm sorry I said that." She cleared her throat, "But if you ever want to be Sammy's dad again," Eddie flinched, "then you've gotta pull your head out of your arse and take a break from drunken sleepovers with Mick."

"Stop beating around the bush and say what you mean."

"You remembered why I'm here yet?"

It didn't take Eddie's eyes long to fill with dread. "Sammy!"

Ros smiled and slapped her leg. "Got there in the end."

"Oh fuck me."

"Appreciate the offer, but if you're late again—"

"Oh bollocks."

"And you owe me 200 quid." She pointed to the parcel.

"What would I do without you?"

"Drown in your own vomit, I suspect." She wasn't smiling now.

"And you wrapped it too. Thanks, Ros."

"I got a card. You'll need to write it though; you ought to do that bit yourself."

Chapter Two

Friday 29th May

Henry was late.

He didn't even know where Beaumont Drive was, for Christ's sake! He looked at the satellite navigation screen in the Jaguar's dashboard, at the cracks running through a rainbow of crushed liquid crystal, and regretted not being calm enough last month to stop the car and turn around when the friendly female voice told him to.

It was Friday morning and the traffic into Wakefield along Leeds Road was heavy and slow moving. Strangely, the traffic coming out of Wakefield was light and fast. Henry groped around the leather passenger seat for the phone; his eyes sharing their time between the road, the search for the phone and a chance encounter with a pen.

His morning schedule was busy; he had five appointments booked, and there was no way of servicing more than four without appearing hurried—

"Shit!" Henry stabbed the brakes. Everything on the passenger seat slid into the footwell, and the nose of the Jaguar stopped but an inch or two from the Fiesta in front. The driver shook his head. Henry screamed, "Tosser!" All that for a phone.

And then the phone rang.

Henry grew increasingly agitated. The phone continued to ring. Where the hell was Beaumont Drive? It was now ten o'clock and the need to relieve himself had developed from nowhere. The phone still rang and Henry, foot on brake, leaned into the passenger footwell and fished about under paperwork, pulling crossword puzzle books, colour brochures and letterheads aside in his haste to answer the damned phone – the damned phone he needed in order to find Beaumont Drive. The traffic moved on. The need to pee grew. And then, just as he saw the phone, just as he reached that little bit further, a cramp grabbed his left side just below the ribcage.

Behind him, a horn sounded. He peeked up over the dashboard, and noticed the Fiesta was a good forty yards away. He released the brake and the Jag rolled. The phone still rang and he lunged for it, caught it, sat upright – teeth bared against the cramp, and nearly slammed into the Fiesta for the second time in only two minutes.

"Fuck!" he shouted. It was 10:05, precisely 300 seconds late for his appointment. He pressed okay, held the phone to his ear, and listened to the sound of an empty piece of plastic. "Bastard!" Why did that happen? Why did they always ring off when…

Henry grew hotter. He pressed the AC switch, and though the light in the centre of the dial illuminated, nothing happened. He breathed deeply of the fumes coming through the vents and called the office. The traffic moved again slowly, more horns, more heat, a growing concern in Henry's bladder section, and nobody answering the phone in the office. What was wrong with—

"Smith, Pryce, and Deacon, how may I help?"

"At last," Henry said. "Listen, Julie, it's me—"

"Henry, is that you? Henry?"

"Yes, it's me, Julie."

"I can barely hear you. You'll have to—"

"Can you hear me?" He couldn't remember booking the day from hell, surely that was yesterday, wasn't it, when dear old Daddy laid down some new rules. *That* was the day from hell; today, it seemed, was the sequel. "Julie, how do I get to Beaumont Drive? I'm lost."

"What's wrong with the satnav?"

He stared at the cracked screen. "Just fucking tell me, Julie, I'm not in the mood."

There was a long silence.

"Julie?"

More silence.

Henry sighed, rubbed his face. A horn sounded from behind him, and almost absently, he flipped the bird as a response. "Julie, I—"

"It's Beau*ford* Drive. And I want a word when you get back." The line died.

"Whoa, hold on! Julie don't you fucking hang up on me!" Spittle flew from his mouth and his face glowed a mellow crimson. The bladder situation had grown painful, and sweat popped out on his forehead and under his nose. "I *own* the fucking company," he shouted at the phone, "I'm your boss!" He threw it into the footwell with enough force to shatter its screen and spill its innards across the carpet.

Someone banged on the window.

Henry jumped. The car behind was minus a driver, and he guessed that the tramp standing by the Jaguar gesticulating angrily was the man on the receiving end of the bird.

Henry stared at him, and as he did so he bit his bottom lip. His nostrils flared and he could feel the heat in his chest growing ever more intense. The tramp ranted, and the pressure in Henry's mind was reaching a critical point.

The tramp seemed appalled at the lack of physical or verbal response and banged on the window.

Henry waited.

Henry stared at him, and finally his teeth sank into his lower lip. Blood trickled into the crease of his chin and dripped onto his suit, but he didn't notice, didn't take his eyes off the tramp. The world was silent, his field of vision shrunk to a circle a few inches across, encompassing the slitted eyes of the man, with hatred leaking from them.

Henry waited.

The tramp banged on the window again, spitting on the glass as he shouted. Horns sounded from behind, onlookers laughed at them.

The world crowded in on Henry. Fury shredded all trace of common decency. He saw the bus coming, and shouldered the door open as hard as he could into the man's face and chest. The tramp staggered backwards into the path of a bus. The bus locked its massive tyres as the tramp folded and then disappeared beneath the smoking rubber. The passengers lurched forward alarmingly. Onlookers screamed. Car horns ceased to blow.

The Fiesta disappeared around the corner, and Henry realised he had wet himself.

From his mind's trivia department, a friendly female voice, sounding very much like the dead satnav lady, said *T-plus 600 seconds and counting*. Henry turned forward and closed the door, engaged gear and planted his shaking right foot hard on the throttle.

* * *

Henry saw the driver step off the bus as a thousand people swarmed the road, several of them with mobile phones to their ears. He was shaking as the scene disappeared into his rear-view mirror.

The sign for Beauford Drive sailed up toward him. He turned the Jaguar and swept up the narrow street as three police cars sped by the junction. Henry didn't like the police; he always managed to fall foul of them. Okay, he'd been guilty, he conceded, but that was beside the point. Other guilty people got away with things.

Dear old Daddy's going to love this.

Somehow, a smile emerged, and then a small laugh fell out of his mouth as an image of Mr Tramp replayed on the Technicolor screen inside his head. He stopped the car, unclipped the seat belt, and laughed so hard that it turned into a coughing fit.

The ache in his belly left him alone and the smell of urine in his lap killed the last of the giggling. He was approximately twenty minutes late in showing the good Mr and Mrs Richardson around what could have been their new house.

"What am I doing?"

There would be plenty of witnesses to say that a green Jag was involved in pushing the tramp under the bus. *Yes, yes, of course, the tramp had started it,* they'd say, *but the fat bastard in the green Jag pushed him under the bus; oh, yes, I saw it all officer, I did, honest.*

Henry had dug himself into a hole so deep they didn't make a rope long enough. The heat under his collar billowed again, the pressure in his mind pulsed, and the thought of losing business filled him with an anger equalled only by the thought of his father's threat. All he could think of was getting the hell out of here as fast as he could; that, and his father's words: "Any smear you bring to yourself, Henry, rubs off on me, and if anything like this happens again, I'll smear you across the fucking wall. Does that make sense?"

Henry took his foot off the brake and dropped it on the throttle.

His father's threat grew to the point where nothing else mattered. The tramp was dead and consequently Henry would be smeared *across the fucking wall.* He was way beyond fraught.

The sun was high and hot and it turned the road ahead into a bright orange glare. The AC still refused to work, no matter how hard he beat the damned switch. Terrified, Henry just wanted out.

Chapter Three

Friday 29th May

– One –

The parcel crinkled under his arm.

Wobbling only slightly now, he turned back to his own front door and knocked again. "Come on, Jilly, for Christ's sake."

The key turned and Jilly's cold face peered around the door at him. "You need a new watch."

"Sorry." He noticed she'd had new locks fitted. Did she think he wouldn't respect their agreement, that he would creep back in the dead of night and steal all her Richard Clayderman and Barry Manifold CDs?

"Why should you be sorry? If you need extra time to sober up, Eddie, why did you make it a morning appointment? Why not make it evening instead?" She had spiteful eyes. "He was so giddy an hour ago…"

"Can I come in?"

She paused, then stood aside as he entered. The door slammed, semi-darkness came between them, and she stared at Eddie and his parcel. "Well?" She sniffed the air. Eddie thought he might have over done the aftershave and the breath fresheners a bit.

On the hallway wall was the framed cutting from *The Yorkshire Echo* showing him as a hero receiving a commendation from the chief constable. And below it was the commendation itself. He turned away from the picture and the ultimate cause of him feeling like a stranger in his own house. "Where is he?" Patting the parcel, Eddie stepped into his old lounge and looked around, and then turned back to Jilly whose arms were folded beneath her bosom.

"He got fed up of waiting. He's gone round to Josh's."

"Ah."

"Why can't you arrive on time just once, eh? He'd be thrilled. And I'd be amazed."

"I know, I—"

"You're three-quarters of an hour late, Eddie. And that's a lot to a young kid."

Maybe Ros had been right. "I brought him this." He held out the parcel.

She took it, put in the corner by the others. "I said he could open them. But he wanted to open yours first." Her eyebrows rose. "Said the others could wait."

"It's a PlayStation," he said. "I heard Josh had one, you know, and that Sammy—"

"You've let him down."

"I know I have, and I'm sorry." He fidgeted with his keys, and glanced at her only occasionally.

"Save it for him."

"I will. But I'm saying sorry to you too. You probably have things you could be getting on with and I've—"

"I'm fine with it. I had nothing planned but a lazy day in front of the TV." Her eyes were cold; it was as if he were a stranger selling double-glazing at the door. It was as if the last fifteen years counted for nothing.

"Don't have time for a cuppa, really, do we?"

"He's waiting for you."

"Yeah." Eddie looked at the floor. "Do you think…" He waited for the rejection first so he wouldn't be embarrassed by asking. "Do you think we could have a cuppa sometime; just you an' me?"

"I know you want to move back in, but it's not the same, and it never could be." Stepping aside, she encouraged him to leave. "It sounds like I'm rubbing salt in, but you've ruined things. You, all by yourself, have ruined things, and I can't even think of trying again until you're dry. And even then…" She stalled, leaving an uncomfortable silence hanging between them. "Well, let's just see, huh?"

"I *am* trying," he said. "I haven't had a—"

She looked out of the window, not listening anymore. "You know if you get caught driving with alcohol—"

"I know."

"Don't worry," she said, "I won't say anything. But be careful how you drive when Sam's in the car."

No, she wouldn't say anything, because if she did, he would lose his job and she would lose his money and she would lose the house.

Her spiteful eyes were gorgeous. He missed her.

She turned away. "Better go now, before he gets really upset."

"Yeah," he said quickly. "On my way."

* * *

Drink was the most ruthless mistress imaginable. She, too, had gorgeous eyes, always changing colour, depending on your poison, and always seductive. She was a hard bitch as well; once she had her claws in your back it was game over.

Even if he could ditch the booze, it didn't follow that Jilly would take him back. And even if she did, he'd be on permanent probation. How could he live like that; afraid to have a row in case she revoked his licence? Life was shite.

Driving across the estate to Josh's, he had the windows down, letting the breeze rip away at the mess in his head. And through the window came a sound so familiar to him that he was inclined to ignore it: that of a siren.

– Two –

Sam crouched, elbows hovering above his knees. From across the garden, Josh placed the ball and stepped back. He ran and kicked, aiming top left. Sam dived, got a finger on the leather and knocked it clear over the wall more than twenty feet away. Sam hit the dust elated because he got to the damned thing, he made contact – God, he was good!

"Shit!" Josh shouted.

"Josh!" shouted Mrs Potter.

"Sorry, Mum." He strode over to Sam. "You knocked it over the wall, dummy."

Sam grinned, slapping the dust from his tracksuit bottoms. "I saved it, Josh. I saved a penalty."

"As a reward, you can go and get the bloody thing, I went last time."

"You shouldn't have kicked it so hard." Sam put his hands defiantly on his hips. "You go."

"Think of it as a compliment, Sam; I *have* to kick it hard to get it past you these days."

Sam's chest puffed out. "Okay," he said, walking to the gate, "but it's your turn next time."

"Absolutely."

– Three –

Henry sped down Westbury Avenue, thinking of nothing other than getting home and lying low for a few years. "What's the sentence for manslaughter now?" His father was working on something big, spending a lot of time in Whitehall with policy-makers on this committee or that committee. It was something big, he'd say, but wouldn't go into detail, other than saying crime would be cut drastically for the first time in modern British history.

"Shit!" Henry swerved the Jaguar. The tyres squealed as he slewed to the left. A ball flew across the front of his car, and Henry almost had a heart attack. His eyes were wide, searching for the youth who would invariably follow the ball. None did. It was okay to kill a tramp, he thought, but not so good to cream a fucking kid!

He dragged a sleeve across his face and noted the stench of warm urine drifting up from his lap, and then noticed the smear of red on his sleeve. "Oh God, I wish I could wake up at seven o'clock this morning and start again."

The Jaguar roared past the bouncing ball and was only a hundred yards away from the tee-junction and freedom when a police car cruised past. It stopped. Its reverse lights came on.

Henry's heart boomed. His flabby jowls tightened. He brought the Jaguar to a swift halt, turned quickly in the road and set off back the way he had come. He studied the rear-view mirror, and saw the police car turn up Westbury Avenue, saw the blue lights flash. Henry pressed the throttle harder.

– Four –

Sam saw the green car speed past.

He trotted across the road after the ball, catching hold of it as it settled in the gutter.

As he walked back he bounced the ball, checked his watch, and discovered his dad was over an hour late. It was an hour less time they had together.

He pulled down the peak on his New York Yankees baseball cap and hurried across the road towards Josh's gate.

His dad was a fucking *drunk!* Mum said so. *He's always late because he's always* drunk. He could see it in his mum's eyes, and he even saw it

Mrs Potter's eyes, and what did *she* know? He might be a drunk, but he was Dad. And he really was wonderful.

Sam was a yard from the kerb when the roar of an engine pulled him free of thoughts of his dad. For the briefest of times he saw the green car and he saw the windscreen, the sunlight glancing off it, and through it he saw a fat man with blood smeared across his face.

Then he saw no more.

– Five –

Henry sped back up Westbury Avenue, thinking of his dad, his arse still slipping in a puddle of piss, and somewhere not too far behind, a police car was screaming after him. He rounded the gentle bend and smacked the AC knob again with his fist, desperate to cool down. And then he stared into the rear-view mirror. How far behind were they, how much of a lead did he have? And then he glanced into the frightened eyes of a boy who was no more than twelve.

The kid met the Jaguar in the very centre of the bonnet. There was a hideous crack as his legs snapped and a dull thud when his head hit the windscreen. The floppy body flew silently over the back of the car; milliseconds grew into days.

Henry screamed as the car slewed to a halt against the kerb, and then held his breath, knuckles white, heart on pause. He waited for the briefest of times, looking in his mirrors. The ball bounced away out of sight and a New York Yankees baseball cap fluttered to the kerb.

The kid didn't move.

Henry took his foot off the brake and applied lots of throttle.

* * *

Henry stopped at home just long enough to change his clothes and to mop up the foul-smelling liquid from the seat. He was shaking, mind working so fast that it wasn't working at all. He grasped the enormity of what had just happened and it flew away from reason just as quickly as it plunged into a desperate panic, and all he could think of was driving away from here and a double manslaughter charge as fast as he could.

They would already be looking for him, well, looking for the car, and here was the first place they'd check, assuming they had the car's registration number. And if they didn't have it... well, that was just too optimistic to consider right now. How long would it take them to run all the British racing green Jaguars in Yorkshire through the system and begin checking their addresses?

Henry set off on his last journey behind the wheel of his beautiful green Jaguar.

Chapter Four

Friday 29th May

Near a village called Great Preston, there's a place that is as abandoned as it's possible to get in West Yorkshire. At one time it was part of a vast mining community, great opencast mines with machines as big as a block of flats dragging the coal out for power stations. It's quiet now. Dead, deserted. Acre upon acre of slag mounds covered in thin, unhealthy weeds that swayed in a warm breeze.

Meandering between the slag mounds was a track that led to the old site office, a wooden building with smashed windows, something nature was busy reclaiming. In places, the track was almost green right over with soft brome and Yorkshire fog growing, hidden from the gentle hum of everyday life that went on in Great Preston half a mile away.

Henry thought about the track, and what an ideal place it would be. He'd played there as a kid, only a few years after the coalmine shut down and the cobwebs grew freely on the great iron gates into the compound. Rusting machinery stood by the flat-top where the coal was stacked, and the small concrete admin offices and weigh-bridge looked like something from a WWII aircraft base complete with its own lookout tower.

It was a great place to play, a wonderful place to be whoever you wanted to be. SAS; that's what Henry wanted to be, and he'd stormed that old fortress where the encryption device was, or where the terrorists were holding a British ambassador, or where the missile battery was, more times than he could remember. His childhood was wonderful, what little he was allowed to have.

Things began to get ugly for Henry not long after his first visit to the track as one half of a newly formed courting couple. He remembered it being dark, but his erection had pulled him along the twisting track as though it was equipped with night vision. The anticipation was overwhelming. Launa Wrigglesworth was his first conquest and he still recalled the way she squirmed and groaned beneath him, and by the time they'd finished losing their virginity, his jacket, laid out on the long grass of a slag mound, was a crumpled testimony to how well it had turned out. His knees, covered in the grey muck of years-old clay, and scratched and torn and bloody, were testimony to how one emotion – ecstasy – could easily blot out another – pain. *Pity that particular talent faded as you accrued the years and the knocks,* he thought.

His father had moved into politics shortly after Henry had moved the earth and that was about the time his world turned into a downward spiral of strict discipline, a change of school and an enforced adulthood that frightened the crap out of him. He wanted to be a kid, he wanted to be Superman, he wanted to be Peter Pan and never grow up. But party politics forced it upon him as it forced weeklong attendance in London on his father, and weekend beatings for Henry. It was the stress of junior politics that loosened his teeth and turned Henry's eyes the colour of overripe plums.

The old site office and the lean-to that was the manager's car parking space, was where he had ended his short relationship with Wriggler Wrigglesworth. She refused to oblige one night, a night when Henry felt particularly virile. So he punched her in the jaw and walked away, massaging the bulge as he went. She landed flat on her back, out cold.

Twenty years later he found himself in the very same spot where she fell. It was dark again but the moonlight was strong enough to see that the old lean-to had rather more lean than it used to, and the site office had fared equally badly; its windows smashed by the creaking old building moving on its foundations. The door had warped and fallen inside leaving a dusty old shell with creepers growing through the floor and fungus sprouting in the joists. *No place to bring a potential conquest now,* Henry thought.

He turned in the dust and looked at the black shape of his beautiful green Jaguar, moonlight kissing its curves, dancing in the crazed glass of the windscreen. He tutted, kicked at the dirt and opened the boot. He found the torch and stared around his steed one last time. It had killed two people today and it could kill a third – him – if he were found in its company again. And Henry quite liked his life; shitty though it was. Time to part company.

He needed a rag of some description and spent ten minutes searching until he cursed his bad luck and ripped a sleeve from his expensive designer shirt. He took off the fuel filler cap and stuffed the sleeve into the tube as far as he could, leaving a dangling cuff. And then, wondering why he ever gave up smoking – a cigarette lighter would have been fairly useful now – he reached into the car and pushed the cigar lighter into the socket. He sat wondering why these things happened to him; he wondered why he had a shitty father, why he had no woman, and then he smiled, "Cause you're a wanker, Henry Deacon, that's why."

The lighter popped out and Henry popped back into reality. He snatched it and ran to the cuff, pressing it hard onto the cooling coil until wisps of smoke drifted into the silent air. But that was it. Just a tiny glowing ember was all he could manage and blowing on it succeeded only in extinguishing it altogether. "Bastard!" How come the car thieves manage to set fire to things so damned easily?

He plugged the lighter back in for a second go, and while it warmed up, he pulled the sleeve back out and brought it into the car, ready this time for full heat. This time it caught, this time he didn't have to blow and the smoking cinder produced a beautiful orange flame that took quickly. "Shit, shit, shit." Henry scrambled around to the filler, flames licking dangerously close, and pushed it towards the tube. But the sleeve was blazing now and he couldn't get it inside. The fire was hot, the shirtsleeve curling, turning a crispy grey as he shouted and screamed for some good fucking luck for a damned change.

And then his hand felt hot, he felt the hairs on it curl away, smelt the singe of flesh and cried out in pain. But he kept pushing, almost not daring to touch it but having no choice, and when it was in the tube and he was about to run to safety before the car blew up in his face, the flames grew thinner and thinner and then died.

The world turned dark again and Henry leaned against the flank of the Jag, head in hands, wondering what to do now.

It was a long walk to the nearest bus stop.

Chapter Five

Wednesday 3rd June

Life soon caught up with Henry. He came back from Great Preston wearing tattered clothes, and with a blistered hand that throbbed.

"Damned thieves," he made himself say over and over again, until he almost believed it. It was them, he thought, who had hurt his hand, it was them, he said, who made me miss all my appointments.

"There." Julie put a coffee on his desk, and sat opposite her boss. "What happened then?"

Henry's good hand massaged the bandage on his left. He sipped coffee and tried out his story on Julie. "They robbed me." His voice was hurt, his chin wobbled, but he looked her straight in the eye. If Julie believed him after all the times she'd caught him lying, then the police would be a walkover. "Damned thieves. They car-jacked me! You hear all this stuff on the news, how these thieves wait for you in multi-storey car parks, or while you're at a red light, and then, wham! They pounce, shouting and screaming at you until you don't know what the fuck happened."

Julie raised her eyebrows, but didn't yank back on the reins simply because he swore.

He couldn't hide a smile; it was a smile of impending triumph, but he dressed it up nicely by adding, "I'm sorry about that, Julie, I shouldn't—"

"Never mind," she said, concern etched across her face. "Go on, dear."

He shrugged. "Well, they hauled me out, punched me in the mouth." He pulled out his lip so she could see. "Tooth went right into it." She looked closely and hissed. "They gave me a kick in the back of the head just for good measure, and when I stood and tried to… I don't know what I tried, but I stuck my hand back inside, either trying to get them out of my car, or trying to get me back in, I don't know. But when I tried, they slammed the bloody door on my hand." He lifted the bandaged hand. "Throbs," he said.

"Oooh, bet it does, too."

"Anyway, I went home." He looked up with his best puppy-dog eyes, and for a moment, he thought she was going to cry for him. Inside he laughed. "I couldn't stand going out, and I didn't answer the phone," he glanced away, "I felt… Julie, I felt raped; I thought they were going to kill me." Was that a tear in her eye? Fucking jackpot! "I'm sorry for not answering your calls. I know you rang a thousand times, and John and Chris too."

"They called around a few times as well."

"They hate me, don't they?"

"No," she said through a laugh, "don't be preposterous. No one hates you. They thought you'd just vanished, though; with your car not being there and there were no lights on, they—"

"I just couldn't bear it. Has anyone been looking after my appointments?"

"Henry," she soothed, "always thinking about work, even at a time like this. Stop worrying, we all mucked in and took care of everything."

"That's great. I owe you all a drink, eh?"

"Several!" She smiled at him, a motherly smile. "Have the police contacted you?"

"I gave them the details over the phone, and they said they'd be in touch."

"And they haven't?"

He shook his head. "Service is appalling, isn't it? I mean, my car could be anywhere by now. Wish I'd had a tracker fitted."

"Oh, you poor boy; you've not heard, have you?"

"Heard what?"

She looked away.

"Julie, heard what?"

"It's been all over the news, and every vidiscreen in town is plastered with it."

"What, dammit!"

"They killed two people."

His heart speeded up, and he knew this because his hand throbbed faster. But he kept cool, didn't glance away, didn't blink, and even refused to allow his eyes to widen; he'd known this was on the cards and was prepared for it. "*Who* killed two people?" He looked suitably confused.

"We don't know. Someone driving a green Jaguar knocked two people down. It happened on the same day they stole your car."

Henry looked shocked. Now he allowed his eyes to widen. "Those poor people," he said as though shocked. "That's awful; what did they do? How did it happen?"

"I'm not sure. Except that one of them was a young boy, about ten, I think. Dead instantly."

"Oh my dear God."

"The police'll catch them, and when they do, Henry, they'll be on a Rule Three, and then *they'll* die instantly."

"Wait a minute, you think someone stole my car, and then they…"

Julie nodded.

"Well that explains it, then." He bit his lower lip and winced.

"Explains what?"

"The police. They think I did it; they think *I* ran those two people over."

"No."

"That's why they haven't been to see me yet; they're gathering evidence, aren't they? They're formulating their plans."

"Henry," she laughed again, "you're overreacting. They haven't even found the car yet, so how can they gather evidence?"

"*You* think I did it, don't you? I can't believe you, my own—"

"Henry!" she snapped. "Calm down this instant! If you say you had your car stolen, then I believe you. And anyway, no one said it was *your* Jaguar that killed them; could have been another. There's no proof one way or another, so stop fretting. When they find the car, we'll all be able to sleep better."

Oh, they won't find the car, Henry thought. *Not in a million years.*

The Yorkshire Echo.

PAC founder and eighteen children murdered in school firebomb

By Michael Lyndon

EIGHTEEN children and four adults burned to death in an East Sussex school yesterday. The shocking news erupted shortly before lunch as firefighters battled for an hour to bring the blaze under control. The Chantry House School and nearby houses in Blackstone were evacuated.

Among those thought to have perished in the blaze is Josephine Tower (38), one of the co-founders of the People Against Crime (PAC) movement, and her six-year-old son, Ben.

A Sussex Police spokesperson said that a preliminary examination of the scene suggests arson, and if that is the case, then a full murder investigation will be launched. The spokesperson went on to say that enquiries are still in their early stages but it seems the classroom was engulfed in a fire ball strong enough to blow out the windows. Police are refusing to speculate whether the attack was meant personally for Mrs Tower, or was an act of sabotage against the school. Terrorism has been ruled out.

The school is not expected to reopen for a month to give investigators time to gather evidence, and to allow for rebuilding. The funerals of those killed will be announced by the coroner later next week. A full service will be held at St Mark's in Blackstone this coming Sunday, with a contribution from Sir George Deacon. Police are still urging any witnesses to come forward in what surely ranks as one of the most horrific crimes on English soil this century.

Mrs Tower's co-founder, Emily Cooper, was unavailable for comment today, but PAC issued a statement expressing sorrow to those killed and expressing disgust at the perpetrator. PAC's statement continues: "This is precisely the kind of crime we have campaigned against for so long and we greatly regret that The Rules were not put in place earlier." There is no shortage of objectors to the legislation and speculation will surround this crime until the offender is brought to justice.

The deputy head of The Chantry House School Janet Nugent said the local community was extremely distressed by the tragedy. She added that her staff are utterly distraught. Josephine Tower's father, the Right Reverend Clive Chapman, Bishop of Chichester, was not available for comment.

Chapter Six

Friday 5th June

– One –

For an hour or so, Eddie and Jilly had spoken about the arrangements and decided it was best to bury Sam on his birthday. The funeral director had managed to get them together, and it was he who had suggested it.

To an outsider, that might have appeared a little strange, even dipping its toes in the fringes of morbidity. But there was logic behind it.

Sam was born 5th June; he died 29th May. They were two dates to add to the diary; black dates with red circles scribbled around them, dates that would hurt for years to come. Eddie and Jilly decided not to create a third.

* * *

Ros had bought Eddie a black suit. And she'd bought him patent shoes, a smart white shirt and a thin black tie. She told him he looked good, but Eddie wasn't even there. That morning he had stood before the bathroom mirror and just stared at himself, feeling nothing, no pain, no inebriation, nothing. He was just a block of wax crafted into a face by some art student who hadn't really got the hang of human anatomy, it looked wrong. It looked twisted, not human.

Catatonic feels like this, he told himself.

An hour later, he was back in front of the mirror, shaved, a shirt collar and black tie visible. His eyes were red. His face pale. And some time after that, he was aroused from his catatonic state by a knock at the door. And here he was in the kitchen. The cutlery drawer was open and he was looking at the paring knife.

He answered the door to Ros who wore the dark grey suit she used for court. She had pity in her eyes – as everyone these days seemed to – and then she moved forward and threw her arms around him. He cried the first tears of the day.

* * *

It had been more or less the same for Jilly. Except that she had her parents there to field any phone calls, to accept the flowers at the door, and to pick up the cards that dropped like tears through the letterbox. She sat before her dressing table mirror in bra and pants and let time drip away, watching a face she didn't recognise and feeling raw emotions eat away at the drugs she'd taken.

– Two –

A breeze skittered across the car park, pushing sweet wrappers and discarded cellophane sheets from bunches of flowers along towards the fence where a congregation of rubbish gathered. The sky was clear and warm, and Eddie suddenly realised she was talking to him.

"Sorry?"

"You still okay to make your own way home? I have to get to work."

Eddie nodded, and on autopilot, said, "Thanks, Ros."

"It was a lovely service," she whispered.

Together at the stone narthex of St Mary Magdalen, they watched as Jilly and her entourage gathered in the central aisle of the nave. He was her husband but didn't feel part of the family anymore. Ros discreetly squeezed his hand, and when Eddie eventually turned to look, she had gone. He stepped outside and saw her leaving through the lych-gate. From there a man watched him.

"Eddie," someone inside the church called.

It was time to carry his boy into the churchyard. Eddie trembled.

– Three –

Eventually, the sextons stopped their work and just looked at him. He was sitting on the highest part of the backfill; they had practically scraped the earth from around him. "Sorry," he said and stood, scooping up the bottle of brandy as he went.

One last time he glanced at a photograph of Sammy that was paper-clipped to a floral tribute just out of his finger's reach, and then he ambled towards the gate, slipping the bottle inside his pocket for later. His face felt sore where she'd punched him, and his ribs did too. He had a hunch there were one or two scratches on his body waiting to be discovered once he got out of his not-so crisp new suit. There was a hole in the knee, and mud on the jacket.

Eddie took out his cigarettes and sighed in despair at the crushed packet.

"Here you are, mate, have one of these."

Eddie looked up as he approached the lych-gate. It was Mick Lyndon. Eddie walked right by him, "I'll pass, thanks."

"Eddie, come on."

Eddie stopped and turned. "Thought I told you to piss off and leave me alone."

"I thought I'd said sorry."

"Whoopee doo."

"What do you want me to do, print a retraction?"

Eddie swung a fist towards Mick's face. Mick screwed his eyes shut, and braced himself. Eddie's fist stopped an inch before Mick's nose, and then his arm fell to his side.

Mick opened an eye, then both. "Look," he said, "I *am* sorry. I thought I was doing the right thing; people don't have enough good news, and they love a hero—"

"I am not their fucking entertainment. And I am *not* a fucking hero! Given the choice, a hero would do exactly the same again. I wouldn't. Okay?"

Mick held out his hands.

"That shit you came out with was four months ago. A lifetime ago. We argued about the hero stuff back then, and you said you'd never pull a stunt like it again."

"I am so—"

"'Hero's son dies', I think you said."

"Okay, okay, I'm sorry, Eddie." He offered the cigarette packet again.

Eddie looked at Mick, and then took a cigarette.

"Drink?" asked Mick.

The Yorkshire Echo. 17th June

School murderer caught
By Michael Lyndon

IT WAS the worst act of murder seen in England this century, and the public outcry was unprecedented. On Thursday (4th June), eighteen children and four adults burned to death in Chantry House Church of England Primary School in East Sussex.

In a planned operation, police arrested a lone female from a nearby housing estate. She is being held in custody and questioned about the incident. The police caught the perpetrator after finding the remains of fingerprints in blood – not believed to be human – on the petrol container in the false ceiling above the classroom.

But only chance ensured her capture. Mrs Margaret Bolton, 28, works for an East Sussex fireworks factory – for which employees routinely have their fingerprints taken. Police confirmed that the crime scene fingerprints did not match any of the 200,000 sets of fingerprints on their computer system. But an internal audit at the company showed several ignition items missing – the same items used in the school fire.

A source revealed that the arsonist, Mrs Bolton, a single mother, allegedly felt aggrieved at the treatment of her son by the headmaster and local education authority.

An unnamed source suggests that he was a disruptive and often violent pupil who terrorised his classmates to such an extent that the LEA expelled him pending the results of an assessment.

Parents of those children who remain at the school, and the families of those who have lost loved ones in the disaster, are calling for more stringent checks on disruptive children and their parents.

Startlingly, Mrs Bolton left a message for the world with a neighbour prior to her arrest: "I would not have done this had The Rules been in force; I didn't want to die, just wanted to be out of the rat race and have my boy properly looked after".

That might be of no consolation, but it is vindication that The Rules will be seen by would-be criminals as a deterrent.

Ironically, had Mrs Bolton been caught or had confessed before the 15th June to her crime, she would have spent life behind bars as she'd wanted. Her death is scheduled for some time in the week ahead.

Chapter Seven

Thursday 18th June

"Mr…?"

The old man looked up. The cap he fidgeted with lay crumpled in his lap. "My name is Lincoln Farrier."

The clerk examined the register and said, "Ah yes, Mr Farrier. Sir George will see you now. Please go through."

A large suited man to the side of the clerk got up out of his chair, but the clerk shook his head, "Look at him," he whispered as the old guy struggled to his feet, "I don't think he'll cause any trouble." The man shrugged and retook his seat.

Mr Farrier knocked on the door. This was the first time he had ever wanted to see his MP; this was the first time he ever *needed* to see his MP. And the fact that his MP was Sir George Deacon, the new Justice Secretary, wasn't lost on Lincoln Farrier. Old he may have been, stupid he was not.

The rich mahogany door swung open before him, but the butterflies he anticipated never came; he only ever looked the world in the eye when that eye needed a good prodding. Today was such a day.

He held on to his cap and stood on the varnished wooden floor in front of a grand-looking desk where a grey-haired man made notes with a fountain pen. This was the great Sir George Deacon.

"Sit."

Lincoln blinked at the man's abruptness. He closed the door and sat in the chair opposite the crown of Deacon's head, waiting until the great man spoke. He wondered where to begin.

"Mr Farrier." At last he put down the pen, took off his half-rimmed glasses. "What may I do for you today?"

Lincoln shifted in the chair. "I want manners to return to England."

"I beg your pardon?"

"Everywhere you go, everything you want to do is governed by fear. Dare I go into the Post Office anymore? It was robbed only a week ago. The local pub was burgled, and two holiday cottages was burgled and another set alight." He put down the cap. "Things are getting too bad for normal folks to cope with anymore."

"Is that all you came—"

"The police – armed because being a bobby is dangerous now – the police catch them and sometimes," he pointed a shaking finger at Deacon, "the little buggers get sent to jail. But when they get there, it's like a holiday camp for them! Did you know that in each room – not cell, mind – *room*, there is a television, and they get to select what DVD they'd like to watch each evening?"

Deacon said, "I didn't know that."

"Oh aye. And they get cash donations so they can buy tobacco or drugs. Them outside send it in to them, cause them outside are still burgling!" Lincoln paused for breath. "Them law-breakers are laughing at me. Well, they're laughing at you too, but I couldn't care less if they laugh at you or the courts or the police, really. But I *do* care if they laugh at me. They are wiping our noses in the shit!" Lincoln covered his mouth.

Deacon waved him on.

"The prisons are filling up with young people who don't care for others' rights. They care about themselves more'n anything else in the world, and that's not what life is about. So long as they're getting their drug money, they're happy. These days, no one believes in working to get the money to buy what they want. They believe in getting things for nothing. And that is wrong."

Deacon nodded.

"Once they're in prison, they get Legal Aid to fight things they should not be entitled to fight, and that makes the system a sham. Far as I know, Legal Aid was invented to help poor people fight wrongs. It's not there to line the pockets of the judiciary, or set the criminals free."

Lincoln fidgeted again with his cap. "Is this makin' any sense, or should I just bugger off and leave you alone?"

Deacon considered it. "I'm grateful you're being so candid, and I welcome—"

"Bollocks," Lincoln said. "What are you doing about it? What are you *really* doing?"

"I'm not at liberty to discuss in-depth policy revision, Mr Farrier, but one titbit I can offer is vasectomy."

"Come again."

Deacon laughed, and played with the fountain pen – definitely not made in China. "We commissioned a study to look at the last fifty years of incarceration in Britain. Its findings are eye-opening. I don't suppose we'll get it through Parliament, but I'll tell you about it anyway."

"I'm listening."

"People who go to jail breed people who go to jail. If you are a convicted felon, you are three times more likely to produce children who themselves will be jailed later in life. So I'd like criminals to be sterilised."

"Really?"

"And the Sentencing Guidelines Council is looking into banning early release for good behaviour. If you're sentenced to four years, you serve four years – *if* you behave. If you don't, you serve longer; we're switching the way it works away from favouring the criminal. That's why we're building more jails. These are the things we're doing about it."

"Impressive."

"It is."

"But do you think more could be done quicker if a cabinet minister was shot dead by a lunatic?"

Deacon slowly nodded. "It was a very sad day for the country and the Great British Independence Party when Roger King—"

"Sod Roger King." Lincoln threw his cap on Deacon's desk and brought out a gun.

Deacon dropped the pen. His mouth fell open and he stared at Lincoln, horrified that he was about to leave office the same way as the previous Justice Secretary. Violently. "They didn't search you?"

"They said it would be okay to bring it in." Lincoln squinted. "Why would they search an honest pensioner? Trouble is, this pensioner is sick to fucking death of being trampled on by the scrotes and then by the state. I want something done about it." Lincoln brought the gun up with such powerful resolve that Deacon recoiled and raised his hands. "If you shout, I will shoot you immediately. If you don't," he smiled coldly, "you may be able to talk your way out of it. That's what you politicians are supposed to be good at, isn't it?"

Deacon's heart leapt to 120 without changing gear. "Why are you doing this, Mr Farrier? I have nothing here of any value—"

"Don't ever put me in the same league as those law-breaking youths we've been discussing." Lincoln's manner changed as though he'd pulled off the mask and the real nutcase was out and running free with his axe.

Chapter Eight

Thursday 18th June

– One –

He could feel his legs trembling, and he thought of shouting. Sirius, the man outside who formed part of his armed close protection squad, would monitor, contain and then… what did they call it? Defuse, disarm, something like that. But he could be dead before Sirius even put down his coffee.

"Then what *do* you want?"

Lincoln Farrier was a brave man, Deacon decided. But greater still was his foolishness. There was a level of persuasiveness that Farrier had exceeded; he had made Deacon truly afraid for the first time in his life. And that was unforgivable. Utterly punishable.

No one threatens me, old man. No one. With his left foot he searched the floor for the panic button.

* * *

He stared into the politician's frightened eyes and chose not to show his regret, but to keep it repressed until the bravado he hid behind had served its purpose.

Deacon tried to smile. "Then what *do* you want?"

"I want my son back."

"I'm not with you."

"If you promise not to try any funny business I'll let you put your arms down."

"Where's your son?"

"Prison. And he's there because the parole board won't give him early release." Lincoln saw Deacon's eye twitch as he mentioned prison. "And before you leap to one of your conclusions, let me tell you that I ain't never been in trouble with the law, let alone been sent to jail."

"I would never presume—"

"My boy was home watching the footy one night. He went to get a beer, and finds this fellow in his kitchen, just climbed in through the open window. And in his hand is my boy's wallet, mobile phone, and car keys!"

His finger feathered the trigger. "Stephen is a good boy, a law-abiding citizen who used to visit me once a week regular as clockwork with his wife. Anyway, he's shocked to see this man in his kitchen and stabs him.

"The long and the short of it is that my boy went to jail because someone else was doing something they shouldn't have been."

Deacon moved his foot away from the panic button. "How do you think killing me might help you exactly?"

"Don't get flippant with me. My hand gets awful shaky when I'm angered, and I've known my index finger, which is the little bugger curled around the trigger, twitch ever so forcefully when I'm enraged. Do you see my point?"

"I see your point very clearly."

"Don't think you're home and safe 'cause this old guy don't know nothing about guns. I know that where I point the tube end is more or less where the bullet is gonna go."

"For a man who claims to stand on the moral high ground—"

Lincoln rode over the statement like it was roadkill. "My son was rejected for early release because – and this will pull your sense of justice right back into the Stone Age – because 'he was still a danger to burglars'." Lincoln said the words very slowly. "He was still a danger to burglars. I went wild. This is where an old man's *Victorian* way of thinking gets in the way of progress, but hear me out; if a fellow is burgling your house, then he is doing something fundamentally wrong. If he didn't do this fundamentally wrong thing then he could never expect to be hurt by law-abiding citizens. Am I talking bollocks or does it make sense?"

"I—"

"Where is the logic in locking up a man trying to prevent a crime in progress when the criminal shouldn't *be* there?" Lincoln was almost screaming now, and he slammed the butt of the gun into the beautiful desk. "Inside, the burglars get a DVD player," he hissed, "and I can barely afford my fucking TV licence!"

Deacon almost leapt from his chair as someone knocked on the door. "Sir George? Everything okay in there?"

* * *

The gratitude Deacon felt at the interruption was like the relief of finally reaching the surface when you thought your lungs would burst. But he kept his demeanour cool, like he'd just stepped out of a freezer. He pressed the intercom and cleared his throat, staring at the frail old man who was as proud a man as he had ever met. He said, "Everything's fine; we were just having a heated discussion. No need to panic."

Unforgivable. Utterly punishable.

* * *

Lincoln looked through slits at Deacon and wondered if he'd just been buggered by some kind of secret word. He gave it ten seconds, and when he found himself still sitting in the chair and still breathing, he thanked Deacon for his benevolence.

"I understand your angst, and I agree with your sentiment entirely."

Lincoln sat up straight and said, "I don't even know if this thing works." He offered the briefest of smiles before pride snatched it away. Then he spun the barrel. "But it's still got six in the hole." He saw a flash of fear in Deacon. "I'm not going to kill you; I had to make myself heard over the do-gooders who've never been burgled or robbed or had their property set on fire. And I had to make myself heard over the crap rattling around inside your head. I knew I was just another disgruntled nutter here to bother you. I had to change that."

Deacon defiantly poked a finger into the barrel of Lincoln's gun. The old man swallowed. The threat looked decidedly more feeble now than it did a moment ago. The path to victory was paved not with bravery, but with calculated risk.

Lincoln pulled the gun away, steered it around Deacon's finger, the one with a fading red circle on the end, and reasserted his point.

Deacon slammed his fist on the desk. "You disgust me. You come in here talking about decency, preaching at me like a law-abiding citizen. And you point that thing at a minister of Her Majesty's Government! At the successor of a minister who was shot dead!"

Lincoln jumped. The threat was dead, if ever it had drawn breath to begin with.

"You could go to jail just for having that thing. You could be in the *room* next to your boy."

Lincoln slid the gun away. "My dad was a soldier. He died so that the burglar could smile at my boy while he stole from him. And then that burglar laughed at my boy, and that burglar *pissed his pants* when he got Legal Aid to *sue* my boy. And that burglar got himself a DVD player and three squares a day for less than half the time my boy is doing. Is that fair?"

Lincoln grabbed the chair and made an effort to stand. "I know perfectly well that I sound like an old fool with nothing better to do than whine to busy people like you, but the world today really *is* what people make it. You have the power to make it good again. You have the power to make it fair."

"Mr Farrier." On shaking legs, Deacon was at his side, helping the old man stand. "I got your message."

"Can you help us? I've tried every other avenue. S'why I'm so desperate, Mr Deacon." Lincoln scooped up his cap, and said, "I've been foolish, I shouldn't have—"

"No, you shouldn't, Mr Farrier." Deacon's stare was grave.

"You gonna call the police?" he asked. "You have every right."

"I don't work like that." Now Deacon's eyes moved away, unable or unwilling to make eye contact.

"Will you see what you can do about my situation, Sir George?"

"Count on it."

– Two –

Deacon closed the door behind the old man.

He wished he loved his own son as much as Lincoln obviously loved his. He wished he loved his own son at all. Back behind the desk, he reflected how he had shaken like a pneumonia victim when Lincoln pulled the gun; could see his career ending very abruptly before he'd achieved his ambition.

He pressed the intercom, "Sirius. In here."

Moments later Sirius appeared in the doorway. "Sir?"

"The old man who just left?"

"Sir."

"He pulled a gun on me."

"Sir?" No change of expression. Though the tone had raised an octave.

"Make him have an accident with it." Deacon put his spectacles on and looked back at his notes, providing no elaboration on the request, except to say, "His son, Stephen, is in jail, and he misses him terribly."

The door closed.

Deacon ignored the intercom and screamed, "And next time search everyone, you imbecile!"

Chapter Nine

Thursday 18th June

– One –

"Thank you." Lincoln stepped down off the bus, shielding his eyes from the glare of sunlight.

He respected Deacon for listening to the drivel coming out of an old man's mouth. On the surface he seemed okay. But there was something beneath the "okay", something that left a trail like a slug did; Deacon was slime. And this wasn't a generalisation; Deacon came across as your good old-fashioned baby-kissing politician, but there was something strange underneath it all.

Over the last two years he'd written to every parole board, each tier of governor at Stephen's jail, to the old PM and the new PM, to the late Roger King and anyone else he thought might listen.

Yet there was still one institution left to raise the issue with, and he patted the letter in the left breast pocket of his best tweed jacket. From the bus stop, he headed for the post box set into the wall outside the Post Office. He paused with the letter in his hand, when Mrs Walker appeared in the doorway and called him over.

She was peering around the doorframe, hand clasped there as if holding on.

"Mrs Walker." He smoothed down his tweed jacket, felt the bump under the right breast pocket, and successfully ignored it.

"How you doing, Lincoln?" Her smile revealed a perfect set of dentures.

"Better, Mrs Walker," he made his way into the little shop that fronted the Post Office. "Just come from seeing Sir George Deacon."

Mrs Walker's face lit up and she stepped closer. "I wondered where you were going when I saw you get on the bus. Oh I am pleased you finally went to see him. How did you get on? Was he a fair man?"

"Well," Lincoln shifted, "It went alright. He said he'd see what he could do, but the wheels of politics turn slowly—"

"But he must have given some commitment?"

"Well, you know—"

"Were you persuasive, Lincoln? Were you forceful? You know these fellows won't do anything unless you put a gun to their heads."

Lincoln stared at Mrs Walker, blinking. "You'd have been proud of me."

"I already am."

"I was posting this…"

"Oh, give it here. You don't need to use the box unless we're shut." Mrs Walker took the letter and sneaked a glance at the address scrawled in Lincoln's forward-slanted writing. "And I have something for you." She slid around the counter, and held out a letter. "I knew who it was from," she said, "so I wouldn't let Ricky take it back to the depot."

Lincoln licked his dry lips, and reached out for the letter.

"It has to be signed for," she said in a high, excited voice. "It's from Stephen."

– Two –

Sirius parked in *The Blacksmith* pub car park in Methley. He took out the paper with Lincoln Farrier's address on it, memorised it and climbed from the car. The place was busy; holidaymakers filled the beer garden with laughter. Kids played on the slide and the squeaking swing out back. And the main street, out to the front, was a throng of colourfully-clothed shoppers weighed down with bags, calling at their misbehaving youngsters as they frolicked in the bright afternoon sunshine.

Sirius took off his tie and tossed it back into the car, slung his jacket over his arm and closed the door. Five minutes later, he left behind the hustle of the main street, its shops, the pub, the restaurants, and ice cream parlours in exchange for serenity and peace. Cottages lined the roadside.

He left the road, turned down a dirt track in between two cottages and let himself into the back garden of the one on the right. It was the last dwelling as you headed out of the village and it was secluded.

Through a well-kept gap in the hedge at the end of the garden was a wooden structure that looked like a small barn, and from here he could just make out through the darkness inside, the bellows of an old furnace. Over the door was a sign: The Farrier's Den.

The shadows were short but dark, the day hot, a day you'd choose to sit out in such a wonderful garden with a cold beer watching the shadows grow longer.

Sirius knocked on the door. There was no reply. He tried the door handle, discovered it was locked, and peered through the keyhole.

He stepped back, looked at the old building, and noticed the window to his right was ajar. It took him no time at all to get inside Lincoln Farrier's neat little house. And it *was* neat, free of bric-a-brac, clean and tidy.

Everything was just so; the TV newspaper was squared away on the tiny coffee table in the centre of Lincoln's lounge, the curtains were tied neatly back, and although the carpet was threadbare in places, it was clean. And the strangest thing perhaps, he noticed, there was no smell of piss you'd normally associate with elderly people; it smelled of…nothing at all.

With gloved hands, Sirius searched the polished bureau and the sideboard drawers, looking for something with the old man's writing on.

These were the kinds of jobs he enjoyed. They gave him a lucrative challenge. He was an officer of the Close Protection Squads run by SO19, a reclusive department based in New Scotland Yard. The job involved Sir George's security, clearing potential hazards, and cleaning up his mess. Each CPO knew his host almost intimately, and often did little "favours" like this for them; though not all officers carried out favours quite so extreme.

Deacon trusted Sirius to be discreet, and he knew Sirius would administer the favour with skill, making it appear accidental, or in the case of this old guy, self-inflicted.

From the bureau he took a letter which bore the House of Commons heading. It was from People Against Crime founder, Emily Cooper. And stapled to the letter, which promised to look into "this kind of thing", was a handwritten note from Lincoln. Sirius sat in the bureau's chair and studied the letter, paying attention not to the actual words used, but to their construction, their fluency and style.

In the same bureau, he found the pad on which Lincoln wrote all his correspondence; a textured fawn paper that added elegance to his remarkable way of writing. And next to the pad, the old guy's fountain pen, and a book of stamps and a wad of envelopes. Sirius slid out the bureau's writing desk.

– Three –

Mrs Walker had practically barricaded the Post Office until Lincoln opened and read the letter. The parole board, those demigods with the power of granting freedom, had finally agreed to let Stephen walk at last.

Lincoln's heart fluttered alarmingly when he read his boy's news, and Mrs Walker had guided him to the wooden bench in the corner of the shop. "He's coming home, Mrs Walker," he said with a voice that was crackly, breaking with the strain of happiness. The letter shook so much it was almost illegible. But he'd made out the important words: *freedom* and *home*. "Next month," he said.

It took a full ten minutes for Lincoln to regain his composure. He stood with his chest out, feeling proud once more and feeling that there *was* a God after all. This morning's trip to see Deacon was now redundant.

Lincoln bade Mrs Walker farewell and left with Stephen's letter tucked into his trouser pocket, eager to read it again in private this time, to really get a feel for it. His hurried journey home was a blur.

He closed the back door behind him, grasped the lounge door handle and stopped dead. Lincoln breathed deeply, trying to figure out where the strange smell was coming from. Something was wrong here, and he had half a mind to turn around and let himself back out. The other part of his mind told him to stop being an idiot. It told him to go sit in his armchair, take out the letter and savour it. He swung the door open and looked at his lounge.

It was just as he'd left it this morning. Except for the fragrance.

"Hello, Lincoln."

Lincoln shrieked, and his heart cracked. The adrenaline surge damned near made him faint.

In the corner by the kitchen door stood a large man. He stepped forward, his jacket over one arm and sunglasses tucked neatly into his shirt pocket.

"Who are you?" Lincoln backed himself into the edge of the lounge door. "What're you…" and then he stopped. "You're that fellow from Sir George's surgery, aren't you?"

His face held no expression at all; no friendliness, no hate, nothing. He advanced.

Chapter Ten

Friday 19th June

She screamed at Eddie, right up to his bloody face, she screamed at him like a sergeant major screams at a recruit. She beat him, and they all looked on, everyone stood by and watched her attack him. The vicar shook his disgusted head at Eddie and then turned away.

Jilly pounced on him, and Eddie's face hit the gravel, grazed his cheek until the blood formed in tiny spots. She kicked him in the back and he rolled over, grunting, bringing his hands up to protect his face, and he could see through his fingers a kid, no more than twenty, laughing at him, pointing something at him.

Eddie closed his eyes and began to scream. Jilly kicked him again and again, screaming the word *murderer* at him until it reverberated around his echoing head. He tried to turn away but couldn't; something stopped him and he screamed again to be set free, but it had him. And when Jilly kicked him again, he felt the brandy bottle slip. He tried to catch it but it fell out of the pocket of his new black suit, tipping end over end, spilling brandy the colour of tea into the sunlight only to darken as the shade inside the hole grabbed it and swallowed it. The bottle banged on the coffin, bounced, banged again.

He watched in horror as it bounced again and again, banging, banging, banging on the lid of the coffin, and still he was trapped and still he screamed, tried to move to cover himself but they had him, and her parents held him tight, and Eddie disappeared into a black hole of panic.

But the brandy bottle spilling the golden liquid onto his dead son's coffin banged on the lid like someone rapping on a door. And then the lid squeaked. It squealed as though it were being opened from inside and that's when Eddie could take no more and he covered his eyes and

* * *

screamed.

"Eddie! Wake up." She slapped him across the face.

His eyes snapped open. He panted, sweat rolled down his neck and he panicked for a moment because he couldn't move. He was trapped between the sofa and the coffee table. And then he looked up, saw a face over his, and gradually brought it into focus.

"You are one screwed up fella, Eddie Collins."

"Ros." Eddie closed his eyes and sobbed.

* * *

"You are one screwed up fella, Eddie Collins." She looked down into his wet face. Tears glistened in the whiskers on his cheeks, and formed small pools in the recesses of his ears. His hair was wet with sweat and his skin was pale, and it reminded her of a body awaiting an autopsy. Ros tutted.

"Ros." He cried like a kid having a nightmare.

"Oh, Eddie."

He put his arm over his eyes, trying to cover the tears, embarrassed by them, and continued sobbing. His chin quivered. It was horrible to see him cry like this, and she felt sorrow that he tried to cover his emotions up. "Come on, Eddie, get up, eh?" She tapped his arm, folded her hand into his and eased him into a sitting position.

She crouched before him, watching as the sobbing grew lighter until he took away his arm and through tear-filled eyes, looked up at her. The tears rolled away into his stubble.

"Same one?"

He nodded. "It always ends there, though; I never seem to get to the part where he—"

In the corner, folded up like an old duvet, Mick coughed himself awake, and stretched hard enough to cause the ashtray in his lap to spill onto the floor.

Ros let Eddie's hand go, and then stood. "Fancy seeing you here," she said to Mick.

"Huh?"

"Did you need him to prop up your ego again last night?"

"Ros," Mick rubbed his face and picked sleep from his eyes, "you should have joined us. We had a good ol' time, didn't we, Eddie?" Mick unfolded his skinny legs, and gawped at Eddie and his tears. "What's up with you?"

Eddie shook his head slowly and looked away.

"Get your stuff and get out, Mick," Ros said, hands on her hips.

"What's wrong with him?"

"You deaf?"

"I'm only concerned for his welfare."

"Welfare, my arse. You're despicable! You found him when he was low and you propagated him, turning him into—"

"Hey, hey!" They looked at Eddie. "I'm here, you know. I haven't left the room." He stood and dragged a sleeve across his face. "He didn't force me to drink, Ros. I wanted to drink." He looked from Ros to Mick. "And it's way past the time you weren't here, Mick; I have things to do."

Chapter Eleven

Friday 19th June

– One –

The auditorium was the size of an indoor football stadium. It had foldaway seats arranged in rows at the front and around the sides, but leaving space by the stage for the press. Around the periphery, lighting gantries trained on the large D-shaped stage jutting out from the back wall like a giant bubble caught on the side of a bathtub, immersed the glass podium and the discreet row of plush chairs off to the left, with dazzling white light.

During rehearsals early this morning, their voices had ricocheted off the walls and ceiling, echoing as though they stood in the Grand Canyon. But things had changed considerably in only a few hours. There wasn't a square inch of floor space left. A constant low chatter droned as people took up their seats, jostling for the best view of the stage, while sound engineers and cameramen made the final adjustments, where photographers sat cross-legged down at the foot of the stage, plugging in flash units, and checking white balance.

The Prime Minister, the Justice Secretary, and several other senior politicians filed in and took up the positions in the plush seats, staring at the gathering of hundreds. After the national anthem and the introductions, the schedule commenced. The lights dimmed slightly and Sterling Young strode centre stage, waving to the party faithful, beaming at his audience as though this were a pop concert and he was the headline act. The cameras caught it all, their flashes bouncing off the glass screens behind Sterling like a dogfight in a Star Wars movie.

The crowd hushed, Sterling rested his hands either side of the lectern. And then he began to speak of the progress his party had made in all spheres of government in the last two years, and each category of improvement, each broad-grinned pause won him praise from the fans. But this wasn't intended as a party political speech.

This was the launch of something big, and it commanded the attention of the British public, and it sparked interest and derision from Europe, interest and admiration from America. Legalised killing. Wherever you lived in the world, Britain's reinvigorated capital punishment programme was big news.

Journalists captured each word, each nuance, as Sterling boomed out his speech in a deep commanding voice. Stills cameras flashed, and as Deacon watched, he counted seventeen television cameras recording every word and every expression for later dissection in the studio with a "panel of distinguished guests". Yes, this was the launch of something big, and the world wanted to be there to catch it.

Sterling paused to let a powerfully delivered point sink in. Ten thousand eyes were upon him, and the room was silent. Deacon felt the hairs on his neck stand up, and felt the sweat on his palms, knowing the time for him to speak approached quickly.

"This year marks the dawning of a new age in Britain," Sterling yelled. "People will come to wonder how we ever managed without this new legislation. It is a show of defiance against those who would betray their fellow Britons and deny them what they have strived for. It is a crackdown on criminals the like of which has never been seen before." He paused, head turning left to right, promoting the tension. "I am proud to have worked alongside the man at its helm, the man whose vision for a truly just society where decent people are once again cherished, and where those who make life a misery for others are punished. I am proud, ladies and gentlemen, to introduce the Minister of Justice," Sterling turned to Deacon, beckoned him with a wave of his arm, "George, come on up here."

Deacon stood and waved, grinning widely as the crowd erupted into a booming applause, and felt the make-up he wore crease and stiffen. The cameras belched into a frenzy as he approached the glass lectern and shook Sterling by the hand. Sterling returned to his seat, applauding as he went.

Deacon waited. Thousands of people peered at him. He checked his autocue on the tilted glass platens arranged in a fan of three in front and at the sides, arranged so that he might turn to the whole audience and deliver his speech in a flawless manner.

The crowd quietened, the whistling stopped, the clapping dribbled to a halt and those with seats retook them, notepads and recorders poised. But he did not speak for a long time; instead, he gathered their attention and then almost ceremoniously turned his back on them. On the wall at the back of the stage was the new Great British Independence Party emblem; a depiction of a flaming torch held aloft by two lions overlaid across the British Isles. "*The new Great Britain*", it proclaimed. Gone were the fluffy flowers of the departed Labour party, and the crudely drawn trees of the old Conservatives –

now it was about teeth, and it was about claws and the depiction of fairness – at last – fairness protected by a lion. The press loved it.

The background began to change. The lions remained, the torch remained, but the picture grew smaller and from the deep blue background emerged a title that grew clearer and bolder. Deacon applauded the title and turned around to face his enraptured audience. A wave of approval began in the middle rows where the party faithful gathered, but with a warm smile, he raised a hand and hushed it.

Power.

"Like all of us, our Prime Minister was deeply saddened by the death of the late Justice Secretary, Roger King, and our hearts still go out to his widow and his children. Two years ago he was taken from us. Even now he is dearly missed." Deacon looked down, remembering what the PR team had said about projection, and about timing. He bit down on his lip, and then looked up, eyes narrowed as though preparing for a fight. "And we were all *sickened* by his murder!" The applause came again, amid murmurs of agreement. "From that day, our Prime Minister decided that this country was fighting a war on crime. The country had had enough!" He brought a fist down hard onto the lectern. He stared around the auditorium, eyes wide now as though genuinely angry.

"This party came to power in the wake of his death, and in the wake of the terrible events caused by Terence Bowman when he slaughtered twenty-three innocent people for no other reason than he was bored. We built a memorial to his victims. How much better if those innocent people were commemorated not by stone, but by a change in society so far-reaching, so radical that no memorials would ever need to be built again? Being in government gave us the opportunity to introduce a justice system that this country has long cried out for, the justice system it deserves."

He gazed out over the crowd, lost in memories of that dreadful day.

Eventually he said, "I had a speech prepared for today but I'm not going to use it." There were mumblings, and from the plush chairs, Sterling Young looked at him anxiously. "I care deeply enough about this subject that I don't need any prepared words. I feel passionately about my job and duty to this great country of ours." He moved away from the lectern, strode around the stage, the blue of the diamond screen behind him like a sunlit sky. Cameras tracked his every move. "You know," he began, "I was asked to fight that war; I was asked to take away the privileges of the few who think they can disregard the lives and safety and property of others, and I was asked to ensure those privileges went to the people who were made victims by the criminals. I felt honoured to accept.

"For too long the victims suffered and the criminals laughed at us. For too long the words 'reform' and 'understanding' went hand in hand with tax hikes and misery. They took masses of money from law-abiding citizens to fund illogical, unworkable programmes to reform the character of criminals who were beyond reform; who sapped the country's wealth, and went back out into the community to commit crime all over again. And what did the victim get from the old regime?" Deacon gazed around at the silent faces. "Nothing."

He turned around to the huge blue screen behind him. The words *"Fairness in Punishment"* glowed in bright red. Beneath them, *"Criminal Justice Reform Act"*.

"If the victims had items of value stolen from them, their insurance premiums went up. If they had been attacked, they couldn't work and lost earnings. The list," he said, "goes on. And the old regime shrugged its shoulders and gave away their money to pay for a criminal's lifestyle and their Legal Aid." He raised his finger to the ceiling, brought it slowly down and said, "It stops here. It *stops here!*" The crowd applauded again and the cameras snapped. In the corner, Sterling Young rose to his feet and applauded too.

"Last year the Criminal Justice Reform Bill went through parliament at an astonishing speed, and it was wholeheartedly backed by many diverse groups of people, not least among them, People Against Crime. And if I may just take this opportunity to express my gratitude to Josephine Tower who so tragically died earlier this month in the most horrific of ways along with eighteen of our wonderful young people." He spoke over a ripple of polite applause. "She and her colleague, Emily Cooper, have accomplished so much in their work on this new act, and of course, we miss her very much, and the tireless way in which she sought solutions to what appeared insurmountable problems."

They applauded again, and Deacon paused respectfully.

"Together we ensured that The Rules, as they have become known, are indisputably fair, that they cannot lead to the death of an innocent person, and the safeguards within the act have ensured the approval even of religious and humanitarian organisations. The level of public support is unprecedented. And four days ago, The Rules came into being.

"The underlying message is simple: if you commit crime you will be punished!" Deacon thrust his head forward with such force to emphasise the words that his hair swung onto his forehead. Nonchalantly, he swept it back, and continued. "Since we took office, we have come a long way. We have seen the introduction of routinely armed police to guard against the more violent offenders, to protect themselves and the public. We are proposing vasectomy for persistent criminals because it is proven that criminals breed criminals – and why provide for them when in later life when they will steal from you or kill you? We have outlawed certain kinds of pornography; we are cracking down hard on drug offenders and prostitutes; all things that taint a good, clean society and all things that attract crime."

He waited for the appreciation to settle, strolled around to a new part of the stage and then continued his performance. "I was visited only yesterday by an elderly gentleman from my constituency in Yorkshire. He was a proud man." *And he held a fucking gun to my head.* "And do you know what his request was? His request was for politeness to return, his request was that decency and manners and safety should return to the country. 'Victorian values,' he called them. And he was right! Why should we put up with people whose sole intention is not to contribute to society's wealth, but to ruin the lives of those who *do* contribute? People are fed up with them, claiming the police don't do their job, claiming the judicial process is weak and cannot cope. Until now, they were absolutely right. But, it stops here.

"The judiciary…"

Deacon paused for the unscheduled applause to settle down.

"The judiciary has teeth now and has been instructed to use them. We have undertaken a massive prison building programme, because we thoroughly expect there to be a bigger prison population—" he held up a finger "—only for the time being. When those criminals experience life behind the bars of a new reformed penitentiary where there are no entertainment facilities except a pack of cards and a communal television, when their DVD players and private TVs are removed, when they work for nothing except their board and lodgings; and more importantly, when they see that The Rules *do* work, and that the guilty are punished by paying the ultimate price, that swollen prison population will shrink very quickly!

"And another thing that the criminal will not like: any costs incurred by victims, that includes items stolen, that includes increased insurance premiums or time taken off work to aid the investigation, will come out of the criminal's bank account. He literally will pay for his crime!"

The cheering had begun before the last words pounded out of the loud speakers. There were whistles and boisterous applause. Stamping feet became the bass accompaniment to raucous shouts of agreement as row upon row of people stood to lend their weight to the speech. The cameras spewed flashing light into the arena, turning Deacon into a strobe-lit figure walking the boards.

He looked at them; they were like a hungry mob. *They are sheep.* "Of course," he began again, quietly, ready to build to a climax, "reform and rehabilitation are offered. We all would prefer those who slip for one reason or another into criminality, to come back into our community as decent citizens, and we congratulate those people. However, hardened criminals who are determined to test the teeth of the Justice Ministry, will be sent to jail for a long time... but will receive help so as they may reintegrate into society. And then, when they reoffend, *if* they reoffend, they will be given an even longer sentence, but still offered further help, they will be offered treatment, but most importantly of all, they will be given a warning: offend again and you will be put to death!"

He continued to speak over the cheers and whistles, but inside he grinned as wide as his imagination would allow. Deacon loved the adulation and could almost fool himself into thinking that they loved him too. He briefly allowed himself to wonder if anyone would want his autograph as he left the arena.

"Murderers," he continued calmly, "go straight to Rule Three where it is at the discretion of the court and the Independent Review Panel to impose the death penalty or send them to labour camps for a life sentence. But the courts are under strict guidelines to punish by death unless it is against the public interest to do so, unless there are overriding mitigating circumstances.

"And it is with regret that I have to inform you that murderers already serving their sentences cannot be retried under The Rules, but those murderers who have evaded capture, who are still at large in our communities, *can* be routed through the new Criminal Justice system, and they will receive the full weight of the law.

"You know, it costs us £30,000 each and every year to keep a prisoner for life. It costs fifty-eight pence for a bullet and £140 for a pine casket. Money well spent, I believe." He smiled at the giggling audience.

"I've told you about the elderly gentleman I saw only yesterday in my constituency; well, I'll tell you another story of what happened while I visited Leeds only last week. I went to the railway station to see how they had progressed since that awful explosion there a few years ago. I laid a wreath at the plaque." He quietened. And then he looked up, hate in his eyes, "Those bombers are the very antithesis of what our country needs!" He strode, and then waved lazily with a floppy right arm, as though exhausted by fighting the good fight. "I digress," he smiled. "Forgive me. I was there to see how the station was coping with the drug problem it has, with the graffiti and with the anti-social behaviour it experiences, behaviour which people find distressing, depressing, frightening." His voice cracked on the final word.

To those in the rows closest to Deacon's feet, it seemed as though he were crying, his eyes looked damp as he recalled his tale, and as though he felt the utter despair that some people had to live with. It was this image, the weeping politician, which would sweep the front pages tomorrow. "People want safety on our streets and in their homes, and by God they have a right to expect it!" Hastily, he wiped a hand across his face. The cameras clicked, hundreds of them.

He walked around the stage and then he stopped, looked at the audience and began to laugh. "I apologise to you again. I *told* you I felt strongly about this, didn't I?" Deacon smiled at the photographers. "Where was I? Oh, yes. While I was there, I saw a group of seven or eight youths, mid-teens, hanging around, hands in pockets, smoking." He raised an eyebrow. "Up to no good. Nearby a group of pensioners were obviously afraid of these kids. One of the kids, a girl, began kicking at a phone booth, really kicking at it hard. And I wondered why she was doing it, she couldn't get money from it, it was a card-only phone. She smashed the handset against the card slot and continued kicking it. I was flabbergasted. The elderly people circled around her, keeping their distance and hurried away. I didn't blame them; she was making *me* feel nervous.

"But she was doing it because she wanted to, because she had no regard for property. She was doing it because she knew there would be no consequence. Who would stop her? What would happen to her for causing criminal damage to a phone box? Nothing. That's what would happen." His eyes scanned the silent audience, who listened with nods of recognition. "No one dare do anything; clip her round the ear and you'd end up in court, and if she clipped *you* around the ear, you'd end up in hospital." He opened his arms to the audience and asked, "Why should we put up with it any longer? Why should those pensioners be scared? People want to feel safe in their homes and on their streets and they don't!" He paused. "But they soon will. Soon you'll be able to sleep soundly in the knowledge that people don't commit petty damage anymore, people don't burgle anymore.

"When you wake up in the morning, your car will still be there, undamaged. Your shed won't have been broken into and all your tools stolen. They won't dare do it," he smiled. "We'll see to it. Give it a year or two," he shouted, "and I'll be surprised if there's any crime left worth talking about. Of course, let's be realistic; there *will* still be crime about, you'll never stop it completely; but the kind of premeditated serious crime will be almost non-existent, the kind of spontaneous petty crime will have all but stopped too. The only crime left that affects the people in the street will be spontaneous serious crime. I hate to admit it, but that's the kind of crime we may never stop. The Rules are there as a deterrent to the petty criminal and to the serious criminal who gives thought to his actions. And particularly against gun and knife crime, something that puts the very fear of God into every mother's heart up and down the country.

"And when these criminals are caught, they'll learn not to do it again; society will not allow them to. If you want to kill serious crime, you have to kill serious criminals!"

Flashguns blazed as Deacon raised his arm and grinned in a parting gesture. The crowd stood, their applause deafening, whoops and cheers and whistles. Even party-poppers erupted, something that caused Sirius, who waited in the wings, to grow nervous. He peeked around the curtain and watched his boss take the adulation before accepting Sterling's hearty handshake and gliding gracefully off the stage, waving to his fans as he went.

"How did it go?" he asked Justine Patterson, his aide and member of the PR team, after he was safely away from the microphones.

"Looked great to me. It looked spontaneous, especially the part where you said 'Where was I? Oh yes…'. That was wonderful. I congratulate you, George, on remembering it; it was word perfect."

– Two –

Outside the conference hall, the police had cordoned off a section of the main road and the square. Large truck-mounted screens pumped Deacon's speech out to the masses while other smaller screens, the vidiscreens, had crowds gathered around them. For the most part, the demonstrations were timid, mild-mannered affairs, where people expressed their opinion with a grunt or a nod. But there were two distinct factions to the crowd: one for The Rules and one against. And even in the 'for' camp, there were divisions. "Why do it with a bullet?" someone shouted. "Yeah, let's hang the bastards," someone replied.

There were hundreds of people gathered in the square, some listening to the speech, most jeering and chanting loudly, drowning out Deacon with bullhorns. Banners swung in the breeze: "hooray for sanity"; "death to murderers"; "forgiveness is divine"; "help, not death". There were posters showing the faces of children used and then slaughtered by paedophiles and other assorted twisted elements in society, and counteracting these were graphic depictions of dead men handcuffed to scarred wooden posts; more of freeze-frame shots showing a bullet passing through a human head; the tip of one breaking through the rear of the skull.

Each faction had its point of view and each tried to outdo the other in words and volume and pictures and arguments, and in the middle, in the grey areas where the two elements joined, were the scuffles amongst PAC representatives and Freedom for Life campaigners.

A female PAC member went down as a blade pierced her heart.

Chapter Twelve

Friday 19th June

Inside Jilly's darkened lounge the tears still fell from eyes that were incessantly tired. They were immersed in loose dark folds of skin that filled the hollows of her skull like some Halloween mask. By God, you'd have thought the tears would have ended by now, maybe returning only intermittently, but no, here they were rolling down the same cheeks they had dampened for the last three weeks. It was a pain she couldn't describe, even if she'd felt inclined to.

She had rejected the offer of counselling; choosing instead the drugs and a deep trough of grief. Sammy was dead. And her heart was in two. The TV blared somewhere in the background as Jilly brought the cold coffee cup up to her lips; she was surprised to see it empty. Blankly she stared at the TV, a distraction that no longer distracted, just noise to fill an otherwise silent existence. Some politician, Deacon, spouted about the rights and wrongs of a society that was in jeopardy of not giving a damn anymore. She shrugged her shoulders.

"The only way to kill serious crime is to kill serious criminals!"

Her eyebrows rose at that statement. "Oh how wonderful. I'd like to pull the trigger," she said without enthusiasm. "What a wonderful law." She wondered where her son's killer was now, what he was doing. Was he enjoying a pizza, flushing it down with a beer, laughing with his chums about how fucking clever he was? Or was he at home, sitting in a darkened room like she was, wondering about the point of it all? She suspected the former.

She put the cup down, finding a place for it on the carpet among the other half dozen or so. Jilly stood and shuffled into the kitchen. The house smelled, the sink was full of dishes with dried-on food, flies munching away happily, undisturbed and likely to remain that way for the foreseeable future.

Her slippers scuffed the floor on the way to the drawer where she kept her medication. Aspirin and Hedex, indigestion tablets, and Calpol for when Sammy got a fever. Her Protromil nestled among it all and she greedily swallowed two capsules, feeling sick as the cold water splashed her stomach. In the cupboard beneath the drugs was the booze. Brand new booze. When Eddie still lived here she'd cleared it out when it became apparent he was in trouble with whisky and brandy. Now she had restocked it. Just in case. She looked in there, sighed and closed the cupboard again. Not yet.

And then it happened. A knock at the door. Jilly froze, her eyes startled wide like the look on a young kid's face just before a car hits him.

She remembered that this was how it all began – the nightmare, with a knock at the door. The knock that was going to scoop her insides out and leave her barely able to stand, merely a shell with nothing good inside anymore.

Only an hour before *that* knock, everything had been fine. Sammy had wandered off out the front door. "I'll see you this afternoon, Mum." He'd walked dejectedly down the drive, hands in pockets, NY baseball cap shading his eyes from the sun.

"Go careful," she'd shouted after him. He waved absently over his shoulder, didn't look back.

She never saw him again.

And now, another knock brought it all back in a flood of tightly ordered memory, despite the sagging state of her twisted mind, and Jilly almost fell over in the kitchen there and then. But she clung on to the worktop until the fogginess evaporated, and only when the knock came again did she feel the urge to move towards it, like some inbred command: need to pee, go to toilet. Knock at front door, answer door.

Eventually she made it there, swallowed hard before reaching for the catch. Her mum smiled sympathetically up at her from the doorstep, a small bunch of roses clutched to her chest and a warm, endearing smile bathed in the day's sunlight. "Aw, Jilly…"

The Yorkshire Echo. 19th June

Deacon's passionate introduction for The Rules: "The criminal will pay"

By Michael Lyndon

"IF YOU want to kill serious crime, you have to kill serious criminals."

Social networks around the world are buzzing with Sir George Deacon's words, which will send a shiver up the spines of those who would commit crime on the United Kingdom mainland.

Earlier today, Justice Secretary Sir George Deacon disregarded a prepared speech for the introduction of the Criminal Justice Act.

At London's Earl Court, Deacon mesmerised the audience as he tore into an ad lib monologue setting out his reasons why The Rules were a just – and justified – piece of legislation for the UK, despite continued pressure from home and abroad to abandon the changes.

Deacon made a strong reference to the murders of his predecessor, Roger King, outside his Kensington home two years ago, and that of PAC founder Josephine Tower, who died alongside eighteen children and two other adults in an arson attack on a school in Sussex at the beginning of June. He said major incidents such as these, and like that on the London Underground, which highlight easy firearms acquisition, were the catalysts for this legislation.

For a more in-depth appraisal of Deacon, turn to page 14, where we compare his style to former great orators including Blair, Obama, Churchill, and Thatcher.

Chapter Thirteen

Saturday 20th June

– One –

The room was dark. It was quiet. The smells in here, mainly linseed oil from the cellar and the lingering odour of gas from the camping stove meal an hour ago, mixed with dampness; even in this hot June, dampness still lingered, reluctant to depart the old house. Two candles burned in the corner nearest the scabby mattress, throwing twists of smoke into the air, their radiance a flickering symbol of hope in a dreary and dangerous world. Spiders' webs glistened in their light and swayed in the tiny updrafts of warm air.

Christian smiled at his lot. He wasn't rich by any means. In the eyes of the state he didn't even exist. He had no National Insurance number, no police record, no bank account; didn't know where his birth certificate was, if he'd ever had one. He'd never owned an ID card, fingerprint, retina or otherwise; and never had his DNA or fingerprints taken. He was Mr Nobody, as transient as the candle smoke, and as vague as its flame. It was just as he wanted it, yes, Mr Nobody.

He looked at the bare brick walls – the dampness had pushed most of the plaster off about three years ago. The ceiling was naked too, a network of laths with only hints of the horsehair plaster that once resided between them. He looked at the rotten window frame, half the glass missing, covered by a piece of swollen chipboard. A grey net curtain, torn and snagged, fluttered against the remaining glass. A breeze squeezed through to sway the candles' flames. No, he wasn't rich, but he was lucky.

He crouched by her side and looked into her face, watching as the candlelight caressed her skin. Beneath the crimson tangle of fine veins running through the yellow tarnish of her eyeballs, there was still the old Alice. And somewhere beneath the black chaos of hair falling across her spotty face, Alice lived still.

The drugs had toyed with her for four years, but she was still in there somewhere. And sometimes, on the days when she felt good, when the drugs slackened their grip enough for her to sneak into the world they used to share, he could see her the way she was back then. That was Alice. And she would come back to him one day. He hoped.

When they first met, she had been on coke, and that was okay; it was tolerable. But the dealers and the other junkies got to her. And now she was a junkie too.

Beneath the candles' light, Christian's smile fell away and he knew it was time to provide for her. There was the stash hidden in the cellar for emergencies, but so far the need for it hadn't materialised. And if tonight went well, he could delay that need for another week or two. He pulled the old quilt up over Alice's shoulders. The net curtain billowed into the room and he could see moonlight, white and pale, through the gaps in the boarded-over window. It made him think of his latest project. He had time just to peek, didn't he?

Christian stood and crossed bare floor where the smell of linseed blew up through the cracks from the cellar below. He opened the door to the kitchen and quietly pulled it closed after him, his footfalls echoed around the bare walls, grit underfoot sounded like sandpaper on an empty pan. He turned towards the cellar door, letting his eyes grow accustomed to the lack of light. No moonlight in here, and he couldn't even switch on his torch; he daren't, for if the dealers found them, death would be the least of their problems.

"Maybe later," he said, and collected his tools and trainers as he headed for the corrugated iron sheet covering the back door. A sliver of moonlight crept through the gap between it and the wall, and further spots of moonlight beamed in through rusting nail holes, and lit up the floorboards like a private interstellar show.

He pulled the corrugated sheet closed and studied the cobbled lane and the black wasteland beyond it, scanning for movement in the night. He saw none and headed out quickly.

If all went according to plan, one day they wouldn't need to live in places that were fit only for pulling down. It was not beyond hope, and the way to achieving his goal was not by using the tools in his pocket, but by using the tools in his heart and in his mind. It was near, that one day.

– Two –

Robin McHue whipped the covers back and sat up in bed cursing his inability to sleep. It was the meeting that did it. The important meeting he had tomorrow with that fucking pillow-biter of a boss.

"What's up, love?" His wife slurred the words, still half asleep.

"Never mind."

He thudded across the bedroom floor, tramped down the stairs, and collided with his golf clubs stacked in a corner of the hall. Still cursing, he poured himself a large glass of whisky and sat in the dark lounge listening to the frigging clock ticking, and watching a band of moonlight creep across the carpet towards the kitchen. He dug his nails into the leather suite and grunted his anger into the silent room. That's it, he'd had enough, and tomorrow after the meeting, he vowed to make an appointment with the doctor and get this insomnia shit sorted once and for all. It was responsible for dropping his performance at work; he'd missed three targets this year already, and the lack of sleep was as certainly to blame for it as sodomy was for his boss's high-pitched voice.

He sighed and then noticed the light in the kitchen. He turned his head and watched it. At first it made him jump. But as he watched through the archway he realised it was the beam of a very small torch jittering around the walls.

Robin McHue climbed slowly to his feet and rested the glass back on the counter.

– Three –

He was a fair burglar. He stole from the rich – and only from the rich – to feed the poor, and he did it with no violence, if possible, and with no mess. He left behind anything sentimental, and took only cash, and maybe credit cards if they were the old ones that had a PIN number, and if that PIN was to hand.

Forty minutes from home, on a good street up in Meanwood, he walked by a suitable target. The house was a large detached job with a double garage and two cars on the drive. He couldn't see an alarm, and the window around the back was open!

No need for the tools with this one. But he still changed his shoes. It was Christian's habit. From each house he burgled, he always tried to take a pair of trainers, and he wore them at his next job, abandoning them later, keeping his own shoes for living in. It prevented the police getting a picture of his working habits through footwear identification. He was thorough, and he thought about things before he did them, like he thought about his ideals and the way he conducted his travels through life. This was all part of the big picture.

He placed his own shoes under the hedge at the front of the house and then strolled around to the rear, getting inside the gloves as he went. He shone his small torch through the open kitchen window, scanning its corners for passive infrared sensors. There were none, and so he hauled himself silently up onto the window ledge and took a last look behind him. He put the torch away, relying on the moonlight and his night vision to get him the riches.

He stood at the edges of the polished wooden floor, lessening the chances of it groaning, and listened to the house.

Christian's eyes sprang wide. He held his breath. Silently he glided forward and crouched, peering around the corner and into the doorless archway that led into the lounge. His eyes were drawn to a slat of bright moonlight lying like a neatly folded sheet on the lounge floor, spreading out and getting wider as it approached the kitchen area. A shadow spoiled the sheet. It moved slowly, and it held a golf club.

He had a choice: He could turn and quietly clamber back out through the window with his tail between his legs or he could confront the man, and consider Alice's needs. This was an excellent opportunity, he reminded himself. How many houses of this standard did you come across, and further, how many houses of this standard did you come across with the window wide open?

Christian approached the threshold as silently as a fog creeping over a graveyard. He looked at the elongated shadow. The golf club lifted.

Am I brave, or am I stupid? More to the point, which is he?

The club wavered, looked as though the guy was preparing to take his shot, waggling his big arse, adjusting his grip, waiting for the ball to show itself. Oh, yes, he was a hit first, fuck the questions, kinda guy. Christian ran the tips of his fingers over the rough stubble of his cheeks. He watched the golf club, saw the shadow fingers tighten his grip, flexing, waiting. He pulled in a long silent breath through an open mouth, considering his options.

"Who's there?"

Christian blinked and held his breath. It was always the question asked by people who weren't expecting visitors.

The man with the golf club cleared his throat and the shadow fingers gripped tighter. "I said who's there?"

"I heard you the first fucking time." Christian heard the shriek, a small surprised little thing that a squeezed diaphragm forced through a clenched mouth. "It's me," he said in a friendly, soothing voice, "Mr Nobody."

Chapter Fourteen

Saturday 20th June

Alice stood and dared to look into the dark ribs of the spider-encrusted ceiling. She saw that Christian wasn't here; and she hoped he was out doing the business, getting her some gear, otherwise… well, otherwise she'd go fucking berserk! Simple as that.

"Hurry, babe," she whispered; and with arms again folded around her breasts, she walked over to the bed and looked down at Spencer. She smiled, and touched his hair, stroked it with a mother's gentle fingertips, felt the softness of his skin and…

the hammer smashed into his skull and shattered a spray of blood and warm brains across her face

…heard the tiniest of snores coming from his puckered lips. Spencer's eyes flickered but stayed closed. She breathed hard and walked away, squeezing the bridge of her nose. "Fuckin help me," she whispered. The sugar had all but gone, the Pepsi and the Lucozade were gone, and she needed something fast before she shrank into a black ball of spiky hatred in a corner, before she became *dangerous* to be around.

Why wouldn't he give her the fucking cash? She could go out and make her own deals, she could…what, exactly?

You could get ripped off again, you could come back with no stuff and no cash and probably with your fanny on fire because you got raped by a dealer just before he robbed you.

Fuck! Why did he always leave it until she'd run dry before he went for more? Just what was his damned game? He had no right to… why not keep a little on standby in case something shitty happened? Was that too—

Hold on. Maybe Christian *had* hidden some.

The blackness of her eye sockets creased a little as she squinted.

He brought Spencer into the world, Alice. He did that and he cared for you both like a decent man. Don't mock him, girl; that, out of all the things you've thought tonight, is the lowest you've got.

* * *

She swung the cellar door open and the smell of linseed punched her in the face.

The candle flickered as she descended the stone steps and into the bowels of the rotting old house. Her hand cast flitting shadows on the whitewashed walls and she shuddered as the temperature dropped another five degrees.

You know he'd be furious if he caught you down here, dontcha? He's told you before to stay out, hasn't he? And why did he tell you, huh?

"If he had nothing to hide from me, why would he ban me from coming down here?" The smell grew stronger.

She swallowed and straightened. "I have a right to see it, whatever it is. I have a right to it, half of it's mine."

Hey, come on, leave the guy alone; it's his only privacy from you. Come on, look what he done for you, how he stood by you. The least you can do is respect his wishes—

"Fuck his wishes." The candle wavered. "What's he ever done for me, eh? Got me pregnant is what he did, the bastard, and that made me depressed and, and…"

Alice began to cry.

He gave you a family, Alice. You think on that, girl. He gave you stability.

"You call *this* stability?"

You ain't got a mortgage and you ain't got no rent to pay, but you got a roof over your head, you safe and you free, and that's what you both need more'n anything.

"I need a fucking *hit* more than anything." She held the candle out in front of her at arm's length and shuffled into the blackness of Christian's realm.

Chapter Fifteen

Saturday 20th June

The knock came. "Who is it?"

"It's me."

Eddie put his coffee – coffee! – down on the table and answered the door. He hadn't seen Mick in over a week. Maybe Ros had been right when she said Mick only wanted to sink into the gutter with some company, and his chosen company was Eddie.

"Come in, Mick."

Mick closed the door behind him. "Hey," he pointed at the coffee. "What the hell's that?"

"I'm back at work Monday. Thought I should try and be—"

"Fuck that. Grab the glasses; I brought us some Metaxa."

"Honest, Mick, I—"

"Now, now. I don't wanna hear any bollocks, Eddie. Sit ya bum, Mick's here now."

"I need to go to bed." He looked into Mick's bloodshot eyes and then burst out laughing.

Mick didn't laugh, he just grabbed two glasses off the wonky sideboard and perched in his usual chair by the window. "I have news, Eddie."

"Hi, Eddie, how're you feeling?"

Mick smiled. "Hey, I'm sorry; I forgot my manners there for a minute." Fake concern smeared itself over Mick's whiskers and even the crow's feet smoothed out a little. "How are you; no, I mean it, Eddie, how are you doing these days? Things any easier?"

As if you care. "No, things are not any easier. I wake up every morning – if I'm lucky enough to fall asleep, and I realise my kid is still dead. How's that? I feel like slitting my throat. Next?"

Mick ignored him, eager to feel the burning sensation of brandy flowing into his gut. "Speaking of throats," he said, smile growing all the time, "come on, get some of this down yours; it'll fade the blues until they're almost tolerable." He handed Eddie half a tumbler of brandy, chinked glasses and slumped in his chair, leg cocked over one arm in his usual fashion. He lit a cigarette and exhaled as though he were in his own lounge.

"I doubt it." Despite his earlier good intentions, Eddie took the glass, as the justifications began to pop into his head. The little voice inside put up a fair fight, but in the end, addiction always won over reason. Hell, he was celebrating his last weekend before returning to the job; and hell, Sam was *still* dead! Both of them were top drawer reasons to enjoy that glass of Metaxa. He nodded the glass at Mick and drank with a free conscience.

"Guess what."

"Me and guessing games are not the best of friends."

"Christ, you are touchy tonight, aren't you? Job freaking you out; going back after a long time off can—"

"Get on with it."

Mick took his leg off the arm of the chair and sat forward, cigarette in one hand and glass in the other, and waved both at Eddie as he told his tale, smile right back on his face as though it were glad to be home. "The first Rule Three death is next week!"

Eddie shook his head. "Rule Three?"

"Oh come on," he said, "you had your head up your arse all year?"

"I've had one or two distractions, yes."

"Fair point. Margy Bolton is due to go before the gun tomorrow. You remember her? She's going to be famous."

"That bitch is already famous."

"She's going to be in all the papers and on all the stations. She's more famous than the fucking PM, is Margy."

"They're not televising it, though? Tell me they're not."

"No, no. Christ, that would go against the decency legislation." And then he winked. "But there *is* a loophole. They can broadcast the *sound* of her dying, of her being shot. No visual, but plenty of audio. The fucking ratings will soar, I promise you."

"You're looking forward to it, aren't you?"

"Damned right. I tell you, Deacon has risen in my estimations no end since he brought The Rules in. They're calling him the new hero of the twenty-first century."

"Who's 'they'?"

"Most of the people I've interviewed think it's about time we got tough on the killing culture, as they call it. And it spreads wider afield than good ol' Blighty. The Yanks are applauding us big style; they think it's wonderful, and those states that already employ the death penalty feel vindicated."

"What about those that don't?"

Mick shrugged. "Dunno, really. Like always, they're saying it's wrong to kill people, but there are more in favour of capital punishment than against it. I mean, most of Europe nearly had a coronary when The Rules came in; no way Deacon could've got it through European legislation – The Sixth Protocol, Article 1, abolition of the death penalty – had we not pulled out of Europe altogether.

"But who gives a shit about Europe anyway? I certainly don't. And I'll tell you something else, Eddie, when The Rules kick in, the crime rate will drop through the floor." He stared into thin air, and with arms outstretched, drew out an invisible banner, "I'm writing it up as this: people will be able to leave their doors unlocked as they did back in the 1940s; Britain will once again be great." His eyebrows rose. "What do you think?"

"Do you think that'll ever happen? Because I don't."

"Well, maybe people won't leave their doors unlocked, but once criminals see their brethren die – or hear them die, should I say – they'll think twice before burgling, robbing and murdering."

"Some, maybe. But not all."

"Hey, I'll accept some, that's a good enough start for me. Crime will drop, overcrowding in prison won't be a problem anymore, and Britain will be more prosperous for it in the end."

"I don't agree with killing someone."

Mick sipped the brandy, peering over the rim at Eddie, obviously wondering whether to pursue the matter. He decided he would. "If you found the green Jag man, would you still say that?"

Fair question. Christ, it was a good question. Eddie thought about it, drank his drink, and lit a cigarette before he could even formulate a response. "Yes. I don't agree with killing someone. I admit that finding that bastard would probably test my principles."

"Good enough answer for me, Eddie." Mick topped their glasses up. "I've written a good piece about her forthcoming demise; Rochester liked it, and it's rolling on page two on Monday if things don't change."

"Who's Rochester?"

"Editor."

"And what could change?"

"You *are* behind, aren't you? They haven't even finished the London and Birmingham slaughterhouses yet. Or should I say, the

'Termination Buildings'. The one in Leeds is done apart from carpets and paint, and some final testing; it's where the kiddie-killer bites the bullet, literally. And then I hear they haven't even finished selecting the executioner yet. Shit, can you believe it; I mean I know they probably don't have any apprentice-trained candidates to choose from, but Christ, come on!"

Eddie shook his head, laughed. "I think Deacon is full of shit. He gives off this air of supremacy. He's a baby-hugger, but I bet behind the scenes he's a bastard, and I further bet he gets his way on most issues."

"Who cares what he's like when he's out of the public gaze, so long as he doesn't smother the babies when he hugs them, he's fine by me."

"I'm surprised there haven't been more objections to it. I mean how can you put a gun to someone's head in this day and age and get away with it?"

"Happens all the time, Eddie. But you never hear of it."

"How do you mean?"

"Well, if the government is under threat, either by terrorists or by infiltrators, the heavy mob gets involved and the threat just disappears." Mick clicked his fingers. "In a cloud of dust."

"Who's the 'heavy mob'?"

Mick shrugged. "I don't know; they keep it to themselves, don't they? But I guess there are men with big guns, like your MI5 or your NCA crews. They're the clean-up brigade; they're the ones who make all the nasty things go away so the government and the public can make believe everything's okay."

"Who was it said 'keep taking an eye for an eye and the world would go blind'?"

"Huh?"

"If you live by the gun, you die by the gun."

"Are you pissed already? You're making zero sense to me, Eddie."

"I'm talking about killing, legally killing. If you kill people who have done wrong, there'll be no bugger left before long, and the eye for an eye thing means that no progress is ever made if you just solve your problems by killing them."

"Bollocks. Kill your problems and you *have* no problems. You speak to most decent citizens and you'll realise that they're sick of being treated as the chaff while the wheat – the criminal – is afforded all the powers and rights he could wish for. They want tougher sentences, they want—"

"Retribution. Whatever happened to reform; now you're saying everyone is out for punishment."

"Hoorah." Mick put down his drink and applauded. "You got that one right. Did you know that it costs you and me nearly £30,000 a year to keep a man in prison? And did you know there are currently 889 lifers in prison under the age of thirty? And since life actually means life now – not like it used to when life meant fifteen years before being let out to kill again – that means that each one has on average another thirty years to do. Do the maths on that, Eddie, and you end up paying a bill of around a billion pounds. That's a mighty fine wad, wouldn't you say? How many hospitals could you build for that?"

"That's Deacon talking. But you're missing the point. There's a host of reasons why it's wrong to kill someone."

"Oh, go on then, wise one, let's hear it; should be good for a laugh."

"I'm not laughing. And I'm the one directly affected by someone who would now be on what, a Rule Three? for killing Sam."

Mick nodded. "If he's found guilty of murder, and it's proved beyond all doubt – hear that, Eddie, beyond *all* doubt – that he killed your boy, he faces the gun."

"I would like him to spend the rest of his life in a cell."

"A lot o' money going to waste."

"It's not wasteful; it's punishing him, month after month, year in year out. He has nothing to look forward to except death. Why give him what he wants on a fucking platter?"

"Fair point. So you're in favour of long sentences for punishment, but not for reform."

Eddie drained his glass, tossed the dead cigarette into the ashtray and lit another, sighing the smoke out in a long stream. "Couldn't give a monkey's toss about reform; what has he got to reform about? He can't bring Sam back by reforming his character, can he? I want him punished. Anyway, what should worry the public is the police."

"Why?"

"What happens when the evidence they have inadvertently puts some innocent man in the slaughterhouse? It's happened, sometimes not even on purpose."

"Oh come on, corruption is dead."

"For a journalist, Mick, you're fucking naïve. Coppers have been doing it for centuries. And they'll be under more pressure to bring in the results now. They'll be inclined to cut so many corners it'll be round when they've finished."

"Won't work. All evidence for Rule Three cases gets sifted by the Independent Review Panel; they're forensics people, law people—"

"And coppers?"

"So what? They're independent."

"Okay, so what happens to the poor schmuck in the wrong place at the wrong time, whose evidence fits if you look at it in a certain light, but is actually innocent? At least if he's banged up for a few years, there is the opportunity to set him free."

"It'll never happen, Eddie. Mark my words; it'll never happen."

Chapter Sixteen

Saturday 20th June

Christian looked back at the open window, checking that the escape route was still there, just in case. "You give me no trouble, and I'll give you none."

"Get out of my fucking house. Now."

Christian silently climbed down onto his front, feeling the coolness of the floor on his hands and on his belly where his T-shirt had pulled up a little. This was the time when normal burglars would have slid back out the window, thankful to have gotten away with their life and their arse intact. But Christian was different; he felt different, almost felt as though he had a God-given right to be there, because what he was doing was *right*. He had selected the target and the target was his until he'd milked it, and no one, not Mr Golfer, Mrs Golfer or even the fucking police would sway him until he was finished.

It was a shame that it had come to this, a confrontation that neither man wanted. But he had a woman at home and both of them could use a little fattening up, and one of them could use a little escapism. Escapism wasn't cheap. The man in there, the golfer, seemed wealthy enough, and Christian didn't think that donating a couple of hundred quid would force him to sell one of his cars.

"I said get out now or else I'm calling the police."

He crawled further forward, past the refrigerator – one of those large American jobs – and closer to the archway giving onto the lounge. He watched Mr Golfer's shadow grow nervous. Christian's mouth watered. And he would be lying if he said he wasn't nervous himself; of course he was, but the nerves were tempered by the challenge and they were calmed by the goal.

The threshold with the lounge was inches away from his face. He could see Mr Golfer's bare foot around the corner of the archway, could see the shadows beneath the moonlit window and could make out half of the leather chair Mr Golfer had presumably sat in before he took up his stance. All the man with the club had to do was look down and take another small step forward, and he could stroke that full head of free-living hair with a five iron, and then be patted on the back for it later. But he didn't move.

From his breast pocket, Christian took the coin and the small black box. Without making a sound, he flicked the 'on' button, listened to the tiny whine as the capacitor charged up, and waited patiently for the LED light to glow. And then he tossed the coin across the lounge. Heads or tails? It tinked into the glass door of the DVD cabinet and moments later, he lunged.

Christian leapt, closed his eyes in readiness and tripped the flashgun with the thumb of his right hand. Mr Golfer shrieked again as his world turned instantly white, overexposed, and then sank into a land of green shadows punctuated by a bright orange dot. And that's when he screamed.

Christian opened his eyes and punched the man in the balls. The golfer folded, gasping for air, retching, his free hand groping wildly in the air between them. And then he stood.

Why don't you be a good victim and hand over the cash and let me walk away with it, huh? Why make things so damned difficult?

He watched the shock on the golfer's face turn to anger. Christian swung his right fist, but Mr Golfer was surprisingly quick as he drunkenly stepped aside, and in the same movement, swung the club around his back. Christian tried to move, he could see what was about to happen – how the club would smash into his skull, how the blood would spray across the lounge walls and then the police would arrive, pin a medal to Mr Golfer's chest, arrest Christian and throw away the key.

The club was already on its arc down towards his head. He saw it – *heard* it whoosh before it crashed into the ceiling lamps. Glass shattered, plaster fell like snow from the ceiling, and the club's arc changed, deflected like a car bouncing off another car in a road accident. Unluckily for him, the light didn't deflect it much and it still travelled toward him.

The club smashed into Christian's thigh and he went down screaming. For a second he wondered if his leg was broken, since all the sensation had evaporated apart from a throbbing tingle at the edges of the numbness. And then he thought he'd better shut up and stop screaming before the club found him again and came back for a second go. But it was too late. The scream gave away his position and there was another loud whooshing sound. Christian closed his eyes.

The club smacked into the skirting board, and Mr Golfer screeched furiously at him. Christian grabbed the man's pyjama bottoms and yanked. He could think of nothing else to do. For the time being, he was paralysed and lay on the lounge carpet like he was a tee on a practice green. The pyjamas slid down but Christian kept on pulling, yanking hard until the golfer lost his balance and banged to the floor on his bare arse. Face to face.

In the near-darkness, both men grunted and screamed. Christian leapt at him, knocked him backwards and sank a punch into the golfer's belly. The man's breath rushed out and his face crumpled. His hands went to his stomach and he dropped the club. He rolled over and glass crunched beneath him, the breath streamed in through clenched teeth hissing like a punctured tyre. Christian got to his feet, ran a hand quickly down the side of his leg, and felt light-headed as the real pain bypassed the numbness and seized his mind. There was damage there; he didn't know how bad but when he tried to put weight on it, it ignited a fire that burned furiously.

"I'll fucking have you, you bastard!" The golfer coughed, and Christian let his knees fold so his weight fell onto the golfer's balls again. More rushing air, bulging eyes, and groans.

"Where's your money?" He ignored the pain in his leg, pulled his mind back to the job and back to the predicament he found himself in. He could still be caught, and so he'd better focus on getting the money and getting out of here. He held his right fist a foot above the man's squinting eyes. "Tell me where, or you'll have a broken nose to go with your flat balls."

"Fuck you," the golfer spat through clenched teeth.

Christian didn't hesitate. This was for his family, it was for his way of life, and now it was for his freedom too. The nose cracked and the man screamed again, hands smearing the blood across his face. In this light it looked like black sludge. "Next time it'll be your teeth. Tell me where you keep your money."

"I haven't got any."

The fist mashed the golfer's mouth, and more blood trickled down the side of his face. His hands fell to his sides and Christian wondered if he'd gone too far and knocked the fucker out. But his eyes were still open, their moistness shone in the moonlight; his breathing still shallow and fast, and he stared at Christian without malice, without feeling, and then he whispered, "It's over there in the bureau, right hand side."

"You'd better not be pissing me about."

"I'm not." And then his eyes closed in a long blink that scared Christian a little; made him wonder if he'd caused the man some real harm, something he didn't want on his conscience. He almost felt like kicking the silly bastard for making him go so far. There was no need for all this, and he felt the anger swell up in his chest again, because it was for nothing, all this, it was pointless – the man could and *would* claim this back on the insurance.

He grabbed the flash unit off the floor and then stood and limped across the lounge. He opened the bureau and saw nothing.

"In the tin," said the man. "In the tin on the right."

And there it was. In a Cinderella tin, no doubt bright and colourful during the day, but only various shades of grey now. "This your holiday money?" He pulled out a wad wrapped in a plastic bag.

And then Christian was blinded.

Chapter Seventeen

Saturday 20th June

Henry sat in the chair and massaged his bandaged hand. He felt like shit and he looked pretty much the same. He waited in the drawing room like some guest at a hotel rather than being allowed to see the old fart right away. His father, the revered George Deacon – *Sir* George Deacon, champion of the common man, if you don't mind – was busy polishing his golden letter opener in the study, by God; but *he* was the one who summoned *Henry*, not the other way round. Henry tapped his fingers on the arm of the chair. It was a mixture of nerves and anger.

He was cold and he was hungry, and these sensations, coupled with the anger, meant he shook uncontrollably. His hand throbbed beneath the bandage and if it had been just a little tighter, he could imagine the skin popping out between the wraps like an inner tube through a hole in a tyre.

It had started three weeks ago at the very end of May; a day that could only have been hotter if you were sitting on a furnace, and he was angry *that* day too. But his anger then was caused by being stuck in traffic while his sale walked out the front gate and drove away.

"Henry."

Henry jumped and almost fell off the Chippendale.

"Henry, where have you been?"

"What– what do you mean?" Henry stood, put his bandaged hand behind him and took a step away from his advancing father.

"I invited you to my after-speech party. And what's more, boy, I expected you to be there!"

Didn't invite me to the fucking speech itself though, did you? "I couldn't make it, I'm afraid. I had—"

"What? What did you have? Stomach ache, a sore head, or perhaps another appointment in the syph clinic?"

Henry ground his teeth. "I had things to attend to."

Deacon spun and began walking back to his study, and Henry followed him down the dimly lit hallway with deep red carpet underfoot, and carved wood flanking the walls. Over his father's shoulder, he saw a man sitting in a chair at the end of the hall. A discreet wall lamp cast its glow onto the newspaper he read. As they approached, the man looked up, nodded at Deacon and became engrossed again. Sirius, the lapdog; Henry recognised the big man even from that one small glance, and he too was on the hate list, the slimy bastard. Henry followed Deacon into the study.

Deacon closed the door and silence cloaked them.

Henry looked around at this sanctum that he had visited once before without his father's knowledge. For a study, it was a large room, easily big enough to accommodate a snooker table and a bar. Thousands of books lined its walls, all neatly stacked on mahogany shelves, and they gave off a musty, comforting smell. And then there was the desk, a thing so large it probably had its own Ordnance Survey reference. It had two flat-screen monitors and two phones on it – one of them bright red. The Bat Phone, Henry immediately christened it. He sat in the chair facing the enormous desk and Deacon busied himself at the drinks cabinet. Lead crystal decanters tinkled against handcrafted tumblers.

"Tonic?"

Henry looked over. Shook his head. "Neat." He already felt intimidated, not only by his surroundings, but by his father. Politics had turned him from the one man to whom he could tell anything into the one man from whom he kept everything. He'd become a vapid businessman whose cronies included ministers and lords, whose name was not on the Prime Minister's printed Christmas card list, but on the handwritten list instead.

He nodded thanks for the drink, and downed it in one.

"Fill it yourself, Henry, would you?" Deacon sat, slackened his tie. "So what did you have to attend to that was more important than my after-speech party?"

"Personal things." Henry sat, readied himself for the interrogation.

"Am I not your father? Can't you tell me personal things any longer?"

"I'm surprised you have the time."

"Was that a flippant remark, Henry?"

"Yes, it was. Strike that from the minutes, would you."

The dictionary struck him on the knee and fell to the floor. Henry jerked, banged his bandaged hand and spilled his drink. He stared at Deacon, and in that instant, hated him.

"Would you like to start being civil to me, Henry? As you can see, I have no shortage of books."

Henry refilled his glass.

"You should have come to the speech. Though I say it myself, I was wonderful. Even Sterling commented upon my performance."

"I'm sure you did a wonderful job, Father."

"I gave a heart-rending speech about the Criminal Justice Reform Act, Henry. Do you know anything about it? The Rules, some people call it."

Henry shrugged, kicked aside the book and retook his seat. He saw something in his old man's eye, and knew that he was playing games. The tone of voice, the insinuation threaded through the question like a certain track near a certain village threads through certain slag heaps. "No, I don't…"

"The Rules, Henry, are a radical new way of dealing with criminals. Basically, you get three chances to reform, three chances given to you by society to keep your nose clean."

"*My* nose? You say it as though you're—"

"Bear with me." He said this with a smile that was far too warm, far too friendly to belong to idle chat, more in the vicinity of the end is nigh. "However, the rule of three only applies to petty criminals, or rather to those who don't pose a serious personal threat to anyone. It doesn't apply, in its fullest form, to those who kill, or to those who have killed and have not yet been caught." He stared directly at Henry.

Henry looked away.

"Those people go straight to Rule Three. The gun." Now Deacon did not smile.

That comment was aimed directly at him. Being an estate agent gave you an instant malice-o-meter; you knew when people hated you enough to talk to you while drawing the dagger behind their back.

But that wouldn't bother you*, you bag of shit. They could break down the doors to this place, drag me screaming out into your grounds and put a bullet through the back of my head, and your only concern would be for the damaged door and the blood on your roses.* "Why have you called me down here, Father? You never call me down here." And then he thought more about it. And he could see why his father *would* be bothered. Not because of the death thing: that wouldn't cause his heart to flutter – did he *have* a heart? He would be bothered because his reputation would be soiled. He recalled, after his last little excursion from the path of righteousness, how dear Daddy had him up against the wall, threatened to smear his face across it. He wouldn't risk the PM crossing him off his Christmas card list.

"I never call you down here while I have government business—"

"Or while there are people here I could embarrass you in front of."

Deacon's eyebrows rose. "True," he said.

"So why have you summoned me? I'm busy with the business, I can't—"

"You can't take an evening off and spend it with your father? What kind of son are you?" He sipped his drink, staring at Henry over the rim with cold eyes. "I'm what, thirty miles away from your home? That's nothing to a man who drives like you do."

Ever seen a trap door, Henry thought, *and gone over to have a look anyway?* He swallowed. "I don't drive quickly."

"Quite," was all Deacon said. "What about the business? Gone bust yet?"

"What a thing to ask! No, I haven't gone bust yet; it's doing alright considering the climate we're in."

"So you're *nearly* bust."

His hand throbbed.

Deacon laughed and reclined in his seat, arms folded, enjoying his son's visit.

"Okay," Henry said, "cards on the table, why am I here?"

"Cards on the table?" Deacon reached into a drawer and pulled out a blue folder, all the while keeping his dark eyes on Henry. From the folder he took a sheet of printed A4 and slid it across the desk to Henry. "Treat yourself."

It was a copy of the statement he made to the police two weeks ago about some nasty scrote who relieved him of his beloved Jaguar. Astonished, he looked up at Deacon. "How did you get hold of this?" Henry's chest grew tight over a hammering heart.

"I am the Justice Secretary, Henry. I pull so many strings, they call me the puppet master." Deacon laughed at the expression on Henry's face. "I'm only kidding about the title, I just made it up, but it has a certain ring, wouldn't you say?" Deacon stood and marched around the desk, and Henry pushed into the back of the chair. "I like to keep a discreet eye on what's happening in your life, Henry. To an extent, we are estranged, and well… I don't want you getting up to any mischief; I don't want your old tricks to re-emerge."

"You're keeping tabs on me!"

"Steady," Deacon said, "this isn't *Nineteen Eighty-Four*, you know. I take an interest, that's all."

"Bollocks!"

Deacon swung his fist with such ferocity as to knock Henry sideways out of the chair. The chair crashed on top of him and hadn't come to rest before the study door burst open with Sirius filling its frame. Henry looked up and screamed. Deacon waved Sirius away and when the door closed, reached down and pulled the chair off his son, providing his foot with unhindered access.

As each blow struck his back, all Henry could think of was that he wished he were in the SAS, because if he were…

Henry curled up on the floor and Deacon took the opportunity to stamp on his bandaged hand. That brought Henry's mind round from the greyness it was sinking into, and he surfaced with venom in his veins and hatred in his mind. He rolled over just as Deacon was about to lay another well-aimed foot at his kidneys. "Stop!" He made it to his knees, and Deacon, grunting like a boxer about to deliver the killer blow, pulled back just as Henry's fist made contact with his balls.

Deacon stopped dead. His spindly old legs buckled, and he sank to his knees, groaning and clutching his balls.

Henry brought his reddened face within inches of his father's and hissed at him through clenched teeth, "If you ever touch me again, you old fuck, the world will find out what a hypocrite you are. You'll go from a seat in Westminster to a seat in the slaughterhouse in record time."

Deacon's eyes widened with surprise, both with pain and at the sudden display of a spine from his wimp of a son. But behind the surprise was something else. Fear.

"What do you know?" Deacon's words fell out of his mouth in a rush, blurred together by that fear. He stood, propping himself against the desk, and then shuffled back to his chair, trying to hide his astonishment. "Out with it!"

Henry climbed to his feet. "You bastard." He held out his bandaged hand and saw the blood seep through it. "It was beginning to fucking heal!" He spat blood onto the carpet and looked reproachfully at Deacon.

Deacon arranged his shirt, pulled his tie back into position, and said, "Tell me what you think you know."

"I don't *think* I know anything." The anger resurfaced. "I *do* know."

Deacon stared at his son for what must have been a minute, then calmly asked, "What happened to your hand, Henry?"

This was turning into the best fucking day of his entire life – except for Launa Wrigglesworth! – and he wondered why he hadn't used the threat before. It was two years old, he'd had it in him for two whole years, and in all that time he had taken the beatings and the humiliations, rather than use the old man's tactics against him. And now that he *had* used it, it worked better than a razor blade chastity belt. But he did not gloat.

"I burnt it."

"Why did you burn it, Henry?"

There was a tentative understanding in Deacon now, almost a grace that Henry had never seen before; and he wondered if this was how politicians dealt with everyday life, whoever had something over someone got the prize. And when someone had something on you, you obliged, you conceded gracefully and you never mentioned it again. That's life in the great game of politics. Deacon wore an expression that Henry had never before seen: compliance. He really *did* have him by the balls.

"You know why my hand is burned; you know how I burned it too, I guess."

"I want to hear it from you, boy. You tell me exactly what happened, and I'll try to help you."

"Why would you do that?"

"Because, for the time being, I believe your threat is real, and I have a lot at stake at the moment. Things that I would rather not lose. If you mess things up, it taints me." He looked derisively at Henry, like he was a piece of shit. "You know," he said, "if they catch you for this, you're going to die for it? I'll look bad for siring such an abomination, may even be voted out, but *you'll* die, boy!"

"Abomination?"

Deacon said nothing.

"So what's the deal?" Henry leaned forward. "You help me out this once, and the next time I mess up you kill me?"

"I hope there will not be a next time." Now Deacon leaned forward, and his voice dropped to a bare whisper; "This is the only time this threat of yours will work. The next time you try to use it, be prepared to die. Do you understand me?"

He stared into Deacon's hateful eyes and nodded, "Yes."

"I mean it, Henry. Next time it kills you."

Henry nodded again. They understood each other for the first time since Henry ploughed his clumsy way through adolescence. And it was something to be celebrated. "Drink?"

"Did you kill that man on Leeds Road?"

Henry sighed, "Yes," and went on pouring the drinks.

"Why?"

"He was annoying me."

"Did the twelve-year-old boy annoy you too?"

Henry blinked. He held his head high, breathed in deeply though his nostrils. "That, sir, was an accident, pure and simple."

"You sounded as though you were giving your pre-prepared answer from the dock of a courthouse then." Deacon tipped the glass. "You were travelling at an estimated fifty-eight miles an hour. You were in a thirty zone. That's two deaths in one day; quite a feat. Even for you."

"Spare me the funnies, please. I have been over it a thousand times, and there's nothing I can do now that will change either of those deaths, the tramp or the kid." Henry sipped and then winced as it bit into his cut lip.

"You almost sound as though you care?"

Henry shrugged. "No, I don't care. It's sad that the kid died, but—" he shrugged again, "—shit happens. I need extricating from this mess before it turns around and bites me." And then he looked up. "Bites us."

"Have you destroyed the car?"

"No."

"What! Why the hell not?"

Henry held up his hand. "I tried to burn it," he said. "But it burned me instead."

"How did you explain that to the police when they asked for your statement?"

"Said the car thief slammed my hand in the door."

"They believed you?"

"I was in pain! They believed me. Why would they think I was lying, carjacking happens all the time."

"I can't believe no one saw you kill either of them, especially the man on Leeds Road, in rush-hour!"

"It all comes down to witness statements, and you know how unreliable they are. My story stands."

"So what if they find the car and it's got your prints all over it?"

"It's bound to have my prints over it: it's my damned car!"

"Steady on, Henry; we have an agreement, that's all. It doesn't turn me into your underling."

"Sorry."

"I'll have Sirius destroy it." Deacon searched the ceiling, looking for some kind of answer, and in relief, Henry sat back down and let him work it out. "Can't be tomorrow or Monday, I have places to go." He looked back at Henry. "We'll have to make it sometime on Tuesday."

"Why wait, though? Why risk anyone finding it? I mean, if you'll help me, then we could sort this whole thing—"

Deacon shook his head. "If anyone had found the car we would know about it, the police would have knocked on your door by now. Another couple of days won't hurt. In the meantime, keep going as though nothing has changed."

"Well," he said, "if you're sure."

"Where is the car?"

Henry smiled. "Remember Great Preston?"

Chapter Eighteen

Saturday 20th June

– One –

Christian breathed hard, holding a wad of cash; maybe five or six hundred pounds. He stared at the man on the floor who groaned and writhed about in the glass from the smashed ceiling lamp. Standing above him in the doorway was Mrs Golfer, wearing a towelling dressing gown, eyes furious with what she saw.

"Get out of our house." Her voice was strangely calm as she looked from her husband to her burglar; her own private burglar. "I have called the police."

"I would have done that too." He looked down at the wad, wondered if they could get by without all this money. "What was this for?" he asked Mrs Golfer.

"That's none of your damned business, my lad."

"I'm not your lad," he whispered. "I only—"

"Get out!"

Christian limped across the lounge, heading for the kitchen, hoping to find the keys dangling in the back door. As he passed Mr Golfer, he looked down, saw the pain in his eyes, the embarrassment.

"You'll fucking hang for this, you bastard."

"Don't think so." Christian stuffed the cash into his jeans pocket and quickly left the house. He was a quarter of a mile away on Kirkstall Lane in Headingley, near the stadium before he saw two police cars speeding past, blue lights flashing, but no sirens. After another quarter mile, he suddenly remembered his shoes in the hedge at the bottom of the garden.

Che sera, he thought. Christian walked home.

– Two –

The candle was weak, the darkness oppressive, claustrophobic. And Alice could feel the beginnings of a panic attack coming on. She was naked and cold, a little afraid, and now she could imagine her demise down here in a dank cellar, could imagine the candle rolling away across the gritty floor as she sucked at the dust through her constricted throat.

She held the light at arm's length again and crouched, looking past its glow and into the gloom, towards a set of drawers, wonky old wooden things not fit for the tip, and she wondered if that was where he kept her stuff. It made sense, but it was a little unimaginative. She pulled the brass loops on each of the drawers, and wasn't the slightest bit surprised to see them full of nothing more sinister than painting equipment.

She slammed the drawers shut, and turned, looking for more…

There was a dark, tongued-and-grooved door with a rusty latch, standing right before her. A hundred years ago they had tipped sacks of coal through the grate at the back of this old house, and this was where it landed. And this is where the stash would be. Alice smiled.

A quick sweep with the candle assured her she was alone. Except, there was an easel just to her right. On it, facing away from her, was a canvas stretched over a frame and held in place by some kind of clamp. A protective sheet of plastic hovered above it, suspended from the ceiling by lengths of twine. She bit her lower lip, noted how low the candle had burned and wondered how much time she had left before it died, or before Christian came home. She decided she could look at the pretty picture all she wanted after she got her gear.

Alice lifted the latch and the door pulled noisily outward, scratching an arc in the dirt on the stone floor. She nearly screamed as the candlelight wafted in its breeze and dipped into a dark blue before recovering and illuminating the web hanging like a net curtain before her eyes. In its centre was a long-legged, skinny, hairy fuck of a spider. It looked at her, unmoving, un-frightened, it looked at her through big oily eyes.

She held the candle beneath the web and watched the spider scuttling upwards, disappearing behind the doorframe. The light showed a row of black plastic spines stacked against each other at the wall side. Alice bent beneath the web – expecting that thing to drop onto her bare back and scurry up towards her neck – and shuffled forward, reaching out her hand as she went.

The spines were the edges of canvases stretched over wooden frames. She grabbed one, pulled the plastic bag away, and peered at the dark colours. She couldn't make anything out though, no distinct shapes. There wasn't enough room for that. But she could see fifteen or twenty of them, all about the size of an A3 sheet of paper. "I wonder how much these are worth."

You *wouldn't!*

Well, it would stop her having to rely on Christian for everything, wouldn't it?

So, what's selling his paintings for money, if it's not relying on him?

"I mean, I don't have to go begging for cash, and if I ran low of stuff, I could go and buy the gear myself instead of being kept prisoner in a fucking shithole!"

Hey, you don't wanna go stealing off your man. Please. You don't wanna do that, Alice.

"Shut up!"

She looked around at the pictures, and then her shaking hand reminded her why she was here. Drugs. Where the hell had he hidden them? They had—

She heard the corrugated iron over the back door creak and then grate against the floor. Directly above her head she heard gentle footfalls in the lounge. Her hands tingled. *I gotta get out of here; if he catches me down here, no telling what he'll do. But wait! What if it's not him, what if it's the police or one of those kids that hangs around at the end of the street with his hands in his pockets and eyes that could cut you in two?*

And then she heard him. "Alice," he called softly.

Relief stole away the anxiety, she stood quickly, turned and walked into the spider. It scuttled across her face. Alice screamed and dropped the candle.

She slapped her face, her neck, her chest. And then she just stood there naked in the darkness screaming.

Chapter Nineteen

Saturday 20th June

– One –

"What were you doing down there?"

She pushed the cellar door closed and looked stubbornly at him.

He'd go out and earn the family a crust, and all the while she was… well, what *was* she doing? "Have you been looking at them?"

She nodded slowly.

The bags under her eyes looked deep enough to jump into, her hair was a tangled freak show, and here in the brightening light of a new day, she looked like something about to star in a horror movie. He stroked her chin with the back of his hand. "You didn't touch the one on the easel, did you?"

"It's still under the cover."

Her voice was meek, almost afraid, and that was something he never wanted to invoke in her. He put down the bag and then put both fists on his hips. "I don't want you going down there. It's dark and—"

"I had a candle."

His eyes closed, face blank. Finally, he sighed. "Where is it?"

She shrugged. "Blown out, somewhere on the floor."

Great. Let's start a fucking fire! "So it's dark."

She looked back at the floor.

"It's dangerous, Alice. And you could damage things that belong to me. Things I value."

When she looked up this time her eyes had narrowed; her lips were barely a line on a tight white canvas. "Things that you value? What about me, Christian, do you value me?"

"Hey, of course—"

"Then how could you go out and leave me with no fucking stuff?"

"I've brought some for you, babe. No need to get upset."

It didn't work. "Upset! I'm not fucking upset; I'm going fucking crazy, is what I am."

"Did you go down there looking for stuff?"

83

She looked away again, stood shaking like a demure porn star. And then she was on the offensive again. "You can't fucking blame me."

He held his hands out.

"You left me no choice!"

"You're right," he said, "you're right. I'm sorry."

"You're a bastard to me, Christian. Sometimes," she shouted, "I think you hate me. You want me to suffer because I'm on drugs. You want to punish me and to control me."

"Bollocks. That's the drugs talking." His eyes drifted out of focus. "I wish you weren't on the damned stuff in the first place."

She pointed a finger at him. "Give me the gear before I blow!"

He rummaged inside the plastic shopping bag and brought out a small block of brown resin. He watched her eyes as he handed it over.

"Is that all?" She stormed away into the lounge, found a spoon and a lighter.

"When we finally make it out of here…" Her eyes snapped to him, syringe ready to break the skin on her groin, and he couldn't make out whether it was a stare of impatience, of regret, or hatred. He didn't like this Alice. "When we get out of here, we're gonna get you sorted."

"Don't hold your breath, Picasso?"

"I just need a lucky break."

"Everyone needs a fucking break."

"Won't be long now. This new one I'm working on…"

She released the pressure on her groin, and let the needle fall too. Her eyes rolled and she squeezed a handful of greasy hair. After a while her heartbeat returned to normal, the poison numbed her anxiety, and she looked at him with eyes that could have belonged to the real Alice. "How many pictures are down there?"

He brought the plastic bag over and sat cross-legged on the floor. "Twenty or so."

"Ever tried selling any of them?"

From the bag he brought out sandwiches and shower gel. "I did at first, but I got nowhere. People weren't interested, said they had new artists coming out of their ears, and that new stuff was always difficult to sell, or they weren't taking on new clients… the list goes on. I got fed up of trying, and decided to carry on doing what I enjoyed: painting. I'm not a fucking salesman."

"So how're you going to get us out of here, Mr Picasso?"

"Stop taking the piss."

"You said you were going to get us out of here, but if you can't go out and sell the damned stuff, how you gonna do it?"

"I'm waiting."

"What for, a fucking invitation?" Alice pulled a sweater on, and stared at him. "They won't come knocking on your door, hoping a fucking artist lives here, and hoping he has a fucking masterpiece to sell to them. God, you're *fucking* thick!"

Calmly, he said, "I'm waiting. I've nearly finished this one—"

"And then what? You gonna haul it round the art galleries or something?" She gave him no time to reply. "Like hell you are. You're gonna put it to one side while it dries and you're gonna start another; another one that the critics will really love, another one that'll get us out of here in no time at all." She stopped, panting hard, anger slowly dissipating. "Sometimes, Christian, you are so full of shit. I bet you have stuff down there that's as good as you'll ever paint. Why wait to see if you can paint any better? *They* are all *you*; they are just different pictures."

"Have you finished?"

"Your ideals won't get us out of here. I'm sick of living like a dosser in a place they should have pulled down a century ago. And what are you going to do when he's old enough to go to school, huh, teach him yourself? We should be looking for a nursery already."

Christian looked away. "I'm not going legit," he said. "I won't—"

"'Be a number'? I know. You're a stuck record. But you're not going to get by as a great unknown; you can't live anonymously for ever."

"Why not? I've managed this far."

"How far have you come, eh?"

"I've got you," he said.

"For how long?"

He paused. "You going to leave me?"

"What if we get sick? You need National Insurance for treatment—"

"We'll get by."

"The wonderful Picasso says we'll get by, well that's okay then, isn't it!"

Christian knelt before her, wincing at the throbbing pain in his leg, folded his arms across her bare legs, and stared up into her dark wide eyes. "We're not so badly off; we don't have to sign on at no stupid dole office, we don't owe the state anything." He could see he wasn't getting through, "We can look people right in the eye and be proud that we live by our own means. I won't be a slave to a regular job."

"You need freedom, don't you?"

He nodded.

"So we can look people in the eye as we steal from them to get by? There's a fucking world of difference between living *The Good Life* and stealing to exist in a fucking shit-tip."

"It'll be fine, you'll see."

"I sometimes wonder who's on drugs. Get real. And do it in a fucking hurry!"

He couldn't get angry at her, no matter how much she goaded him, he couldn't do it. He smiled, stroked her leg some more. The night had gone well, and Mr Golfer had been good enough to buy a bit of food for them, and some tobacco for Alice, as well as the drugs, some drinking water and a few toiletries. And there was still 350 quid left. "Hey," he said, "wanna see them?"

"You going to show me your paintings?"

He nodded.

"Make it quick before Spencer wakes up."

– Two –

She followed him down the stone steps, seeing but ignoring his limp as the torchlight illuminated the steps before him.

"Okay, babe, stand still while I connect the lights."

"You got lights down here?" So his "studio" was the only place to have electricity; how could he value his studio above the lounge?

"Of a fashion."

He disappeared into the corner, taking the torchlight with him, and the blackness attacked Alice. "Hurry up, this is freaking me out."

"Relax, I'm hooking it up."

"Don't you go getting no shock!"

"Don't worry," he laughed. "It's DC."

"Oh, that's okay then," she said, not knowing what the hell he was talking about.

"I'm thinking of tapping in to one of the streetlights; see if we can have some mains power in here at last."

She caught sight of a violet spark and then a glow above her head turned quickly white, spreading light right across the dusty room.

"Wow, this is wonderful!" She spun around, staring at the small spotlights, the kind you'd normally find sunk into a kitchen ceiling.

"They're just 24 v spots," he said, "so don't get too excited."

"You never said we had electricity."

"We haven't." He walked back around the corner, rubbing his hands on a rag. "It's an old truck battery that's no good for anything except a couple of bulbs really. I didn't want you to think we could power a cooker or a fire from it."

"What about a TV?"

He shook his head.

"Why couldn't you run a wire upstairs into the lounge, so we could have light up there?" She planted her fists on her hips and looked sternly at him.

"I knew you'd say that."

"You were just keeping it all for yourself, weren't you?"

"No… I just thought that if we had light up there, you know, anything brighter than candlelight, it'd give our position away, and they would know where we were. Anyway, I thought you liked candlelight."

"I'm not a fucking pit pony; I would like to see by proper light every now and then." She looked around at the cellar and the way he "lived" down here, how things were neatly arranged on the walls, on the shelves, in the drawers. She got into his face, "But I could come down here." She didn't wait for a response. "We could all move down here and we could all share your light. How do you like that, Christian?"

"No," he said. "I wouldn't like it."

"But we could have the light on all the time and—"

"It's powered off a truck battery. And when the light dies away I can't just charge it back up again, I have to go and steal another. They're fucking heavy, and I risk being caught every time I do it—"

"But your paintings are worth the risk, right?"

"Why do you always complicate things? If we had light on all the time, we'd flatten the damned thing in a day or two." He nodded over his shoulder, "So far, that's lasted two weeks—"

"Well, there—"

"Because I don't use it all the time!"

She folded her arms, heard him sigh and shuffle his feet. He could be such a selfish bastard at times.

"Do you want to see them or not?"

She looked up into his eyes, nodded.

The smile burst back onto his face. With the excitement of a kid discovering his first hard-on, Christian took hold of her hand and dragged her across the room, around a wooden easel in its centre that was draped with a sheet of plastic, and right up to the rickety door she had encountered only an hour ago all by herself.

He opened the door and brushed aside a spider's web. "I've dreamt of showing you these for ages," he lifted three or four plastic-wrapped frames in each hand, and ushered her back out into the main room. Gently he placed them on a bench against the wall at the far side of the room where the light near the easel shone the brightest. "If you don't like them, you will tell me, won't you?"

She shrugged. "Have I ever lied to you?"

"Well, here goes." Christian unwrapped the first one, and leaned it against the wall, standing back, positioning himself strategically so he could see her reaction. "This is a big event for me."

For a long time, she gazed at it. She brought her hand up to her face. Her eyes seemed to grow bigger as they studied it. For what must have been half a minute she did not breathe, only stood there, half naked and cold, but unaware of everything as, like Mary Poppins falling into the chalk pavement picture, she fell into the painting before her. Silence hung in the air like a delicate web, and at last she exhaled and turned to him.

"Well?"

She looked back at the painting, enchanted, engrossed, lost within the world on the canvas. "It's..." She studied it further, speechless for a moment longer. There was a lake, illuminated by moonlight, calm, placid, surrounded by a dark forest. Into the lake, protruding like a pointing finger was an old wooden jetty, dilapidated, neglected. Ghostly light danced beneath it, reflected from the shimmering water. And up on the shore stood a log cabin, a red light illuminating the shabby curtains, door open giving a glimpse into the kitchen with a steaming pot on the stove. Wisps of grey smoke twisted gracefully into the still air from a chimney hidden by the sunken spine of the shingle roof. Above it all, encircling the large moon, was the Milky Way.

It was more like a photograph than a painting; there were stars glowing with varying intensity, curls of gas clouds way out into the universe, all clearly visible and all beautifully captured in their translucent colours like a rainbow stirred by God's hand. And in the centre of the painting, standing on the edge of the jetty, was a lone female whose silhouette was draped in a light lacy gown that billowed gently around her in a breeze you could almost feel. Her hands were curled around the smooth old wood and she gazed thoughtfully out into the lake.

For a moment, Alice could hear the woodland creatures, could feel the breeze on her damp cheeks and could smell the pine in the air, and could hear the gentle rippling of the water against the mossy legs of the jetty. Alice was enraptured.

She wondered who the woman was, and what she was thinking, where the lake was.

She was about to turn to him, tears – of what? joy, pride, enchantment? – glazed her eyes, but she stopped and looked back at the picture, looked deep into it as though someone had called her name. And she became rigid with wonder as she lost herself in the scene. Through the painting – no, that's wrong, through the paint, the actual scrapes and brush strokes of the oils, perhaps even through the canvas itself, she *could* see it. It was a face, long hair, in ringlets blowing around it. It was a man's face, and it smiled at her with sparkling eyes—

"Do you see him?"

Christian's voice was like an explosion. It wrenched her back into the cellar with its smell of linseed and damp, back into the cold dusty room with grit underfoot and goose pimples on flesh. She gave a shriek and almost collapsed against the bench. Christian wrapped his hands around her. She peered at him; his eyes sparkled and she recognised the man in the picture. "You…"

He smiled still.

"You should grow your hair, Christian. It looks wonderful."

"I'm glad you can see it." He encircled her, and she felt safe, untouchable by the horrors of today. But she also felt troubled; unease trickled through her like a warning, a foreboding that she couldn't tie down. He nuzzled her neck and she closed her eyes.

"You've heard of Realism? I call this style Beyond Realism." His breath warmed her neck. "I invented my own style."

He paints like… he paints like a magician. It shocks you, it startles you and it teases you, draws you nearer and then it mesmerises you.

"Are they all like this?"

"All made with paint."

"Are they all as detailed as this? Do they all—"

"Talk to you?" He shrugged. "I suppose it depends who's looking at them, how deeply they look, how hard they listen."

"Yeah, but they're all as detailed as this, aren't they? They're all," she struggled for the word, "they're all special?"

"Oh yes, they're that alright."

She closed her eyes and dreamed of selling them. What a difference a vein full of drugs could make to an otherwise dull day, and what a difference seeing the magic hidden inside the mind of your man, magic that could command financial independence. At that moment everything was as it should have been.

Alice ignored his earlier lies about trying and failing to sell the paintings, for these things would sell themselves without a shadow of a doubt; and she understood why he'd lied to her. He didn't want to sell them, and she appreciated that; they were wonderful things but they didn't deserve to live hidden in a dark cellar in a fucking squat! She let his stubble stroke her neck, and her hands moved over his body, down to where—

She stopped. Spencer was crying.

"What's wrong?"

"Spencer."

He closed his eyes and sighed. "I was getting in the mood then."

"I wanted to look at that one." She nodded to the easel.

"Not that one. Not yet."

"Oh why?"

Spencer's cry heightened.

"It's not finished."

"So?"

"No one sees my work before it's finished; it'll ruin it up here," he prodded his head. "It's like discussing some idea; it dilutes it, ruins the purity."

"You know how to talk bollocks, dontcha?"

"Anyway," he walked back around the corner to the battery, leaving the naked painting for her to stare at until it all went dark, "I need more paint, can't paint without it."

"Go out and buy some!" She screamed it at him, and then quickly put her hand over her mouth. *Patience,* she told herself. *You'll get to see it soon.*

"I only steal paint, never buy it."

"Why, you have the money, don't you?"

"Got plenty. But I'm not wasting food-money on paint, we have to eat and drink."

"But—"

"Don't worry, I'm going out this afternoon, there's a big demo in town today and it'll shield me." He poked his head around the corner, and she tore herself away from the lake to look up at him. "Stolen paints give you an edge, they give you a buzz."

It all went dark.

Chapter Twenty

Saturday 20th June

– One –

Almost silent. It was as if the building was catching its breath between Friday and Monday. Mick sighed and rubbed the whiskers on his face. It was 11am and he'd been in the office less than an hour. Already he wanted to go home, and already he needed a drink. He looked around to make sure Rochester wasn't peering at him through his office window, and headed through the double doors towards the gents' and a generous top-up.

He'd come directly here after Eddie – Ros, actually – kicked him out this morning, and he guessed that if it was Eddie's first day back at work next week, then who could blame the guy for wanting to be prepared. Mick though, didn't care too much for work, or his personal appearance. If he stank, he stank. *Let them breathe me in.*

The gents' was quiet as it usually was at this time of day, but he was dismayed to see *his* cubicle engaged. "Fuck," he whispered, and stepped into another cubicle, sat and waited. His mind got working on Eddie and his situation. He was a good drinking buddy, and he planned on keeping it that way; they were so rare these days, and to have one that worked for the police had its benefits, not that Eddie realised he was occasionally being pumped for information.

That bitch Ros, was the fly in the Eddie ointment, always wanting to manipulate him.

He heard the sound of a zipper, and the toilet flushed. Mick stood and waited, door ajar. The lock snapped back and footsteps echoed on the tiled floor. Mick froze. The footsteps belonged to Rochester. Mick closed his eyes, standing there, half in and half out of the foreign cubicle, with smell oozing out of his armpits, with a day's growth on his chin and no fucking tie.

The taps turned on and a voice spoke. "Still waiting for that story to land in your lap?"

Mick opened his eyes and sighed. "Hello, Mr Rochester. How are you today?"

"Rather better than you judging by your appearance." Staring at him in the mirror, Rochester rinsed, dried and then turned around. "You look disgusting."

"Sir."

"You are turning into a tramp." He stepped closer, sniffing the air. "You stink."

"Sir."

"You really have gone downhill. You weren't at much of an altitude to begin with."

"Attitude, sir?"

"Altitude. You didn't start that high. Oh, never mind."

"Sir."

"You have turned disagreeably into a slimy toad, Mick. You have grease escaping from every pore that isn't blocked with filth. Your hair is a disgrace; you've worn that shirt every day for the last week so far as my memory serves and," he moved slightly closer, holding his breath, "is that gravy down the front of it?"

Shit, I knew I should have brought a tie in. "Absolutely not, sir!"

Rochester raised his eyebrows.

"It's spaghetti."

"What's your excuse?" Rochester was not pleased.

"I was never very good at twiddling it around the fork and as I sucked it in, it did a helicopter and threw juice all—"

"My office. Ten minutes."

"Shit," he whispered as Rochester walked to the door.

"And Mick?"

"Sir?"

"Find some deodorant first, please."

This was it. The day they forced him to resign.

He went into his own cubicle, slammed the door and punched the wall. He took off the cistern lid and pulled out a bottle of brandy wrapped in a plastic bag.

* * *

Mick sucked on a Polo as he approached William, the office junior. "William?" The lad turned, and his usually permanent smile slipped somewhat. "Have you got any deodorant you can lend me?"

"What?"

"Deodorant. Do you have some?"

"Er, yeah."

"And I need to borrow your tie."

* * *

"Sit down, Mick."

"Sir."

"And close the door."

Mick got up and shut the door, retook his seat and stared into Rochester's widely-spaced eyes. "What can I do for you, sir?"

"You are a disgrace to this newspaper, Mick."

Mick laced his hands. There was a long silence, so long that it angered Mick into saying, "Look, if you're going to sack me—"

"I should sack you, Mick."

Should. The old man said *should. That is a good word. It means won't. But it also means there's a condition attached.*

Rochester leaned forward on his desk, cufflinks tinkling against it. "You've done some reasonably good reporting in your time here."

"Thank you, sir."

"I said reasonable, not good, certainly not outstanding," he said. "You've covered the UK Criminal Justice system. I want you to take it a step further. I want you to go beneath the surface—"

"Undercover work?"

"I want you to get beneath the skin of the system, I want background stories for and against The Rules; I want you to capture the effects they're having on everyday people."

Well at least it wasn't the sack. "Sir."

"You will need a starting block. Something to ease you in."

"Yes, sir."

"Take a look at this." Rochester handed Mick an unmarked brown envelope. "Read it when you get back to your desk. And then formulate an approach, gather information on the subjects and report back to me after you've interviewed them with a basic premise on your approach strategy."

"Right, sir. Read the letter, interview someone and write a story."

Rochester gave a slow shake of his head. "I'm treating this as your first real report. I'm treating you as I would a newcomer to the office, which means that all basic procedures must be adhered to, and company policy is uppermost. I want to see good story, good layout and plenty of feeling. Do I make myself clear?"

"Yes, Mr Rochester, very."

"This is your chance. Hand in mediocre work, and I may give you a reference; hand in work to your usual standard, and I'll have security come and evict you. Is *that* clear?"

– Two –

To Whom It May Concern:

I am writing this letter to you as a last resort. Please don't be offended by that, I meant that I have tried every other avenue available to me but have so far failed.

My son, Stephen, was sent to jail last year. He stabbed a burglar who was stealing his phone, keys and other property from his kitchen. I'm not defending his actions although I think any reasonable person could see it from my boy's point of view.

What I'm protesting about is the parole board keep knocking him back for release because "he represents a danger to burglars"! A danger to burglars? That goes against common decency. Surely if you didn't burgle good honest folk in the first place, you wouldn't be in danger. He's a decent fella in his fifties who don't deserve to be locked away like a common drug-taking rapist or thief.

To add insult to injury, the burglar gets Legal Aid to sue my Stephen for wounding him. I nearly had a heart attack when I heard that. And that's something else that I think the public, if I can bring it to their attention through your wonderful newspaper, would be disgusted to learn. As they will be disgusted to hear that prisoners get a TV in their room and a choice of what DVD to watch every evening. Good living if you're a criminal, eh.

I would very much like you to take up this story on Stephen's behalf and see if you can't get him out of prison and back to his family.

Thank you,

Lincoln Farrier

P.S. I'm going to see Sir George tomorrow, don't know if he can help.

Mick read the letter through twice more and felt the prickle of injustice skitter up his spine. He tutted, reclined in his seat and folded his hands behind his head. He had a feeling for the story already; decided to play it from the sympathy angle, milk it for all it was worth. But then he had another feeling, a genuine interest in this old guy's plight. Maybe he didn't need to give it an angle at all; maybe it had all the angle it needed in its raw, untouched state.

"Can I have my tie back now?"

Mick looked up, dragged away from his thoughts, and saw Williams hovering over him. "This stain is coffee. It'll wipe right off, no problem. Sorry."

Chapter Twenty-One

Sunday 21st June

– One –

Her feet tapped on the cinder path. She stopped, turned and listened. The high hedges on either side stopped the streetlight reaching her, and the moon was out of sight. She thought someone was following her, and almost said, 'Come on, Sammy; hurry up!', but she stopped short, reminding herself that she was alone, literally.

She buried her kid weeks ago and had to begin learning all over again. Learning not to make his breakfast, not to get him ready for school. She shivered. Eddie should be here, but she'd said some awful things to him at the funeral and hadn't seen him since.

Despite often taking twice the dose of Protromil – and walking around like life was on loan – she felt there was an inevitable end to it all, a sinking feeling pulling her in like a black hole pulls in the light. She wasn't coping and instead of the guilt and the shame and the grief abating slowly but distinctly as time passed by, it grew more intense.

But maybe there was a way around it all. It was something reserved for the fruit loops and the desperate.

If he can't come to me, why can't I go to him?

And so she had.

It had been her mum's suggestion, and she'd treated it with derision as though she wouldn't be foolish enough to fall for hocus-pocus like that. But the black hole grew bigger, its pull stronger, and her will to carry on lessened.

Eventually, there came a time when the pull of suicide was equalled by the pull of hocus-pocus, and Jilly came to see a medium. She wasn't a fruit loop, she *was* just desperate.

The night was cool, and a breeze like a refreshing tonic floated over her as she walked the cinder path from the community hall. She smelled the scents of flowers caught in the breeze, and for the first time in a million years she smiled. It had been a good night.

Overhead, the yellow moon was out of focus through a veil of mist that might be the precursor to a storm tonight or tomorrow.

– Two –

Eddie stared at it.

It wasn't much of an altar, but it was a fitting tribute to his little man; the New York Yankees baseball cap perched on the stained mantelpiece was all he had of Sam now. That, and the memories that came and went with the bouts of sobriety and incapacity. Right now, Eddie was in one of his rare sober moments, but his eyes flicked between the baseball cap and the bottle. In the end, the tears rippled both and he reached for the bottle.

The ceremony two weeks ago had left him paralysed from the neck up. It was hard enough to bury your own kid on his birthday, without having your estranged wife beat the crap out of you in front of the congregation because you killed your boy.

If he'd been there on time, Sam wouldn't have been at Josh's chasing a ball down the street; they'd have gone for a Mac and caught a flick.

But less than a week after letting his boy die, he'd stood over the small grave feeling the sun's heat drill into his head, and felt the half-bottle of brandy in the pocket of his new black suit begging him to take a swig. For the sake of his boy, he had resisted and stood there sober while Jilly told him all the things he already knew, and she wasn't ambiguous about it either.

Standing between her parents, Jilly had shouted at him from across the grave, and Eddie had neither the heart nor the motivation to retaliate, because everything she'd screamed was true. "You killed our Sam! You sank him in the fucking earth, you bastard! He was only eleven, he was days from his birthday and you couldn't even make the effort to be there on time for him. Today was supposed to be his birthday."

And that was about the time he realised how much he had damaged her; his inability that morning to get things right had resulted in this, Jilly's heart was broken, and she was crippled by it. He felt like a bag of shit.

Was it possible to spoil a funeral? he asked himself. It was the shittiest day of his life, and the screaming made it shittier. Yes it *did* make it worse, twisted the day into anger instead of smoothing the river of grief in which everyone swam.

Jilly had snatched herself away from her parents and almost ran around Sam's grave to smack Eddie on the face with enough force to knock him down. There were gasps – he got the impression that some of those present were just soaking up the entertainment – and the old vicar called for calm. It didn't happen. Eddie raised his hand to protect himself and Jilly crouched to hit him more. He didn't stop her because he deserved it, every blow and every fiery word; he soaked it up and almost begged for more to lighten the load of his burden.

Jilly stood up straight and panted, looking down at him, her hair a tangled mess, mascara streaks gruesomely etching her reddened face, and she kicked him. And that's when the brandy bottle slipped out of his jacket pocket and fell on the bare earth. If he'd been a foot closer to the grave, it would have slid into the hole and landed, thud, on his kid's coffin. How ironic. Both of them stared at the bottle and then both of then stared at each other. "I hope it kills you, you worthless fuck," she snarled and kicked him one more time.

"So do I," he whispered.

They all left huddled in a group with Jilly and her parents at its centre. The vicar came over, patted him on the shoulder, and asked if there was anything he could do. Eddie looked up, thought about punching him, and then whispered, "Bring my boy back."

The sextons quietly worked around him, almost reverently filling in the hole, and Eddie sat there on his arse, his new suit looking decidedly worn, and stared from the brandy bottle to his boy's coffin until the coffin disappeared and all he could see was fresh earth. Eddie sat there among the silent work, and he cried for the death of his boy.

"Is there anything worse than burying your son," he asked the bottle, "other than knowing you were the cause of it?" It didn't answer, just stared back at him, miming the words, *drink me*. He was a regular at the local Booze King where behind his back they called him "Brandyman". He didn't care, so long as he got his dose of oblivion once or twice a day. No, there was nothing worse than burying your son and knowing you were the cause.

As he unscrewed the lid, he asked himself why tonight was different; why was he sober? Easy. The self-loathing was dominant and it told him he needed a night off the booze so the memories could punish him properly instead of them having to fight through a haze where the pain barely made a mark. Tonight he needed to feel the pain sharp and deep like the thrust of a knife, like the bonnet ornament of a green Jaguar as it tore into his ribcage. Yeah, let the film roll and let me suffer like my boy suffered; go on, give it to me again. He screwed the lid back on and put the bottle down.

And anyway, tomorrow was his first day at work since… he needed to be sober for that, at least to begin with. They would all be scrutinising him, they would all offer their condolences, and he wanted to be able to say 'thanks' without breaking down; hell, he didn't even want his chin to wobble, so best get it over with tonight, and then tomorrow night he could visit Brandypuke Farm and his old friends guilt and hatred. But the bottle *did* look inviting, and it smiled up at him and said, *Come on, Brandyman, take a swig.*

He clenched his teeth, looked at the baseball cap and tried to put the bottle into a place in his mind it couldn't reach. His eyes slid reluctantly away from the cap and the fact that his son's fragile head used to live inside the damned thing, and they slowly came down to look at–

Oh what was the fucking use? *Why prepare yourself for work when you don't want to go back, why deny yourself the booze when you've no intention of going back?*

You know, if you do it tonight, the pain is gone, click, just like that. No more hurting, Eddie. And it does hurt, doesn't it? Yes, do it tonight, eh. And what was the best way, the quickest? Hanging.

With stinging eyes, Eddie opened the door to the kitchen and pulled out the Dirt Devil, unwound its flex and threw it over the door. He accepted the invitation, and took a long swig from his friend, and stood with his back to the door, heart thumping, eyes streaming, thoughts of his first words to Sam: "I'm sorry, son." They blasted through his mind like a small explosion as he wound the flex around his neck. Eddie took a last look around his "home", his eyes settled on the baseball cap, and then he tensed.

Do it. Just drop, just let your legs buckle and it'll all be over in a couple of seconds.

He closed his eyes and tensed up. Then he let go.

His backside hit the floor with a mind-numbing bang and he could feel the small vacuum cleaner climbing the other side of the door. "Fuck!" The Dirt Devil banged against the door. "Can't even fucking kill myself. You useless piece of shit, Collins." He wound off the flex, and let the Dirt Devil clatter back to the kitchen floor.

He stared through the tears at the cap and then the bottle.

The phone rang. Eddie jumped. The screen said "Jilly". He swallowed, and if he'd been wearing a tie, he would have straightened it, would have freshened his breath too, just in case. He reached for the thing, avoided video, pressed talk instead. "Hi, Jilly."

"Eddie, put the screen on."

"Why?"

"Just do it, please."

Icy cold. He opened the flap on the mobile phone and pressed video. A wonderful colour image of Jilly leapt out at him, and he almost flinched, expected her fist to come through the screen and punch him in the nose – *just for old times' sake*, she would say, and hang up.

"Are you sober?"

What? Whatever happened to *Hello Eddie, how are you? Long time, no see. How you copin' with your grief?* Are you sober, shit. "Don't piss about with small talk, Jilly."

"Well, are you?"

"Yes, I'm sober, for Christ's sake. Why?"

"Come over."

He looked into the screen, saw her eyes avoid his own, as though she was suddenly embarrassed. This wasn't like her; he squinted, suspicious. "Why do you want me to come over? Have you got your dad with you, gonna let him have ten minutes with me? Going to kick some more crap out of me, Jilly?"

She pursed her lips, and though the screen had reasonable resolution, it wasn't quite good enough to pick out the full extent of her blushes. She was feeling guilty about the scene at Sam's funeral, and wanted to apologise.

Only she wasn't the forgiving kind, wasn't Jilly; she was the punishing kind. Even the poor resolution showed that in her eyes. "Why do you want me over?"

"I have some news. Please come over."

"News? What news, why can't you tell me over—"

"I won't ask again, Eddie."

Chapter Twenty-Two

Sunday 21st June

– One –

He sat in his own lounge feeling awkward. He said thank you when she handed him a coffee, smiled politely. It was as though they were back in their courting days, long before the time when he felt relaxed enough to fart in her company.

He wanted to ask her what she wanted at this time of night; didn't she know he was going to tie a knot in the Dirt Devil flex? Didn't she know how difficult it had been driving past Booze King? He needed a drink, and somehow he knew coffee just wouldn't hit the spot. Instead, he looked around politely, as though admiring her choice of décor, and felt like asking her if she came here often. The presents in the corner had gone, and on the walls, photos of Eddie had gone too, and in their place were more of Sammy, lots more.

He sipped the coffee, put it on the floor and sat forward in the chair, elbows on knees. "So," he clapped his hands together, "what's so important?"

She sat on the settee opposite him; legs tucked underneath just as she always did, cuddling a cushion. "You know the problems we always had with the heating system and with the lights fusing all the time?"

"Yeah?" His suspicions were aroused further.

"Well, I know what the cause is. The fuse box in the cupboard under the stairs has been wired up wrong, or it has a fault inside it."

Eddie blinked. "At last I'll be able to sleep soundly."

"There's more." She took a large breath. "I went to see someone tonight and they told me about the fuse box, told me I had to get it fixed urgently before something horrible happened."

"Okay."

She stared at the carpet.

"If you haven't dragged me all the way over here to beat me up again, then what have you got to tell me?"

"You'll think I'm crazy."

"Too late."

"See! I knew you'd make this hard for me."

"Come on, I'm here listening to talk about the fucking fuse box—"

"Sam's okay."

His heart stopped. He couldn't take his eyes off Jilly, who now met his stare. His mouth fell open and he cocked his head to one side. "Say again."

"He's okay," she whispered.

"What… what do you mean, he's okay. What are you talking about?" No sooner had he asked the question, than the answer ploughed into his mind. And yes, he did think she was crazy. "You've been to a…" he clicked his fingers, searching for the title, "A medium? You've been to see a fucking psychic?"

And then it all came out in one long blur of words. "He was good, Eddie; he told me about the fuse box, and he told me he could see a young man, coming up for a birthday. He said he was a smart little fella wearing a cap with NY on it." She rushed through the sentence, probably to limit the time Eddie had to ridicule her. "He said he loved you."

What do you say when someone tells you that your dead kid still loves you? "Jilly, please—"

"I know what you're going to say and you can save it, Eddie. This man came out with all sorts of things that no one else—"

"Enlighten me."

"He knew you'd bought Sam a PlayStation!"

"So?"

"He knew how he died; said he was playing football with a kid called Joshua and was hit by a green car while retrieving the ball."

"How many newspapers has that little titbit been in? Jilly, he's a con, they all are. They're just playing with your grief and they're taking your money. They're scum and should—"

"Shut up."

"They're using you."

"Like you always have!" She screamed at him and then threw the cushion at him too. She unfolded her legs, leaned forward and she was all snarls and claws, and she looked at Eddie with eyes that flashed red in the pupils. She had gone wild. "He told me that he loved you still – though God knows why – and he told me to tell you that he didn't blame you." Her eyes narrowed and she leered at him. "Fuck knows why; because I still do, you drunken piece of shit."

"Jilly, he's pulled the wool—"

"Then how did he know about the wiring?"

"They prey on people like you," he said, "that's how those vultures earn their living. You don't believe in all that bollocks, do you? I thought you were a sensible woman."

"People like me? People like *me!* You cheeky bastard; you practically threw Sam under a car and then you have the cheek to tell me they prey on people like me! People who are grieving, you mean. People who—"

"Who need to reach out and still feel Sam's hand, yes. They're not stupid, Jilly. I don't know how they found out all this crap about the electrics, but they did and they used it to pull you in like they do every other sucker!"

"You're wrong!"

"They are out to con you, to manipulate you, can't you see that? What they're offering you is a chance to," he searched for the phrase, "to not let go; they'll give you snippets of him, tell you things you'd like to hear—"

"What about Sam saying he loves you? Don't you like to hear that?"

Eddie fell silent, heart racing, cheeks flushed and the desire for a drink so strong it almost pulled him off the seat and out the door. "I'd rather hear it from his own lips, Jilly." He swallowed and looked up at her, eyes wide, sorrowful. "But he's gone, babe."

"He's reachable, dammit!"

"He is not," he whispered. "It's a con. We sank his body in the ground two weeks ago. And nobody, not even you, wants him back more than I do—" he felt the familiar sting of tears, but he swallowed, coughed and carried on "—but it's not going to happen. Let him go, Jilly. Don't keep on punishing yourself by seeing these vultures."

"They're not—"

"They are!" he yelled at her, and then he shook his head. What was he doing? She was upset, she needed comforting, she didn't need a row, dammit. But she didn't need false hope either. "You'll grieve forever if you believe he's out there somewhere in the ether or flying in between the stars just waiting till you contact him again. You have to let go, you have to recover."

She cried. In great sobs, she cried into another cushion and Eddie almost got up out of the chair and went to her. But he couldn't; she didn't want him anymore, she wanted Sam, and she would do anything to have him back.

"Hey, you're so desperate, Jilly—"

"I hate you."

"I expected you would. But I thought you should know about them, the mediums, that is, and if I've shattered their carefully fabricated illusion of a reunion, then I'm sorry, sort of. But I think you need to get a grip and move on."

"Oh, good idea!" She looked at him, and her eyes were red and puffy already. Their lashes stuck together. "I could do what you do, couldn't I? I could just get pissed all the time to cover up my feelings and to blot out any memory—"

"It wouldn't matter how much I drank, Jilly. I could never blot out my memories of Sam. He'll be with me always in here," he patted his heart. "I don't need no psychic bullshit to tell me he loved me; I *know* he did, despite all my failures. And I don't need no man in flowing black robes with a fucking crystal ball to tell me—"

"Oh shut up. I've heard enough."

Eddie felt sorrow like he never had before. Jilly was such a strong woman, the way she always told him to quit drinking or he'd be out, and he always thought, *yeah, yeah*. And then she did it, she kicked him out. And how strong did she need to be to do that? She was strong, but look at her now.

And his heart went out to her, but his hands feared to follow, just in case her claws and her red eyes and her venom came back. But it made him sad that she was so much in grief that she couldn't see the way they fooled her. She missed Sam so much that she was willing to lay her head under their guillotine and take part in the charade. Grief made a fool of everyone, even strong people.

"I'm sorry I couldn't be more positive about it, Jilly."

She said nothing, looked at the wall, tears falling from her trembling chin in a silence that was almost scary.

"I wish I could believe the way you do; but they're out to make money out of you, and to bring you nothing but false hope so you'll keep going back for more." Still she said nothing. "Will you go again?"

She blinked and more tears fell, though at least now she looked across at him. "Yes, I will," she sniffled. "Because I believe them; they say things that aren't generalisations. They say things that are spot on. And I think Sam's communicating with me through them."

Eddie plucked up the courage to get off his arse and go and cuddle his wife. He made it almost to her shoulder before she looked up at him.

"What?"

"Nothing," he said, "just thought you could do with a hug, that's all."

"Leave me alone." And then the venom came back, the claws came out and the eyes turned a deep shade of crimson again. "I never want you to touch me again. I want your sorry fucking arse out of my house and I never want to see your drunken, bag o' shit body again until it's in a fucking coffin! Now get out!"

Eddie retracted his hand and stood still as though stapled to the floor. "Jilly—"

"I said get out."

"But—"

She looked up at him with such pure hatred in her eyes that he thought she could kill him in an instant.

Through clenched teeth she said, "Get out now while you still can."

– Two –

He threw the keys onto the coffee table and reached for the bottle and drank greedily, staring at the baseball cap.

Maybe I should *try the vacuum cleaner flex again.*

So much for keeping sober until tomorrow. "What the fuck," and then he threw the bottle at the wall. The glass shattered and brandy sprayed into the air, dripped down the wallpaper and formed a puddle on the carpet.

The Yorkshire Echo. 22nd June

Margy Bolton takes a bullet
By Michael Lyndon

MARGY Bolton (28) from East Sussex, has the unenviable notoriety of being the first person put to death in England since 1964.

In record time, the Crown Prosecution Service passed Bolton's file across to the newly formed Independent Review Panel who took a single day to establish that all evidence against her was true and accurate. That means that the court's decision to impose the death penalty stood as correct and the slaughterhouse was put on standby.

Bolton appeared behind a glass screen briefly in court five at the Old Bailey where, through shouting and jeering from the public gallery, she confirmed her name. The Hon. Mr Justice Shaw adjourned the hearing for four hours while Bolton was moved to a video interview room where the rest of the case was heard.

Police arrested Bolton on the 16th June, just hours after the commencement of The Rules, enabling her to be tried under the new legislation. She was charged with the murder of eighteen children and four adults in an arson attack on the Chantry House Church of England Primary School.

Calls for The Rules to deal only with cases that happened after 15th June this year have been dismissed by the Justice Ministry, who reiterated that their stance is to try people arrested after midnight on the 15th using the new system, irrespective of when the crime with which they have been charged took place.

It comes as no surprise to learn that Sunday 15th June was a busy day for the police, with over 950 offenders handing themselves in to be tried under the old system.

Conversely, say opponents, it can be shown that arrests prior to the date slumped as police officers waited for the deadline to pass so the new tougher laws would apply to those they arrested.

The Yorkshire Echo. 22nd June

The Bloody Code
Facts of English execution
By Michael Lyndon

Margy Bolton is the first citizen of this country to be put to death since 8am 13th August 1964, when Gwynne Evans and Peter Allen were hanged in Manchester and Liverpool respectively for the murder of John West.

All those years later, we see the beginning again perhaps of the Bloody Code, but using different techniques.

Now we use a nylon bullet fired under pressure from a source of compressed air into the brain stem. There are two sizes of bullet and various pressure settings available depending upon the subject's build and density.

The idea, suggests a government document, is to sever the spinal column and the brain stem in the quickest way possible without unnecessary distortion or disturbance of the body.

There are three Termination Buildings in England: Leeds, Birmingham, and London (within the grounds of the Old Bailey). Ironically, the slaughterhouse, as it's become known in Leeds, was only completed two days prior to its first use, and several technicians worked through the night to overcome a reliability issue.

The problem occurred when the projectile misfired repeatedly in tests, causing damage to the apparatus by jamming in the muzzle.

Its first proper use, however, went without a hitch. Harry Allen and Robert Stewart, the last two chief executioners, calculated weight and rope length in their days whereas their modern-day equivalent is 54-year-old Edward Donaldson, a grandfather who lives in Derbyshire, who determines structure and density using X-rays.

Two further candidates are expected to be confirmed in role within two weeks.

Chapter Twenty-Three

Monday 22nd June

– One –

"I don't know what I'd do without you, Ros." Eddie shaved three days of stubble away, wondering if this was how it felt being on fire.

"We have to leave in ten minutes," Ros called from the lounge.

The smell of coffee wafted into the bathroom, and Eddie stared at himself in the cracked mirror over the sink. *Is this it? Is this all I have until I curl my toes up?* He sniffed the coffee. *Why does she do this? What does she get out of supporting a no-hoper like me?* "She should be out catching herself some young hunk with pecs and a dick to die for." A thin smile showed itself.

Ros was a twenty-nine-year-old woman who wasn't exactly blessed with stunning looks, but had not fallen out of any ugly tree either. She was nicely shaped, and was good with people, especially those who needed a little TLC.

But she's not after me otherwise she wouldn't encourage me to get back with Jilly.

"Here's your coffee, you tosser."

He watched her in the mirror. She put the pot on the side of the bath, looked at him standing there in his towel, the cream towel that showed all the stains, the one with the fucking big hole right about where his arse was now.

"You're so good with words."

"It's easy where you're concerned. Now get a move on, don't wanna be late today." Ros left the bathroom.

"Almost done." From the shelf, he took down a plastic bottle of shampoo. The label was faded, worn away as though it had taken a lot of use in its time in Eddie's bathroom. He drank from the bottle and it tasted good. Brandy warmed through him, sent him a little light-headed and he could feel the liquid singe away the taste of toothpaste lingering in his mouth. He took another swig and hoped nobody ever wanted to wash their hair in his bathroom.

* * *

The uniform felt foreign to him. The dark blue polo shirt felt tighter than he remembered it. The West Yorkshire Police badge over his left breast looked faded and the trousers shiny. He looked the part, but he felt abstract, as though no amount of police blue could persuade him that he truly belonged. He drank the cool dregs of the coffee.

– Two –

He slammed the door and sat looking through the windscreen, feeling nervous and wondering how they'd be with him after such a long absence. Would they all talk about him behind their hands; would their whispering cease abruptly the moment he entered the room?

"All set?"

He looked across, shrugged, and looked ahead again.

"That good? I thought you'd be raring to go."

"You'd be wrong."

She handed the cigarettes and the newspaper across.

"Cheers. How much—"

"My treat." Ros engaged gear and set off.

He scanned the headlines. *Dignity, Purity, and Hope*. It was the slogan for PAC. One of their bigwigs, the one who was involved in the meetings with Deacon to bring about The Rules, had been slaughtered in an attack on a fucking school of all things, and still they marched on towards their ultimate goal. And that was another thing he thought often of, the marches, and how people were caught by the debate.

You were for The Rules or against them.

But even in the for camp there were divisions: yes, they should be killed, but it should be in a humane way, such as by lethal injection, or by gas, not shot. And then there were the radical opposition who said shooting the bastards was too good for them, and that they should be hacked to bits by the victims' relatives, or they should be starved to death in full view of the public. Either way, Eddie guessed shooting someone behind closed doors wasn't what life in the twenty-first century called for. But if they'd made their minds up to dispatch a habitual or serious offender, then on balance the gun was probably the best and quickest of methods.

Beneath the banner headline was another proclaiming *Why The Church Backed Down*. According to the paper, the Church had been brought into line by three events. One was a siege in a small parish church in Cumbria eight months ago where an escaped paedophile sought sanctuary from a group of vigilantes.

It had ended in a frenzied bloodbath. Probably caused by the fear of being cornered by a mob, the paedophile had killed the vicar and a parishioner who had become caught up in it all somehow. The paedophile had died too; it seemed the armed police were a little slow in reacting to the situation.

The second thing to bring about the change of collective heart was the invocation of an Independent Review Panel, now in place and functioning. It had been promised for a long time, and indeed was supposed to have been instrumental in negotiating the fine detail associated with The Rules; but as they often said, better late than never.

The IRP's task was to scrutinise all evidence relating to a conviction leading to a Rule Three death. It was a group of professional people from a forensic background, or a law background, who were conversant with police procedures.

Yeah, like hell, Eddie thought.

Their first case had been Margy Bolton. It took them a single day to check things out and sign the paperwork. They were new; they wanted to be liked.

And the third factor that convinced the Church to accept The Rules, was a certain Right Reverend Clive Chapman, whose speeches on several levels – at the General Synod, the Diocesan Synod, and also at the House of Bishops – finally convinced them that an eye for an eye may be the way forward in this unholy century of ours after the abhorrent loss of his daughter and grandson in the Sussex school arson.

A picture of the Justice Secretary, crying as he gave a speech introducing The Rules, had its own headline: *Deacon, a Man of Integrity.*

They drove in silence for almost ten minutes, and Eddie became more nervous and increasingly twitchy as their destination grew closer.

I could murder a drink.

"What you thinking about, Eddie?"

Eddie jumped. Could she see inside his mind?

"You look pale."

"Why are you doing this, Ros?"

"Doing what?"

"Taking me to work."

"So I know you'll get there. It can't be easy, your first day back after… after a long time away."

"You can say it, you know. I won't bite you or curl up in a corner crying. You can say 'after Sammy died'."

"Well, that's why I'm doing it." She cleared her throat. "What's the headline?" she nodded at the paper in Eddie's lap, changing the subject swiftly, aiming for subtlety but failing quite dramatically.

"Talk about The Rules."

"Good," she said.

"You agree with them?"

"Damned right. How many times have you dealt with aggro from some complainant saying the courts never do anything with burglars even if we catch 'em? They say it all the time, Eddie. I'm sick of hearing it, and I'm sick of saying yeah, yeah to them, pretending it's the first time I've heard it. I'm glad they're finally doing something."

"But don't you think killing someone's a bit extreme?"

"They have three chances."

"So why are you really helping me?"

Ros tightened her grip on the wheel, and Eddie noticed her cheeks flush slightly. But she wasn't so easily intimidated, and came right back with, "How did the meeting with Jilly go?"

Touché, he thought. That was a poke in the eye with a pencil. "She kicked me out again." He avoided eye contact, felt too embarrassed. "She went to see a psychic, and she claimed to have received a message from Sammy, and I…"

"You forgot to take your tact pills, didn't you?"

"Er, yep."

"Didn't nip into the diplomacy school on your way over?"

"Slipped my mind."

"So you told her they were charlatans?"

"Something like that."

"You told her she was stupid for falling for their trash." She turned to him, a slow shake of the head. "You silly boy."

"I'm not the sharpest knife in the drawer, am I?"

"More like a spoon." And when she looked around this time, her eyes had warmed, and her smile was friendly. "Give her time, Eddie. I'm sure she'll call again." She patted his knee as though knowing he had switched off, and when he turned to look, she asked, "How's the drinking? Do you think you can control it while you're at work?"

He shrugged. "I'll have to." He knew the spiel and didn't need lessons in perseverance versus resignation. "Mind if I smoke?" he asked without even realising he'd said it.

"Yes, I do. Wait till we're at work."

"Thanks."

"Welcome."

He'd wondered whether she would remember the dual carriageway as they travelled to work this morning, and avoid it. But she didn't. They drove along it now, and Eddie's eyes were drawn to the right, to the fence and the little patch of land over by the other carriageway where a sleek gymnasium and office complex used to be a building site. Without knowing, he massaged his leg, and Ros looked across and saw him.

"Oh God, Eddie. I'm sorry, I didn't think—"

"Don't worry about it."

"Why didn't you say something? I could have gone a different way."

"I have to drive this road some time or another. Might as well get rid of all that's bad in my life in one day."

Her raised eyebrows asked him, *How can you get rid of that much badness in just one day?*

His hands were clasped in his lap, knuckles white.

"I'll help you."

Hadn't she come round to soothe away the grief when Jilly kicked him out, and hadn't she been there when Sammy died? She saw him crying and she didn't leave, she didn't coo at him, didn't fuss with him, didn't sit in judgement and blame him, and she didn't laugh. She was just there to catch the vulgarities and mop up the puke. Ros was a stayer and she was a good friend.

But *why?*

"How's Stuck-up Stuart, these days?"

"Still a tosser."

"Great."

"Actually he's worse now. He failed his CRFP, has to do it all again."

"Stuart? Failed? How come?"

Ros shrugged. "He won't give out details. He thinks only a few people know about it, but we all do. No one says anything to him though, it's more than their lives are worth."

Eddie grinned, rubbed his hands together. "Not so perfect, is he?"

"Not a word. Right?"

They arrived at the office five minutes before eight.

He climbed from the car, felt the twinge in his leg and felt the need in his mind.

The SOCO building was a stand-alone single-storey brick building on higher ground, roughly level with the cell windows at the back of Morley Police Station. It was the old district mortuary. Its windows were higher up than you might expect. They were the kind you had to stand on tiptoes to see in through, if you were that way inclined. There was an obvious large access doorway where once they'd wheeled the dead in, gurney wheels a-squeaking on the lino floor. They'd bricked up that entrance, leaving just enough room for a squeaky blue-painted door and a slim window next to it.

Ros locked the car.

He laughed. "I'm sweating."

"Don't let it bother you."

"Oh, okay," he said. "Why didn't I think of that?"

It was already bothering him. He'd worked from this particular office for five years, knew each of the CSIs, knew Jeffery, the new supervisor, enough to know that he would be led back into work gently, probably accompanying someone until he felt able to cope alone. "Cope alone?" he whispered, as he followed Ros around to the doorway. *Hell, since I've been away, I've lost my wife and my kid and should really be dead through alcohol poisoning.* What made everyone think he could cope?

He followed Ros almost cautiously over the threshold and smelled the dirty smell of crime work. He glanced around the small entrance foyer, which doubled as the notice board and signing-in wall, where the access to the small kitchen and toilet were. *Nothing changes,* he thought.

In the main office, Mr Perfect was sitting at his desk, writing. Stuart looked up, registered who it was, and then went back to his paperwork.

From behind him, the door to Jeffery's office opened and a crowd of people shouting and screaming hemmed the new guy in.

People patted him on the back, and for a moment, Eddie felt a panic attack coming on. There were faces so close that he felt claustrophobic; he needed to get out of here and run away.

They were all over him. He reached the point where he was about to scream and run. He could feel it inside, something real with edges and form, something creeping up into his chest, into his throat ready to escape like a spray of hot vomit, when it all stopped.

"Eddie," said a small voice from behind the crowd. They quietened, stepped aside. Jeffery smiled warmly, edged his way through, and held out a hand. "Good to have you back with us."

Eddie didn't smile. Nervously, he looked around at his colleagues and saw anticipation in their eyes, saw their smiles falter slightly. *They expect me to be the same old Eddie, the one who tells the rudest jokes, the practical joker who crawls along the floor, reaches under someone's desk and grabs their leg to make them scream.*

But I don't have a sense of humour anymore. I'm just a twisted, sarcastic cynic who hates all of you equally. And the only screaming today will be inside my head. I will not perform the magic for you anymore.

He reached out and shook. "It's good to be back," he lied. He smiled and the banter sprang up again. The patting began again, and Jeffery urged him to turn around and look up the office to where his desk – surely covered in spiders' webs and moss by now – was decorated in home-made bunting, where balloons, tied in threes, with *Happy 40th Birthday* printed on them, hung from the light fixture over his chair.

Eddie tried to give them what they wanted. He smiled and said, "Aw, you guys… hey, what can I say?" There was dampness in his eyes, and it made them aw and coo. He had given something, and it was just enough, thankfully.

Please don't ask for a fucking speech, because I will walk out. I will.

"We couldn't get any 'Welcome Back' balloons," Terri said. She squeezed his arm and gave him a peck on the cheek, and then she walked by him, her long black hair swishing this way and that, just as it always had. But it was good of her to be so friendly. Andy and Helen, it seemed, knew he was verging on embarrassment, merely slapped his arm and shook his hand, and said almost in unison, "Good to have you back, mate," as they walked to their own desks.

Ros disappeared back around the corner, "I'll put the kettle on," she said, "make us all a brew." Eddie stared after her, wishing she'd come back.

Stuart glanced his way, through expressionless eyes, and even though he smiled at Eddie, it was false, a lie etched onto a face as cold as the bottom shelf of a freezer. They knew. They all knew about Sammy, and they all knew about Jilly kicking him out, and they all knew he was floating on a swamp filled with brandy. They knew it all. Stuart's eyes said so, but no one said a word about it. And provided it didn't interfere with his work he would be accepted back into the fold.

"Get yourself fixed up with a coffee, Eddie," said Jeffery, "and then we'll have a natter. Okay?"

Chapter Twenty-Four

Monday 22nd June

– One –

The door closed behind them, and suddenly there was silence. Eddie felt trapped and alone. Jeffery hung up his expensive jacket and sat behind his desk. He was small, had a Roman nose and close dark eyes; not unfriendly but probing. He too wore the perpetual smile of a man tainted by too many bodies, and too many polite meetings with people he hated. "So, how's it going?"

He shrugged, "Okay."

"Any trouble from the leg?"

Eddie flinched as his mind made Jeffery's mouth say, *'So, how's it going, Eddie; Sammy still dead then? Oh, good, that's good. Wife still screwed up in the head over it too? Yeah, great. What? You're a fully-fledged alcoholic now? That* is *good news; do you need special training or can anyone try?'* He caught himself, pulled his wandering mind back into Jeffery's office and tried to focus on the man. "It aches sometimes. Especially when it's cold; I think it thinks it's arthritis." He smiled, trying to be polite, since Jeffery had been so courteous.

"That's the pleasantries out the way, let's get down to the truth."

Eddie recoiled because whatever was wrong in his shitty life, there was one important thing he definitely wasn't ready for, and that was the damned truth.

"I know what's happened to you recently." Jeffery leaned forward on his desk, hands together as though in some kind of prayer. "But I won't pretend to know how things are up here," he pointed to his head, "because even if you explained it to me, I still wouldn't get it. I can't imagine what you've had to go through and what you've had to do to get through each day. Though, since you've made it back here, I have to put down on record that I admire your strength."

"I have no strength. Just stumbling from one crisis to another."

"I'll do all I can to ease you back into the routine. If there's anything troubling you, anything that makes you feel uncomfortable, or you just want to call time-out, tell me, okay? I'll help you if I can."

"Thanks." Eddie felt humble, and a little emotional. He hoped Jeffery would leave all that horrible stuff alone now before his lip starting quivering and he fell off the chair in a lump of grief onto the carpet.

"How do you think you'll cope with normal volume crime, burglaries, car crime, that sort of thing?"

Eddie shrugged. "Truthfully?"

Jeffery nodded.

"I have no idea. If it wasn't for Ros, then I probably would have found it easier to stay in my flat than come back here."

Jeffery thought for a moment, a stray finger hovering over his lips. "The welcome wasn't my idea; *I* thought you'd like to just slip behind your desk and spend the first day or two catching up with developments. But everyone was determined to officially break the ice and welcome you back." He raised his eyebrows. "Do you think it was a good thing, the welcoming committee?"

"It was kind of everyone. I would have liked to slip back in, but I guess this way we get all the intros over quickly." Eddie noticed his fingers trembling. Was that drink-induced or was it the nerves of starting all over again? "I just... I don't want any sympathy though, you know?" And then it all simply fell out of his mouth. "I don't want people crowding me. You know when you visit someone in hospital, and you're one of three or four people looking down at the guy in bed, and you're all asking how it's going and do you want any grapes bringing in, and have you got a newspaper, do you need change for the payphone? I feel like the guy in bed, looking up at all these faces, who are looking down at me asking inane questions, when you know all they really want is the gory stuff, the *real* stuff – not because they're all creeps, but because they want to walk in your shoes and see what it would be like, see if they could handle it. Who knows?" His eyes narrowed and his cheeks rose slightly, "I'm not making any sense, am I?"

Jeffery nodded. "Perfect sense."

"I don't want the sympathy. I just want to be left alone to get on with things. I'm sorry if it sounds ungrateful, and I understand that they all want answers. But I don't want to give them. I've lived it, I don't want to talk about it."

"Do you want me to tell that to them? Or are *you* going to do it every time one of them asks awkward questions?"

"I think I should do it, don't you?"

"Your call. But if that's what you want, you or I should do it today."

Eddie nodded, fingers tingling now.

"What about the other things, the more serious jobs, how do you feel about them?"

"You're asking me things that I don't know. I'm still at the point where I have good days and bad days; I have no..." he stared around, searching for the word, "I have no consistency yet."

Jeffery reclined, folded his arms. "This is what we'll do. You spend a week or two with Ros. Shadow her, see how you feel. If a biggy comes in and you're not up to it, then I'll send someone else. That sound okay?"

"Sounds fair to me."

"How about road accidents?"

How about them indeed?

Traffic officers only called CSI to road accidents when there was a fatality, or likely to be a fatality. They were invariably not pretty sights; clumps of crumpled metal that used to be shiny cars, wheels pointing in the wrong direction, doors that didn't open anymore, rooflines that looked like tents because the concrete streetlamp won the impact competition; skid marks, splashes of blood on the airbag, windscreen glass with tufts of hair blowing in the breeze. Footballs deflated, trapped beneath screaming tyres. And the tears. And the paramedics and the fire brigade with their cutting equipment. Baseball caps with no one's head in them.

Death. Death. Orphans, widows, and widowers.

He squinted at Jeffery, and all these thoughts rattled around his head; and the need for a drink accompanied them and turned the trembling into a shake. "I'll leave off the road accidents for a while, if that's okay."

"Fine. But after a month, I want us to meet again. I want us to talk honestly about how you think you're doing versus how I think you're doing, and take it from there. I'll not rush you into anything, Eddie; but eventually I want you back fully operational."

Eddie nodded. That was okay; he was right to expect that and for the moment he couldn't see a problem with it. The real big problem was still some days away. And that problem would be out of Jeffery's reach, well out of his league.

– Two –

The office was still a dark and dingy place. It always felt cramped too; too many bodies and not enough desk space. But it was always warm, and on days like today, it was too warm; the place was crammed with computers and even though the windows were open, the heat was stifling, adding to the claustrophobic feeling. The walls were police-issue magnolia. The shiny, well-worn carpet tiles, and the white paintwork was decidedly yellow interspersed with black hand marks as though some kid had run amuck after a finger-painting spree. All the desks bore the battle scars of twenty-odd years' life working for the police.

Over in the far corner, screwed to the wall, was a white sheet of chipboard with registration numbers printed on it and van keys dangling from hooks beneath them. And below each one was a charger for the phone, radio, satnav, and Maglite, and a laptop docking station. In shelves below these were little storage pens for the digital cameras and flash units, and their respective chargers.

The chairs were creaky things, and now, sitting in them patiently, after Jeffery made his brief announcement, were Eddie's beloved work colleagues; people who sat with their arms folded, or leaned against the desk, propping up their faces with a fist.

But one thing they all had in common was anticipation. They wanted a show; they wanted a piece of someone's life that they could only imagine. And why? Because it made their own lives seem a little more normal, a little less fragmented by comparison. They could laugh after he'd gone out, they could all gather in a circle and be grateful that this shit didn't fall on *their* shoulders. Each and every one of them waited for the story that made their own lives appear tolerable. They stared, waiting.

"I've been off work since January," and even *he* noticed the quiver in his voice, "and I guess you've all had extra work to get through."

"We never noticed!" Duffy shouted out. It brought a welcome ripple of laughter.

He patted the leg. "It's getting better; I still take painkillers and some days it still hurts like a bitch, but most of the time, I hardly notice it's there."

Stuart interrupted. "Are you on light duties?"

"No."

"Will you complete a risk assessment for each job?" On the surface, it was a fair question, but one laced with insinuation: if you can't do the job, why are you here, hampering us?

"Eddie will carry out a dynamic risk assessment at each job, Stuart," said Jeffery, "as all of you do as a matter of course. And he is on recuperative duties, not light duties."

"And will you be double-crewing?" Stuart's face was still blank, but behind it was trouble, as though he begrudged Eddie being here at all. Traditionally they'd got along together like two dogs fighting over a bitch in heat, and it seemed that, even after all he'd been through, he wanted to continue where they'd left off.

"Let him get on with it, Stuart, please."

"I'll be crewing with Ros. Just to get me back into the swing of things. If you don't mind, that is, Stuart." He stared at Stuart, and the same old hatred surfaced. He looked at him, at his ski-ramp nose, turned up to expose narrow black nostrils; at his round, wide-apart deep blue eyes; and at his receding hairline and slicked-back black hair over large cabbage ears. No Mr Universe was Stuart. And the way he spoke grated like someone scraping their nails down a blackboard; when he opened his mouth to speak, the voice came out of his nose, and sometimes it was hard not to laugh but most times it was hard not to punch him.

Stuart shrugged. "No skin off my nose." He picked up his pen and turned away.

Eddie noticed how Toni, Duffy, and the others, shook their heads at Stuart. "I see you're still a wanker, Stuart."

"Keep to the point, Eddie," said Jeffery.

Eddie went on to tell them about Sammy, and gave an overview of how that had ended his family life. He asked if anyone here had done the scene, and everyone shook their heads.

"Out of division," said Jeffery.

"The car? Has it been found?"

"Don't think so."

And then, just for the record, to save the gossipmongers a job, he told how Jilly and he had split up; not how Jilly kicked him out because of the drinking, which got out of hand somewhere near the end of February, just that they had split up. He noticed Stuart look up then, and how he stared between him and Ros, a sliver of a smile on his face, before going back to his writing. And Eddie rounded off the talk by saying, "Now I'm back, battered and bruised, but otherwise my old self—"

"Oh good," Stuart said without looking up.

Eddie ignored him. "I'll be a bit slow on the jovial front," he looked towards Duffy who sat there respectfully engrossed, "but hopefully..." he stumbled for words, voice growing ever more quiet.

"You'll do it, kid," Duffy said.

"Yeah, give it some time."

"Why are you telling us all this?" Stuart looked around at the others and assumed incorrectly that they felt as he did.

"So you won't have to whisper behind my back, and so that pricks like you don't start any rumours. Plus I think you deserve an explanation without being embarrassed to come and ask for it. You can tell anyone what I've told you today. But if you have any questions, ask me. Don't be afraid of hurting me. I promise that none of you can hurt me any more than I already hurt myself."

The unexpected then happened, and it caused Eddie to nod gracefully and remove himself from the office for a cigarette. Duffy began it, but soon they all applauded; one or two even whistled and cheered. Eddie went red, and Stuart remained silent.

Chapter Twenty-Five

Monday 22nd June

Rochester had given him a fair story to get him back on track. It had everything he needed to show how cruel and desperate the world had become, and it had everything he needed to secure his job, if he handled it right. On his way here, he thought about how desperate the old guy must be to have written a letter like that. He was looking forward to meeting him, this Lincoln Farrier.

It was Monday morning, the 22nd of June, and it was another scorcher. The traffic through the city was abysmal, but it had given him time to rationalise his stance on The Rules and what they stood for.

Mick had written thousands of words, hundreds of column inches, on the subject, taking the stance that The Rules was a just way forward; and he saw the meeting with Mr Farrier as just another point of view along the same theme, nothing to really stretch him too far.

He pulled up on the main road in Methley and killed the engine.

* * *

He rehearsed the questions he had in mind for Mr Farrier. Nothing too taxing; after all, what he couldn't get out of the old guy, he'd embellish – his job was on the line, remember. He'd stick with what the parole board said, how Farrier's son – he rustled quickly through the typed version of Mr Farrier's letter, just to refresh his fogged memory – Stephen, yes that's it, Stephen. Anyway, he'd stick with how the parole board thought this fifty-year-old man called Stephen Farrier still posed a threat to burglars. Still posed a threat to burglars? That's like saying a rapist could sue his victim if he caught syphilis from her!

The ratings would go through the roof. And of course, it would be his by-line. No bad thing when looking for future employment. But he wanted to feed Farrier The Rules too, and see what stance he had. He expected that an old guy like him, obviously a man of good character, would see them as a breath of fresh air, something hard to hit back at the thief and the burglar with, something to kill the murderer with, too.

Mick slipped his digital recorder into his jacket pocket, climbed from the car, and peered around. *Nice,* he thought. *One day I'm gonna retire somewhere just like this, where the high point of your day is finding out just how many pints of beer you can sup before barfing into the weeds.* It brought a smile to his face, and it brought a thirst to his lips; Mick reached into the glove box for the bottle.

He felt the sun on his back as he walked with his head down watching his shadow ripple over the undulating path towards Lincoln's back door.

Mick stopped at the door. It was open, but so was the small window just further along the building. *Trusting,* he thought, *or stupid.*

He knocked on the shiny door.

Absently, he brushed dirt off his jacket, waiting for a reply, and then straightened the tie he'd bought on the way here, the tie he promised to offer William to replace the one he'd ruined. He knocked again, louder. "Turn your fucking hearing aid on, old man." He peeked through the letterbox and quickly pulled away again, shuddering. His throat closed up and he turned away, feeling the tightness in his chest. *Old folk,* he told himself, *they piss everywhere, don't they? But look around, Mick, look at the guy's garden, look at his door – it shines like a mirror! The old man's not a doddering fool; the old man's simply a man who is old.*

So what's with the smell, huh?

Maybe he fell asleep and, well, you know, had an accident. But it didn't smell like piss. Mick pictured dead goldfish floating on a crusty skin of rancid water. This smell was like that.

"Explain those then," he whispered as two bluebottles buzzed out through the open window. "Like flies around..." He knocked louder, desperate for a response. The door swung open. "Hello?"

His eyes were drawn inside Lincoln Farrier's home, into the hallway with flowery 1960s wallpaper, with a deep green carpet running up the stairs in front of him. The centre of the carpet had worn thin. But his eyes couldn't stay there for long, they were pulled to the lounge door.

All was quiet. Except the flies.

He stepped into the hall. "Hello," he called again. Nothing. Only the smell and the flies.

He shouldn't be in here.

You should go back to the car and you should sit there, taking little sips from the God-help-me bottle, and you should wait until a frail old fella walks up the path. Then you could ask him if his name was Lincoln, and when he says, "Yes, it's Lincoln, who are you?" you could breathe that sigh of relief you've been promising yourself, and you could pat him on the shoulder, and you could laugh at him and say, "Hey Lincoln, think it's about time you changed your fucking fish water – it smells like someone died in there!"

He touched the lounge door handle. His heart thumped irregularly.

"Get a move on, Micky," he said. "It'll be fucking dark soon!" And that helped, that little chip of humour sent the ghosties and ghoulies flying off with the bluebottles and got him smiling at this nonsense he'd created.

He'd simply step into the lounge, leave the old guy a friendly 'while you were out…' note and then go.

Mick stepped into the lounge and froze.

* * *

Mick had walked in; the smile he'd prepared in advance wasn't needed after all. Without realising it, his feet were already inside the room, and though he wanted them to stop and turn, they walked on a few extra steps and came to a lazy halt by the table, literally a couple of yards away from the maggots crawling inside Lincoln Farrier's nostrils.

He watched in silence, with a repugnant fascination at the maggots, a tiny writhing mass, wriggling in the hole, and it seemed strange that all that movement was going on, and yet no one reached out a finger to scratch at the annoying tickle they caused; how could you put up with it!

The top of Lincoln's head had left home. Parts of it were buried in the wall along with a spray of dark red blood that had dripped and run towards the bureau, the bureau that had collected most of the old man's brains and the blackening fleshy bits that used to surround it. Splinters of bone were everywhere.

The front of the old man's shirt was awash with a large blackened stain, as though he wore a warlock's bib, and his hands, strangely similar to a dead chicken's claw, how all the fingers seemed drawn together, were pale save for the liver spots, and were draped as though he were asleep, one in his lap, the other over the side of the chair, hanging in mid-air.

At his feet was a gun.

And on the table was a note. Mick tried to sidestep the emotions he knew were coming his way, and he tried to read the note, but it may as well have been written in Arabic for all he could see or absorb. He could see the single droplet of blood though, high up in the right corner of the note, just one droplet of blacky redness. It was abhorrent as though that was the icon of the scene as a whole, the exclamation mark at the end of Mr Lincoln Farrier's life.

As he looked back at the old man, whose eyes were sunken white things in sockets that were six sizes too large for them, he felt something move in his stomach; something unpleasant with a smell not too dissimilar to that now enjoyed by his nostrils.

His eyes let go of the old man's, his feet turned rather raggedly and tried to make their way to the exit. He stepped along toward the daylight, ignoring the flies and the smell, and out into the back garden of a dead old man who would never again tend his roses. He rested his back against the cold brick of Lincoln's house, breathing deep, cleansing breaths.

Then Mick doubled up and threw up onto the path, spraying his grubby shoes with puke.

The next thing he knew, he was gulping down mouthfuls of foul-tasting brandy and marvelling at the lumps of vomit clinging to his new tie.

Chapter Twenty-Six

Monday 22nd June

– One –

An hour after giving his speech, Eddie had deleted almost 3,000 worthless emails and familiarised himself with yet more new procedures concerning DNA recovery techniques; had charged up the Multi-Layer Protein Dye latent fingerprint enhancement canister, installed new batteries in the mini-sequencing machine and checked out his personal-issue laptop, ready for a day of fighting crime. He slurped the coffee and then sneaked off to sip the brandy in the toilet, feeling the familiar buzz as it hit his brain and took the edge off what should have been a steady reintroduction to crime scene examination. "What have we got then, Ros?"

The sheet came out of the old laser printer and she logged off IBIS and sighed. "I've tried to keep it low-key," she handed Eddie the list, "but I think I've hit boring by mistake."

"Today I like boring."

Ros stood next to him, reading the list over his shoulder. "Have you," she whispered, pulling at his arm, gaining his attention, "have you had a swig of the hard stuff?"

Eddie looked at her, and then over towards Jeffery's office. "Don't know what you mean."

She didn't whisper this time. "It's okay if you can't quit in order to get back with Jilly, but don't you touch that stuff while we're on duty!"

He held out his hands. "Okay, I get the message."

"Well make sure you do." Ros grabbed her coat. "Now, come on."

– Two –

Eddie whispered, "Twenty minutes."

Ros shook her head. "Fifteen, no forced entry."

"Okay, fifteen, cash, no electrical goods."

The man looked tired. He answered the door and his eyes were tiny, shiny things hidden somewhere in great folds of dark skin that were sunken beneath outcrops of hairy brow. His moustache flicked up and down. "Yes?"

"Hello," Eddie said, "police fingerprints."

The man ran fingers through his thinning hair. "Are you CSI?"

"Yes."

"Well why the bloody hell didn't you say so?" The outcrops grew heavier.

Eddie and Ros looked at each other. "We're sorry we couldn't get here yesterday," Ros said, "only we—"

"Don't give me your excuses, I'm not interested in excuses. Just come in." He stood aside, let them in and slammed the door. "Through here," he snapped.

"Where did they get in?" Eddie asked, realising the same old questions, asked in the same old concerned voice, were already tripping back out of his mouth as though he'd never been away, as natural as exhaled air.

"Kitchen." He walked away from them. "Through here."

"Kitchen," Eddie whispered, miming behind his back, waddling behind him. Ros poked him in the ribs. "Did you leave the window open?"

"Is it a crime?"

"No, just wondered, that's all."

"It was open."

"Thanks awfully," smiled Eddie. *I'm the one who needs cheering up, and look what I get lumbered with: Mr Happy! I'm gonna slit my wrists before today is over.* Eddie struggled to keep up because his leg ached again, and as they walked through the lounge towards the back of the house, he noticed a dent in the skirting board the size of a fist.

"I was sacked today," Mr Happy said to no one in particular. "There," he said, folded his arms, nodded his head, "he came in through there." He stood back, watching them closely.

"Right," Ros said, "I'll start outside. Okay, Eddie?"

"Are you sure?" he pleaded, "I mean, I don't mind…"

"I'll be fine." She stepped outside.

"Okay," Eddie smiled sarcastically, showing teeth and all.

"Sacked after fourteen years. It was all *his* fault too," the man grinned with irony, like he was a road accident victim picked up by a life-saving helicopter, only to be told there was a bomb on board, "the fudge-nudger." He looked at Eddie. "He sacked me for straight-talking," he grunted again, "for not being sympathetic enough, for not bending over and taking it up the shitter. The bastard! And then *this* happens and I have to take the day off. He says it's not good enough, that I look like shit! But what's he expect? I went six rounds with a fucking burglar." He put his face close to Eddie's, nodded outside to Ros. "What's *your* boss like?"

Eddie opened his kit, didn't look up. "We get along well most of the time."

"Mine was a wanker! A poof! Ha. At least he *was*; I don't work there anymore, I don't fucking work anywhere anymore."

"I'm sorry to hear that, Mr McHue." Eddie took out the MLPD spray and squirted it on the glass. Then he bent and took out his squirrel brush and jar of aluminium powder.

"Yeah, I bet. You do this day in and day out, and I bet you hear this kind of shit all day long. Why would you care, you'll go home at the end of every day to your swanky little house where wifey has tea ready for you—"

Eddie stiffened.

"Hey, that's enough." Ros stood in the doorway, watching.

"I can see it in your eyes; you don't give a flying fuck that I got beaten up. You couldn't care less that some bastard came into my house and beat the crap out of me!"

Bet it took ages, Eddie thought. He noticed Ros watching, thinking the same thought, and he half winked at her, just to let her know he was in control of the situation, and yeah he was fine, and no, he wouldn't let this guy wind him up. Eddie stood again, folded his arms and watched McHue blame the world for his troubles.

"And do you know what, he took it, he took my fucking savings. I mean, I have some put in the bank, but *that* was special, see I knew he was going to do it, I knew he was going to fucking sack me, that bum-bandit—"

"Please," Eddie said, "cool the language down a bit."

"And I knew… what? What did you say to me! This is *my* fucking house! I was attacked and robbed in my own fucking house, and then it takes two days for fucking forensics to finally get their arse in gear and come out to make a mess in my house, to tell me there's nothing—"

"Calm down, sir." Eddie put the jar of powder down.

"Don't you tell me to fucking calm down."

"Hey! Hey!" Ros stepped into the kitchen. McHue looked at her and slammed the door on her foot. Eddie dropped the brush. He grabbed the man by the scruff of the neck and pinned him against the wall.

"Eddie!" Ros screamed.

"I'll ram this torch down your bastard throat, you little wanker, if you don't keep a lid—"

"Eddie!" Now Ros screamed at Eddie, not at McHue, not at the pain in her foot, but directly at Eddie. "Let him go."

Eddie stared into his face, stared deep into his tired eyes, and he actually felt sympathy for him, but then McHue spoiled it all.

"Go on," he croaked, "do it to me. See what happens. I don't care what you do next, big boy; I'll have the last laugh." And then a chuckle fell out into the air between them. "Go on," he said, "get out of my house, you piece of shit, and take your chemicals and your fucking girlfriend with you. Go on, back to your wife and your little bastard kids..." He spat the words into Eddie's face.

Eddie went cold.

Mr McHue's words faded. The coldness spread out quickly from his head, through his shoulders and into his arms. And he thought about how he would go home to his little wifey and watch his little bastard, Sammy, as they played on the carpet waiting for tea to cook. Eddie's eyes grew wide and his grip tightened on Mr Happy's reddening throat, until Mr Happy's eyes changed from irony to fear. They flicked between Eddie and Ros, a kind of pleading in them now. "Get him off me! He's fucking crazy, get him off me now!"

"Eddie," Ros whispered his name. "He's not worth it, Eddie."

Eddie relaxed the grip. He blinked and then the ferocity left his face.

The man breathed again, rubbing his throat as Eddie stepped back. "What's your name?" He looked at Ros.

"Why do you—"

"You're his boss, aren't you? I want your name."

"Hey come on, sir. I think we should all just calm down. We're here to—"

"What is your name?"

"Do you want us to carry on with the examination?"

"Is that a threat, young lady? I ask for your name, and you imply you will cease to carry out an examination if I carry out my right to complain about being held by the *throat*," he looked at Eddie, "by one of your gorillas?"

"No, I only—"

Eddie moved forward and Ros held him back. "Well if he's gonna sue, I may as well get my fucking money's worth."

"No! Eddie, please, it's not worth it; leave him alone and lift the marks you found. Ignore him, do your job."

"That's right, Eddie. Do your job." McHue turned to Ros. "Write your details down for me now. I won't ask again. And write his down, too."

Eddie lifted the aluminium powder marks off the inner sill, along with a partial footmark. The MLPD marks on the window were of no value. He had some evidence, but for the life of him couldn't come up with a reason good enough to help this ignorant bastard more than he already had.

He sealed the lifted marks in an evidence bag and plugged the cap back on the MLPD spray bottle. And then he looked at the man, at his straggly hair, his unkempt features, eyes that needed a year's worth of sleep just to start looking normal again, and he wondered why he had said those things; Christ, they had never met, why would he want to say those things... he almost felt sorry for him. Was he the cause of his own bad fortune, or the result?

Did I look like that? Do I look like that now?

"Listen," Eddie said, fighting back the words he dearly wanted to use, "I understand you've been through some bad times—"

"Bad times?" McHue smiled for a moment. "Bad times! You don't know what fucking bad times are, you snivelling piece of shit." His eyes darkened and his head sank into his shoulders, hands turned into claws. "You collect your nice *huge* monthly pay, pay that I provide you with, and you couldn't give a sideways fuck about people like me!" McHue closed the gap down and prodded Eddie in the arm with each syllable of his snarled words. "You've no idea what bad times are. You go from one fucking job to the next, like parasites feeding on the misery of others, and you file your fucking paperwork." He brought his black eyes right up to Eddie's, and when Ros tried to intervene, he merely turned his eyes to the side and growled at her. He looked back at Eddie. "Come back to the real world, you pumped up piece of shit, and come back to where bad things happen to nice people. You'd fold in seconds if it happened to you!"

Eddie gritted his teeth, felt the heat in his chest intensify, and felt the tears come to the surface. "You want a fucking competition on the Bad Times League?"

"Enough!" Ros said.

McHue saw something in Eddie that made him flinch and take a couple of steps back. "Is that it?" He saw the evidence bag in Eddie's hand. "Is that all you got?"

"I'll wait outside for you, Ros." Eddie picked up his kit.

"Don't walk away from me while I'm talking to you!" McHue reached out and took hold of Eddie by the shoulder.

Eddie turned and rammed a well-aimed elbow in his stomach. McHue coughed and folded up, holding himself off the floor with the fingertips of his right hand, while his left rubbed his gut. He shrieked in pain, but cursed Eddie, promising to have his fucking job, and every penny he had.

Well you won't get much, Eddie thought and walked away.

Chapter Twenty-Seven

Monday 22nd June

– One –

Stuart looked across the empty office to Eddie's desk.

He had finished his morning's work with the ease of a pro; had accumulated fingerprint and footwear evidence in his usual diligent way. Stuart was perfection personified when it came to his work, his *craft*. He was the one with all the knowledge, the man who rarely referred to a satnav to find his way around the city centre, and the man who never made mistakes in his clerical duties. He was punctual, and smart to the point of being annoying. His black trousers had a crease so sharp up the centre of each leg they could have been cast from iron; his shoes were so shiny that you could see a reflection of the ceiling, and his hair was slicked back covering a slight bald patch on the crown of his head – his only imperfection – with such precision that it could have been drawn with a black marker pen.

He was the one who organised the Christmas parties and forced everyone to attend; he was the one who administered the tea fund with such efficiency that he could easily have been the Chancellor of the Exchequer. He was the unofficial judge of those around him, checking their paperwork as though the supervisor had died and he'd put him in charge. And he was the one who brought their discrepancies to the supervisor's attention, and always with great pride.

He munched his square-cut sandwiches, and watched the BBC TV news showing the demonstrations surrounding Margy Bolton's death on Sunday, the first to die by a bullet.

Stuart's eyes strolled around the office and fell on Collins's desk again, the most untidy desk here; and he shook his head at the accumulated papers scattered across it, at the bulging in-tray, at the unfulfilled statement requests and other assorted detritus lurking there. He was a disgrace to the service, was Collins. Why they hadn't turfed him out was a mystery.

The man was a lower-class caricature, an ensemble of tramp-like qualities: scruffy, hair a mess, face a parody of eagerness, clothes un-ironed, and with a slack attitude and abysmal way of speaking to complainants that was appalling. Stuart detested Eddie Collins and all he embodied. Sure, the man brought in results, when he was here, but you could train a monkey to do that. He had no finesse and held the mystique of the job in scant regard, and Stuart found his unprofessionalism intolerable.

And now he was an alcoholic. Oh, it wasn't widely known, but Stuart knew; could see how pallid his face was, could read that absent look in his eyes, and this morning's little speech cut no ice with him; all that teary nonsense about his kid being run over and his wife kicking him out – *hmph*, a separation, he'd called it. She kicked him out because he was a drunk – and West Yorkshire Police should follow her example. And the kid, sure, that was tragic, but come on, life goes on, the job goes on and it seemed Eddie couldn't grasp that, and turning to the booze just displayed his inherent weakness and unsuitability for this work.

It had all stemmed from last January, when he tried to be a superhero and save some woman's handbag. Stuart couldn't understand why he had bothered; after all, the robber was wearing gloves so there was no chance of a fingerprint ident; and low copy DNA was out too because the weather and type of contact between assailant and victim rendered it unsuitable. So why risk life and limb for no forensic yield, no statistical benefit?

Stuart made sure the office was empty, and then he couldn't resist the urge any longer to have a peek in Eddie's desk drawer. The temptation of finding something juicy in there was just too strong. He put down the sandwich and slid his chair across the shiny carpet to the untidy part of the office, the Eddie Collins part of the office.

The top drawer was full of pens and batteries and paperclips – none of them compartmentalised – and the bottom drawer, the one large enough to accommodate files, was full of minute sheets, and changes to working practices, statements and ident sheets, and all crammed in any old how. Stuart's nostrils flared at the inefficiency.

He was about to slam the drawer shut when he saw something shiny underneath the rack of suspended files. He glanced around again and then delved deeper. It was an unopened bottle of brandy, ready for the time when the stress got too much for Eddie. Stuart thought about how he could get this information back to supervision without declaring his method.

The phone rang and he jumped, slamming the drawer shut and scooting away back to his own desk as though his chair was turbocharged. He turned the TV off and grabbed the receiver, heart hammering. "Stuart Tunstall, CSI." It was control, and he slowly regained his composure, reaching for a pen as the controller talked about a scene that had just been shouted in. The scene they wanted examined was on the far boundary of their division, and it was a suicide, nothing special, nothing to get the circus out for; it probably just required a few photos. Stuart scribbled down the details. "I'll get Collins to examine it this afternoon. Yes of course he'll be okay with it," he smiled, "it's only a suicide." *And if anyone's used to death in this office, it's Eddie.*

– Two –

Ros emptied her arms of equipment and folders of paperwork.

"Had a good morning?" Stuart asked as Eddie fell into his chair.

"Put the kettle on, Stuart, and don't ask stupid questions."

"Job too hard for you now?"

Eddie looked at him. "No," he said, "but the people are still arseholes. Now don't forget, I take my coffee white, point-two millilitres of milk, and 2.4 grams of coffee powder. Can you remember that?"

"Lost none of your sarcasm, I see."

"Where you're concerned, Stuart, I like to make an effort, and it's not sarcasm. It's contempt."

"Pack it in, you two. Christ, you've only been working half a day and already you're at each other's throats."

"Nonsense, Ros," Eddie smiled, "just good old work chums getting reacquainted. Ain't that right, Stu?"

"After your lunch," he looked between Ros and Eddie, "there's a suicide for you. I thought about you straight away when it came in."

"Oh, why's that?"

"I thought it'd be a nice easy job to get you back into the swing of things. No stress."

"You're all heart, Stu, do you know that?"

Ros stepped in, "We'll take it. It'll keep us out of the way of Joe Public for a while."

"Oh?" Stuart grew interested. "Had some bother this morning?"

Eddie's face turned dark as images of McHue up against the wall came back into his mind, images of an elbow in the ribs. "Just an irate complainant, that's all."

"Oh yeah?"

"Have you polished your shoes this morning, Stu?"

Stuart headed for the kitchen, "Some of us think image is still important."

"Damned right. Shine your head too?"

Although her voice was angry, Ros couldn't help smiling as Stuart disappeared. "Why do you have to wind him up, you know what he's like—"

"I'm just having a little fun, that's all."

"Well choose someone else to have fun with. He doesn't have a sense of humour; and he can make life difficult for you right now. So just remember that. Fool."

Chapter Twenty-Eight

Monday 22nd June

"Ignore the vomit. It's mine. Not too good with dead things."

"How long have you been here, Mick?" Eddie unshouldered the camera bag and folded his arms. "Why have they kept you waiting around?"

"I don't know," he drew on his cigarette. "I found the dead guy and I suppose they're punishing me for ruining their day. Either that or they think I did it and are going to cuff me after they finish their coffee." He shuffled from foot to foot. "How the hell do you do this job?" He looked at Eddie, his face screwed into a tangle of bemusement. "How do you play about with dead people?"

"If you start thinking that it's an old man who's lived through the war, and has kids and grandkids, and that he was thinking about preparing chicken for his lunch when the urge to do away with himself took hold, then you're in trouble. Forget it all, and just do your job."

"You're a freak."

"Tell me something new."

Ros stopped dead in her tracks, forensic kit in one hand, slip of paper in the other. "What are *you* doing here?" She stared at Mick, eyes cold.

He couldn't even raise a smile. "I had nothing better to do, and I know how much you like my company."

"Why do you look so green?" Her eyes narrowed.

Mick pointed to the vomit.

"You've been *in* there?"

"He found the body," Eddie said. "Now let's get on with it."

"How come *you* found the body?"

"What makes you think it's a suicide?" Eddie asked.

"There's a suicide note."

Ros asked, "What were you *doing* in there, Mick?"

"I had a story to cover. He wrote a letter to my newspaper—"

"Just cos you found a note, doesn't make it suicide," Eddie said.

"What letter?"

"I can't—"

"You can," Ros said. "Have you got it with you?"

"No!" Mick took a step back, holding his hands up. "You come near me," he said, "and I'll throw up on you, I promise."

"Leave him." Eddie took off his jacket.

"Said something about his son being in prison, and he was distressed at it all and hoped *The Yorkshire Echo* would broadcast his story. I was going to *get* his story and I wanted to know what he thought of The Rules, that's all. Nothing wrong with that is there?"

"No, go on. There's nothing more we need you for, is there, Ros?" Eddie looked at her.

"Ready to rock?"

Eddie was smiling at her, but already he was sweating. "Thirty minutes."

"Might have a bullet to dig out. I say fifty minutes."

"Pessimist."

"Is that the pot calling the kettle grimy arse!"

* * *

Using a gloved knuckle, Eddie pushed the lounge door open. He peered around the corner and was hit in the face by a bluebottle. Ros laughed and almost fell over, and even when both saw the old man with half of his head running down the wallpaper, still they giggled. Neither thought it necessary to wear protective clothing, or a mask. It was only a suicide scene after all. The white suits and overshoes, the hoods and two pairs of latex examination gloves were reserved for scenes where contamination would be a worry; the only problem here was the flies.

"Let's take a look around," Ros said.

Blood. There was so much blood, and even the conversation he'd had on the doorstep with Mick about being detached, seemed ineffective in here. He was worried that the Old Professional had abandoned him, that he was back to being just a rookie, that he would follow Mick's example and throw his lunch and the swig of brandy he'd had in the toilet earlier, right back up over the old man and his congealing brains.

He felt woozy, he suspected, because sitting in that chair with his hands white and stiff in the shape of some bird's claw, with the top of his head missing and a huge black stain down the front of his checked shirt, was Sam. The old man's face, alive with black flies and white maggots, his eyes glazed, their lashes stuck together, was the face and the eyes of his dead son. This is how Sam was now; this is what he looked like after that car left him in the middle of the road. This was him as they sank him into the ground: lifeless.

Eddie turned away quickly, taking gulps of stale air. His hands shook and he reached out for the table, careful not to move anything.

"You okay, Eddie?"

"Fine."

"Looks like he took care of himself, doesn't it? I mean, it's a lovely clean place he had here."

"It's a fucking treat." Eddie took the weight on his feet again and made himself stare at the old man, feeling his history, feeling his kids and his grandkids, feeling the war he lived through and the passing of his wife. And suddenly Eddie felt like crying, he felt hurt for the guy that his life should come down to this, to a fifty-minute exam before his old blown-away carcass was shipped off to the local morgue for a quick hacking and slashing session; and the only person in the world who probably gave a flying fuck about him was locked up in jail somewhere and probably didn't even know his old man was dead yet.

It was a shame.

Eddie blinked but still he stared at the face, made himself do it, made himself care less and less, made the old man's history dissolve into the smelly, fly-ridden air of the room. He was a corpse, a stiff, a body; something to fill in the day before going home and starting all over again tomorrow. This was his job, and if he wanted to keep it – and that glimmer of hope of keeping Jilly – then he'd better get a grip on himself right now.

On the walls were pictures of the old days. Here was one with Lincoln in a smithy. Behind him the furnace burned bright, giving off a white glare in the black and white photo, smoke disappearing into the rafters somewhere, and Lincoln posed over an anvil, holding a hammer over a glowing piece of bent metal, sweat on his brow, but with a pleasant smile on his smooth face. Next to that was a colour photograph showing a graduation ceremony with his son collecting a rolled-up piece of paper wrapped in a red ribbon, from some be-gowned man on a stage. Below the picture, in neat calligraphic script, *Stephen Farrier, BEng Hons, 1985.*

History.

Eddie turned away from the wall. "I'll set the camera up. I want to get the hell away from these bloody flies."

"You sure you're okay?"

"Fine."

They quartered the room, took pictures of the front door, inside and out, to prove there was no lock damage, and then they closed up on the body itself, taking images from all around, showing the position of the gun, proved safe after a quick visit from an authorised firearms officer who couldn't cope with the smell. And they took another half dozen of the head and its debris on the wall behind.

"Okay," Ros said, "we'll finish off with a quick one of the note, and then we can get back for a coffee. What d'ya say?"

"Sounds good to me." Eddie checked his watch. "Told you forty minutes."

"Hmm, do you think we ought to retrieve the bullet?"

Eddie looked at the wall, dripping with black flaky old blood. "What's the point?"

Ros shrugged. "It proves the weapon on the floor killed him."

"You get the bullet. I'll swab the weapon to prove he was the one holding it, and then I'll package it."

"Low Copy?"

"From the grip. We'll have the barrel superglued; might get some marks and an easy ident," he smiled at her.

"Christ, you sounded like Stuart then, keen as mustard to get an ident."

Eddie looked back at the old man, puzzled by the circumstances of this whole scene.

"Can't understand why he killed himself. It's not as though he would never see his son again, was it?"

Eddie looked at her.

"Oh shit, Eddie, I'm sorry, I didn't mean—"

"It's okay. Don't walk on eggshells around me, Ros."

"Sorry."

"And stop being sorry, woman. If you want to make yourself useful, start getting the bullet out the wall, eh? I'll photo the note before I dick about with the gun."

He brought the camera up to his eye and peered at the last scribbling of an old guy with a broken heart. He squared the note up in the viewfinder, tried to capture the old fountain pen too, just in the right side of the frame. Then he let the autofocus bring the letters sharp, and then he stopped. Dead. He blinked, took the camera away and stood there motionless for a moment, thinking. He read the letter.

*To those who find me, I am sorry to cause you so much grief.
I'm sick of my Steven being locked up for no good reason, and
I can't take it no more. Steven, I love you, please forgive me.
Lincoln Farrier.*

Then he walked to the wall, the one with the photos on it, and
specifically to the one where Lincoln Farrier's boy was getting his
degree. "Ste*v*en," he whispered. He read the words below the picture
of the young man wearing a black gown and mortarboard. "Stephen.
Ste*ph*en? You'd think a father could spell his own son's name right,
wouldn't you?" he whispered. And then he looked again at the other
picture, the one where a younger Lincoln Farrier was beating the shit
out of a glowing piece of metal using a hammer. A hammer, noted
Eddie, that he held in his left hand. He turned and saw that the pen
lay on the note's right side as though the author had finished writing
and automatically put down the pen to read his own work. And he
looked at the gun, and saw where it had landed. By Lincoln's right
side. "Erm, Ros?"

"What?"

"Leave the bullet, dear."

"Why, what's up?"

"I don't think this is a fifty-minute suicide. I think we have
ourselves a little murder."

Chapter Twenty-Nine

Monday 22nd June

– One –

It was nearly midnight when Eddie closed the door to his flat and switched on the light. He wasn't expected in at work tomorrow until ten o'clock under the late-off late-on rule. The first thing he did was chuck four slices of bread in the toaster and down a glass of brandy, and never had it tasted so good, and never – well, almost never – had it been so well deserved. He was exhausted, and it was the third glass that finally managed to take the edge off the day. After the fourth glass, his toast popped but by then he didn't feel hungry anymore. Eddie saved his legs and sat down with the bottle, and only minutes passed before some inconsiderate bastard knocked on his door and disturbed his self-pity. "Go. Away."

"Eddie, it's me, Mick."

"Go. Away. Mick."

"I have to talk to you."

Sighing, Eddie let him in, and returned to his chair and lit a cigarette. "Go on, I'm all ears."

Mick sniffed the air. "You had toast?"

"Didn't get the chance," he smiled, tipped the bottle at him.

"Good man. Mind if I have it?"

"Fill yer boots."

"Ta." He headed for the kitchen. "It was interesting, wouldn't you say, that suicide today?" he shouted.

"Oh yes, interesting is what it was alright."

Mick came back in munching hard toast. "It wasn't a suicide, was it?"

Eddie raised his eyebrows, drank brandy.

"I did a little research while I was in the village. And though it pained me I talked to people in the pub," he laughed, spitting crumbs across the settee. "And then I spoke to an old girl in the Post Office."

"I'm enthralled."

"She was devastated when I told her the news. Had to shut up shop."

"Still enthralled."

"Listen!" Mick sat down, put the plate of toast on the carpet, grabbed a glass, and lit a cigarette. "Lincoln Farrier was murdered. I know it."

"Bully for you, we'll make you into a PI in no time. What should we call you? Mick the Dick? How's that sound?"

"The old lady, Mrs Walker, says he called in on his way home, and was on cloud nine when he left her because of a letter she gave him."

Eddie's face crumpled, "I'm tired, mate, and I don't really want to listen to a pile of bollocks about some old couple having it away in the back of the Post Office."

"Will you shut the fuck up and listen!" He glared at Eddie, and when Eddie waved an apology, he snatched the bottle off the table and helped himself. "Thank you. Now," he continued, "Mrs Walker handed him a letter from his son; a letter that said the parole board had finally granted him release, and he was due out of prison in a couple of weeks." He watched Eddie's face, noted how it suddenly appeared slightly interested after all. "You tell me, my forensic friend, if *you* were so sad about your boy being kept under lock and key by an unfair system, and then, listen to that," he pointed a finger, "and *then* you found out he was coming home, would you go and suck on a gun? Would you?"

"No. I wouldn't."

"Exactamundo. Exacta-fucking-mundo." He downed the brandy and refilled the glass, and then he looked at Eddie, saw that his rubberised face had slipped back into uninterested. "How did *you* find out it wasn't suicide?"

"I can't—"

"Off the record, Eddie."

Eddie stared at him.

"No, I mean it, off the record. I won't quote you, or use anything—"

"For a second there, Mick, I almost believed you."

"Eddie, an old man was shot through the head in his own home, and someone tried to pass it off as suicide. I'm going to the police with everything I have tomorrow—"

"After you've run the fucking story, no doubt."

"Hey, I'm hanging on to my job by its foreskin, I kid you not, and I have to make this work. But it doesn't mean I can't take a personal interest too. And I do, I *have*."

Eddie relented. He told him about the photographs and about the spelling error in Lincoln Farrier's alleged suicide note. And he finished his brief résumé by adding, "If any of this, *any* of this gets into print, I will dutifully collect my P45 and then come straight round to your house and pull your legs off. Do I make myself ultra-clear, Micky-boy? I *really do* mean it; I have a job to keep too, remember."

Mick held up his hands, "Absolutely, no problemo, I promise."

"Good, now pass the bottle, you pisshead."

"I knew about the spelling error anyway."

"How?"

"I saw the note, remember?"

"You were chucking your load, Mick; how come you took notice of the note?"

Mick was silent for a moment. "I've never seen anything like it. It was abhorrent but... mesmerising."

Eddie stared a little longer, then nodded his understanding.

"So tell me what happened after I left."

"We called the circus out, that's what happened. CID eventually showed up, Jeffery came along too."

"Did they call a biologist?"

Eddie nodded.

"And a ballistics expert?"

"You know more about this job than I do. Yes, we did all that, and we called in the forensic pathologist and then we had tea and biscuits in Lincoln's lounge while the horseracing was on. Went through a full tin of fly spray but I won twenty quid."

Mick wobbled his head side to side. "Oh, ha fucking ha."

"Well, what do you want me to say, Mick? We went through the whole shit-n-shaboodle, start to finish; that's how come I've just managed to plonk my arse in my own chair after a sixteen-hour shift. And even then I end up talking about the pissing job. *And* I need a shower; I've got so much ali powder on me that I feel like the tin man."

"You smell of death."

"You smell of body odour."

Mick nodded. "I wanted to know what evidence you found."

"I'm not telling you that, you plank. Not only would I lose my job, I'd end up in jail for perverting the course of justice."

Mick put his hand on his chest, the smoke streaming around his chin. "This is me you're insulting."

"I couldn't care less."

"I've already promised—"

He groaned. "You're worse than a kid, you know that?"

Mick smiled.

"We took the gun, we'll get low copy DNA from the butt and we'll try for fingerprints off the barrel. The bullet can't be examined cos it's too badly damaged, and the shell will go for fingerprinting along with the note too. We fingerprinted the house, including the doors and the windows and found forty-seven marks – probably all his, and maybe Mrs Walker's too if they were having it off. That's it. Tomorrow," he looked at the clock, "later today rather, the chemical boys will go in there and spray ninhydrin all over the walls and maybe, in a couple of days, they'll find another dozen marks or so. Okay?"

"Thanks. No need to be so gracious."

"I wasn't."

"I know." He poured himself another drink. "What about the PM?"

"I wasn't there, Mick. I don't know."

He paused. "I can't understand it; who would want an old boy like Lincoln dead?" He stood. "Want some fresh toast?"

Eddie shook his head. "You go on."

"Ta. I'm going to run the story as a tragic suicide, how an old man couldn't bear to live without his wrongfully imprisoned son. And then, the next day, I'm running it as fucking murder."

"Run it as what you want, Mick. Just don't mention me or anything I've told you. Got it?"

"I won't, I promise, I'll mention what Mrs Walker told me, that's all. That way, it'll keep the murderer wondering if the police know something or not, or if it's just speculation in print."

"I'm trusting you here, Mick."

"And you're trusting me, my forensic friend, because I've never spilled your beans in print before. Have I?" Then Mick blushed, "Apart from that once and that wasn't anything to do with a job," he reinforced the point by waving a finger.

"And—"

"Okay, twice. But that wasn't anything to do with a job either."

"And don't mention Stephen's name; if the murderer sees it in print, he may panic if he cottons on he's spelled it wrong."

"Gotcha, big boy."

Mick left the room, and Eddie heard the bathroom light click on. He sighed, rubbed the stubble around his chin and downed the last of the brandy, coughing in that wheezing way as it stung his throat. Five glasses in twenty minutes and he still felt sober. "It's becoming more and more expensive to get pissed these days." And that simple sentence was the catalyst he needed to drop from a superficial – *artificial* – level of feeling okay with things, to falling three floors down the lift shaft and into a decrepit feeling of despair.

He tried to count his blessings, as his old mum used to say, and he was finding it difficult to come up with any he could actually label as blessings, more "not disasters".

He sniggered, felt light-headed. "At last," he said, and thought about Jilly. Maybe he should attend one of those crank nights at the Crystal Ball Club with her, where some schmuck feeds you a plate of hope, when all you can really taste in your mouth is bullshit.

The toaster popped. "You're out of margarine," Mick shouted.

"Scrape some grease off the top of the cooker."

"Barrel of fun, you are."

"You know where the door is."

Mick walked back in, spilled brandy down his chin and slammed the glass on the table. "What's your problem?" He stared at Eddie, dark eyes narrowed, cheeks throbbing. "Why can't you be civil just for one evening?"

"Because I don't have to be fucking civil. No one invited you here, you prick! You came here to squeeze me for info about the dead pensioner. Oh, and you came here to eat my fucking toast." They stared at each other. Eventually Eddie dropped his gaze, watched the pattern in the carpet float this way and that. "I'm sorry." He looked up again. "I nearly punched a guy who'd been burgled today. He said something that I would normally have brushed aside, but I had the bastard by the throat up against his own kitchen wall."

"I bet *he* had margarine."

"I feel like punching everyone I meet. Stuck-up Stuart nearly bought a dental appointment twice today. I can't hack it anymore, Mick."

"Hey, come on."

"I just want to sit in the corner and drink brandy until I piss brandy, you know what I mean?"

"Yes," Mick said earnestly. "I think I do." He topped up both their glasses and sat opposite Eddie in his accustomed fashion, one leg draped over the arm of the chair. "I admire you. I think you've coped well since Sam's death. And today, wow," he shook his head, "I don't know how you go into places like that and fuck about with corpses that carry their own livestock."

"It's not just the job. I actually hate being alive. If I was a braver man, I would be sitting in this chair looking a lot like Lincoln Farrier right now." He blinked and a tear fell. "I miss my kid, Mick."

"I know you do. You were a good dad, Eddie; anybody can see that." He lit two cigarettes, threw one at Eddie, and stared at the ceiling. "I never had kids," he said. "Couldn't see the attraction."

"Couldn't find anyone dumb enough, you mean."

Mick laughed. "No pulling the wool over your eyes is there?" And then his face straightened. "Never had the opportunity, if the truth be known."

"Oh? Why?"

He tipped the glass at Eddie. "Who wants to marry a pisshead?"

Eddie looked away.

– Two –

Jilly sat in the darkness. She could smell him on the teddy. She held that damned thing in her arms so tight that she had pins and needles. It smelled just like him, and it took her mind back to the happy times, the really good times where they shared a wonderful family life. All three of them. She buried her nose in the soft fur and breathed in, and there he was, large as life, good old Sam. He would never admit to any of his friends that he had a teddy – a boy of twelve did not have such things – but he loved it all the same, and his secret was safe with her.

The Yorkshire Echo. 22nd June

'Justice' to blame for death of a lonely old man

By Michael Lyndon

THIS reporter found the remains of a sad old man who had taken his own life. Lincoln Farrier (78) killed himself after suffering the absence of his son for an intolerable length of time.

The tragic story began with Lincoln's son being imprisoned for attacking a burglar. Despite repeated pleas from Lincoln and his son's family, the parole board insisted he was still "a danger to burglars".

I believe everyone has a right to defend their own hard-earned property, and it is unethical for a so-called "justice system" to keep a man locked up for doing just that. Furthermore, doesn't the parole board consider burglars to be in the wrong place at any time? This phrase of theirs gives burglars the right to a life of crime and gives those defending themselves and their property no rights at all.

I had intended asking Mr Farrier his views on The Rules. Those now will never be known, but his honest lifestyle and the neat and orderly way in which he kept his life, indicates his wholehearted support for decency, and for The Rules.

Would it be wrong to assume that if they had existed prior to his son's house being burgled, the burglar – who has been free for some time (presumably to burgle again) would have been on a Rule One already, and that alone may have deterred him from committing crime again? That in turn would have left this wonderful old man and his son united, and, of course, wouldn't have seen such a tragic end to a proud man's life.

I hope those bureaucrats responsible for this horrendous slant on British justice, rethink their policy on those defending their right to enjoy their own possessions and property, and comes down hard on those who would steal it.

The Ministry of Justice refused to comment this morning, claiming individual cases are for the relevant authorities to deal with.

Surely, that relevant authority is they. Is this another case of the blind leading the blind, or of simply shifting the responsibility? We have The Rules, why don't we use them?

Chapter Thirty

Tuesday 23rd June

A little bell tinkled over the door when she opened it. She stepped in, intimidated, a little afraid of being here, and more than a little afraid of being in the city, especially without Christian by her side. It was something she could never recall doing before. He was protective, always had an arm around her, always on the lookout for trouble and guiding her away from it.

She suffered panic attacks wherever there was a crowd, and that, she supposed, was the drugs' fault. But today, necessity overcame panic and she had trailed bravely through Leeds for two and a half hours by herself, feeling the sweat trickle down her back, watching them, the crowd of people who stared at her like she was some fucking freak in a sideshow, making sure they kept their distance. She should never go out alone, he said. *The world is a bad place,* he said. And she believed him; why wouldn't she?

The door closed and the calming silence welcomed her. The shop was stuffy; it was crowded with *objets d'art*, or whatever they called this crap. Her eyes floated around and her feet slowly edged their way over the shiny wooden floorboards. There were globes of all descriptions: etched, gold, silver, porcelain, standing on intricately carved legs, some even doubling as drinks cabinets.

There was a shelf of cameos, another of miniature paintings in tiny gold frames, there were countless clocks – none ticking – stuffed animals, and books everywhere. There was furniture scattered around the place, at one time arranged deliberately, she supposed, but now, shuffled backwards, forwards or just out of the way so the owner could cram more crap onto the overburdened floor. Lights, they were everywhere, dangling from black cast iron hooks in the ceiling.

But what took her eye more than any of this collection of dust-gatherers, were the pictures. They were everywhere, popping up between each piece, standing on the floor, leaning against the walls and against chairs, against tables trimmed with lace. And across the walls, too; wherever there could have been a spare patch of wall, there was a painting. No prints, just original paintings.

Alice stepped around a rocking chair, slid sideways towards the near wall and let her eyes roam.

Oh boy, was she in the wrong shop – again. This was her sixth, and she couldn't grasp how difficult it was to place modern art – no, not modern art, but recent art, you know, where the artist is still actually alive. So far, most of the shops had suggested car boot sales and hockshops, they didn't even want to see the sample she had brought. Wrapped in this bin bag was fine art, dammit, "but this is an antique shop", they all said. Wankers. What did they know?

"Ahem."

Alice gasped. She turned, almost knocking a carriage clock onto the floor, catching it with her spare hand just in time. The little balls smacked noisily against their glass dome. Eyes still closed, she steadied the clock, and then, with an apologetic smile on her face, looked up into the eyes of a weirdo. Across the shop floor, standing beneath an arch she had failed to see before, was a strange little man wearing a bright yellow waistcoat and tiny round spectacles that hung on the end of his nose. He had no neck: his head fitted directly onto his round shoulders. Alice stifled a laugh. "You made me jump."

He stared, made her feel uncomfortable; the way he eyed her almost slyly as though weighing her up and categorising her, reading her date stamp and hallmark in the blink of a well-experienced eye.

"May I help you, madam?" His hands were laced daintily in front of him, and he wore only the merest hint of a welcoming smile.

"Sorry," she said, "I er…" She sidled her way back into the main aisle, a section of bare floorboard about eighteen inches wide that had nothing on offer except a scratched shine. "I was wondering how interested you might be in purchasing something."

Alice, don't you do this, girl. Get outta here now. You'll ruin it all.

His little eyebrows rose slightly and the portly fellow stepped out from beneath the archway and into the comparative brightness of the main shop. "May I ask what you have there?" He held his chubby hands together tightly, rubbing them.

"Yes, yes," she said, "this is what I have for sale." Alice yanked off the plastic bag. "It's a—"

"Ssshh," he said. "I like to try and guess."

Alice wondered whether to tell him he would not guess the piece or the artist unless he had a degree in psychic ability. But she thought that pissing on his bonfire might not be the best way to go.

The man took the picture, stepped back and held it an angle to catch the light from a chandelier. His face creased, and then he smiled, looked at her and said, "I have to admit, my dear, I'm not totally familiar with the work," and then he looked back at the painting, "though it has certain connotations of, er, of," he clicked his fingers, "Ralph Shephard."

"Really?"

"You don't agree?"

She shrugged.

He looked back at the painting. "Oh yes," he said, forming a greater interest now, studying it with an ever more inspective eye. "Very similar anyway," he mused. "Maybe James Preston."

"It does?"

"Fine Realism artists."

Realism. That's what Christian had called them. Beyond Realism.

Oh yes, he did, girl. And you know, he also said he loved you and he said he cared for you, and what you gonna do for him in return, huh? You gonna stab him right between the shoulder blades.

I am not!

How much thought you given to handing the cash over to him? How many times have you told him in your imagination that you found a buyer and by Christmas you'll be in an apartment where he can paint in comfort? None. You outta your mind, girl. You a traitor.

"It does indeed." He looked up, Alice blinked and stepped back. "It has a clever play with light."

"You sound very knowledgeable."

"What can I say; I like paintings, my dear. But this is no painter I ever saw before." He looked at her, knowingly yet ignorant, hoping for a clue. "It's modern, isn't it?"

"You could say that."

"Well," he said, "I can't deny it, young lady, you have me at a disadvantage." He appraised *her* again now instead of the picture, and she could see the figure he had in mind dip by around ten per cent. She wasn't his usual kind of customer; a little more rough and ready, and clearly a little more desperate. He smiled, almost friendly. "Who painted this?"

Alice played it cool, which for someone who was as desperate as she, was a risk. "You like it?"

"Take a look around my emporium, dear." He waved an arm across his fine treasures like a magician about to say *voilà!* "I like paintings, all different kinds," and then his smile faded, "except abstract expressionism – I hate that shit." He looked to see if she was offended by the word – she hadn't even noticed it. "I have lots of paintings, and I can tell that you have no experience of trying to sell them. Let me be honest, what I'm trying to say is that I don't need the picture as much as you need to offload it. Am I making myself clear?"

"Erm, no, not really."

"Where did you get this?"

"My boyfriend."

"Ah, now we're getting somewhere." He stepped closer. "And er, where did *he* get it from?" He winked at her.

Alice narrowed the gap even further, aware now that he thought it was stolen and okay, yeah she was walking around inside a skin that shouted JUNKIE. And so he thought she'd be glad to settle for next to nothing; just enough for the next fix, just enough for the boyfriend to "find" more of these pictures and build some kind of underworld relationship, a mutualistic parasite-host bond. "Do you like it?"

"Of course I like it. And if *I* like it, I know others who will like it. I won't ask if you have come by this art legally or not," he held up a hand, looked away and closed his eyes, "that is none of my business. But what I will ask is that—"

"That's enough."

He looked at her through the corner of his eye.

"I can see you think this is stolen so forget the whole thing!" Alice snatched at the bin bag, pulling it over the painting.

"Now wait a minute, dear; let's not be so hasty."

She stopped trying to get the torn bag around the rough edges of the canvas and looked him straight in the eye, jaw pronounced, eyes half closed. "The picture is *not* stolen. My boyfriend *painted* it."

The man stopped as though slapped by an invisible hand. "He did?"

Alice nodded.

"What's your name, my dear?"

"Why? Do I need to fill in a form or something?"

The man laughed. "No, no. I just wondered. My name is Max; and I own this fine emporium." He smiled the smile of an old friend.

"Alice."

"It's funny," he said, "I always imagine girls called Alice to wear a bright blue hairband and an old-fashioned blue dress with white stockings." His eyes slipped to her bare arms and the track marks in the crook of her elbow. A far cry from Carroll's novel. "Is it yours to sell, Alice, is all I want to know?"

"Yes it is. And what if it wasn't?"

"If it's yours to sell, then we don't need to consider that question, do we? Now, let me see it again."

Chapter Thirty-One

Tuesday 23rd June

– One –

Rochester's nostrils twitched and flared, and he looked up from the scattering of papers on his desk. "Michael, that smell…"

"Ah yes, sir; that would be my tie, I'm afraid."

"Why can't you take up chess for a hobby instead of drinking and seeing how far you can throw up?"

"I threw up on it after seeing a dead body!" He stood there feeling the air turn slightly noxious – nothing to do with the tie – and feeling ever so slightly embarrassed that he stepped on Rochester with such ferocity. "It's nothing to do with the drink. I saw a body yesterday, the old man? And well, I smelt him too, and it kind of… well, you know, it upset my delicate constitution."

"Can't you afford a new tie?"

Mick stepped forward, placed a slim wad of printed paper on Rochester's desk. "That sir, depends on you."

Rochester took his time in looking at the story and then paused. "Would you please throw that tie away; it stinks to high hell and I can't concentrate. God knows how you've managed to work with it dangling right under your nose."

"Oh, yes sir, no problem." Mick slipped the tie off, crept around the desk and dropped it cleanly into Rochester's big stainless steel bin.

"I was thinking of a bin in another room."

* * *

"How long have I known you, Mick?"

He shrugged. "Ten years?"

"And would you say I have a reasonably keen eye for a good story?"

"Without question, sir, yes."

Rochester leaned back in his chair, laced his fingers behind his thinning mop of grey hair. "Ergo, I have a flair for picking out the odd dud story. And let's be honest, Mick, since your career rests on it, more than a few of those duds belong to you."

Mick's shoulders slumped. He imagined himself walking from this big old building, the door grating closed after him for the last time, the slot reserved in his wallet for his press card, now empty.

"Is this a dud, Mick?"

"No."

"Do the police think this old man was murdered?"

"Yes."

"By whom?"

"I don't think they know, sir."

Rochester's eyes narrowed into their customary slits – the lie detector slits. "Do you?"

"Well… no, not really."

"You sound as though you do, but for some reason are reluctant to share it with me."

This was the moment of truth, as they said. This was the time when he would either hand the press card over and sign the security book for the last time, or crack open a fresh crate of the good stuff. He whispered, "Do I buy myself a new tie, sir? Or not?"

At last Rochester smiled. "It's well written. Does it have anything to do with The Rules, this old man's killing?"

"I have an idea that it might, sir."

"Is this actually leading somewhere?"

"Somewhere very big, I think. Exclusively too."

Rochester tapped the wad of paper. "I always preferred silk ties, myself. Paisley."

– Two –

She watched him dress and then she watched him leave. The corrugated door squeaked across the kitchen floor. Christian couldn't abide being cooped up in here all day with just a whinging woman to annoy him; it turned his thoughts rancid and nothing good came of rancid thoughts, nothing good ever appeared on canvas when he was cooped up.

Alice threw back the duvet, wincing at the throb in the crook of her left arm. It had bruised; the whole inside of her arm. Max had paid her handsomely for the painting yesterday. Fifty quid. She patted her jeans pocket and pulled out the change. Just over ten left. "Shit."

She stood and stretched, then reached under the table in the corner, her long hair tickling her thighs as she bent and retrieved the small black box from underneath a scrunch of newspaper. Just to get her into the swing of the day, she injected roughly a quarter of Christian's painting back through the bruise in her left arm. The world swam and Alice rolled over backwards, feeling the warmth flow through her, feeling her own kind of inspiration come to the surface like a fisherman's float. She lay there naked on the dirty floorboards, arms outstretched, gazing in wonder at the black ribcage of the ceiling.

In the cot above the stash, Spencer began to fidget, and before she could finish dressing he had woken completely and was crying for his breakfast, so busy with his own needs that he cared not a jot for those of his poor mother. "Spencer," she said softly, "come on, Mummy's here." Spencer ignored her and cried louder than ever. "Shut up!" Alice put her T-shirt and denim jacket on and lit a roach. Before she had even pulled on her jeans and boots, Spencer had hit the high notes. "Shut up! Fucking kid!"

The cellar was as dark as ever but she got to work quickly, blocking from her hazy mind any thought of right or wrong, and any thought of Christian. Even Spencer's pained screams couldn't pierce the barrier she had constructed inside her mind. *Better get it done and quick, better just get the gear and get the fuck out of here.*

Bravely, she opened the door to the annex and swept a hand through the new web that stretched across the doorway. She bent and grabbed two this time, feeling the texture of paint through the thin bag. She pushed the door closed and left the cellar, throwing the candle aside as soon as she reached the kitchen.

She slammed the corrugated door behind her and stood on the step, taking deep relaxing breaths. Spencer had reached orbit, but even when she tried to hear him, there was nothing more than the faintest sound. Almost undetectable. Tolerable now.

– Three –

Christian chose a window table and set to work on his Big Mac with gusto. He watched the huge crowd grow larger as it thundered along Boar Lane, turning left up Briggate in a convoluted path towards the Town Hall. There was another demo, probably of a similar size and probably making a similar racket, already congregating outside the Crown Court building, having arrived via Park Lane. Several hundred police officers and several blocks of Leeds city centre kept both groups apart.

As with all the demos, the police filmed them; and trotting alongside the fringes of the crowd were news cameras. Outside broadcast crews took in the sun and recorded the growing madness about to erupt on the streets between the Crown Court and the Town Hall; something of a focal point for marches concerning justice.

Christian slurped black coffee and watched the large vidiscreen on the Corn Exchange's wall flicker the Crimestoppers hotline number. Then, in ten-second intervals, faces appeared, names beneath them in large red letters and then the words that made the crowd shout louder, that made the bullhorns belch into a frenzy of electronic noise, the words "wanted. Rule Three violation. Reward for conviction".

Christian studied the faces; half hoping he knew one of them. They were offering £10,000 for information that led to a prosecution and conviction. These days, it meant £10,000 for information leading to a sudden death. The number in the corner of the screen said 3/256. The state wanted to kill 256 people. That was a lot of lives, but he wondered how many people had *they* killed or made suffer?

Alongside the protestors marched mounted police, and plenty more on foot, all armed. The protestors' banners indicated they didn't wholeheartedly agree with the state. "Killing is still killing," said one. "Two wrongs don't make a right," said another. And then there were the personal attacks on the guy who masterminded the whole policy. Death Deacon, they called him. It seemed that a great number of ordinary people despised the new act, despite it being introduced to protect them and discourage the current wave of murder that hopped, skipped and jumped around the nation in sporadic bursts of semi-automatic gunfire.

Christian craned his neck, and could make out the last of the protestors as they marched in less flamboyant mood up Boar Lane, and that's when he slurped the dregs of his coffee, mopped his goatee and walked briskly from the shop, turning left, and heading up Briggate to where all the fancy shops were.

– Four –

"Sirius?"

Deacon's door opened and Sirius stepped inside. "Sir?"

"Get hold of Henry. We have to get this car business sorted out once and for all."

"Sir." Sirius held out a hand, stared at Deacon.

It was so unusual for him to interrupt, that Deacon stopped immediately and looked at his man. "What's wrong?"

"May I speak candidly, sir?"

Deacon nodded.

"Is it necessary for Henry to accompany me? I can—"

"Yes it is. For one thing, it'll keep him out of harm's way, and I want him to witness how ruthlessly efficient you can be." He raised his eyebrows. "Do I make myself clear?"

Sirius nodded.

"I also want him to see that I have kept to my part of the bargain." He looked away, lower teeth bared as though expressing regret. "I should have killed him at birth," and then he noticed Sirius's smile and shook his head. "No. Let's keep to our word. I'll give him his final chance."

Chapter Thirty-Two

Tuesday 23rd June

– One –

The bus hadn't even stopped before Alice bounded onto the pavement, buzzing with life. From the bus, she'd seen a huge crowd, maybe two or three thousand, outside the Crown Court, spilling onto the roads and the steps around the Town Hall. A warm breeze rippled banners that proclaimed how wonderful it was to finally kill the dross of society: "Deacon for PM" and "Don't Shoot 'em, Hang 'em!" and "An Eye for an Eye, God is on Our Side" and "Bravo The Rules". Bullhorns screamed.

Mounted police, sidearms tucked neatly into sexy thigh holsters, kept the demonstrators in line, enough for her to walk straight past them without feeling the slightest bit nervous. The crowd was a blur as she carried two precious paintings wrapped in dirty black plastic bags that trailed twisted cobwebs; nothing could detract from her goal.

She hurried up The Headrow and past the entrance to Park Lane, watching the faces on the vidiscreens, along with the legend beneath them: "Wanted. Rule Three violation. Reward for Conviction". *Wonder how much they're offering.*

She passed another three vidiscreens before she reached the summit of The Headrow and then took a quick detour into a tobacconist's.

Once back outside the shop, letting its canopy shade her from the sun, she lit the cigarette, paintings held between her knees as she shielded the flame. To her right was more noise, the sound of bullhorns that bounced from building to building, ricocheting its way up to The Headrow.

She walked away, blending into the bustling crowd. Over the natural low roar of a crowd of shoppers and commuters, there was another sound that grew as though someone were steadily turning up the volume; the sound of a gathering that chanted in unison. It had an electric quality; a false, crackly quality.

Alice stood and stared in awe at the rabble and the police escorting them, at the TV cameras surrounding them, running alongside as though their viewers had never seen a demonstration before, and at the banners. "Killing is still killing," said one. "Two wrongs don't make a right," said another. And then "Death Deacon," said yet another.

"What the hell is happening to the fucking world? What's all these demos for anyway?"

Alice tightened her grip on her treasure and headed down Eastgate, looking out for the discreet sign held out from the wall by a golden hand. "Bookman Antiques" it said. Her own private money fountain.

The bell tinkled, and although she didn't think she would feel nervous, a little trepidation trickled down her throat and made her gag

no, hon, that ain't no trepidation, that's guilt.

but she shook it off, swallowed it and bid it good riddance, and waited for Max to show his little rotund self. It was quiet, the sounds of the demos, soon to be on top of each other, surely, soon to erupt into another riot, faded into a backdrop that was so slight, it was easily forgotten,

like you easily forgot little Spencer

and easily hidden beneath the ticking of Max's grandfather clock to her right.

"And what have you brought today, my dear?"

The cigarette fell and bounced on Max's shiny floor.

"If you could spit it *outside*," he said, picking it up by the filter as though picking a rat up by its tail, "that would be better for the fire regulations."

"You made me jump, I—"

"Did I?" He bolted the door. "Come, show me what we have today."

She followed him through the bead curtain and into the back room. "Did you manage to sell the first one I brought you?"

"These things take time. I'm sure I'll have a buyer for it sooner or later." And then he stopped by a table, brought a lamp across and plugged it in nearby. "I don't think I can command as much for it as I had hoped." He took out his round-rimmed glasses, and peered up at Alice over their tops. "I did try, my dear, but the market these days is saturated."

"Stop talking bollocks. I'm not asking for thousands, and I know you're making a handsome profit. So don't come the poor old man routine, and definitely don't come the 'I'm doing you a favour' routine."

Max simply rolled up his sleeves. "Come on, I haven't got all day."

She pulled away the plastic bag from the first painting and propped the second against the wall.

He brought the light over and studied it, giving little away, but he couldn't hide the delight in his eyes. "I have to admit, Alice, this boyfriend of yours paints exquisitely."

"Yes, he does."

"So my dear, what is this one called?"

She shrugged. "Fuck knows."

Max was aghast. "You literally are in this just for the money, aren't you? You care nothing at all for the image, the painting, or the artist."

See, even a complete stranger wonders how you came to be such a hard bitch that could sell her man's blood and tears for a pittance, just enough to fill her arm a coupla times. You a waste of space, girl.

"How much are you going to pay me, Max?"

"Don't you have any idea what its title is? I really would like to know."

"Well, let's see." She snatched the painting from his hands, and he yelped, hovering over it. "What's it of?" She held it at an angle towards the lamp's soft light.

It was summer. A glowing sunset soaked a meadow in deep orange and burgundy. The shadows it cast fell long across the castle walls that glinted as brightly as a diamond, and there were smaller diamonds dancing on the surrounding water. The grass by the golden river seemed to sway to and fro, and...

"Sunset Meadow," she said at last. She ignored the smiling face that appeared like a hologram inside the painting. It was Christian's face.

"What?"

"Meadow, see? And the sun's setting. What's wrong with that?"

"Nothing," he concentrated on the painting. "It's fine."

"I want a hundred for this one."

"Nonsense." Max stared sharply at her. "What do you think this is, madam, a pawn shop? I do not bow down to pressure from people like you. *I* appreciate the work that's gone into paintings like these; *I* appreciate the talent and the skills—"

"Then you'll be willing to pay for it."

Max was lost for words, but his old dealer's tongue soon found first gear. "And indeed I will. Fifty pounds. It's a fair price, I assure you."

"Listen, I may be a junkie, I may understand as much about art as you understand what it's like to give birth, but I understand this much: you've already sold the last one I brought." Max's mouth fell open. "Haven't you?"

Under the rims of his golden eyeglasses, his wide eyes showed a flicker of fear. "I told you," he stuttered, "I'm struggling—"

"I can spot a lie at forty paces. How much did you make off the last one?"

"That, my dear, is privileged—"

"How much, dammit?"

Max pouted, his cheeks flushed. He was definitely not used to customers like Alice.

"Very well, my dear," he said quietly. "I will pay you one hundred for it, but I must stress that you have dented our business relationship."

She smiled. "Do you want the other one or not?"

Max mulled it over, taking his time. "I think," he whispered, "I could help you out, yes. How many more do you have?"

She shrugged. "Don't know; maybe ten, maybe twenty. Never counted them."

"And when could I expect you to visit me again?"

Chapter Thirty-Three

Tuesday 23rd June

– One –

Eddie was showered, shaved and ready for Ros this morning. He could manage the ten o'clock starts, no problemo – as Mick would say.

And she smiled at him this morning when she came to pick him up. "Wow, I needn't have brought the Domestos this morning."

"You saying I live like a slob?"

"That about sums it up." She studied his face. "You've even shaved. Your public *will* be flattered."

"Any more complainants like yesterday and my public will be flattened."

"Fingers crossed," she chuckled. "Mick come around last night?"

"Why? You my part-time mummy now?"

"I just think he's a bad—"

"I'm a big boy now, Mummy. I can shave myself without getting blood over the bathroom and I even managed to put my shoes on the right feet this morning."

"No need to take the pee." She turned, ready to leave.

"I'm sorry," he said. "I've made up my mind to try and sort this lump of shit they call life out at last."

"Really? You're going to quit the booze?"

"I'm going to cut down."

"So you know it's becoming a problem then?"

"It's only a problem when I can't get up for work because my head's stuck to the pillow."

"You are gross."

He laughed, and her wrinkled-up face made him laugh more. She was cute, was Ros; a slim, small woman but with a matron's ferocity. And she had quite a disarming smile. Put that together with her deep brown eyes, and there was an attractive combination there.

* * *

She stopped the giggle and the screwed-up face and she stared right back, wondering what he was looking at. He had never looked at her before – oh sure, he'd *looked* at her, but he'd never looked *at* her, not in that way. She blinked, and they both cleared their throats and tried to speak in unison.

"Should we—" they laughed again.

* * *

They ignored Stuart when he greeted them with, "Aw, it's the two love birds. How nice to see you both."

Eddie ruffled Stuart's hair and groaned as his hand came away sticky with gel.

"Oi! Pack it in, Collins."

"Ooh, touchy," Eddie grinned.

"Not as touchy as you'll be in half an hour."

"Why?"

"Better fix yourself a drink," Stuart rearranged his hair, scowling at Eddie, "Jeffery wants to see you both. He'll be back in a minute."

Just the smug look on Stuart's face, the way his perfect mouth hinted at the trouble that was to come, made Eddie's stomach turn. "What's happened?"

"Dunno," he said. "But make sure when you do fix yourself a drink, it's just coffee. With no additives."

"What the hell are you talking about?" asked Ros.

"Your boyfriend not told you?"

"He's not my boyfriend—"

"Don't rise to him Ros; he's a tosser."

"I went in your drawer yesterday for some DNA forms…"

Eddie's eyes widened.

"…and I came across—"

"You snivelling little bastard. You're a worm, do you know that?"

"What, what did he come across, Eddie?"

"He came across a bottle of brandy." They all turned, and Jeffery stood in the foyer, finger beckoning Eddie towards him. He glared at the three of them, and then disappeared into his office. "Now, please, Eddie."

"I ought to—"

"Careful, Eddie," Stuart said. "I think you're in enough trouble already."

"I find it strange," Eddie whispered, "that you can find a bottle in someone's private drawer—"

"It's police property!"

"I have a key to it."

"Then you should have used it."

"I shouldn't need to. Strange how you can find a bottle, but you can't examine crime scenes properly." Stuart's face changed like the enthusiasm bubble had burst and left incomprehension dispersing in the air. "You're crap at your fucking job, and the only way you can make yourself look good—"

"Is by comparing myself to you."

"The CRFP don't give a shit about your silly comparisons. All they care about is whether you can perform as a forensic practitioner." He began walking up the office, "And I'd say you can't."

– Two –

"Explain this." Jeffery pointed to the bottle on his desk.

"It's unopened. I have never attended work while under the influence."

"You can take that high and mighty stance with him out there, but don't try it in my office, or you'll be out of here before you can call your union rep. Clear?"

Eddie nodded, and his eyes sank to the floor.

"I'm aware it's unopened, but I'm also aware that alcohol is banned on police premises. *You're* aware too, I shouldn't wonder. Which brings me to ask, even though it's unopened at the moment, when were you planning to open it?"

Eddie thought for a moment and all he could think of was beating the shit out of Stuart. He had no excuse and no reason to offer Jeffery. "I don't know."

"You'll face disciplinary for this. I can't allow it to happen, and since it was discovered by a certain member of staff, I *have* to act on it, I can't just ignore it."

Eddie shook his head. "I understand. Do what you have to do."

"Oh thank you. How gracious." Fists on hips, Jeffery leaned forward. "This office has an excellent reputation, and you've singlehandedly bollocksed it up!"

"I'm sorry, it won't happen again."

"Damned right it won't."

"No, really. It won't."

"Good. But that's only half of the bad news coming your way this morning."

"Now what have I done? Flicked a bogey at an old woman? Farted in the cake shop?"

Jeffery's eyes darkened. "You're on a warning." He paused and then almost whispered, "I know about the shit you've had lately, and I'm prepared to bend a little because of it. But you'd better fix this problem," he nodded at the bottle. "And you'd better consider getting on Stuart's good side because, like it or not, he can make life tough for you. This animosity ends today; I will not have my section pulverised by petty battles. Is that clear?"

"I hope you're going to tell him that too."

"Already done."

"You failed. He's still an obnoxious prick."

"Speaking of obnoxious, I had a call from the head; we've have a complaint about you."

"About me?"

"Hard to believe, isn't it?"

Eddie sighed.

"Remember McHue? He's the man you had by the throat yesterday."

"Ah. I can explain—"

"Save it. You'll have your chance soon enough. Is it true?"

"He was a bad-tempered bastard who said—"

"I do not care. While ever you wear that uniform, you represent West Yorkshire Police, and West Yorkshire Police do not beat up victims of crime!"

No matter which way you sliced it, when you put it like that, he had a good point.

"God, it's good to be back."

Jeffery stared.

"So what's next, then?"

"Next is a meeting with the head. You'll have the opportunity to make a formal statement and then, if McHue wants your arse, it's further disciplinary action which could result in suspension."

"Great."

"And if he wants it, he can have you for a Section 47 assault. And I'll let you guess what that means."

"It means a Rule One, doesn't it?"

"Correct. And it could mean your job, Eddie."

Chapter Thirty-Four

Tuesday 23rd June

Eddie crouched, his back against the cold brick of the office. The cigarette in his hand did nothing to alleviate the stress.

Things had begun to slot back into that well-worn pigeonhole inside his head marked NORMAL. But now NORMAL was growing moss while the one next to it, DESOLATION, shone with the regularity of letters and minutes that flowed in and out. It seemed that the better your life was, the harder the blow when it all went wrong.

He flicked the cigarette away and tucked his head into the crook of his crossed arms.

"You're a sorry little wanker, Collins, do you know that?" Stuart stood above him.

Eddie didn't satisfy him with a reply.

"I don't know why they keep you on. There are plenty of better people out there who'd die for the chance of doing your job."

"Unfortunately, you're not one of them."

Stuart flinched.

"Please, just go away." Eddie took out another cigarette.

"And miss the chance of seeing you fall from your perch?"

Eddie dragged on the cigarette and smiled. "I get it. You're jealous of me. That's why you're so desperate to see me gone, isn't it? You can't stand the competition. And since the CRFP highlighted how bad you were at your job—"

"Why would I be jealous of a chain-smoking alcoholic?" Eddie's smile left on the wind. "Who loses—"

"Be careful how you tread. I'm not in the mood for—"

"The truth? You're a loser. That's why your missus threw you out."

Eddie stood, flicked the cigarette away.

Stuart pulled back a step. "They had you down as a hero after what you did in January. But it didn't last long, did it? Then the true you came tumbling out, the pisshead, the louse." He took a few more paces backward.

Eddie walked forward, eyes dark, fists curled tight at his sides.

"I bet she threw you out because the booze made you impotent."

Eddie growled, advanced.

Stuart retreated, mouth pulling Eddie's strings like a skilled orator wooing his audience. "And then, when your sprog died—"

Eddie leapt towards Stuart.

"Stop!"

Both men looked around.

Ros stood watching them. "Can't you see what he's doing, Eddie? Are you so dumb?" He stared at her, eyes just slits, nostrils flared, and fists ready for action. "You're right in front of Jeffery's window."

Jeffery was standing behind the reflection on the glass, hands resting on the sill, looking out into the back yard. There was disappointment in his eyes before the clouds floated by and blocked out the view. Eddie felt ashamed.

And when Jeffery disappeared from the window, Stuart stepped forward and slapped Eddie's face. "That's for the CRFP jibes."

Eddie stood there, too stunned to move as Stuart walked. "Did you see that?"

Ros came closer and turned to watch with Eddie as Stuart rounded the corner, flicking the bird as he did so. "He'll try anything to get you out."

"I hadn't noticed. He slapped me. The bastard actually slapped me."

"He was the kid at school who started all the fights and then ran to teacher with a bloody lip and got you detention."

Eddie's cheek throbbed.

"I bet he's been like that since he was born."

"He wasn't born. He was hatched."

Ros chuckled.

"He's going to a lot of trouble for nothing."

"What do you mean?"

"Remember McHue, the fellow I had by the throat? He's complained, seems he wasn't too happy with me yesterday."

"You're joking?"

Eddie looked at her blankly.

"I'll vouch for you, it was a clear case of provocation, and I don't mind standing up in front of whoever and telling them that."

"If I were you, Ros, I'd distance myself from Eddie Collins as much as I could. There's no point ruining your career for the likes of me."

"You'll have me crying in a minute."

He looked across at her. "I'm serious. What's the point in us both going down?"

"The point is that it's wrong. And I'll tell you something else, Eddie Collins; being the Olympic champion at feeling sorry for yourself won't get you through."

"Gee, thanks for that."

"Well, come on, Eddie; it's true. Start to straighten up a bit—"

"And how the fuck would *you* feel if people kept kicking your legs out from under you each time you started to straighten up? Every time I give it a shot I get slapped by arseholes like Stuart, or I get verbally abused by the McHues in this world, or I get Jilly—"

"So show 'em! Show them you won't let them walk all over you!"

Eddie sighed. His frustration dribbled away and he turned his back on her. "Just… Ros, I don't mean this how it'll sound. But you'd be better off leaving me alone."

She was silent for a long time. The first tentative raindrops fell between them and then the skies darkened further. Still she said nothing; both stood around the side of the CSI building getting slowly wetter. "Eddie," she finally whispered, "you're a good bloke and I hate to see you like this. Is there nothing I can say—"

"No. Thank you."

"You know I'll help if I can."

"I just want my life back." His voice trembled slightly. "And the more I try, the further into the shit I sink." His head bowed and behind him, Ros sighed. "Everything I touch turns bad. So do me a favour; stay away from me?"

Ros walked past him.

Eddie sighed inwardly. He turned but Ros had already disappeared.

He sighed again, aloud this time. Eddie Collins felt the tears sting his eyes.

He whispered, "I'm gonna kill you, Stuart."

Eddie went inside, grabbed his jacket and shouted to Jeffery, "I'm taking the afternoon off. That okay with you?" He didn't wait for an answer, just slammed the door behind him. He headed for the bus stop.

* * *

Ros came back into the main office as Jeffery poked his head out of his doorway. What was happening out there? First the hotheads nearly bust each other's face, and then Ros comes back in wiping away the tears. "God, why couldn't I have had an easier section, why here? What did I ever do to offend you, eh?"

He crept outside, dismayed to see it had begun raining, and peered around the corner. Eddie Collins was still out there, back to him, standing in the rain. He was about to say something, maybe offer some kind of consolation when he heard Eddie mutter words that sent a shiver down Jeffery's back. "I'm gonna kill you, Stuart."

Chapter Thirty-Five

Tuesday 23rd June

– One –

"Art for Art's Sake." What a wonderful name for a shop.

It was ten o'clock and the day was a warm and hazy envelope of luxury that held you safe from all the nasty things in life. Christian shielded his eyes from the sun and noticed the grey cloud off to the west making its way over here into the city. It looked threatening, but for now, everything was as it should be. Calm.

He'd walked past the shop twice and took a good look inside each time. It was always busy, just how he liked it. Out here on the pavement was even busier. The noise from the demo was deafening. "What do we want!" they cried through bullhorns. "Justice," came the natural reply. Over and over. Monotony on the breeze.

They advanced down Briggate like a dark army, like the grey clouds advanced on the city, relentless, eerie. The ground beneath Christian's feet seemed to quake like the bass you could *feel* in the nightclubs. They were massive in number, forming one huge barrier, banners flapping overhead in the breeze, individual shouts, and outriders on cycles weaving in and out of the mounted police, catching and holding the attention of the news cameras that panned the scene. It was impressive, or was it *de*pressive.

Christian peered again into the shop and noticed the fake CCTV camera in the corner near the drawing pads. He smiled at the "thieves beware – CCTV in operation" sticker on the glass door. "Yeah, right," he said, and entered. He didn't see the other sticker on the other of the two double doors, the one that said, "We always prosecute".

The stickers were new.

And so was the camera over the till area, and the one over the technical drawing paraphernalia. And these cameras worked. No one had replaced the batteries in the fakes because they had the real thing now.

The door swung closed behind him, and the incessant racket of the demonstration was reduced to something easily obliterated by a preoccupied mind. There they were, the oil paints. Christian's mouth began to water as he ambled up the aisle opposite them. *Red ochre. Burnt umber. And anything else you can get your hands on in a hurry,* he thought.

He pictured himself in the cellar, small dusty bulb casting its glow over the huge canvas. There it was, almost complete, stretched over a simple wooden frame and draped against a home-made easel. And soon it would be finished. Dejection would settle on his shoulders, and a dark mood would slowly crush him from the inside out. And he'd be back in reality with a junkie woman and her stupid imagination.

There they were, each in a rack, like a thousand spices lined up in a kitchen. Christian licked his lips and reached out for the white tubes. Burnt umber slipped into his jeans pocket. Red ochre next, two tubes, and a tube of white, followed by a sable brush which stuck out from his pocket like a flag.

The few people at the till were engrossed in conversation; others in the aisles looked at goods for sale. Christian slipped towards the door, fingering his goatee as he went.

"Excuse me, sir!"

He swung the door wide and leapt into a throng of people who cared little for the morals of errant artists and who cared perhaps equally little for the lost profits of an overpriced art shop. He mingled, caught hold of the flow and went with it. The shouts of the shopkeeper were as dead as dust, lost in the noise like a droplet of water in a rainstorm.

Christian made his way through the crowd, avoiding the thrusting arms and jostling that was part of its momentum, and emerged on The Headrow, straight into the path of an armed officer.

– Two –

Behind her, lost to the sounds of agitated shoppers and buses slowly ploughing their way up Eastgate, a small bell tinkled. Max locked the door and searched the bustle of people for the druggy-girl in the floaty top and tight faded jeans.

* * *

Her pocket bulged with cash like never before. Max had paid her £250 for the paintings. And they enraptured him; he was in her palm like the beads of sweat that nestled there now. He was hers, and he couldn't get enough. She knew he was selling them for a huge profit, probably made a couple of hundred on top of what he paid her, but she could live with that. Everyone was happy, as the saying so stupidly went.

Christian wouldn't be happy when he found out. But only for a short time, because she had found that elusive gateway into commercialism, into hygiene, into running water, and into light for all. She was the agent who had at last done what Christian could not. Surely for that alone, he ought to be pleased.

Cigarette dangling in her mouth, Alice headed back up Eastgate towards The Headrow. She had one thing to do before climbing aboard the bus back home, and that was to spend a tenner on a lottery ticket.

– Three –

Christian froze. His feet were stuck to the pavement; his wide eyes stared at the officer.

The vidiscreens pumped out the Crimestoppers number and flashed images of wanted felons, and for a moment he thought he saw his own image among them.

"Been doing a spot of shopping?" The officer smiled so widely that Christian knew he'd been caught. He sighed, and that was enough for the officer to slap on a pair of black plastic cuffs and speak some garbled rubbish into the discreet mic on his lapel. The officer looked in Christian's pockets and found the paint. "Planning a spot of redecorating, son?"

Christian whispered, "Something like that." He looked away as a girl walked past him and into a tobacconist's shop. She wore a floaty top and tight, faded jeans. Ten yards behind her, a rotund man in a waistcoat followed her.

Chapter Thirty-Six

Tuesday 23rd June

"But why are there two?"

Mick wiped his nose on his sleeve and then looked from the officer to the tray where his cigarettes, lighter, wallet, and two Dictaphones were. "They go through batteries just like that," he clicked his fingers. "And anyway, one of 'em is a little temperamental." He scratched his head and whispered, "But I'm not sure which one it is. And if I mess this interview up, that's it," he shrugged, "I'm out of a job."

Mick thought he would be asked to leave one behind. "Okay, go on through." The officer grimaced at the vomit on his tie. "Might want to smarten yourself up a bit first."

Mick waved without looking back, "I'm fine, thanks." Pompous bastard.

Another officer outside Deacon's door checked Mick's details against his list before knocking. As he opened the door and ushered him into the hallowed room, Mick pressed record on the Dictaphone that he'd slipped back inside his pocket. Wearing a broad smile on his homely face, he walked in tall, exuding loyalty to Deacon as though the man were an icon. "Sir George," he held out a hand and strode towards the great man, "so good to meet you again."

"Mick, please," they shook, "sit down, sit down."

Mick loved the way Deacon ignored the stain on his tie – always a sign of a good upbringing, was that. He sat, placing his notepad and pencil and his Dictaphone on the desk between them. A picture of the Queen hung resplendent over the fire; silver candelabras adorned the mantelpiece. Oak was everywhere and books too, hundreds of them, and the carpet... well, you could trip over and fall into it, it was so deep. "It's a while since we had our last chat, Sir George; I hope you don't mind this imposition at such short notice."

"Not at all, I know you're quite a fan of The Rules and so," he smiled warmly, "you're always welcome here; helps spread the word, you know."

He found it surprisingly easy to imagine Deacon in an angry or violent temper. He was quite weighty on the top half, had "ruthless" stamped right across his wrinkled forehead and razor-sharp eyes that searched for and exploited weakness. "You're aware that I and *The Echo* are great supporters of The Rules, but I wonder, sir, if I may begin by asking for your reaction to the public opinion on them."

He switched on the recorder, and Deacon held up his hand. "Mick, Mick. Slow down, would you." He stood, slipped off his jacket and strode around to the shiny wooden cabinet. "How about a drink first?"

Mick licked his lips. It was a thirst that tea or coffee couldn't combat, and anyway, it would help Deacon open up. "You've twisted my arm, Sir George. You know I could never refuse a good malt."

"Who says you're getting the good stuff?" Deacon bellowed with laughter, and Mick joined in, keeping the volume lower than his host's. "There you go. Sip it slowly, now," he laughed again. "Anyway, I know you like a drink, Mick." He winked. "I do my research, too."

Mick tipped the glass at Deacon, and sipped. "So, Sir George; what is your reaction to public opinion?"

"I presume you mean the positive opinion we have received?"

"There have been a number of calls from the Church and from campaigners overseas for The Rules to be abolished."

Deacon took a deep breath. "Well, the Church has many different voices and it expresses its doubts over the state taking a role in humanity that it deemed the sole responsibility of the Lord God. I fully understand that position, and while most of Great Britain's subjects are Christians, the overwhelming voice they speak with tells me we are doing the right thing. Even the Bishop of Chichester is a convert, I'm pleased to say." He raised a finger to stifle Mick's next question. "Consider this, how many innocent lives have we saved by killing the murderers and the rapists?"

He stared at Mick as though expecting an answer. "We have saved, it is estimated, sixteen. That's sixteen people living today who would be dead, and sixteen families not grieving, not torn apart. And that's in just a week! How many more people have been saved from assault, rape, burglary? That is a question I can't answer with any degree of certainty; but it must run into hundreds, and for that, I am grateful. And I suspect," he smiled, "so too is the Church."

"And the overseas campaigners?"

"Now you're talking about countries where the death penalty has been out of existence for many years, hundreds of years in some cases. Maybe they have their crime under control and don't need such a forthright approach to securing the peace enjoyed by their nation. Though I doubt it." He sipped again. "France, Belgium, Germany and the like are tied into European law and ECHR; since Great Britain left the union, we are bound only by our own laws. I suspect that if their peoples had the choice, they would follow our lead."

"But there are still a lot of dissenters, Sir George."

He dismissed the statement with a wave of a nonchalant hand. "Bound to be. It's a heck of a law; one that gives the state the right to kill a citizen." His hand curled into a fist. "Make sure your tape recorder is working, and listen carefully: if a person takes another's life unlawfully, or they are a persistent offender who ignores the counselling provided to them, why should innocent citizens put up with them on the streets, or pay through the nose to keep them in jail?"

"Carry on," Mick nodded to the recorder, "it's working fine."

"Do you know how much it costs to keep a villain in the comfort of a modern jail?"

Mick shrugged, knowing the answer, but guessing wrong to promote Deacon's sense of conversation. "Twenty thousand a year?"

"Try thirty thousand, per year per prisoner."

"Some would argue that incarceration is the best form of punishment."

"Naturally they would. But it's expensive, reform is unlikely and in most cases – particularly with sexual deviants – impossible. And do we really want these people back on our streets again at some time in the future? I don't think we do.

"And then there is the deterrent factor. Hotly disputed over many years, but research indicates that most offenders would not have committed serious crime had The Rules been in force prior to that crime being committed. The Rules work. And for those on Rules One and Two," he picked up his glass, "well, would you burgle or rape again if you knew death was but a fingerprint away?" His eyes narrowed. "And anyway, what's wrong with good old-fashioned punishment?"

"So what do you say to the woman who kills her husband after years of abuse? You going to kill her too?"

Deacon sat back in his squeaking leather seat. "We have been through all this before, and you know it. But I'll refresh your memory. I have great sympathy with those unfortunate enough to suffer at the hands of a supposed loved one. Not all murderers deserve the same fate; some, as in your example, who suffer diminished responsibility or mental incapacity, deserve an alternative to punishment for a crime they unwittingly committed or committed while under duress. And for those, there is every chance of reform, of reintegration where they pose a risk to no one. Medical treatment will always be available to that class of unfortunates – we are, if nothing else, a just and tolerant society employing a just and tolerant government to administer the law as it sees fit.

"Don't think of it as a 'bloody code', like the one used in the nineteenth century; we're not out to slaughter those who commit crime through no fault of their own—"

"Maybe not, but what about appeals?"

"You're moving off the point of the discussion here, I think. But since you ask; the appeal system is fairer now than at any time in the history of British law. Do your research, Mick, and you'll find that appeals against capital punishment went where? To the Home Secretary – a politician! Surely, decisions of such a magnitude where aspects of legality and proportionality, where aspects of law and mitigation are to be considered, should be made by an expert in the law, not by someone governed by the doctrines of politics. That's why all appeals quite rightly go to the Lords Judicial in consultation with the Independent Review Panel."

Mick abandoned the sipping and slurped the whisky, then placed the empty glass under Deacon's nose. He smiled.

"More?"

"Go on, then." *So far, so good,* he thought. The interview, designed to cloak the real issue, meandered on the fringes. *Wait,* he told himself, *choose the right moment before asking him what you really want to know.* "What do you think of Margy Bolton's execution?"

Deacon handed over the glass, returned to his side of the desk but did not sit; instead, stood there pondering the question. "You know I can't talk of specific cases." His answer was cold, not at all the jovial host.

"You must have an opinion."

"I do, yes. But not specifically aimed at that one case."

"Margy Bolton is the first woman—"

"To be executed by the state since Ruth Ellis in July 1955. I know my history, and I also know she wouldn't have killed those kids after the 15th of June – proof of the deterrent value." Deacon's demeanour had changed; the warmth he extended to Mick began to wane and as he gulped his whisky, his sharp eyes looked at nothing other than Mick. Deacon sat and sighed, as though waiting for the next nonsensical question, as though obliged to appease this parochial journalist.

Mick cursed; he asked these questions as a way of engaging Deacon in conversation; but instead he was turning Deacon away from him. He tried to bring him back on side. "All I'm trying to say, Sir George, is that the state is impartial when it comes to executions." He smiled warmly. "And that's a good thing. After all, she killed a class full of youngsters, she killed three teachers and she killed Jo Tower. The nation was outraged and it demanded justice—"

"No it didn't! It demanded retribution. And it got retribution. The court, however, did not acquiesce to their cries of retribution, it stuck rigidly to the guidelines set down in the act, and it administered the trial and passing of sentence perfectly. The Rules worked."

"Yes, yes, Sir George." Mick reached out and switched off the Dictaphone. Then he looked back into Deacon's eyes. "I'm not trying to make you look bad or to trip you up here," he said, "I'm trying to cover all the bases and have The Rules appear impartial—"

"They *are* impartial!"

"I know!" he shouted. Then he closed his eyes, could hear Deacon puffing. "I'm sorry, I didn't mean to raise my voice." Fuck, this was all going wrong. "Shake my hand." Mick reached over the oak desk.

Deacon looked confused. "What?"

"Go on, shake my hand."

He did, slowly, cautiously as though Mick was wired into the mains. "What was that for?"

"How about we forget that last episode, and start again? I meant no offence—"

"None taken."

"Really?"

"What do you want to ask?"

It hadn't worked. Deacon was still as frosty as a winter's morning, eyes just as dark, too. He was going to have to bring the conversation down to a more human level; comical, even. "I'm not here for anything specific, Sir George." Mick sounded deflated, eyes roaming the lower regions of the room, a sigh leaked out of his loose lips and then he reached again for the whisky. He shrugged, looked up; "I'm wasting your time, aren't I?"

"What's the matter, Mick? You don't seem your usual self."

Mick shrugged again. "I dunno; I think I'm losing my touch, not that I ever had a very subtle touch in the first fucking place. Oops," he held his hand over his mouth, "sorry, Sir George."

"Forget it." He nodded to Mick's glass, "More?"

Mick held it out, didn't make eye contact.

"Were you at my speech last Friday?"

"I was there. I thought it went very well; even though the audience were selected to applaud in the right places."

Deacon laughed, and Mick sneaked a sly glance at him.

"You noticed then."

"I thought you spoke with real passion, *real* passion, I mean."

"I did, didn't I?"

"Was your anecdote real?" He looked up as another whisky came his way. "Don't worry," he nodded towards the Dictaphone, "it's turned off; I really do have discretion, you know."

"I had to get my point across to the nation. It's a game. Power is everything; give the public what they want and they'll vote you back in. It's a *game*."

Mick showed the slightest nuance of being uninterested, trying to make Deacon feel safe, as though what he said mattered little anyway. He puffed and sat back in the leather chair. At last the drink was having a calming effect, and with it came a tinge of bravery, and he tried to turn the conversation away from the dull grind of work and politics and on to a friendlier, more personal level. "So," he said, "how's Henry these days?"

Deacon would either clam up altogether and dismiss the interview as a non-starter, or he would just slip into the small-time rhetoric of one worn out middle-aged man talking about life's disappointments with another.

"He's okay. Business seems to be floundering. But the market's poor for real estate just now." He paused, looked at Mick to make sure the "uninterest" was still there, and added, "He'll never amount to anything; he's a waster."

"I'm under the cosh at work as well."

"He's thirty-seven and still can't control himself or his own life."

"I've been told to pull my fucking socks up," no apology this time, "or find another job. Bastards."

"Every couple of weeks I have to get him out of trouble, it seems."

"Oh go on, what's he done now?" Mick tutted.

"Is your job threat serious?"

Damn! Deacon wasn't a soft touch, and Mick must have been stupid if he'd thought he would spill his innermost secret after only a couple of glasses. He breathed hard, itching for a smoke. "I'm doing stories on crime and justice." He opened his hands, stared at the room. "That's why I'm here. But, and this is how shitty my luck is, I went to interview this old bloke whose son was locked up for knifing a burglar, and when I got there," he giggled, "the bastard had killed himself!"

"Nothing to do with your scintillating company?"

"Yeah, thanks for that, cheers."

Deacon laughed.

"Landed me in a heap of shit with my editor and the police. They accused me of destroying their scene! I *found* the bastard!"

Deacon roared with laughter.

Mick shook his head, feigning disconsolation. "It was only a bleeding suicide, anyway. Would've made a great story."

"I read it; it *did* make a great story."

"Thanks." Mick swallowed. "Turns out he was murdered."

Deacon's own smile froze. "Really?"

"No doubt about it."

"But he left a suicide note. He *did* leave a suicide note, didn't he? I mean, they always do, don't they?"

Inside Mick's numb brain, his hands were raised and he was dancing a hooly-hoo. *But he left a suicide note. That, Sir George, was a statement. It was not, repeat not, a question. And look at his eyes, see how shifty they suddenly are?* "Oh yeah," Mick said absently, "he left a note…" And then he paused, wondering whether to give the game away just for a reaction.

"And?"

"And what?"

"You said he left a note."

Mick shrugged, "Yeah?"

"Well, it sounded as though there was a revelation to follow."

"Tragic. An old man dying like that." He sipped. "You knew him, Sir George, didn't you?" He asked the question in the same manner he'd used to ask how Henry was, nonchalant, unchallenging, not caring.

"No, don't think so."

"Oh yes, he came to see you that morning, the day he died. Came to see you in your surgery."

"Really?"

"Lincoln Farrier? Old fella, seemed nice though. All there," he prodded his head.

Hesitation. "Ah, was *that* him? I remember now, delightful old chap. Dismayed about the dishevelment of today's society, if I recall correctly." Deacon glanced at the Dictaphone. "What makes you think he was murdered?"

"Whoever wrote his suicide note..."

"Yes?"

"I don't think I should say. The police told me to keep schtum."

Deacon's smile twitched. "You can tell me."

"If I do I'll lose my job. How do you go about being a private security guard, you know, like Sirius, I mean?"

"Do the police know he was murdered?"

"They know."

Deacon tapped the desk. "Good! I can't abide gun crime."

Mick's fingers tingled. He looked at Sir George with renewed interest. That was it; that was the proof! And now he'd had the suspicion confirmed, he had to get away and think things through. But first he had to hide his surprise.

"What's wrong?"

"I think I pissed myself."

"Oh not on the leather!"

"No, no, I think it was just a dribble." He smiled, shame evident on his face. "I'm sorry, it's a condition I've—"

"What about the note?"

"Oh yes, the note. Whoever wrote it spelled his son's name wrong."

Deacon slowly looked away, pale faced.

Chapter Thirty-Seven

Tuesday 23rd June

"Over here."

Christian looked up. The copper was pointing at him.

"Yes, you. Come on, I haven't got all day."

Christian sloped across the custody area and stood in front of the high desk where the edges were surrounded with foam rubber, and where the monitors were shielded from violent "customers" by thick plastic. The sound of metal doors slamming filled the air, of keys on chains and of echoing voices; subdued, monotonous, and others shouting obscenities. Christian's dejection plunged into hopelessness.

"Do you understand English?"

"What? I was born—"

"Any printed material handed to you will be in the English language. Is that okay?"

"Yes, but—"

"It can be supplied in any other language."

"No, English is—"

"Name?" The sergeant positioned his hands over the keypad and waited.

"Christian Ledger." He looked around; there were three other sergeants performing the same duty, and there was a queue of miscreants that wound around the custody area like customers in a bank. He expected to see till numbers in flashing LEDs above each counter, and waited to hear "sergeant number three now serving". It never came; only the gruff voices of people working too hard and too quickly, of bored faces peering along the lines of the never-ending queue and wishing their shift was over. Around the periphery of the room were half a dozen armed police officers and detention officers who gossiped among themselves, enshrouded by a ring of bars. In total, Christian counted fifteen CCTV cameras.

Each time the custody area door opened to admit another offender, he could hear the West Yorkshire Police flag slapping against its pole outside. It flew at half-mast: another officer had been shot yesterday.

Christian felt dejected like never before. And all for a couple of tubes of paint. His dejection was only partly caused by being caught;

184

the greater part of it was that he wouldn't get to finish his masterpiece. Life could be so cruel.

"Under the Theft Act 1968, superseded by The Police and Criminal Evidence Act 2010, you are charged with theft from an establishment by the name of Art for Art's Sake, Park Row, Centre, Leeds, on the morning of Tuesday 23rd June." The sergeant didn't look up, simply continued to recite, "You do not have to say anything. However, it may harm your defence if you do not mention when questioned something which you later rely on in court. Your attitude and demeanour, any intimation you offer, and anything you do say may be given in evidence. You will be appointed a solicitor if you do not have the funds to appoint your own; the costs will be deducted in instalments from any state payments made to you in future and may accrue interest at the current rate." He slid a leaflet entitled *Paying for Your Legal Costs* across the counter. "Do you need to see a police surgeon for any reason?"

"What?"

"Do you need to see a doctor?"

"Why should—"

"Do you have any physical debility that we should be aware of?"

"No."

"Do you have any mental debility that we should be aware of?"

"No."

"Have you ever been in a mental institution, been declared sub-educational, suffer from any disease, communicable or otherwise?"

"No."

"Are you on any medication?"

"No."

"Do you partake in street drugs?"

"No," he sighed. His mind ebbed away from here, receding into a shadowy place made redundant by painting. This was as far away from his idea of utopia as it was possible to get.

Beneath the counter, a printer spat a form out. "Sign here and here." The sergeant pointed to two red crosses on the paperwork.

Christian did, the pen retracting on a chain back to the sergeant's side of the desk as soon as he placed it on the counter.

"You gonna make any trouble for us, Mr Ledger?"

Christian slowly shook his head. "No, sir."

The sergeant looked across the room. He whistled, "Tom, over here." To Christian he said, "Go with him; interview room four. You are being monitored. Need I tell you more?"

"No."

* * *

"Your name?"

"Christian Ledger."

"Address?"

"17 Shaftsbury Court, Holbeck."

Tom had a logo in red across the right breast pocket of his shirt: *Seven Security Services*, it said, and on his black epaulettes, silver stitching proclaimed DO901. A Velcro badge on his chest proclaimed *Tom Vincent Detention Officer*. "That's a residential home, isn't it?"

"Yes."

Next to Tom, a man in a suit with a briefcase by his side made notes on a laptop computer. Around his neck was a lanyard with *Pennant Solicitors* in script across it. His name was scrawled beneath it, but was illegible.

"You will be charged £48 an hour, plus VAT at 25 per cent," he told Christian, "so it'll be in your own interests to keep it short, create no trouble."

"I won't give you any hassle."

"Okay, Mr Ledger, I need to read this to you, so pay attention."

Christian nodded.

"Under the Police and Criminal Evidence Act 1984, you have been searched and your personal effects seized under the Administration of Justice Act 2012, and are securely lodged here at Millgarth Police Station, Leeds, in locker A87. Cash money to the value of £326 was among your belongings, an amount not greater than fifty per cent, that being £163 has been confiscated as full or part payment of compulsory legal advice and representation. Any balance is payable by yourself or your estate as detailed in the above act should you be subsequently found guilty of, or plead guilty to, the charges made against you. Any balance in your favour will be paid upon completion of this process. A leaflet explaining this payment is offered to you now."

From a drawer, Tom took a leaflet and passed it across to Christian. Its title was: *Helping to Pay Your Debt to Society*.

Tom stood, stretched nitrile gloves over his petite hands and donned a face mask. "I'm taking your DNA now. It won't hurt, just a case of rubbing a couple of swabs inside your cheeks, okay?"

"Fine."

"Have you been in trouble with the police before?"

Christian waited until the swabs came out, and replied, "No, I haven't."

Tom sheathed the swabs and sealed them in a plastic bag with FSS stamped across it. "Glad to hear it. I'll take your fingerprints next and you'll be pleased to hear I've already taken your photo." He pointed over his head to a remote video camera on the wall. Beneath it, a warning to those who worked here: "Everything you say or do is being recorded".

"What happens then?"

"Once all this is out of the way," Tom said, "you go home and we'll file the paperwork with a magistrate."

"I don't have to go to prison?"

Tom laughed. "You really *haven't* done this before, have you?"

"No, why?"

"You'll get a fine, and have to do fifty hours community service. In the meantime you go home with a Rule One violation against your name provided you're pleading guilty to the charge of shoplifting?"

Christian nodded.

Tom peered through the laminated glass in the interview room door, "Very busy these days, Mr Ledger," he grinned, "no time to send folk to jail over a misdemeanour anymore. It's like a conveyor belt out there; you do the naughty, we ship you in and process you."

There was a glimmer of light after all. Christian's heart dared to lift.

"Okay, place both hands in the gridded squares on the glass platen." Tom indicated to a machine the size of a photocopier that protruded from the magnolia wall below the video camera. "We'll take your prints in a jiffy. Don't move your hands though, or we'll have to start over, and that'll cost you more."

£48 an hour, plus VAT.

There was a flash of red light, like the kind you see on supermarket checkouts, as a scanner criss-crossed his hands.

"What's your ID number, Mr Ledger?"

"I…" He looked between Tom and the solicitor, who suddenly stopped typing and looked up at Christian. "I don't have an ID card."

Tom stopped operating the machine. "How can you *not* have an ID card?"

Christian shrugged. "Don't know. Just never got round—"

"You know it's a civil offence not to carry an ID card with you, let alone not have one at all?" the solicitor said.

"Is it?"

"Yes."

Tom pursed his lips. "That's another half an hour, Mr Ledger."

"You on bonus?" Christian asked him. "You seem keen not to have me in here too long."

He laughed. "I'm on performance-related pay. But that's how we keep the public happy; it keeps costs down, see, keeps you fellows in here for the shortest time, and—"

"Keeps me free for others who need my services," smiled the solicitor.

"Better get the forms out," Tom said.

Before he even got the gloves off, the scanning machine buzzed and a red light pulsed on the screen. Tom seemed confused and then went to have a closer look. "So you haven't been a bad boy, Mr Ledger?"

"What's it say?"

The solicitor looked up hopefully.

"Burglary is what it says." He tutted. "Sit down, this'll take some time. I have to take a statement from you and update the computer systems."

"Will I still be going home today?"

"I expect so, but you'll be going home with a Provisional Rule Two stapled to your arse, and you'll be bailed to appear before a magistrate."

"Shit!"

The solicitor typed furiously on his machine.

"Where were you overnight on the twentieth of this month, Mr Ledger? That's last Saturday?"

"I can't recall."

Chapter Thirty-Eight

Tuesday 23rd June

– One –

Alice scraped the corrugated metal door back into place and watched the kitchen recede into a semi-darkness that put a dampener on her previous buoyant mood. Here she was, back in the fucking slum.

It was silent.

"Spencer!" Alice hurried into the lounge and over to the baby's cot – the wooden crate that Christian called a cot! He had screamed this morning as she headed out the door and she didn't have the time or the inclination to feed him then. And now she felt guilty, and expected to hear from the nagging voice. Like the house, it remained silent.

She peered in, pulled aside the grubby blankets and stared at her son. He was sleeping; his chest rose and fell and his little eyes never opened once. "Aw, bless," she whispered. "I'll feed you, Spencer," she smiled, "just as soon as I get some food, eh?"

Cigarette smoke curled up her face, and she put the packet on the table, on top of the lottery ticket, and then crouched beneath Spencer's cot. She pulled out her stash and a fresh needle. The drugs flowed and Alice shuddered as normality chased away the torment.

The corrugated iron door banged. She caught her breath, went cold, and she slid her drugs back beneath the cot. On the windowsill was Christian's hammer. She took it and held it up ready for action. The door banged again and she wondered if it was the police come to sort out the squatters. Or maybe it was the kids at the end of the block come by for some entertainment or to steal her drugs. Her heart pounded as she made her way to the door.

The light creeping between the door and the scored kitchen floor was obstructed by the shadows of legs. She raised the hammer and waited. "Alice?" A voice, little more than a whisper, crept around the door.

Who the hell *was* that?

"Alice, it's me. Max."

She exhaled a long breath and let the hammer fall to the floor. "Shit."

"Can I come in?"

"What do *you* want?" Her voice echoed in here. It made her cringe.

"Just to talk, that's all."

"We'll talk next time I come to see you."

His voice smiled at her through the door, "I'm here now; might as well have a chat. We could talk about your boyfriend's work."

She said nothing, only played with her nail-bitten fingers.

"He's not in there, is he?"

If I say he is, then he'll want to talk to him, and that's my fucking cover blown. If I say he's not, then he'll want to talk to me, and he'll know I'm vulnerable. What do I do?

You start prayin, girl. That's whatcha do. You should have thought about all this nonsense before.

"I don't mean you any harm; nothing to be afraid of, my dear."

My dear. She made small nervous steps towards the door. "You can't stay long. He'll be home soon."

"He doesn't know about our little arrangement?"

She sighed, "You know he doesn't."

"We'll keep it our little secret. No one need ever know."

When she opened the door, the light burst in and for a moment, she squinted against it.

"There," he said, "nothing to be afraid of."

She stepped well back as he came in, taking no chances. His eyes adjusted to the gloom and then appraised it the way he'd appraised her when they first met. And the strangest thing was how nervous she felt. "I told you I'd try and come by tomorrow."

He stepped in further, peering around corners, peeking into the lounge as though he were a prospective buyer! He turned, hands laced behind his back. "Just popped by, hoping I could accelerate our transaction."

"You followed me!"

"Are they here? The paintings?"

"I thought you had trouble selling them? Why is it so urgent you get your hands on more?" Alice clutched her arms tightly around her chest; she looked outside, hoping to see someone, anyone, just in case she had to call for help.

"Why are you looking so scared? I followed you, yes, just so I could buy a few more of them here and now." He winked at her,

"Give you a good price for them." He came closer. "Got 200 in my pocket right now."

Alice thought of the hammer.

His hand curled around the edge of the door, teasing it closed. "Maybe we could have a quick look at the paintings? I could be gone before he gets back. What do you say?"

* * *

The candle's flame trembled. "Watch your step, Max."

"Right behind you. Following you into wonderland."

Alice felt cold, could almost feel him breathing down her neck. What was she doing in the cellar with a stranger, anyhow? How stupid could you get? In the horror films this was where the heroine got her skull split down the middle because she was too stupid or too greedy to run away.

She could make a lot of money here today; make this her final day in this squalid shithole. She shuffled around the covered easel and swung open the annex door. The big spider stared at her, daring her to cross its threshold. She held the flame beneath it and watched it scurry up the remnants of its fluttering web.

"Alice," Max called from behind her. "Can I have some light please, dear? It's awfully dark back here."

She looked over her shoulder. "Leave it alone, that one is *not* for sale."

"Oh," he said, "shame."

"You need to be over here, this is where all the sale items are kept."

"Would you mind me taking a look at this; just a quick look, you understand, just to satisfy my curiosity?"

She sighed and brought the candle closer to Max's face, saw it filled with anticipation. "I told you," she said again, "it's not for sale."

His eyes didn't stray from the dustsheet. "Just a look."

"Make it quick, I'm bricking myself."

He lifted the sheet up. His eyes fell on the work and there they stayed.

Alice cooed. She had not seen this before, either.

They stared at it together. "See," she whispered, "it's not finished."

"A little red here, maybe a swish of crimson there, but apart from that, it's as good as done." He looked across to Alice. She too was mesmerised. "It's beautiful, isn't it?" He smiled at her. "I would take it off your hands now, my dear, in its current state for five hundred."

She blinked, seemed to come out of a trance, and she frowned at him. "Come on," she said, "the ones for sale are over here."

He nodded slowly, and peered at her over the top of spectacles. "Very well," he said, "I will offer you one thousand—"

"You could offer me ten thousand and I still wouldn't sell it. I couldn't do that to him."

"How controversial, that you can stretch your betrayal so far, but not this far?"

"I couldn't live with myself."

– Two –

"Okay, Mr Ledger," Tom said. "Sign there on this form and," he slid another two across to him, "also there and there on the other two."

"What are these for?"

"The first is an application for an ID card; you'll still be fined for not having one, but at least we've tried to put that right. It'll look good for you in court. And the second one is your conditions of bail, and the bail slip itself. It states on there that you will appear before a magistrate at the time and date shown, and this," he handed Christian a leaflet, "explains about your visit to court, about who may represent you and about the costs you're likely to incur.

"It also sets out the possible consequences of your crime, and tells you about the Offenders' Charter, which is designed to help you not to reoffend. The last form is your copy of a Rule One proposal. It sets out the crime you have committed, the case the police have against you, your agreement with the charge, and the consequences of reoffending."

Christian looked up, a frown across his face.

Tom sighed. "It's all to do with the Criminal Justice Reform Act. Basically, you're already on a Rule One because of the shoplifting. If the judge finds you guilty of the burglary last Saturday, you'll go to a Rule Two. So you're walking on very thin ice. I strongly suggest you do nothing illegal before your court date, Mr Ledger. If you commit any offence deemed more serious than offences against property, you could find yourself on a Rule Three." He stared at Christian with solemn eyes. "You know what *that* means, don't you?"

"Death?"

"In one, my friend, in one."

Christian swallowed.

"If you find yourself on a Rule Three, you'll be given a brief trial, then the Independent Review Panel breeze over all the evidence for and against and make recommendations to the judge. Then it's curtains." He sliced a finger across his neck. "But, I don't expect we'll see you back here again, will we, Mr Ledger?"

"Definitely not."

"So what's the damage?" Tom asked the solicitor.

The solicitor punched numbers on his laptop's calculator. "£137. Including VAT."

Tom said, "Give me five minutes. I'll get your stuff out the locker, be right back with your change and a receipt, okay?"

* * *

Christian stepped outside and the door swung shut after him. Over in the distance, he heard the demos finally coming together outside the Town Hall and the Courts buildings. He heard the screams and the shouts and the sirens. And then it all went strangely quiet, where the only sound he could hear clearly was the flag flapping in the wind. There was a loud crack like a circus master lashing a whip. It made Christian jump.

There was a roar from the pro crowd and jeers from the objectors; the furore resumed at a quieter volume, electronic voices massaging the crowds on megaphones, sirens screamed down the roads and undecipherable chants bounced off each building.

Full of dejection, Christian headed home.

– Three –

Mick didn't notice Mr Rochester behind him. He carried on punching the computer keyboard with his two index fingers, looking up every now and then, searching the ceiling for inspiration. It was only after a sustained pause where his finger resisted the urge to type and instead meandered its way in and out of his right nostril that Rochester coughed and made his presence known. Mick swivelled, "Ah, Mr Rochester."

"Any further forward with the copy for tomorrow's edition?"

"I have some new info. And it's in the gel stage." He smiled, "Sort of, anyway."

"So it'll make my hair stand on end, will it?"

"As a matter of fact, it'll make your cock stand on end. Sir."

Chapter Thirty-Nine

Tuesday 23rd June

She took the light away from him and he sighed when the dustsheet fluttered back over the painting. "Come on," she said, "they're over here."

"Of course, my dear."

"We don't have time for you to have a good look at them. Just take a couple, pay me and go."

He followed her towards the curious black hole, and laughed, "You can hardly expect me to hand over good money without inspecting the merchandise first, can you?"

"Inspection is fine; just don't spend all day wanking over them and asking what they're called."

"Your choice of words is, as always, no surprise."

* * *

She held up the candle, and pointed to the plastic-wrapped treasure. "Don't you ever come here again. I will not be forced into selling in my own house."

"My dear—"

"Is that clear? Come here again, and I'll find another buyer."

"You make yourself understood. I have no intention of distressing you further."

And then she heard a noise. Her eyes widened, looked up towards the ceiling, and froze. She held her breath and when Max opened his mouth to speak, she hushed him immediately.

"I didn't hear anything," Max said.

He's back! Christian's home! Her heart pummelled against her ribcage and she stood rigid with fear. *What the fuck is he going to do when he finds* him *here?*

Should 'ave thought about all this before you let him in. You should never have brought him down here, girl; now you in all kinds of pain. Or you soon will be.

"Shut up."

"I didn't speak," Max said.

"Ssshh!"

He's gonna come down them stairs, feeling his way in the dark, and he's gonna see the candlelight—

"Will you shut—"

He gonna see the little fat man there. And then hell itself will erupt, girl. Oh, you done it now.

"What's going on, Alice?"

Alice caught her breath. Stared at Max. Listened. There were no more noises. Maybe it was… "Just Spencer waking up. He needs feeding."

"Spencer?" Max looked around as if he expected to see someone standing next to him.

"My son."

Agitated, Max said, "Look, can we just get this over with and I'll be out of your way."

"Take a couple. Peel back the bags and have a quick look."

"I need more than a quick look. Please, I—"

"Take the candle. I'll wait upstairs; at least if he comes in, he won't catch me down here."

Max's smile widened. Greed leaked out. "What a splendid idea." He took the candle and then asked, "He's a bit violent is he, this chap of yours?"

"I don't know what he'd do if he found out about this."

"Bet he'd be none too pleased." There was a sparkle in Max's eyes.

"If you pull a fast one on me, I know where your little empire is, and believe me, I know how to throw a petrol bomb."

He took a nervous step back. "Right you are, my dear. I'll not let you down."

"Just remember which side of the bread your butter's on." In a swift movement Alice was past him, engulfed by the darkness.

She rounded the stone stairs and daylight illuminated her way to the top. Once there, she checked the lounge, peered into Spencer's cot, relieved again that still he slept soundly. She sighed hard, took another cigarette from the packet and breathed the smoke. Of course, her heart still hammered in her chest—

"Alice?"

Alice screamed. She dropped the cigarette.

"Why's the front door open?"

"You frightened the *shit* out of me; don't ever do that again."

Christian walked towards her, feet scuffing the bare floorboards, and an ashen look on his face. "You okay, babe?"

With a shaking hand, she picked up the cigarette. "Spencer's being playing me up."

"I've had a shit day, too." He peered into the cot. "Only mine was real."

She puffed on the cigarette and fidgeted with her hair.

"Got arrested for nicking paint. You're looking at a Rule One criminal, now." He waited for a response, but she was too busy sucking on the cigarette, too engulfed by tension to respond. And then he saw the table. "A lottery ticket?" When she said nothing, he picked it up and studied it as though he'd never seen anything like it before. She didn't volunteer an explanation. "How did you get hold of this? And the fags, it's a new packet, isn't it?" Then he had her by the arm. "Where did you get the money from?" His voice was almost seductively smooth.

"Money?"

"For the ticket and the cigs."

She laughed. "I found a fucking twenty!"

There was a rustling. He turned his head away from her and towards the open front door. "Wait there."

Alice squeezed the bridge of her nose and prayed for it to be over.

A whole minute went by before she heard him slam the corrugated door. Trouble with that door was, when you slammed it as hard as he just did, it bounced open again. Dust rose into the lounge and through it walked Christian. He looked very unhappy, but too engrossed to be bothered slamming the door shut again.

"Where did you get the money from?" He stopped in the doorway, arms folded tightly across his chest.

She edged closer to the hammer on the floor by the cot. And what sprang into her mind was a hell of a lot safer to tell than the truth. "You know them kids at the end of the block, always hanging around, leering?"

"Go on."

"They said they'd give me twenty quid if I flashed my tits at them."

Christian's mouth fell open. "You are kidding me."

She said nothing.

He dragged his feet into the lounge and snarled, "So you're a whore now?"

"I am *not* a whore."

"Jesus, I can't believe you. You're hooked on some drug that makes you feel ill if you don't take it, you've got delusions of being a good mother – no wait, you've got delusions of being a mother, full-stop! And now you show your tits for twenty fucking quid! What next, eh? You going to show your fanny when you run out of cigs?"

"You shouldn't keep me on such a tight rein."

"The next time I burgle a house for cash to keep you from going under, to keep food in your belly, will you be *going down* for the price of a cigarette, I wonder? Or will you be going horizontal for some brown?"

"I would never…" *This is when he hits me*, she thought. Her foot nudged the hammer.

"You disgust me." He turned his back on her.

She felt like crying. He wasn't going to hit her; she ought to have realised he would never do that. Whereas she was above nothing. Tears sprang into the corners of her eyes and she recalled telling Max that she couldn't live with herself if she sold the big painting. Now she wasn't sure she could live with herself anyway.

Like flicking a switch, the tears dried up. He was a high and mighty man, a proud man, a pious man – *and she was fucking sick of it!*

She looked at Christian's back, his arms folded, head down. Nervously she reached for the hammer.

Don't you be stupid, girlie!

Her fingers touched the hammer shaft; she watched him constantly.

Christian turned around and faced her. She stood quickly, brushing the hair from her face. Meekly she smiled at him. The hammer lay at her feet.

"You know, I'd rather you took everything I held dear than spoil yourself for cash." He spoke barely above a whisper. "You mean more to me than…"

Her eyes were so wide they almost fell out of her stunned face.

"Alice?" he stared at her. "What have you done?"

Chapter Forty

Tuesday 23rd June

Down in the cellar, Max paid for his purchases. He propped the paintings against a wall, pulled out the 200 and wondered where to put it, where only Alice would find it. He slid the bundle up into the rotten old doorframe that was the spider's home. He patted it, and sincerely hoped she found it – the safety of his shop could depend on it.

The transaction complete, Max licked his lips and returned to the easel where he lifted the sheet up enough to get the candle and his head beneath, to gaze at the beauty on canvas.

He fell in love with it all over again and wondered if he could make it out of here with this masterpiece as well. He didn't think he could. Not this time.

Reluctantly, Max let the dustsheet go, hooked his new acquisitions and shuffled along the dusty floor to the stairs. Halfway up he stopped dead, heart thudding like someone tapping a brick against a dustbin.

He could see the silhouette of a tall man with hair draped around his shoulders. He peered outside for a long time before grunting, slamming the old metal door and storming off into the lounge.

A wave of dust blew into his face and blew the flame out. It went dark for a moment. Then the door rippled, wobbled back open, and Max chewed grit as the daylight crept back into the cellar stairs.

The open door was only a few yards away. But the kitchen doorway opened into the lounge, right to where Christian and Alice were. If Christian was looking this way… Max crept along the kitchen floor and squeezed between the metal door and its rotten frame, out into the open at last.

Behind him, Alice screamed.

* * *

He raced down the steps, Alice's scream still in his ears as his footfalls echoed around the cellar. He stopped, sniffed the air, and his eyes closed down to a cynical squint. Candle smoke.

When he was level with the old desk, he bent and flicked the light switch. He yanked the dustsheet aside, and then ran a finger across the nymph's face, grateful it was still there and undamaged. But then he noticed the rotten annex door was wide open. Christian never left the door open. He saw the resident spider, and gently lifted him aside, crouched down and inspected the stock.

His fingertips glanced along the line of bags. At least four missing. He slumped to the ground, and pulled at his hair. What was she doing to him? She was turning herself into a whore for drugs money, and she was letting people take his paintings, or was she selling *them* as well?

He screamed in fury and leapt the cellar steps. His eyes were wild, they were insane as he strode into the lounge. "You *bitch*!"

* * *

Alice stiffened; hammer knocking at the side of her leg. Tap. Tap. Tap. Spencer howled. *Shut up! Shut the fuck up, boy!*

She licked her lips, and her eyes flicked to the cot. Tap.

Christian closed down the gap, eyes narrow slits of hatred.

Spencer screamed at the top of his lungs, his arms and legs writhed beneath his crude blanket. Christian advanced towards her. She squeezed the shaft. Tap.

"I fucking detest you."

Teeth bared, fingernails white, she lunged and brought the hammer down.

"Nooo!"

* * *

Christian walked towards her, gritting his teeth, watching the madness in her eyes. He glanced to the cot he'd rigged up for her. *Build a cot for my baby,* she'd said, smiling at him, while she stroked its hair and while she forced a bottle into its mouth.

The girl was mad.

The room was silent except for their own heavy breathing.

By her leg, her hand twitched; it briefly caught his attention but couldn't hold it, and his gaze locked on to her unblinking eyes, wide, reddened.

"I fucking detest you."

It took him a moment to work out what was in her hand but by then it was too late.

"Nooo!" The hammer glanced down the side of his face, ripped into his ear and smashed his collar bone. That's when the world erupted into an explosive white mass of pain that engulfed him, and he sank to his knees.

He scrabbled quickly backwards as she advanced, and then he was on his feet and made it clear just as she swung the hammer again.

Everything happened so quickly. The pain in his shoulder was almost more than he could bear, and when she swung again, he moved left, banged into the cot. Alice paused, and Christian reached inside.

"No!" she screamed. "You leave him alone, you bastard."

He grasped the thing by its neck, and circled around her. "You're fucking crazy!"

Her mad eyes followed him, then focused on the doll. They appeared to be pleading to it, almost pained as though it was screaming at her. She held her hand out, fingers trembling, "…and promise to look after you, and Daddy won't hurt you."

A shiver ran up Christian's back. Just how mad *was* she? He raised the doll with its nappy hanging in tatters from its plastic hips. He saw its blue eyes swing open and then swing shut. He squeezed.

"You're frightening him!"

"*I'm* frightening *him*? You mad bitch!" Christian threw the doll to her right.

She dropped the hammer and made a grab for it. Her fingers brushed its dirty plastic feet and it landed on the floor between them. Christian twisted and smacked her hard in the face with the back of his hand. Her hair whipped around. She staggered back a few paces and then stood still, panting. Blood dripped from her nose.

Despite his left arm hanging limply by his side, and a deafening buzzing in his ear, Christian was happy he'd made her stop the craziness. He picked up the doll with his right hand, passed it to the tingling fingers of his left.

Alice snarled.

He reached for the hammer.

"No, Christian," she screamed. "He's only a baby… He's your son!"

He let the doll fall to the floorboards and brought the hammer down.

Eventually, Christian dropped the hammer, stood straight and punched her in the face. Alice hit the floor in a crumpled mess.

He stood there panting, engulfed by a physical pain and a mental torment. He looked at the cash, at the lottery ticket and the cigarettes.

And then he left the house.

* * *

Max slammed the tailgate shut and rested against it, gasping, looking around to make sure he was safe. This was the worst neighbourhood he had ever dared venture into.

He felt well out of his depth, and his busy eyes saw everyone and everything as a potential threat. He had been brave coming here at all, especially dressed in his working garb: gold waistcoat, smart trousers and neat cravat. They created the image, and helped to promote his wealth of knowledge. But here, he stood out like a dot-to-dot at a Rembrandt auction.

Inside the car, he tapped the wheel, thinking about the dryad nymph. And how to get it.

His eyes were drawn across to the terrace of old houses again. The corrugated door opened and a bedraggled creature stumbled out into the yard. Was that him? Was that Christian? He walked in a crooked line up the cobbled street, heading straight for him. Max held his breath and, with pummelling heart, slowly sank into his seat.

He's coming for me; he knows I have his paintings, he's going to demand them back, he's going to fight me for them, and he's going to hurt me.

Max leaned across the car and delved into the glove box, readying himself for an assault. Only a minute passed before Christian walked within twenty yards of him. There was blood down the left side of his head, it tangled in his long wavy hair, and his right hand was never away from his forehead, where it massaged a headache, maybe. His left hand hung limply by his side. Max watched him stagger away up the street, sighed, and slid the knife inside his waistcoat.

Alice was alone, she was vulnerable again.

* * *

He approached the open corrugated door and listened carefully before entering. Creeping forward, he peered into the gloom of the lounge, and saw her lying prone on the filthy floorboards. She was completely still. Next to her lay the crushed remains of what looked like a plastic doll, batteries by its side, head caved in. He wondered if she was dead. Should he go and… no, no; get the nymph and get out. He might come back.

Chapter Forty-One

Tuesday 23rd June

Though he could see almost nothing, Max could feel its beauty. He could almost feel his wallet bulge in anticipation. He licked his lips and then slid the home-made tethers away. He took its weight and felt the tension in his stomach, felt the sweat tickle the crack of his backside, felt more running down the sides of his face and arms. He turned and then he froze.

From above he heard a noise.

Afraid, he peered through the darkness and up the stairs towards a tinge of daylight.

"What now?" he whispered.

He had no choice: he had to climb the stairs, he had to get away and if that meant facing Christian, then face Christian he would. He had to have this art, and if it meant paying the lad off and promising to keep quiet about Alice's death, then he'd do that too. Anything to get the nymph into his shop.

With sweat dripping from his face, he reached the summit and peered out into the kitchen. No one was there, and whatever the noise had been, it didn't bother him now. He stepped out of the shade and into the brightness of the kitchen and stifled a scream.

Alice grinned at him.

At her side a hammer tapped against her leg. The hammer had blood and hair on it. Max stared at it, then at the blood oozing from her nose and at the tears making her cheeks glisten. "Alice, my dear." His voice was shaky, and he knew she detected the fear in it. "I was going to wake you," he forced a smile. "But I thought I'd just leave the cash for you to find; didn't want to disturb you."

"Fuck off, Max."

"Alice, please… Are you okay? You look terrible, my dear."

She sobbed, but stared coldly at him. Tap.

"Did he hurt you, my dear?"

"Put that back!"

"I have a thousand pounds here. You could have a nice flat; I could arrange that for you. You could be out of here within the hour. We could get you fresh clothes, help you start over—"

"My baby," she whispered. "He killed my baby." Tap.

"We can get you another." The beginnings of a frown turned her eyes dark, "No, we could," he refreshed the smile, "we could make everything better. How would you like that, Alice?" Max put the nymph down. "I have the money right here," he said, reaching inside his waistcoat. "And I already left you 200…"

Alice lifted the hammer.

Max didn't wait for it to come at him. He stepped closer and thrust the knife forward, pulling her onto the blade, feeling her slight weight collapse against him. The hammer fell to the floor and Max opened his eyes.

She stared right at him, and he watched her sad eyes slide shut.

He had a dead body leaning against him. And for a moment, he was horrified. He glanced down at the nymph making sure the falling hammer hadn't damaged it. It was safe.

In one slick movement, Max spun on his heels and pushed. Alice tumbled down into the darkness, her head cracking against the cold stone steps, her pale hand disappearing into the shadows as it scraped a swath of blood down the whitewashed walls. The knife was smeared with redness and faint traces of creamy white fat, and he shuddered. His hand had her blood on it too; his waistcoat had smears of redness melded into the fine golden thread. None of it mattered; he had the nymph, and it was even more glorious by the light of day.

He folded the blade away and dropped it back into his waistcoat pocket. As the sweat cooled on his face, he grabbed the painting and then slid through the open corrugated door, shaking with fear and exhilaration.

Chapter Forty-Two

Tuesday 23rd June

With rainwater still dripping from his hair, Eddie rounded the stairwell, looked up towards his door and he wished he hadn't. "How come every time I come home, you're here?"

"Hey," Mick smiled, "Good to see you too!"

"You wanna move in?"

"And live with a slob? No thanks."

"Look, Mick, I've had the day from hell, do you mind if we—"

"Tell me about it." They swapped glances. "No, I mean it; tell me about it. I'll try and help if I can."

Eddie groped in his pocket for the keys and swung the door open. "You never come round to help. You come round to get me drunk and elicit information."

Mick nodded. "Yep, you're right. But I can still listen to you whine a bit first if you'd like."

* * *

"I'd have hit the bastard." Mick slurped coffee, flicked ash towards an ashtray and missed by three feet.

"Hey, at least make the effort."

"Sorry." He rubbed it into the carpet. "I don't know how you showed such restraint, I really don't."

"Because my boss was peering through his window at the time, and I'm in enough shit without digging myself in further."

"You allowed him to walk away after saying those things? He needs dealing with, and permanently."

Eddie shrugged. "I have to accept there are arseholes in the world; it's just unfortunate that I encounter them all in the space of a week."

"So you could end up on a disciplinary *and* a Rule One?"

"Could lose my job."

"But you know that damned job inside out—"

"I'm thinking of seeing Jilly this afternoon, it's why I came home early."

Mick raised his eyebrows. "After your last meeting?"

"We have something in common. I can't just—"

"Go bollocks." He sat up straight, pointed a finger. "Sod what you have in common! You two know each other inside out, as much as you know your job inside out, and it would be just as criminal for you to let your marriage go as it would be for them to sack you. You go to her with some honesty in your heart for a change and you might stand a chance. You don't fool me, Eddie Collins, so how the hell are you gonna fool your wife?"

Eddie's fingers tugged at a frayed seam. "I think I should go to one of her crazy clubs." He looked for a reaction, and was angered by the head shaking. "What now?"

"What now? Okay, I grant you that it's probably a load of bollocks, this psychic stuff; but come on, cut her a little slack, she lost her son and she wants to keep hold of his memory. Is that such a bad thing?"

"You've changed your tune; said it was—"

"I know what I said. And I was wrong. If she needs a little support, then give it to her; see things from her point of view. Help the lady along until she's ready to stand on her own two feet."

"Should I go and see her, or should I just meet her there? There's a meeting this afternoon."

"Meeting her there shows a little more spontaneity, you know, it shows you're trying to get involved without spouting your good intentions first. *Show* her you care, don't just tell her."

Eddie sat forward, clasped his hands together. "I will." He looked up. "More coffee?"

"Thought you'd never ask; we agony aunts get thirsty quickly."

"Anyway, what have you come around for?"

"Thought you'd never ask that as well." He followed Eddie into the kitchen. "Hey, you've tidied up a bit." He laughed, "Is that a cooker over there?"

"Almost funny, Mick; don't give up the day job."

"I don't intend to. I'm onto something larger than life, my cock-eyed friend. You remember Lincoln Farrier? I found out all the places he went to on the day he died." He counted on his fingers. "He went to the local grocery store for some milk. He went to the Post Office where he posted the letter to the paper and where he collected the letter from his son."

"Keep this up, and you might need to use your other hand."

"I found out he went to a third place."

"The local brothel?"

"As good as. He went into town to see Mr George Deacon."

Eddie bit into the back of his hand and screeched. "Oh no; you don't think Deacon killed him, do you?" He laughed and poured the water.

Mick was silent, arms folded.

"Aw, come on. You don't really think *that* do you?"

"I happen to believe that Lincoln didn't piss anyone off at the grocery store or the Post Office."

"He might have pissed someone off a week ago, or a month ago. Doesn't have to be someone he pissed off on that day, Christ." He handed Mick his coffee. "What about the burglar his son stabbed?"

"Far too elaborate a killing for a burglar," he said. "Anyway, Deacon can be a nasty piece of work when he wants to be."

"I'm surprised one head is enough for all the fucking faces you have. Last week he was a wonderful guy, and he deserved a medal for The Rules."

"Different things entirely. The Rules are a stunning piece of legislation, but the man himself stinks."

"Really?"

"I saw an interview from a few years back when he was accosted by some television colleagues of mine. They asked him a few pretty awkward questions when he thought they had stopped filming. He said, 'You wait till I take office, and I'll show you real power!'"

"I repeat: really?"

"He's evil. I think he's behind Lincoln's death."

"Why would Deacon want to kill an old guy?"

"Haven't worked that bit out yet."

"You surprise me."

"But he did it, definitely."

"And how you going to prove it?" Eddie walked back to the lounge.

Mick followed. "I need the results from Lincoln's PM."

"At last. *That's* why you're here."

"Come on, I did my *best* agony aunt for you, the least you could do—"

"And how do you expect me to get PM results?"

"Maybe not the results themselves, just what the findings were."

"Okay, pop round tomorrow about noon."

"Really?"

"No. Dickhead."

"This old man was shot with his own antique; it's murder!"

"I know! CID knows that too. But if we have no evidence, then it goes in the unsolved file."

"Big, is it," Mick sat down again, "this file?"

"Murders happen all the damned time, even premeditated murders. Not all of them are solvable; some crimes *are* perfect. And even if the crimes aren't perfect, then the means to find the criminal are still *im*perfect. Sorry to shatter your illusions." Eddie sipped his coffee and lit a cigarette. "And sulking with me won't help, either."

Mick sulked anyway.

"Okay, I'll see what I can do."

"Really?"

"Yes."

"Great! That's all I want."

"No promises, though."

"Absolutely, mate."

"Why do you want this so badly? You never cared so much about a murder before."

"*I* found him, remember." He paused. "And he seemed like a nice old fellow; reminded me of my dad."

"You're so full of shit."

Mick looked up quickly. "It's true! And anyway, he wrote to me, asked me to help him with something I feel strongly about: British injustice."

"Now are you going to tell me the truth?"

Mick sipped more coffee. "I need to save my job."

Eddie laughed.

"I kind of said that I thought this murder was linked to someone big, that it had something to do with The Rules."

"You really *are* a dickhead. And what if it doesn't? Thought of that?"

"No. I daren't." He squinted through the strata of smoke floating around the room. "It *is* kind of personal. That's why I care. When I found the old man with his brains dripping down the wall, when I saw his old wrinkled face splashed with his own blood… I don't know. It made it personal, finding him, I mean, rather than being shown photos or just being told about it." He took a breath. "Have you any idea what I'm talking about?"

Eddie only nodded. He did.

Chapter Forty-Three

Tuesday 23rd June

Rain thrummed against the large, curtained windows, and that might have been a slender skitter of thunder, but he wasn't sure. Eddie shook his hand, sat down behind the battered old desk, and appraised him as discreetly as he could. The man wore no black cape, and there were no golden stars or pentagrams sewn into his jersey. He had the eyes of a man, not a cat, and his teeth and nails were… regular teeth and nails. Eddie was a little disappointed.

"Could I have your watch?"

Eddie looked at him through the corner of his eye and smiled. "I thought you took cash these days?"

The man smiled out of politeness.

Maybe this wasn't the place for Eddie Collins. "Sorry." He handed the watch over and looked around the community hall with its scratched parquet floor and stack of chairs up by the stage. All the curtains were drawn against the early evening light; the eight or so tables just like this one, each manned by its own psychic freak, were arranged evenly across that floor. Very intimate. Very becoming. Very production-line. They should have banners around the hall, adverts in the local press: "Come along and meet the dead! Roll up, roll up, Psychic Freaks Inc brings you close to your stiff!"

The bums of the needy and hopeful, mostly women, who all seemed to know each other, who all gabbled incessantly and sipped cheap coffee from Styrofoam cups, filled a row of chairs at the edge of the hall. They were the type that came here week in, week out, hoping for some juicy revelation that would keep them going for seven days until their next spiritual top-up; they came to the entertainment, the gossip; they came to fulfil the need; they came to find Grandpappy's lost treasure and they came to see people in tears. *Whatever,* thought Eddie, *they didn't come for the fucking coffee!*

The man held the watch and closed his eyes. For a reason he could not understand, Eddie's heart kicked up a gear as he waited for some kind of response.

"You're a sceptic, Eddie." The man smiled triumphantly.

He looked back towards the collection of women, hoping to see her.

"You've suffered a loss recently, haven't you?"

"Yes." He looked at the freak.

"It was a boy."

A prickle ran down Eddie's neck, and suddenly the psychic freak had Eddie's full attention. "Yes." He watched him, waiting for the next tasty instalment.

The man turned the watch this way and that, feeling its texture, yet taking something from it maybe. He smiled, closed his eyes momentarily and then opened them again quickly. "He's here, you know."

"Who? Who's here?" Eddie nervously looked around.

"Sam."

He went cold. The colour seeped from his face and sweat glowed on his forehead. Swallowing, he tried and failed to regain some composure. And in the pause, he collected himself, made himself not believe – the way he had always not believed, reminded himself of the ridicule he threw at Jilly, and of all the good reasons not to believe these freaks.

What newspaper have you been reading, he wondered, *what obituary column have you memorised? Yeah, but he seems to know... that's just* it, *he* seems *to know. But he doesn't. Remember that. Put your barriers up.*

"He thanks you for his shrine."

"Sorry?" No one, only Ros, and maybe Mick if he took the blindest bit of interest, could know about the shrine.

"The baseball cap? The one with NY stitched on it. He said thanks for keeping hold of it and putting it on the mantelpiece." The man didn't seem particularly interested in scoring points, in converting a sceptic.

Eddie swallowed again, and was that – no, surely not – a prickle of tears behind the eyes? *It's bollocks, Eddie,* he told himself. *You* remember *that, dammit, it's all brainwashing shit! He's reading your mind! Block it, man, block thoughts of it.*

I don't know how to.

Think about... think about Stuck-up Stuart.

He thought about how good it would feel to hear Stuart's jaw cracking under the weight of his booted foot. And he did it because he could just about grasp the possibility of someone being able to read his mind; it was an easier concept to grasp, a *safer* concept to grasp than the dead coming through a medium on some short-wave receiver that no one but Psychic Freaks Inc could decode.

"And he says he's glad you've started to think of him as Sam instead of Sammy. He says it's okay that you were late picking him up, and he forgives you."

Eddie opened his dry mouth, but absolutely nothing came out.

"He says you should work on forgiving yourself now."

"I… I can't, I…" Eddie stood, grabbed the watch and in a blur, he began to walk away, oblivious now to the chatting ladies.

"Eddie," the voice echoed.

He stopped, didn't look around. *How's he know my name?*

"You have got to stop the booze."

He walked quickly across the wide-open floor, wiping his eyes, listening to the silence that just crushed the hall. He was just trying to put distance between himself and the psychic freak and the monkey's tea party.

His eyes were a blur, his heart hammered in a chest that had begun to heal the misery of loss and had tried to put things into pigeonholes, locked away for the safety of his mind. The pigeonholes had been plundered by a medium who could read minds.

Eddie was in bits. His mind reeled. For the revelation that Sam liked the shrine and had an expanse of love deep enough to forgive the unforgivable. It was like sucking on a live mains cable.

He ran out into the rain, into oblivion in his haste to get out of there, and wouldn't have noticed if a herd of bulls was about to cross his path, let alone the scrabbling, clutching hands of his estranged wife. He didn't see her; tears spilled across his face and all he thought of was running; there was nothing else, nothing else existed. Eddie was frightened half to death, but even the numbness in his legs couldn't stop him running from the ghosts that followed at the speed of thought. And it took a mighty slap to bring him round and allow his eyes to see again.

She was here. He saw her. His breathing was laboured, his face hollow and pale, but at least his eyes could focus now. And they focused on Jilly. He saw the horror on her face, the shock at meeting him, and then the understanding in them. It wasn't such a massive jump for her to conclude what had happened in there.

His numb legs let go and Eddie collapsed onto the wet tarmac. She knelt beside him, pulled his chin up and forced him to gaze at her. His hair clung to his forehead, his flimsy jacket already shiny with water. His lips trembled, and then Eddie shrieked and cried, folding his head into Jilly's neck.

A crowd gathered at the doors. They clasped Styrofoam cups in their hands, exchanged glances and hushed words. But none stepped outside the dryness of the community hall. The rain came heavier, bouncing off the tarmac; he could hear it battering the roofs of nearby cars and could even see it cascading across the car park, a shallow river going downhill – a little like himself.

Chapter Forty-Four

Tuesday 23rd June

– One –

Christian spent hours crying in the corner by the dustbins, trying to keep out of the rain. He mourned two deaths: Alice's and his own. For when the police caught up with him they would kill him too. He wondered if the protestors would hold a demonstration in Leeds for him.

His mind shuffled the day's events, trying to make sense of them. But there *was* no sense. Who would want to kill her? And why? She had become too brave for her own good over the last few days, mixing with the wrong kinds of people; the kind who would take advantage. She was naïve, and crazy, literally insane, and she *had* been since the day they met – well, no, that's not right; she'd been crazy since the day she miscarried. Spencer, they were going to call him. If he'd lived.

Christian let the tears fall and hoped the police caught her killer before they took the easy option – him.

He thought of the paintings – and of course he couldn't go back for them because the place would be crawling with coppers by now, and even if it wasn't, how would he carry so many without a car – and to where?

There was only one objective now: survival. And to survive he needed to get away from the city, needed to head for solitude in the hills or somewhere out in the country away from vidiscreens and bounty hunters and bureaucracy. Away from the police.

He coughed, pulled his shirt tight around his shoulders and stood, wincing at the pain in his left arm. The light was poor, and now would be the right time to head off into town to find some transport.

– Two –

"Your father has instructed me to collect you."

Henry held the phone away from his face, stared at it as though he wasn't sure what it was. "He has? Why?"

Sirius made a point of ensuring Henry heard him tut. "Because it's time to kill the cat."

"What? Will you speak English, man?" And then it hit him: kill the cat, meant destroy the Jaguar – of course; it was code-speak. "Ah, you mean torch—"

"Be ready at two."

Henry listened to the hum of a dead line and rocked his head side to side, "Be ready at two," he mocked, and slammed the phone down. Henry sat in his leather armchair, sipped his coffee and turned the TV off. Why did he have to go along? What could he possibly contribute?

He stood, knocked the coffee over and didn't even notice. "It's a set-up. It's dear old Daddy's way of getting me permanently out of the way." And it was a way of preventing disclosure of Henry's secret. "Bastard," he whispered. "Bastard!" he shouted. Whatever happened to giving him the one chance they'd agreed on?

Henry walked into his bedroom, pulled open the divan drawer and reached up inside the bed frame. It was good to feel the reassurance the handgun gave him. Henry slid it into his belt, patted it and smiled. And now for the paperwork that needed attending to.

– Three –

The rain pounded mercilessly, and Christian wandered through the deserted city centre streets. Thunderclouds gathered, and the storm rolling into town from the west promised all kinds of magic and fireworks. The light had receded into a kind of opaque greyness tinged a rich ochre.

Fear tiptoed alongside, making him snatch his breath as he remembered seeing her lying on the stairs with blood all over the place. Her face stared accusingly at him, and he remembered standing there feeling guilty at what he'd done, but feeling totally vindicated at the same time. But the guilt was worse – he almost felt as though he *had* killed her.

His cold legs, to which his wet jeans clung like a second skin, brought him into Burley and the land of the Victorian terrace; back-to-back prisons that crushed families within their confines as effectively as a razor wire fence, where each window looked out onto more bricks and where gutters tipped the rainwater down the walls. His shoulder throbbed, his ear stung like a burn, and when he discarded the sodden bandage he felt the warm trickle as blood flowed again.

There were few people about, and those he saw paid him no attention. The light dimmed so much so that the street lamps came on, bathing the weeds and the rusting cars in a disgusting orange glow that saddened him further.

Old cars lined both sides of the street. They were rust-spotted, had cracked windscreens, smashed door mirrors and damaged door locks – this was the car thieves' training ground. He turned right onto a road called Turner Avenue, and was only a third of the way along it before his hand came away holding an open door. Quickly he ducked inside, heard the rain drumming on the roof and looked at the damaged ignition, hanging down into the footwell by its wires.

Church bells, three chimes, cracked into the sodden air, and then disappeared without so much as an echo.

He rifled the glovebox, looking for a screwdriver, something to stick in the ignition and get the motor going, but came out with nothing more than CDs and a can of de-icer. The ceiling lamp poured its light over him, and in the darkness outside, he stood out like a lighthouse. He pulled the diffuser away and flicked the festoon bulb out from its holder. A quick glance up and down the street told him he was still okay, and so he snapped the diffuser in two.

– Four –

The windscreen wipers grated intermittently across the screen. The hire car headed north into Leeds, and into a looming black cloud so big it was like a tidal wave in mid-air. The sunlight shrank away from it and an eerie calm fell upon the crowds they drove through.

"All I need from you is an address," he mocked. And then Henry looked across at Sirius. He could see a bulge beneath the flimsy summer jacket he wore, just in front of his left bicep. Gun? "You don't like me much, do you, Sirius?"

"I don't like you at all."

"And why's that, then?"

"Just shut it."

"Frightened I'll run and tell my dad if you upset me?"

Sirius stared forward. "Your father knows how I feel about you."

"Really?" He knew they both hated him in equal amounts; he wasn't stupid.

"Bailed you out more times than you'll ever know."

This was going to be a fun afternoon. "Where're we going?"

"We're going to get someone to help bail you out – again."

"So long as I'm keeping you amused."

"You're not keeping me amused, Henry, you're just pissing me off."

Henry smiled wide; as long as the money kept appearing in nondescript brown envelopes, Sirius would keep on bailing. Men like him were ten-a-penny. "So if all you need me for is an address, why am I here?"

"Ask Sir George."

He sneaked another glance. He had a neck that came out at the ears and blended into the cliffs of his shoulders. Henry grew worried. *Who are we going to meet? Am I going to help Sirius dig my grave? Does he do things like that? Kill people? Bet he does. Anything to keep politics running smoothly.* This made Henry edgy. As they headed for the less respectable part of town, the daylight shrank away from the dark clouds even further, and the rain came down so heavily that the wipers struggled to keep the screen clear.

Out of the side window, Henry noticed a road sign. "Burley? Why are we going to Burley, of all places?"

"We're meeting someone there."

"Who?"

Sirius smiled. "Don't know yet."

"You make no sense at all." Henry shifted in his seat. "You know this is where all the dross hangs out don't you? This is about as bad as it gets."

"Don't you ever shut up?"

"If all you needed from me was an address—"

"Shut up."

Henry did shut up. For the rest of their journey – another ten minutes spent easing the hire car through narrow streets. The rain was a muffled roar on their roof. "Are we heading somewhere in particular?" he asked, "only I think we've passed that burnt-out car before."

"We have been here before, and you need to keep quiet."

* * *

There he was. Out on his own.

Sirius glided in for a closer look. He went by a few minutes ago, and this kid was just rounding the corner onto Turner Avenue, and now he was trying his hand at vehicle recovery. He drove past the kid and stopped in the street fifty yards away and killed the engine. He reached over the seat for his GoreTex and noticed Henry looking at his chest – or more precisely, at the bulge of steel on his chest. Henry looked away. "Yes, it is."

"What?"

"A gun. A legal gun. Now stay here, and don't do anything stupid. While you're out with me, you abide by my rules – your father's words – and if I have to, I'll keep you in line by force." He did not smile.

Sirius climbed from the car, closed the door with a push rather than a slam, pulled his GoreTex on and then he crouched. The weather provided excellent cover; no noise, few people around, perfect for creeping up on some unsuspecting car thief. Sirius wasn't fussy – this kid would do; a burglar would do, a shoplifter would do, anyone really, anyone who had that look of "bad" about them.

He ran across the road, crouched behind a car and assessed his prey. Church bells announced 3pm, and Sirius never twitched.

– Five –

The diffuser snapped cleanly, leaving a sharp plastic triangle that only just fitted into the little slot in the black plastic ignition barrel. He was indeed lucky, not only was the door unlocked, but the ignition had been previously attacked and exposed. He hadn't even started the car before he was planning a drive-by of his old house. If there were no police around, he meant to retrieve some or all of his work, beginning with the woodland fairy. The thought of striding over Alice made him shudder.

After that, he'd head to Scotland, as far north as you could get, where the vidiscreens were infrequent and the friendships stronger. *And who knows,* he thought, *maybe one day I'll come back and I'll find who killed her.*

As he turned the plastic diffuser in the ignition barrel, a violet flash of lightning ripped through the air above him, electrifying it, searing it. He screamed but the shatter of thunder, a crisp cleaving of the air around him, deafened him. He stared at the sky, marvelling at the rain.

* * *

Sirius watched from three cars back. The kid was fannying about with the ignition after having successfully blinded the interior light. The driver's door was open, giving out onto the footpath, an escape for the would-be car thief if the owner happened to show up. He crept closer, could see the kid's sneakered foot and soaked jeans, could make out his damp elbow as his arm worked away at something inside the car.

Directly overhead a spear of violet lightning, followed by a clap of thunder the volume of which he had never heard before, leapt through the air, sizzling raindrops, forming wisps of steam that melted quickly away.

Closer. He was at the back of the car now, creeping silently nearer. The curtains to his right twitched and a smudged face appeared at the misted-up window. Then a hand cleared a circle and distinctive eyes peered directly at him.

Sirius put one dead straight finger in front of his lips and blew a shush at the onlooker. Whether the onlooker thought Sirius was part of the crew about to nick his car or not, he didn't know, but he banged on the window, rattled it, and he was shouting, screaming at the kid in the car.

* * *

Henry sat alone in the hire car wondering what would happen next. Was a gang of miscreants about to rip him from the car and beat him to death? What *was* going on?

Sirius was between two parked cars a little further down the street, and envy tickled Henry Deacon as he peered through the back window. Watching a man crouched like that, pursuing his prey silently in difficult conditions took Henry into a daydream of donning webbing and camouflage, shouldering his M18a and going out to hunt the enemy.

The lightning and the thunder wrenched Henry back into the car, misted-up windows preventing him seeing clearly. He started the car, switched on the AC and the rear screen demister and gently, reassuringly, patted his own gun. Just a little insurance, daddy-o.

And then he saw a little way down the hill, smoke spewed from the exhaust as a car started up.

* * *

He turned the plastic shard and the engine coughed but eventually started, registering its apparent wear by the noise from the valve train – a rattle like someone shaking a tin of nuts and bolts. At the house window, a man banged on the glass.

As Christian reached out to close the door…

* * *

…and Sirius smacked the cuffs over the kid's right wrist. The kid yelped like a girl and fell backwards into the car. Sirius growled and tried to haul the kid free, reached further in and when he did so, the kid tried to kick him off, his shouts muffled by the noise of the rain bouncing on the car's roof. Sirius yanked the cuffs, almost pulling the kid out into the wetness. Then he drew his fist back and punched at the kid's face, but he moved aside unbelievably fast, replacing his whiskered face with a piece of sharp white plastic.

The plastic sliced through the skin covering Sirius's knuckles, glided under it, up the back of his hand. And then the kid's kicking feet won their own battle, sending him back out onto the pavement screaming in agony. And furious that he was minus a prisoner, and minus a pair of cuffs. The car door slammed shut…

* * *

…and Christian crunched it into gear, and set off kangarooing down the street. He shook uncontrollably, and his mind worked fast, scattering its attention over everything. But it gathered nothing except hurriedly compiled inputs of the rain on the roof, of a man screaming at him from the gutter, of something hindering his right hand, of the squelching of water in his trainers, and the unforgiving pain in his left shoulder. A thousand things volleyed across Christian's panicking mind. His heart beat as fast as the engine rattled. Lightning flicked the sky again and made him shriek as he pulled the old Ford up into second gear.

He looked at the hindrance on his right wrist, saw the cuffs. Did that mean he'd just assaulted a copper – and you're on what, a Rule One? Yup; a Rule One today, Rule Three tomorrow. Great, oh this would look good in court. The car gained speed and Christian

221

scrabbled for the wiper switch; torrents of rain flowed down the screen and as his speed increased, the rain wavered in transparent curtains. Then he found the wipers. They didn't work. And he was driving blind, couldn't distinguish road from footpath. Christian screamed and slammed on the brakes.

– Six –

Sirius leapt to his feet, didn't even notice the steady trickle of blood falling from his clenched fist as he broke into a run back across the street to his car. He ignored the shouts coming from a man in a vest who stood on his doorstep screaming curses at him. Henry had started the car already and Sirius didn't even acknowledge him as he rammed it into reverse gear and sped down the street.

"He wasn't expecting us, then?"

Sirius turned on the rear wiper and drove backwards with his left arm over the back of his seat. "Shut up!"

"Didn't seem overly pleased to see you."

"Last warning."

"Your hand's bleeding everywhere!"

He slapped Henry hard across the face. "Now shut up."

Henry looked aghast, and wiped his cheek as though the stinging would melt away. "How fucking dare you!"

"Easy!" shouted Sirius over the scream of the engine and the roar of the rain. "And if you speak again, you'll get another."

His face reddened and very serious now, Henry glanced in the wing mirror and screamed.

The rental car smashed into the old Ford, and Sirius's right foot never went near the brake pedal. The crunch of grating metal as the old Ford ploughed into a graffiti-covered wall was loud enough to get the curtains twitching right up the street.

Sirius was out and running towards the wreck. It leaked orange water down into the gutter, but he concentrated on the driver's door, wrenching it open with his injured hand. He winced at the pain, and fury made him ram the kid's face into the steering wheel, pull it back, scream at him, and ram it again. The kid was a floppy mess, but Sirius's fury was not easily appeased.

"Kick me, would you," he rammed the head, "stab me would you, you fucker," he rammed it again. Blood splashed the windscreen and a groan fell out of the kid's mouth like the blood dripped from his nose. Still growling, Sirius grabbed a hold of the cuffs with his left hand and just pulled until the kid fell out of the car, and then dragged him through the rain, through the gutter coursing with water and litter up to the rear door of the rental. Then he let go and the kid flopped to the road like a discarded toy.

"Oi!"

The man in the string vest – now clothed in an old mac, waddled down the road in his slippers. "Henry," he opened the rear door, "help me. Drag him in, quick!"

Henry reached over his seat, gave Sirius a reproachful look for the red fingermarks on his cheek and then pulled the kid on board with the cuff; Sirius pushed from the back and then slammed the door. "Police business," he shouted to the vest, "go back inside."

"But—"

"Go back inside!"

The string vest stopped and saw the blood dripping from Sirius's fist. He turned and waddled back up the street.

– Seven –

Henry's hands shook and his face was pale as he stared fixedly through the windscreen. He didn't speak for a long time, until they had made their way through the heart of the city and out the other side, heading east, and out of the rainstorm. "Who is he?"

Sirius steered the car using his left hand only; his right was wedged into his crotch, trying to stem the flow of blood from the wound, a wound he still hadn't examined.

"Is he our appointment?"

"Any scrote would have done; suppose it's his lucky day."

"Do you know him?"

"Never seen him before. He's a tea-leaf and that's all that matters."

"Why does that matter?"

Sirius turned the windscreen wipers off. "It matters because when the police find his blood and fingerprints inside your car, they'll be able to pull his name right off the database – and nail him for your bad driving habits." He wiped the moisture from his face, using his knees to steer. "If we used someone without a police record, it would make things very snaggy because they'd have no one to pin it on, except you of course."

Henry asked, "But what happens when the police find him, when they ask him about driving the Jag and he says…" He stopped talking. Sirius was looking at him as though he was an imbecile, as though he still hadn't cottoned on to what was in store for the kid yet.

Henry peered into the back seat. The kid looked dead. His eyes had swollen, his right was black already and was the size of a small plum, and his nose was unrecognisable, just a red mess somewhere in the centre of his face. He leaked blood into the upholstery. "You sure he's up to whatever it is you have planned for him?"

"It doesn't matter; he'll be dead by the end of today once we're finished with him." He smiled at Henry.

"That's why it doesn't matter if the police find him?"

"My, you're bright, aren't you?"

"No," Henry said, "I really don't think I am."

"Well maybe you'll think twice before you—"

"Yes, yes! I know how reckless I've been without you pointing it out to me!"

"About time too." Sirius winced at the pain in his knuckles. "Right; where is this place?"

Chapter Forty-Five

Tuesday 23rd June

– One –

"Hey, slow down," she said, "plenty of time to build ourselves up, you know, the anticipation." She rubbed her hands together.

"Should be taking that statement first, really."

"Yeah," she said, sliding closer to him, as close as the seat belt and her packed utility belt would allow, "should be really, shouldn't we." She laughed then, rubbed his thigh.

"Glad you made the switch to my team."

"It wasn't easy. Anderson put the block on my transfer for over two months. Bastard. Tried to keep me on his team." And then she thought, "Hey, you don't think he knows about us and he just tried to keep us apart, do you?"

"Never mind, Launa, you're here now. Let the good times roll."

She laughed and slapped his leg. The roar of the engine blotted out the police radio. Today, Launa intended getting laid and she didn't want police business ruining it. And now that she was on Mark's team, there was a whole shit-load of laying to be done.

Great Preston called seductively. Launa grinned as he reached across, fingers walking northwards, and she slapped them away, laughing all the while.

– Two –

"Tell me where I'm going."

Henry sat forward again. He couldn't help looking back at the kid all the time. It was a shame, and he felt a tinge of guilt over the whole business. But the lad was a criminal, and his life was worth less than Henry's. It wasn't as though he had any great talent or would be a great loss to society; probably had no aspirations other than filling his veins with whatever foul substances they peddled these days. "Great Preston, near Garforth."

"That helps."

They continued east, outrunning the storm clouds, driving into intermittent sunshine diluted by white cloud. The ground was dry, the roads quick and within fifty minutes they turned onto a deserted country lane. There were a couple of tractors doing what tractors did in the fields left and right, but that was it. The place was idyllic, proper countryside, where birds made more noise than people or cars.

The tiny road got narrower the deeper into the country they went. The hedgerows grew intrusive and the corners ever more acute. Another twenty minutes passed and Henry said, "Right in about a hundred yards. You'll see an old sign that used to say Norburn Site Office."

They slowed but not enough. The junction slid past them and Henry pointed, "There."

Sirius stamped on the brakes and the kid thudded onto the floor. Sirius backed up. "I didn't see a sign."

"I suppose you have to know what you're looking for. Anyway, I think it actually now says Nob Shite Off, or something similar."

They drove between two rotten gateposts set back thirty yards from the road and flanked by tall, dense, bushes. A mix of overgrown blackthorn and dogwood swallowed up the entrance. Guelder rose twisted upwards in an effort to meet those growing downward and it scraped along the underside of the car in protest as the hawthorn scraped along the sides and roof. This went on for fifty yards, becoming increasingly dark and noisy inside the car and then finally opened out into a wider road.

"How the fuck did you come by this place?"

"Used to play around here as a kid; knew it like the back of my hand. There's an old tower over there beyond the slag heaps, and—"

"Okay, okay; it was only a simple question!"

"Forgot you hated me there for a second."

"How much farther?"

"Just keep going." The driveway was rutted with potholes you could lose a child down, but its surface was smooth, hard and dusty where the plants and creepers hadn't reclaimed it yet. Only a minute or two passed before they rounded a right-hand bend and could see up ahead on the crest of the road, the remains of an old single-storey hut at the side of the widest part of the road – wide enough to let the water bowsers turn around back in the old days. And as they drove nearer, the outline of the Jaguar grew clearer.

Sirius raised his eyebrows.

"Told you it was a good spot to hide a car." Henry smiled at his own ingenuity. "It's not a through road, you see. It ends in the old quarry about quarter a mile further on."

They rolled to the scratched Jaguar, and Sirius laughed as he turned the engine off.

Henry smiled in return, but hadn't a clue what was so funny and merely said, "What?" with a giggle running through it. "What's funny?"

"You tried to *burn* that thing, didn't you?"

"Stuffed a rag down the fuel pipe."

"You'd never get it to burn like that, you prick; it's diesel. I can smell it from here." Sirius used his left hand to open the door and then swung himself out, freeing his damp trousers from up the crack of his arse.

Henry climbed out. "What difference does that make?"

"You haven't a clue, have you? Petrol will burn if you look at it wrong. You'd need a fucking blow torch to set diesel on fire." Sirius laughed again as he inspected the car.

Henry was despondent. "What are you going to do with *him?*"

"*We* are going to sit him in the driver's seat of your fine motorcar – your fine *diesel* motor car – and then hit him. We're going to get his blood on all the controls and the seat belt buckle, then—"

"Then are we going to… you know?"

"Gee, I don't know, Henry. What do you think?"

Henry gazed through the dusty window at the crumpled bulk of a street kid lying on the floor. "If we didn't, it would be a loose end, wouldn't it?"

"You'll forgive me if I don't clap." Sirius opened the door and grasped a wet foot. "Sir George does not like loose ends." He was looking directly at Henry, and Henry nervously stepped back. "What is this secret you have over your dad, eh?"

"As a loose end, I'm not likely to share that information with my dad's private killing machine, am I?"

"I'm not a killing machine." He grunted, "Here, give me a bloody hand instead of standing there like a penis." He moved aside, granting Henry a little pulling room. "I'm his personal protection, government sponsored."

"That means you can do what the hell you like, doesn't it?"

They hauled the kid out onto the dusty road like the carcass of a dead animal; his head banged against the doorsill before it smacked the road. He only murmured slightly. "It means I help your father in times of trouble that could impact on national security. So yes, I can do whatever I like."

"Is there anything you wouldn't do if the great Sir George asked you?"

Sirius looked Henry in the eyes and whispered, "No. Remember that." Steam floated off the kid's jeans. Just another job. But one that could cost Henry everything if it went wrong. He was tempted to hang Henry out to dry, to let the police have him and bang him up on a Rule Three – shoot the bastard and get rid of him for good. And what stopped him from letting the police have him? Sir George. If Henry went down for murder, it would make things very awkward. If Henry weaselled his way free, he could imagine the public accusations of duplicity, and of unsympathetic rigidity if he didn't. And besides all that, Sirius imagined Henry would be the chatty type if subjected to a police interrogation. Bad news indeed.

No, Henry's death would happen at a time and place of their convenience away from the public gaze.

"Nothing?" Henry smiled that cock-eyed smile and then said, "Prove it."

"Look around you. I was asked to get you out of the mire, and that's what I'm doing."

"Hmph."

"Hmph?" Sirius dropped the kid's wet trouser leg and back-handed Henry.

Henry took a step back and held fingertips to his lip. There was no blood, but it throbbed. "What the fuck was that for?"

"Don't mock me." He came in close, close enough to smell the aftershave on Henry's designer stubble. "I'll use that toy gun of yours to blow your head inside out. You ever seen someone's brains dribbling down a wall?" He nodded to the bulge caused by Henry's gun, watched Henry's eyes widen at the revelation. "I'm not stupid, Henry."

"How?"

"Never mind." Sirius lifted the kid's leg. "Now let's get a move on, I've got better things to do than—"

Henry's cocky smile was back, and he clicked his fingers. "You did that old fella. The old man from Methley. It was big news, locally. Lot of speculation surrounding it."

"Don't know what you're talking about." Sirius pulled on the leg. "Now pull!"

"You did it, didn't you? You used *his* own gun and blew *his* brains all across the wall."

Sirius stopped pulling. "Mention a word to anyone and I'll give you the slowest death I can think of."

As they pulled, Henry spotted a slip of paper protruding from the kid's jeans pocket. "Wait, wait, wait," he said, and pulled it free. He unfolded it, holding the damp sheet between fingers and thumbs. "It's a bail slip." He smiled across to Sirius. "You were right, scrote through and through."

"I have a sixth sense. What's his name?"

"Christian Ledger."

"Welcome to your last day, Christian Ledger."

– Three –

Mark guided the car along a lane he had never travelled before, as Launa let her hands do the walking. "You know we'll be in a heap of shit if they find us up here? We're well outside our division."

"So?"

"How much further?"

"Just keep going, but slowly." She peered through the dusty windscreen. "There's a sign up here somewhere, it's around one of these– There it is, look. Norburn Site Office."

"That says Nob Shite Off!" Mark laughed until tears squeezed out of his eyes.

Launa laughed so hard that she thought she broke wind. That in turn led to another sharp burst of laughter so powerful that tears welled in her eyes. Just before she wet herself.

"Phwoa," he said, "country air stinks."

Launa bit down on her lip.

"How the hell did you know about this place?"

"When I was a kid I lived in the next village." And then she smiled, "Did my share of courting around here."

"That's what I like, a girl with a sense of tradition."

Branches screeched down the side of the car, and the roof lights took a pounding, but all they did was look at each other and laugh about it. Eventually the road widened, the tearing branches yielded and allowed them entry.

* * *

"Go down the lane and keep an eye out."

"Why?" asked the one called Henry.

"Because I'm a professional killing machine and I just told you to, that's why."

"But you said yourself how little—"

"Just do it! I don't take chances."

His head hurt so much that thinking was painful. He had one good eye but he dared not open it; the sunlight was strong and he just knew it would intensify the headache that throbbed with each hurried beat of his heart. Better keep it closed until he really needed it. And then there was his shoulder; he'd lain awkwardly on it while in the back of the car, and when Sirius, or whatever his name was, braked hard and he had landed on it, he nearly screamed. But fear told him to keep quiet, that playing unconscious was the right way to go.

The stinging rip in his ear still seeped blood down his neck, and sounded like ringing bells, but it was nothing compared to his nose and his face in general. That was the one that kept his chest inflated as some kind of psychological barrier against screaming out in agony. He sipped air through his split lip, past his loose teeth and thanked God he could even do that.

At first, he thought they had nicked him for Alice's murder, but as the journey from the rain-sodden centre of Leeds progressed out here, to wherever here was, where the sun was strong and the day warm, it became obvious they didn't even know about Alice. And they weren't police, either.

It only became apparent what was going on when they dragged him out of the car, and through bouts of semi-consciousness he realised they intended using him for government business. And there was something to do with a diesel car, though most of that conversation slipped by him. Yes, they were serious and no, Christian wouldn't see the sunlight tomorrow if they had their way.

"But don't you need help getting him in the Jag?"

There was a pause, and Christian heard the one called Sirius sigh loudly. "I'll manage. Now piss off and do what I say."

There were footsteps retreating, the sound of angry, stomping footsteps that kicked at the dust.

"Wanker," Sirius said.

Christian dared open his eye a little. Sirius stood with his back to him, peering in through the window of some dark car a few yards away. Steam floated from his back as though demons were crawling over him. It was satisfying to see blood encrusted across the back of his right hand.

While Sirius opened the driver's door, Christian checked his arsenal: it was still tucked neatly in his jeans pocket, the little shard of razor-sharp plastic he had used to start the old Ford, and had used to disable his attacker's right hand.

And then Sirius was back, mumbling about Henry. He grabbed a foot and Christian scraped along the gravel, arms trailing behind the rest of his limp body. His shirt rode up his back, and the grit tore into his bare skin and through his hair where it gnawed at his scalp. The tiniest flicker of hope crept into Christian's mind. *They're going to sit me inside a car, aren't they? They're going to make me touch everything, bleed on everything; what if that car has keys in the ignition? What if it'll start, what if I can drive–*

Sirius stopped dragging Christian, and shouted, "What?"

Henry shouted something from down the road, sounded like "Nepalese are humming".

"Fuck! Fuck!" Sirius growled, and then he shouted back, "Get off the road."

And now he was being pulled around, dragged back to the car they had just removed him from. Sirius grunted and cursed, hissing, probably at the pain in his hand. And then his feet were in the shade of the car again and Sirius let go. Christian snapped his eye open and wondered if now was the right time to run, while they were panicking over something. But then Sirius grabbed his foot again – from inside the car this time – and heaved him back up inside and slammed the doors.

And that was the end of that escape plan. He vowed the next time, if there was a next time, he wouldn't think about it, he'd just do it. And then it hit him. *Nepalese are humming.* No, Henry had shouted *the police are coming!* He was in the company of others who were running from the law.

The car dipped and the driver's door slammed. Sirius was careful not to spin the wheels as he set off; careful, even with the police approaching, not to leave a clue that they were there.

Clever, Christian thought.

* * *

"Anywhere here," she said, already undoing her seat belt and turning the radio off.

They travelled slowly another fifty or sixty yards up the lane to where it bent around to the right. Falling stones caught Mark's eye. They tumbled down the steep banking to his right, and he watched them roll, wondering what caused them to fall in the first place. "Bet there are foxes and all sorts of wildlife round here."

"You wouldn't know wildlife if it dropped its knickers for you."

"Hey, what's that up there?" He pointed through the screen, and Launa's eyes followed to what appeared to be a small hut. "Maybe we should go take a look."

"Do we have to? It's the old site office that's all, nothing special. Nothing that we need interrupt our—"

"Just a quick peek to satisfy my curiosity."

"What about satisfying me?"

"Won't take long."

"You men are all the same," she yelled, "always playing cops and pissing robbers."

"Might as well go all the way, Launa."

She folded her arms, "Chance'd be a fine thing!"

* * *

Henry walked dejectedly from the Jag, kicking dust up with his feet. He heard Sirius call him a wanker, but couldn't be bothered to reply. Being lookout was hardly SAS action was it? He wanted the excitement of punching the kid in the face until he was a sloppy mess – and then he thought better of it; getting blood all over his clothes wasn't a top idea. Let Sirius do it.

Up ahead, the lane bent around to the left. Steep banks on both sides had sprouted clumps of ugly grass and weeds and bushes. And the remnants of old wooden fencing that had bleached white over the years, grown old and rotten, leaned and collapsed intermittently.

And how was I supposed to know that diesel doesn't burn? They never tell you that when you're in the showroom buying the damned thing, do they. "Oh yes, it's a fine model, but if you ever intend setting it on fire, then may I recommend the petrol version…"

As he walked, he glanced back over his shoulder and saw Sirius peering into the Jag, the driver's door open, the kid lying out on the road as though he was dead. Henry chose his spot another hundred yards farther down, sat on the incline and took out his gun. He thought about his father, and how he'd surprisingly stuck to his side of the bargain, and what it would cost him in the long run. When all this was over, George Deacon wouldn't leave himself open to further blackmail, that was for sure.

Henry returned to thinking through his plans of protecting himself should Daddy turn nasty in future; how he could store the secret and make the old man think twice before killing him.

Wait, was that a car engine he could hear? He stood, strode further down the lane and listened again, shielding his eyes from the sun as he peered towards the entrance, maybe 200 yards away.

It was! It was a car, and it was coming up here! And when he caught a glimpse of the bank of blue lights across the roof, Henry was concreted to the ground. "Never in a million fucking years," he whispered. He didn't know what to do, didn't know whether to run towards them and stop their advance, or run away and get to Sirius before they rounded the corner. Shit, shit! He turned, thrust the gun back inside his jacket, ran like hell back around the bend and up the hill, shouting, waving his arms. "The police are coming!"

Sirius looked up from the kid he was dragging. "What?"

"The police are coming!"

"Get off the road. Get up the embankment!"

"Shit, shit, wank!" Henry looked around at the embankments, at how steep they were, how loose their top coverings appeared. He heard the engine behind him, saw Sirius struggling with the youth, and darted to his right, making no particular appraisal, just getting the hell off the road. He scrambled up the bank, pulling at weeds, digging his feet in, yanking breath in by the boatload. Eventually he made it to the summit, through the broken fence, threw himself down flat on his belly, SAS style, and peered back down into the valley of death, panting furiously.

The little bare old lane that *nothing ever travelled up* stared back at him, and then a police car, doing four or five miles an hour, crawled past, window down, eyes inside peering at the earth that tumbled down the bank from Henry's hurried climb. It didn't stop though, just carried on crawling up the lane.

Chapter Forty-Six

Tuesday 23rd June

– One –

Henry saw Sirius drive the rental car past the hut and out of sight. And he drove slowly too, probably to keep the dust down; something Henry's own escape hadn't succeeded in doing. The stones and the dust cloud still rolled and still plumed.

Sweat ran into Henry's eyes and then he noticed how badly his hands shook and how dry his mouth was.

On his belly, he slithered away from the edge, part way down the far side of the embankment and away from the lane. When he could no longer see the embankment opposite, he stood and trotted at a slight crouch up the man-made valley of a slag heap towards his Jaguar and the old site office.

When he got there, he settled and took a minute to slow his breathing, to catch his thoughts, and that was about the time that the enormity of his bad luck struck him. "All the time this lane has been abandoned," he said, "all the time no one ever came up here, even back in the old days, and now this! *Fucking* plod!" It seemed too coincidental, though. Had they been set up? Had someone grassed on them to the police?

He leaned back into the banking, hand on his thumping chest. An hour, that's all it would have taken for them to plant the kid's evidence and get the hell out of here. Why now?

Henry crawled carefully to the crest of the bank, peered between two head-sized rocks and gazed down into the lane below. And what he saw made him gasp.

– Two –

Sirius drove smoothly past the hut and didn't stop looking in the rear-view mirror until the hut and the old lane next to it had vanished around a corner and over the brow of a hill. He visibly relaxed and then pressed the accelerator a little harder.

Three bad things had happened. One: they hadn't planted the evidence yet. Two: Henry was out there alone; and three: the police were here.

Problem three nullified problem one; the police were here, forget planting the evidence; but problem two remained outstanding, aching like his knuckles. He had to get to Henry before Henry did something stupid and got them all caught.

Through the dusty screen, he could see the massive opencast coal mine, probably many hundreds of feet deep and with an incline steeper than Everest's North Face. Nothing that went down there would come back up again, that was for sure. Over the far side of the hole, he could see a road of some kind, a ledge maybe, a pale grey ribbon that corkscrewed its way from top to bottom – but it was half a mile away, maybe a mile.

He turned the car around, facing it back uphill, and parked behind a massive grey outcrop, bald of any vegetation and still bearing the scars of the machine that originally cut it. And then he turned off the engine, listened to the breeze blowing up from the abandoned mine, spinning eddies out of loose dust and throwing them at the car. He turned in his seat, looked down at the kid who lay motionless and blood-caked on the back seat. He breathed still, but only just. Was he unconscious, or faking it? Sirius leaned over and nudged the kid's arm. Nothing. He stretched further and delivered a weak punch, into the kid's chest. Nothing at all.

Good. Now he could take care of problem two in the hope that if the police left again after requesting recovery of the Jaguar, he could still use the kid as he first intended. If the police stayed around until the Jaguar was recovered, the kid would take a dive over the precipice.

He climbed from the car, slammed the door and began walking away. Then he stopped, returned to the car and took the keys out of the ignition. He locked the door and went looking for Henry.

– Three –

Christian felt them drive uphill. The car stopped again and the engine died. He lay motionless and wondered what Sirius would do next. He would go and look for the fat one, Henry. Of course, you would want to know if your captive was faking his unconsciousness, and how would you do that?

Christian tensed his whole body and waited, expecting some kind of slap. And then he heard Sirius turn in his seat, heard the fabric brush against fabric, and then felt the cold eyes of a killer scrutinising him. And now nothing short of his life depended on him being a good actor.

The nudge came as expected, and Christian let his mind float out of harm's way, releasing the tether it had to his body; he would catch up with whatever happened now a little later. And then he heard the seat creak and felt the punch in the chest. It almost succeeded in bringing him back into his body, but he fought it, kept away and satisfied Sirius. The car door slammed and Christian breathed out. He was about to open his eye when the door opened again!

The keys jangled and the door slammed and locked again. This time he opened his eye quickly, and saw Sirius's bulk heading uphill towards the Jaguar and Henry. He counted to thirty, plenty of time for Sirius to be out of earshot, before he began moving about.

He expected the pain, but he never expected it in quite such a pure quality. Dazzling white lights seared his brain and something like an electric shock jolted his damaged shoulder. Together they made him breathless – but he fought it, wouldn't be set free by Sirius only to be tortured by his own body.

Everything spun around his mind like a whirlwind of litter on a street. He had to get out of the car, or he had to be able to drive out in the car. Both meant he had to get the ignition on, since nothing electrical worked without it, including the windows and the central locking.

But there was something he could try first. He looked at the front and rear side windows, determined the fronts were larger and so should break easier. He lay across the front seats, took aim with his feet and kicked. And kicked. And kicked. It rippled – the light shimmered as the glass contorted – but it remained defiantly intact; the only change was the new pain in his feet and the bruised ribs from the handbrake lever. He forced the car into first gear and gently took the handbrake off. The car rocked but stayed steady. He tried again, and put more force into his kicks than he had before, but the glass still didn't break. Sweat flicked from his hair with each kick, and it didn't take long for him to gasp like an old man.

The rental car was a base model Ford D-Max, and there was no boot release lever by the driver's seat, so no chance of climbing through the folding rear seats and to freedom that way. His only remaining option was to smash the cowling away and try to get the ignition on – at least then, the windows would work, even if he couldn't open the doors because of the deadlock. He kicked at the cowling, and immediately a split appeared in the flimsy black plastic. One more kick and the cowling cracked wide open, and Christian pulled at the thing until it broke away in his hand. There, up underneath, was the black plastic ignition barrel.

– Four –

Mark looked around the hut, amazed by the smell in there, of old turds and rotting animals, food perhaps for the fox he had almost seen. But the weeds that grew through the disintegrating floor were astounding; huge, rampant. What a good word. He turned around and looked back at the patrol car. Rampant: that's what Launa was. The old building was derelict, but the Jaguar, well that was only a year or so old; smart green, like British racing green but slightly lighter, metallic. Scratched to buggery now, though. All its windows were darkened, adding to the mystery.

He sighed, dreamed of being able to afford such a car, dreamed of being able to afford the insurance! Christ, what a beast, "V8, five-litre turbo injection."

Launa spoke the location into her mic; she flicked a switch, putting the radio on to loudspeaker mode. "Okay, Charlie Alfa Six, recovery authorised. Should be 10-6 in thirty minutes, over."

"10-20."

"Charlie Alfa Six?"

"Go ahead."

"Charlie Alfa Six, be aware there's a 'preserve for prints' marker against that vehicle, believe involved in fatal 10-11, over."

"Yeah, 10-20." Launa looked at Mark, who wandered slowly towards her, a wicked grin on his face. "XW, can you pass keeper details again please?"

"Charlie Alfa Six; registered keeper is a company: Smyth, Price and Deacon. Insurance affirmed, belonging to that company, over."

"10-20. Can you confirm primary user status, over?"

"Charlie Alfa Six, primary user is Deacon, Henry, born 16.1.1978."

Launa's eyes stared off into the distance. Henry Deacon. *The* Henry Deacon, MP's son and would-be SAS operative. Christ how the memories came back; she rubbed her cheek. "10-20, thanks."

Mark leaned in. "What's up?"

"Memories. It belongs to Henry Deacon," she nodded at the car, "son of the great Sir George Deacon."

"Lucky bastard. He'll be pleased to have it back."

She nodded, "I'm sure he will be, but it has to be CSIed first." She looked at him. "It was involved in a fatal knockdown about three weeks ago."

"They won't get anything off it after three weeks."

In the back of her mind was Henry Deacon's face, how it turned from handsome and placid one minute to snarl and bastard the next, about the time she declined sex that night. He'd punched her and knocked her out. She looked down; it happened right about here, strangely enough. She hoped she would be the one to tell Mr Deacon that the police had found his car, but she knew it would fall to CID with it being a big job.

But then something else struck her: how the hell would they explain being this far out of division?

* * *

Henry stared over the edge and even as Sirius approached in a crouching run that would have been comical had they not been so far up Shit Creek, he couldn't take his eyes off her. He was sure it was her: Launa Wrigglesworth. My, had she changed. In all the right places.

"Have they called for recovery?"

Henry turned to Sirius. "That's my old girlfriend down there," he pointed, "the copper."

"Not the time, Henry. Now, have they—"

"Yes, yes!"

"Shush, you tit, you want to get us arrested?"

Henry looked up at Sirius. "How the fuck are we going to get out of this, now?"

"You said no one ever came here!"

* * *

Twenty minutes floated by. Henry daydreamed about Launa and intermittently thought of the Jaguar. Sirius thought about the Jaguar and intermittently about the kid and disposing of him as soon as he got back to his car – no need to keep dead trash. He dwelled on Henry's problem, getting to the car before CSI did.

Both were pulled from their thoughts as a large lorry, with whole branches of hawthorn sticking out of the roof lights and the bent mirrors, drove up to the police car, turned outside the hut and reversed towards the Jaguar.

Sirius climbed down the far side of the embankment, standing straight at last, and walked back the way he came. Henry shuffled along by his side, sulking. "Don't ponder on irony, it'll drive you nuts." Only minutes passed before they heard the truck revving hard, and then a plume of smoke belched into the air as the driver set off again, down towards the entrance, followed no doubt by Henry's ex-girl.

* * *

The shard protruded from the ignition barrel and the lights glowed red at him. But Christian was lost in thought. *What's wrong with you? Sirius will be back any moment and you can expect a real beating before they finally kill you.*

He shifted quickly, looking for the window switches and then stopped. The car was rocking as though someone outside was gently pushing it from side to side. He cocked his head and listened but heard nothing except a strange crunching.

Christian sat up and looked out of the window. The car was indeed rocking, and the crunching was coming from the wheels as they turned on the gravelly surface. The rocking was caused by undulations as the car picked up speed going backwards, downhill. The ignition light glowed and in the rear-view mirror loomed a hole in the earth as large as the Grand Canyon.

* * *

"That was the only plan I had to get you off the hook."
"What about the kid?"

"We don't need him anymore."

"Can't we follow the car to the garage and—"

"They have security on, never get him in there, and no, we couldn't get the car out either."

They walked west, occasionally seeing the bowed roof of the old hut thirty yards below through breaks in the embankment's edge. They walked over the crest of the hill and down the gentle incline at the end of the embankment, a strong breeze blowing into their faces.

Up ahead, no more than an hour away, was the dark cloud they had outrun from Leeds. It was heading their way and below it was a band of rain that looked like a shredded grey valance.

Without warning Sirius started sprinting downhill.

Henry looked perplexed and followed at a more leisurely pace.

Sirius was in time to see his rental car fall backwards off the cliff, a very alive, very awake and very scared kid peering through the windscreen at him, one hand reaching out as though hoping for redemption. He didn't know why, but Sirius raised his arm too, and watched as the nose of his car disappeared over the edge.

Henry stopped at his side. "Please tell me I did not see what I—"

There was a scraping of metal, then a thud, more scraping of metal and breaking glass, and then a faint pop. They looked at each other. "I *did* see what I thought I saw, didn't I?"

Sirius walked towards the edge.

"I am so sick of fucking walking from here back into town! It took me an hour and a half just to get back to something resembling civilisation, and then a taxi home!"

"Shut up, Henry."

There wasn't an edge as such, but there was a steep gradient and he wondered how fast the car would have been travelling as the gradient turned more vertical than horizontal. He couldn't see the result of that speed, couldn't get close enough. A blanket of dust and some shiny part of the car blew briefly into view, then nothing.

"How far down is it?"

"How should I know?"

"Do you think he's dead?"

He turned. "I am not a fucking psychic, Henry."

"But we need to be certain, don't we; can't have—"

Then a sound came from down the empty quarry that shut them both up. The car erupted in a whoosh that made the air ripple, and close behind it was a mushroom of smoke. They looked at each other again.

"He *was* inside it, wasn't he?"

"Yep."

"Glad it wasn't a diesel car. He's toast. Let's go."

Chapter Forty-Seven

Tuesday 23rd June

The sound of gravel and quarry dirt grinding under the tyres stopped. The car was airborne. There was something approached serenity. Air whistled past the car with the odd tink as grit from the spinning tyres hit the inner wings. Christian whimpered.

For an eternity, Christian saw nothing but blue-grey sky. He felt pressure against his back as the car tilted from horizontal towards vertical. And then there was a shocking bang as it caught an outcrop; the view through the windscreen changed considerably then. The sky disappeared, and the grey subsoil of quarry loomed large. Christian landed against the ceiling of the car as it went into a flip. Papers and coins hit the ceiling around him.

Christian was going to die soon.

In the eeriness of the falling car, things changed again. All the papers, the maps, the pens and coins, fell against the windscreen. Christian fell onto the steering wheel and dashboard. He screamed, his shoulder smacked the dash and his cuffed wrist punched the screen as the car hit the haul road head-on.

In a microsecond, the two airbags deployed and Christian thought he'd been shot. The explosive charges that set the airbags off deafened him and punched him on the ribs and the knees. Surely death would snatch him now.

The car teetered on its crushed nose for a moment and then toppled onto its roof. Christian hit the ceiling again, hard, and the side windows buckled and blew out. Cold air streamed in along with dust and fragments of toughened glass that made him screw his good eye shut and hold his breath.

Christian expected to see Sirius and the fat one, Henry, standing there with the wind whipping their fancy suits around their legs, smiling, pointing a gun into the car.

There was nothing. Just the eddies being tossed about by the wind.

All his senses reported back: there was mild pain in his left knee, massive pain in his left shoulder and arm, more blood trickling into his ear, an ache in his head like someone had mistaken it for an anvil. And a strange smell.

Petrol.

Cubes of shattered glass stuck to his hands and knees as he crawled out from the wreck. And as he did so, he looked up and saw the summit forty or fifty feet above him. "Thank you," he said to whoever had pulled the strings. When finally he stood on shaking legs at the side of the car and looked around at his prison cell he cursed.

The first few drops of rain patted his head. "Bollocks."

Chapter Forty-Eight

Tuesday 23rd June

– One –

The rain flowed down his face as he looked up at her. She held him.

The tears subsided, and the sobs came less often. He looked at the Styrofoam cup brigade in the doorway but eventually they lost interest and ambled back inside for the resumption of their weekly fix.

"He spoke to you, didn't he?"

Eddie ignored the question.

He felt invaded, he felt dirty; as though his inner thoughts had been plundered by a mind rapist. And now, instead of grief being the prevalent force inside him, anger took over and made him stand.

Jilly caught hold of his arms, "Answer me."

"That fucker is reading minds."

She let go. "Right," she whispered.

"Come with me." Eddie clutched Jilly's arm and walked her inside the Memorial Hall. Two pairs of wet footprints followed them over the parquet floor and stopped at the freak's desk. "Excuse me, do you mind?" Eddie pulled the freak's new customer out of the chair and asked her to, "Leave us alone for a moment, please." The woman protested, but Eddie stamped on her words like damp confetti into coarse asphalt. "Would you jump in my grave that quick? I haven't finished here, now give me some space!"

She shuffled away to her coffee-sipping cronies in the corner and shared disconsolate words and reproachful looks.

"Eddie," the freak began.

"Don't fucking *Eddie* me," he sat, "I want to know where you got your information about Sam."

The freak looked up at Jilly, smiled almost apologetically in recognition.

Eddie nodded. "So you two know each other, eh?"

"I now know that you and Jilly are Sam's parents."

"*Were* Sam's parents. And you've been pumping her for info, haven't you? And when dear old Daddy walked in like some schmuck, you gave it right back through both barrels."

244

"Eddie," Jilly said.

"But I didn't know then that you were Sam's father."

Eddie stared. Blinked.

"Did I?"

"Eddie," repeated Jilly.

"Shut up." Eddie stood, looked down at the freak. "Now I'll give you one last chance to tell me where you dug all this shit up from and then I'm gonna make your face look like melted plastic."

"Eddie!" Jilly shouted.

"He read it somewhere!"

"I did no such thing."

"Then you're a mind reader."

"I beg your pardon." The freak stood.

"Please, Eddie—"

"Sir," said a voice accompanied by footfalls in the silence, "may I ask you to leave?"

"Shut it before I nail you to the fucking floor!"

The footsteps ceased and the voice mumbled something about calling the police.

Eddie took hold of the freak's shirt collar and marched him backwards, and all the while Jilly was screaming for Eddie to let him be. Eddie slammed him into the wall, fist under his neck, eyes inches from eyes. "This is the last time I lower myself to your level; now you tell me and my wife where you got that shit from."

The freak's eyes flitted around the room, pleading for help, and when Eddie jerked his crumpled collar, they stopped dead, pointing right at Eddie. "What can I say, I didn't make it up, I'm not an impostor. Please, I'm sincere. You have to believe me."

"Eddie, let him go, babe."

Eddies eyes sprang wide. When was the last time she'd called him *babe*? Must be eight months ago. And her voice had lost its glass-shattering quality. She was calm, serene. Eddie's grip relaxed slightly.

"I didn't read your mind, Eddie."

"Don't call me Eddie. I'm Eddie to my friends."

"I swear to you, I'm genuine."

Eddie laughed. "Genuine, my arse. No such thing." He let the freak go, flexed his fingers and thought hard about punching the bastard. But what would it earn him apart from a night in the cells and an eternal cold shoulder from Jilly. "You stay the fuck away from my wife. You hear?"

The freak looked from Eddie to Jilly and back again, confused.

"Come on, Eddie." Jilly put her hand on his shoulder and he turned, head up, chin out.

"Eddie?"

Eddie stopped in his tracks. Jilly looked over her shoulder at the brave freak.

"Do you know a man called Stuart?"

Eddie said nothing.

"Watch your back around him. He's stuck-up, and he's out to get you."

– Two –

In silence they walked through the rain. They were only a minute from Jilly's front door; maybe the need for talk had arrived, and it was Jilly whose need was greatest.

"What did he mean by that?"

Eddie shrugged, still trying to swallow both episodes of that particular soap opera.

"Do you know a Stuart?"

"Yes. I have to take my hat off to the guy, he was spot on; Stuart is after my blood." He looked across at her through the rain. "Spooky, really. That's my nickname for him: Stuck-up Stuart. Don't you find that a bit… unsettling?"

"I find a lot of things unsettling." Jilly took her keys out, "Coffee?"

Eddie dithered. He'd had a day right from the anus of life, and he wasn't so sure he could handle the splashback. All the games she played these days were going to be too much, despite the whole point of tonight's encounter was to get her back on side. "I think I'll pass, if you don't mind."

"Well, I do mind. Come and get dry."

* * *

She threw the towel at him and then put a steaming mug on the floor by his chair.

"Go on," he said. "Ask it."

"Okay, I will."

"It's why you insisted I came in, isn't it?"

"Partly." Jilly sat, kicked off her wet shoes and took a breath. "What did he say to you?"

"There. Wasn't so hard, was it? You could have asked that right away and saved yourself a cup of coffee."

"My, aren't we feeling sorry for ourselves?" She smiled. Barely.

"I'm having a fucking ball, Jilly."

"So just tell me."

"It's the same shit he told you before, about how Sam still loves me and how he forgives me."

"But you went mad; you were white as a sheet when you came out the first time."

"Sorry," he said, "didn't know it was illegal to feel like that."

"Like what?"

"Like my guts had been on a spin cycle."

"You're so flippant. Why can't you just open up? Why can't you just admit that you got a message, tell me what it was and stop acting like a tough macho idiot."

"I'm not—"

"You are. There are some things even your scientific mind can't rationalise. There are some things that we cannot understand. Try to open up your mind to the things that haven't been explained yet." She watched him, sitting there like a petulant kid, sipping his coffee, clenched up, not letting anything out. "I bet a hundred years ago, if you'd said to a scientist you could catch a criminal by analysing a single hair from his head, he would have laughed you out of the building. Some things just aren't explainable yet."

Eddie rocked his head. "Really."

"Now what did he say?"

His eyes fell away from her as he whispered, "He said Sam thought the altar I made was wonderful. He said he forgave me. Happy now?"

"Oh, baby," she said. "What altar?"

"It was a mind-fuck."

"What altar?"

"His NY cap. That's all. I keep it on the mantel."

"That's nice."

"Nice? It had my son's head inside it, woman! And that's it: nice?"

"I mean I think it's good that…"

"I'd best be going. Thanks for the drink."

"Wait."

He braced himself. Tonight was a stupid idea.

"Don't go."

"Why?"

"I think you need me."

"What?"

"Okay, okay. I think we need each other."

He tried a fake laugh of exasperation. It sounded like a regular sigh. "I've been living in a flat that's one step down from a squat for months, and you finally decide we need each other? I needed you months ago, and I told you that. And now I've had some kind of miraculous contact with my dead boy we can give it another go? Is that all you were waiting for, for me to get in touch with my inner feelings?"

"Eddie, I don't know what—"

"That's it! Now I've shown my caring side by signing up to Freaks Inc—"

"Who?"

"You've decided we can all be one happy family again. We can go down to the Memorial Hall once a week and meet up with Sam and have a good old laugh at the times we enjoyed watching him play football and the birthday parties we threw for him. Gee, that'd be great!"

"You're in shock."

"Damned right I am! And what about my drinking? Is that suddenly alright?"

"Well, I would have—"

"Like fuck." Eddie stood. "You've now decided it's worth another go, this relationship of ours."

"I thought it was what you always wanted."

"It was!"

"Then what's the problem?"

"The problem is your timing's lousy. All this time I've wanted to be back here, and now I've dared to expose these people as charlatans, everything's fine again! I've been drinking this whole time, I've travelled to the bottom of bottle after fucking bottle, trying to pickle myself so I don't have to stand the agony any longer, and now it's all okay and I can curl up next to you in bed tonight. Jesus, Jilly, your motives are shallower than a teaspoon."

Jilly stood, the tendons in her neck bulging. "I want you back, you arsehole, because you gave it a *try*. I never thought you would, I always thought you'd be the stubborn idiot I kicked out, but you're not." She swallowed, and calmed slightly. "I know you don't believe anything he said tonight, and that's fine, and I know you're still a drunken pisshead – not fine – but I do know you're trying. And I know you tried for *me*. And that's the important thing."

"So you'd have me back on a whim."

"You had some kind of contact tonight. I know it because you were shitting yourself when I bumped into you. And whether you admit it, doesn't matter. I *know* Sam spoke to you."

"This is two-faced, Jilly. I can't stand my life where I sit all evening in a rotting green chair and watch a portable TV with a glass of brandy in my hand and a death wish in my mind – but at least I know where I stand. I don't like it, but it's flat, even ground, the kind you're never going to trip up over, no matter how pissed you get. But," he looked around, "I'm not sure I can give up on that for a life with you on a mountain side. One wrong move and I'm back on the floor.

"This doesn't make sense to me," he said. "You hate me for killing Sam, you hate me for drinking, you hate me smoking too much. Jilly, you *hate* me. I kind of got used to begging, but I don't want it if it means setting up a standing order to those fucking freaks back there." He shook his head, looked earnestly at her. "Why would you want me back?"

"You're an arsehole, Eddie. Let's just get that straight."

"Loud and clear."

"But I can see that you're trying to be good again. I can see it now." She brought her palms together, shoulders forward. And her eyes said, *bear with me on this one*. "And I don't hate you. And you can't say I hate you for killing Sam—"

"You've said it often enough."

She sighed. "I have, I know. I was wrong, I suppose."

"Oh, you *suppose* you were wrong."

"Just shut up and let me finish, dammit!"

"Sorry."

"I lost my son," she began. "I had to have someone to blame; can't you see that? I don't know who ran him over, but I figured if you'd been on time..." she shrugged. "I blamed you. Past tense."

Eddie retook his seat, folded his arms defiantly. Headway demanded a hard stance. "And the drinking?"

"I want you to stop. Am I wrong for that? If for no other reason than it'll stop you killing yourself. And I don't want you to kill yourself. I'm not angry with you anymore, Eddie." Jilly flopped back into her seat. "That's why I want you back." Her big eyes never strayed from his.

He searched her face for traces of the hatred he thought she still had for him. And a pang of homesickness, the kind of sweet nostalgic pain that grips your heart and tweaks it, blundered back into his mind like an old friend falling through a door with a six-pack under his arm and a silly grin on his face. It was good to be back.

Eddie almost allowed himself to begin feeling at home again, to take off his coat, kick off his shoes and lie on the settee with his arm behind his head flicking through the channels. Like he would in the old days.

In the old days.

The days when nothing mattered. When Sam was out back playing on his swing and Jilly was out playing bingo or trimming the plants in the rockery.

How strange things can get. You wish so hard for something that you can't quite believe your damned luck when it lands, plop, in your lap as though all you had to do was say please. And when finally your wish comes true, you can't help but treat it with suspicion. After all, how many wishes do you make in thirty years, and how many of the damned things ever come true? So when one does, your eyes slit up, you take a deep breath, and you poke it once or twice, making sure your worst nightmare isn't rolled up cunningly inside.

It was this suspicion that caught Eddie as squarely as a pike on a barb. Two things had happened, like something out of a reverse psychology game show. Both had changed perspectives. She wanted him back. And he didn't trust it; it came too easily. It would have been much easier to close the door behind him and head home to the empty flat in Wakefield city centre, safe in the knowledge that the only pain he would ever feel again came entirely from himself.

Hey, think it over. Surely the offer will still be on the table this time next week. Call it a cooling-off period where either party can change their mind without recourse to legal action. And then, call it a safety net. If she blows hot and cold like this, you don't want it to blow hot when you bailed out of your shitty slum with nowhere to go except the back seat of your car.

"Mind if I think about it?" He looked at her through the tops of his eyes, face downwards, voice quiet, tentative.

She covered her shock well, hiding the embarrassment she obviously felt with an endearing smile. "Sure. But why? I thought you'd snap my hand off."

"It's the mountain thing."

She only nodded, didn't try to hide the hurt this time.

"Tell you what, Jilly. Let's give it a couple of days, and if you still feel the same, I'll bring my toothbrush and all my crap over. What do you say?"

"Yeah, whatever," she puffed the words out through thin lips.

Ten minutes later, Eddie was on his way home with a glowing feeling in his chest and a proud, victorious smile on his lips. He reminded himself how good – and rare – it was to have a wish granted.

Chapter Forty-Nine

Tuesday 23rd June

"You must be mad."

Mick's words took away that feeling in his chest. "It was you who suggested I go—"

"Whoa there just one minute. Don't you dare blame me—"

"Who's *blaming* anyone? It's a good deal, I'm getting back with her, I'm going back home and I can't believe you're not happy about it."

"Hmph."

Of course Mick wasn't happy about it. Eddie could live without the debauched language, the binge-drinking and the sloppy behaviour once he was back home. But Mick would find it difficult. "We could still go down to the pub. It's not as though we have to stop drinking together."

Mick's face said, *Yeah, right. Prick.* "Don't forget how you managed to change your luck. You found Sam. You now share a common theme again."

"No, we don't. I told her we wouldn't be relying—"

"And she believed you?"

"Yes."

"And you believed her when she said that?"

He paused. "Yeah."

"I repeat my earlier response: hmph."

"I could come over to your place, maybe; drink with you there."

"We'll see." Mick didn't look up.

"I've never been to your gaff."

"You're not missing much."

Eddie drank the brandy, stubbed out his cigarette and stared at the dejection that tumbled from Mick like hail from a winter sky. "You're really naffed about this, aren't you?"

"Bet you forgot to tell her you might be heading for the sack, and possibly a Rule One."

It was true, he had forgotten. Genuinely. She would be mortified when she found out. But it was the way Mick said it, as though he was jealous.

The night had crept up on them; the window was dark now, only the subdued light from the snooker hall showed itself, that and the orange glow from outside. Every time a bus passed, light from its upper deck swept briefly across the wall behind Eddie. In here, it was warm, homely. It also stank like the threshold between the bar and toilets in an old geezers' pub. But it was safe.

"How's the investigation going?"

Mick lit a cigarette and looked at Eddie through the rising smoke. "Okay, I suppose."

"What's wrong with you? You've got a face like a bashed crab."

"It'll never be the same, you know."

"What won't?"

"Being together again after a while apart. Things'll feel strained, you know, as though you have to make polite conversation instead of just letting a rasper echo around the room. You'll feel false and you'll try to conjure that old you again, but you'll fail and all you'll find instead is a plastic you with the real you inside begging to be free again. Because you've changed, Eddie; your boundaries have widened and you'll feel trapped."

"Christ, you're cheerful tonight." Eddie wondered who Mick was talking about: him and Jilly, or him and Mick? "Thanks for that."

"Pleasure." Mick looked away.

"Hey, look; either put a smile back on your face or piss off home."

Mick stood.

"Lighten up, I was only kidding."

Mick made it to the door, even opened it before Eddie said, "Don't you want to know the post-mortem results?"

Mick stopped, hand on the door.

"Got them right here. Interesting reading."

"You bastard."

"I know."

Mick closed the door, filled the Mick-sized indentation in his chair and lit a cigarette. "Those things I said about getting back with Jilly…"

"I'm listening."

"I never thought you'd actually do it. I hoped you would, I just never thought you'd have the balls."

"More brandy?"

"Lots more."

Eddie half-filled their glasses and raised his to Mick. "You are a dear friend of mine," he said, "even though all you want me for is information—"

"Hey, that's—"

"Below the belt? Anyway," he said, "it might not work out yet. I'm keeping this place just in case it goes tits up."

"Odds?"

"In favour of me being back here within a week."

"You think so?" Mick sat forward.

"You ever tasted the grass on the other side of the fence and realised it was just as shitty as your old stuff?"

Mick laughed.

"I got a sneak preview this afternoon. I think she'll be disappointed."

Solemnly, Mick nodded. "Where's the PM results?"

"You're all heart."

"I know."

Eddie pulled a sheet of paper from his pocket, unfolded it, smoothed out the creases and passed it across to Mick.

Mick almost danced as he took it, but his happiness faded quickly. "Thanks," he said absently. "I don't understand all the numbers and the bloody Latin." He looked at Eddie.

"Basically, they're all normal. Go straight to conclusions, turn over."

Mick did. "Ah, now I see. He wasn't drunk, had no other drugs in his body other than non-steroidal drugs for rheumatism. Had very early signs of heart disease – but he was seventy-eight, to be expected." Mick looked up again. "All other organs were normal; he was a fit old bird really."

"Until his brain fell out."

"There was light ante-mortem bruising to his shoulders and upper back, also some to his lower arms."

"Could have been a struggle in the chair he was sitting in," Eddie shrugged, "Not too sure though, could be a thousand other things."

"It's the sample list I'm interested in."

"I can guess which bit."

"Nail scrapings."

"They're not in yet," Eddie said. "Definitely some foreign tissue under his nails, but we've no idea who it came from. They're being rushed through the processing right now."

Andrew Barrett

Chapter Fifty

Wednesday 24th June

– One –

Eddie turned off the engine, let the wipers skitter to a stop on the sodden windscreen and sat there watching the car park of Morley Police Station dissolve into a blur of nothingness. He reached for the glove compartment, stalling before he even opened the catch. "No," he said, "leave it."

There was a strong cup of coffee steaming on his desk as he threw his coat over his chair. "Thanks," he said to whoever had made it. He expected Ros to peek around the storeroom door and say, "It's okay. Morning."

"My pleasure." Stuart walked tall out of Jeffery's office, teeth glowing as though he'd gargled with Dulux gloss white only moments before. His tongue was still brown though, noted Eddie.

Eddie moved the drink aside and sat down.

"It's not poisoned," Stuart said.

"Probably not; but I shudder to think what you stirred it with."

"I'm just trying to be friendly, that's all."

"Why, what's in it for you?"

From his office, Jeffery snapped, "Eddie!"

"Only joking; I'm sure it's wonderful coffee."

"Only the best for my good friend."

Eddie whispered, "Piss off, Stuart. I preferred you when you openly despised me. At least I knew where I was then."

Stuart smiled his widest smile and between his row of perfect teeth, seethed, "Fuck you, Collins. You're still a drunken wanker who doesn't realise how close he is to being an unemployed drunken wanker."

And that brought it all back. Last night's visit to Brandypuke Farm had erased it all from Eddie's mind, until Stuck-up Stuart gave him a reminder. And things went downhill from there. Though nowhere near stratospheric, his mood hadn't been in its customary place in the gutter, and he'd even imagined getting through the day without inventing new ways of suicide. Now the kettle flex at home looked ever more inviting, especially with the McHue business and the HoD interview to look forward to.

Eddie thanked Stuart for the coffee and gulped it down.

He spat it out all over his desk and up the wall, and dropped the cup on the floor. He coughed until his face was red and the veins stood out on his forehead. Stuart flashed his glossy teeth and stood at Eddie's side, slapping him on the back, and Eddie struggled to vocalise the profanities queueing up on his tongue. Jeffery came out of his office, and Ros appeared at his side, coat still on, bag slung over her shoulder.

"What's happened?" She flicked rainwater from her hair.

"What's—" Eddie coughed and then gagged again, holding his fist over his mouth as Stuart pounded. "He put fucking salt in it."

"No, I never…" Stuart looked shocked. "I must have picked up the wrong—"

"You twat!" Eddie turned, and knocked Stuart with his shoulder. Stuart doubled up and fell to the floor coughing, holding his stomach.

"Eddie!" Jeffery shouted and ran across the office. "Why did you do that? It was an accident. Anyone could mistake—"

Ros shouted, "They're in different jars, how could he mistake—"

"That's no excuse for elbowing him in the guts." Jeffery helped Stuart stand, guided him to his seat and then turned on Eddie. "Clean this mess up and then appear in my office in ten. Got it?"

Eddie stood there with spittle hanging off his chin, eyes flitting between Stuart, Jeffery, and Ros, unable to believe what just happened. "What's wrong with your eyes?" he said. "You saw—"

"Ten minutes." Jeffery turned to Stuart. "You alright?"

"Feels like my ribs are bruised. But I'm sure he didn't mean it."

Jeffery gritted his teeth and slammed his office door.

Eddie stared at the coffee on his desk, at the coffee running down the walls over his photos of Sam and his CRFP certificate, and at the puddle forming on the floor. The cup was smashed.

Stuart winced, clutching his stomach, and two things grew in Eddie like fungus on dead wood: anger at Stuart, and the need for a drink.

"You want me to come in there with you?" Ros asked.

He thought about it; thought about what he'd said to her yesterday about staying away from him because he was a trouble magnet just now. But she would keep his tongue civil and maybe prevent him being summarily dismissed.

"I don't mind," she said. "It would get me away from the smell for a while." She looked at Stuart.

– Two –

Eddie closed the door and Jeffery indicated that Ros should sit. "I hope you don't mind me bringing Ros in?"

"You're entitled."

"Is this a disciplinary hearing?" Ros asked.

"No, it's not." Jeffery folded his arms.

"But, I—"

"You seem determined to sink further into the quicksand. I'm not gonna be able to pull you out, you know. And now," he nodded to the office door, "there'll be even more trouble to answer for. You can't go around physically abusing your colleagues."

"He did it on purpose!"

"Even if he did—"

"You can't mistake the sugar and salt containers, Jeffery—"

"Ros; you're here to make sure he gets fair treatment, that's all."

"But I'm not getting fair treatment."

"You smacked him in the stomach. What do you want me to do, give you a medal?"

"You should make *him* apologise," Ros said.

"You elbowed him in the stomach. It'll go on your file. And the Head of Department will study that file—"

"You know you're handing me a disciplinary notice, don't you?"

Jeffery leaned forward. "Let's get this one hundred per cent crystal, shall we? If you are sacked or you go on to a Rule One, or you find yourself on a Stage 2 disciplinary, it has *nothing* to do with me. Your name will be at the top of the form, not mine. Clear?"

"No. Not fucking clear. He provoked me, he taunted me and he took a dive like a professional footballer. You saw it. You chose to ignore it."

"Enough."

Eddie closed his eyes. As Ros was about to speak, he said, "Forget it. He's not listening, Ros. Keep out of it before you end up alongside me." He turned to her. "But thanks," he said. Then to Jeffery, "When's the meeting?"

"Yet to be decided. Soon, though."

"Yippee."

"I want you two to stay together; you'll have less chance of getting out of control if you have Ros watching over you. Okay?"

Eddie looked back at Ros again, shrugged an apology.

"Here's your work for today. And it *will* take you all day." Jeffery held a computer printout.

"A car?"

"Yes."

"That won't take all day, not with two of us."

"I said that it will take you all day. Clear?"

Eddie snatched the paperwork.

"CID wants a full job doing. Thoroughly."

– Three –

They walked together up to the window marked "security". A bald man, smoking a roll-up, with a reserve parked behind his left ear, sat behind a clear Perspex window, peered at their ID cards swinging on lanyards around their necks, and waved them through. "I think I'll be with West Yorkshire Police for another three weeks if I'm lucky."

Ros stopped. "You going to resign?"

"Resign? No, they're going to sack me. And the sooner the better."

"You don't mean that?"

Eddie held the garage door open. "Stuart gave him that IBIS log. He manipulated Jeffery into giving us this damned car. He's why I want out."

Ros put down her kit box on a small, stain-covered desk in the corner of the garage. "Let's crack this thing off, eh? You can take me to lunch later."

"Yeah," Eddie said, "I'd like to do that."

The garage was an echo chamber. Its high breeze-block walls were whitewashed yet grimy with years of exhaust fumes and fingerprint powders. The concrete floor spat dust each time a foot went near it, and it stank of damp in here, even in June. Traffic roared past on the busy main road beyond the sliding wooden doors, and behind them, high-speed trains made talking impossible every ten minutes.

Banks of fluorescent tubes dangled from the ceiling on chains, and more were screwed to the walls casting a cold light over the Jaguar's scratched, dusty paintwork. It stood alone in the CSI bay.

"What's the story behind this, then?"

Ros looked at the printout. Scanned its pages and shrugged. "Not sure, really. It's been recovered from Great Preston. Stolen-recovered." She read on, "Wait a minute. It was stolen nearly a month ago!"

"Then why do CID want a full mashings job on it? Doesn't make sense."

"I'll give them a call." Ros perched on a plastic chair next to the desk and held the phone to her ear, talking quietly, eyes roaming as she was passed from detective to detective.

Eddie lit a cigarette and strolled up to the Jaguar. He followed its curvaceous styling from the bullet-shaped bonnet across the rounded wedge of its doors through to the muscular flank of the rear wheel arch. He stepped back; his reflection blurred and then scooted away. He looked at the car, at its darkened windows and scratched paintwork.

It was green. It was a dark green Jaguar.

Eddie held his breath. Smoke crawled up his face as a shiver ran down his back. The cigarette fell out of his mouth, and he stood on unsteady legs, not daring to move in case he simply fell over. His hands began to shake as he turned to Ros, but he saw nothing except shimmering strips of white light.

She was there just as the first tear fell. "I'm sorry, Eddie," she said.

"Is it... is it the one. *The* one?"

"They think so, yeah." She led him away, making him turn away from it. "Come on, let's have a coffee."

The admin office next door was empty and quiet, soundproofed from the road and the trains. It had its own kettle and comfy chairs.

"Why does he get such a kick out of it? How would *he* like it?"

"He'd love it, Eddie. He'd be thinking of the overtime he could get out of it."

Eddie screwed his hands into fists, "I've never wanted to kill someone before."

"Enough," she warned. "Even garage walls have ears."

"Can you blame me?"

"I can't blame you at all. He's malicious. He's done it to provoke a reaction—"

"And I'll see to it he'll get one."

She patted his hands, "Think how disappointed he'd be if you came back to the office smiling about it; think of his face—"

"Oh I do. With a fucking bullet hole in it."

"—when you don't rise to it. He'll be furious."

"And then what will he do next?"

Ros sipped her coffee and Eddie lit another cigarette.

"When it boils down to it, if that's the car that killed Sam, it's a big part of him, wouldn't you say? Jilly and me brought Sammy into the world. That thing took him out of it. That is big." He was cringing as he spoke, because he didn't know if it made any sense or if it made him sound like an idiot. "Sorry. I'm talking bollocks."

"Come on," Ros said, "we'll go back to the office. I'm not having this. Jeffery's gonna hear about—"

"I'll do it, Ros. Maybe Stuart's done me a favour." A smile came to Eddie. "Maybe he's done me a really big favour. I can find out who killed Sammy."

Ros looked worried. "Why would you want to know that?"

Eddie paused for a moment, looked away as he said, "So the police can lock him up. Obviously."

– Four –

Ros watched Eddie as he struggled into a scene suit. He was shaking. And he avoided looking at her; because his eyes shone with tears. Examining the car that killed his boy wasn't right, and the very thought of it sent a shiver up her back and stirred the anger inside.

Dealing with other people's misery became easier after a while; she simply distanced herself, grew detached and though she still sympathised with the victim – how could she not – it was more than her own sanity could bear to let the sadness of a scene be anything more than work. But that didn't apply when it was so close to home.

Eddie set the camera up and Ros began the paperwork. But her eyes strayed to the tufts of hair in the cracked windscreen and she wondered how he would cope with recovering them.

The flash popped and a green rectangle clung to her vision.

She watched him. She still wanted him. The pre-January Eddie would be better; the calm one, the one everyone looked up to, but this version would heal eventually, and then–

"You gonna stand there all day, or you gonna give me a hand?" Eddie smiled, but it was a mask. Plastic.

Ros blinked, cleared her throat. "Where do you want me to start?"

He pointed to windscreen. "I've photoed the hair, Ros, but I can't... would you mind..."

"Go and fix another coffee, would you?"

He said nothing, just put down the camera and walked from the garage.

As the door closed behind him, Ros pulled out the hairs with sterile tweezers and dropped them into a small plastic pot. She packaged and labelled it, and the sliver of scalp, before quickly inspecting the front bumper, the grille and mascot badge, the windscreen washer jets and wipers and then the screen-to-roof joint for further hair, for fibres from the kid's – from Sam's – clothing. Nothing though. No blood, nothing.

"Here you go."

Ros jumped. "Jesus! Cough or whistle next time, will you?"

"Would a fart do?" Eddie set down his coffee and lit a cigarette.

She tried not to smile but found it impossible. It was good to see him trying. "What next?"

"The wadding in the fuel filler pipe. Someone tried to fire it. Bit optimistic considering it's a diesel," he shrugged, "but it's good evidence."

"Maybe they lost the filler cap and were using the cloth as a bung." She peered at the material.

"It's been burnt around the edges. Look. Singed."

"That's a cuff," Ros said. "Yeah, it's a shirt sleeve. You can see the button."

Eddie flicked on the Maglite and looked closer. "It says Oxford & Hunt." For the first time, professionalism was beginning to take over as master; maybe this was teetering towards becoming a job. And that was a good thing.

"That's expensive designer gear. Don't find many scrotes wearing Oxford & Hunt."

"Let's get a macro shot of the button and then we'll open out the sleeve to show the scorching, and bag it. If we can match someone's shirt to that—"

"Fat chance."

"We have to try, Ros. Might even be able to get wearer DNA from it."

"I didn't mean... never mind."

Eddie stood up, turned the torch off and stepped closer to her. "Don't beat yourself up every time something downright tactless falls out of your slack gob."

Ros's mouth fell open.

Eddie smiled. "Now, lighten up."

"Okay," she said, "sorry."

"And stop being sorry."

"Sorry."

Ros pulled on a fresh pair of gloves and eased the sleeve from the filler pipe, laid it out onto a clean exhibit sack. "They look like cigarette lighter marks. You can see the tiny circles of burnt cloth."

"Okay, I'll take a shot with a scale."

Two hours, four coffees, and for Eddie, countless cigarettes, later, they had fingerprinted the dusty exterior of the car using MLPD spray because using a brush and powder would have destroyed any marks beneath the dust. They had taped all four of the leather seats for fibres, swabbed the driver's seat because of a curious odour coming from it, had swept the footwells, fingerprinted and recovered the damaged mobile phone and had begun photographing and swabbing the fine droplets of a dark brown liquid that had sprayed across the passenger seat and partly onto the fawn leather dashboard. "Blood?" They KM tested a site and the filter paper turned pink. "Certainly is."

"Okay," Ros said, "What's left?"

"Interior fingerprinting, and photo and swab the cig lighter." He eased out of the car, stood and stretched.

"Need a drink?"

"I could slaughter one, Ros, but I ain't touching a drop while I'm near this thing."

"Glad to hear it."

The coil of the cigarette lighter was dimensionally the same as the marks in the shirtsleeve, though Ros supposed it proved nothing. It would be the DNA that would put a name to the would-be torcher.

"Aren't these things fitted with a tracking device?" asked Ros.

Eddie shrugged. "No idea. Something like this is approximately a house and a swimming pool out of my price range."

* * *

Eddie reclined in the reception area, bags of evidence surrounding his chair. "Thank God that's over." His eyes were dark, he looked as though he hadn't slept in a year, and still he had that slight tremor in his hands. "I think we have a pretty good chance of nailing the bastard with what's in here," he patted the bags.

"You want me to come to the meeting with you?"

"What meeting?"

"And I thought it was worrying you."

"The head's meeting?" He took a deep breath. "All I'll say is that when I go down, they'll want my supporters to go down too."

"Then it looks like I'm going down."

"Haven't had an offer like that—"

"Eddie Collins!"

"Sorry," he laughed. "I would like you there, Ros."

Absently, she asked, "You making any progress with Jilly?"

"If you can call it progress."

"Well?"

He spoke with a sigh, "She's invited me back home."

Ros nodded, looked away, "That's great. I'm so pleased for you."

"I'm not sure it is."

She looked back. "Why?"

"She's deranged, that's why. She's got it into her head that me, her, and Sammy can be a wholesome family again." Eddie tutted.

"She's trying to cling to him. You can't blame her for that."

"I'm clinging to him too." He thought of the NY hat on the mantelpiece. "But I won't delude myself. Sam's never coming home again. She thinks he will."

"You should give it a try. It's what you've been praying for, you'd be silly to pass the chance up."

"Think so?"

"I do."

"So do I."

Ros sighed.

"But it won't last. We're different people who'll never go back to being themselves."

"You should still try." Ros blew air through her nose. "If you don't, you'll forever wonder how it would have been. And if you do, you may like it, you might both get along great. And that's good. Then again, you might hate each other, and that's good too because at least you'll both know you have nothing in common and you can get on with the rest of your lives." Her eyes glistened.

The Yorkshire Echo. 23rd June

Lincoln Farrier death is suspicious

By Michael Lyndon

This reporter travelled into the countryside on Monday to interview a 78-year-old man called Lincoln Farrier.

He wrote to The Yorkshire Echo *asking for our support in helping to get his son released from prison after he stabbed a burglar.*

Of course, we wanted to help, but I wanted to learn how he saw the country as a whole today, and what he felt about the introduction of The Rules.

I was never able to find that out because Mr Farrier, a grandfather of three, was dead when I got there. Initially I thought he had committed suicide because he was distraught at being separated from his son for so long and with no chance of being together again for some time.

I was wrong. Lincoln Farrier did not commit suicide and the police have launched a murder enquiry.

Readers will be pleased to note that I have furnished the police with all my findings concerning Mr Farrier and would be honoured to help in any way I could.

The Yorkshire Echo *will continue to report on this case as soon as I know more. We can only pray that those responsible for Mr Farrier's death are brought to justice soon, and our thoughts are with his son and his grandchildren.*

That he was concerned enough to write to us after the miscarriage of justice surrounding his son's imprisonment, shows that the Justice Ministry still has work to do in distinguishing what is right from what is wrong.

We hope they get there soon.

Chapter Fifty-One

Wednesday 24th June

Using the last of the daylight, Christian had walked through a thin rain around the haul road that wound its way up to the surface like a corkscrew. His left leg ached where the golfer had swung the club at him, his head was a pit of percussion instruments, and his lips and eyes were still swollen. The walk out of the old opencast had taken hours, by which time Sirius and Henry had vanished.

He made it back to the derelict hut.

Henry had screamed to Sirius that the police were coming. Well, they and the dark-coloured car had left too, and he was alone in total silence, just him and the remains of this old hut. It was okay, he said to himself, he was used to living in dereliction, had done most of his adult life.

He had only been inside it for less than half an hour before the shock bit like a dose of bad street drugs. And that was when the shakes came and he felt icy cold. The cuff on his right wrist rattled. And the more he shook the more pain he experienced in his face and his shoulder especially. He was a patchwork of matted blood and even in the coldness of the old hut, even while suffering the shakes, he sweated like a tenth-round boxer.

It grew towards twilight and Christian merged with it into a dreamless sleep. The rat woke him the next morning as it scurried across his face and dug its muzzle into his ear. He screamed and jumped. And when he jumped, the pain bit and he screamed again. The rat fled. But so too had the shakes and the sweats and that was a good thing.

He peered out of the hut, and the sun was creeping like a thief up the horizon. Its brilliant glow caught the far rim of the canyon, gradually working its way down into the bottom to reveal all kinds of demons and wreckage there.

Christian wiped a hand under his nose. It came away bloody. More bloody wetness down the left side of his neck. He stepped outside and checked his surroundings. They were clear. And when he listened, he heard nothing except his grumbling stomach. He ignored it, because today was all about putting distance between himself and his previous life, and surviving.

How was he going to get away from here without being seen?

He began walking and the aching in his body gradually subsided. Mud squelched under foot and progress was slow, but the sun warmed his damp body and before long, Christian found himself on the periphery of a village. He saw the church first and then houses, farms, a pub, and a shop that also doubled as a Post Office.

The village was small and private. There were terraces of cottages, old farm labourers' cottages, and the odd detached property of a grander nature. As he skirted the village, keeping low behind the bursting hedges of a bridleway, the detached properties grew larger, had more land.

The bridleway opened out into a field that was bordered on its lower part by a small but dense wooded area. And the woods ate into the grounds of a fake Tudor mansion with a BMW and a Mercedes parked squarely on a black asphalt drive along the side of the house. He peered through the trees. All the windows were open, curtains moving gently in a breeze he could not feel.

Christian's feet contacted tarmac and he walked to the side of the house to where the cars were parked. No keys in the ignition.

He moved across to the house, unlatched the open casement window, pulled aside the curtain and peered into the gloom of what seemed to be a dining room. He swung the window wide open, slid a potted plant on the windowsill aside and pulled himself in. There were no visible PIRs, no alarm of any sort so far as he could tell.

Without a sound, his feet touched the wooden floor, and he began looking for car keys.

There they were, hanging on one of six small hooks on a plain wooden board screwed to the wall next to the rear door. He made his way over the floor and was about to reach up for the BMW keys when something growled.

* * *

Christian froze. It growled from behind him, and a shiver flowed through him like a slow electric shock. His hands were inches from the keys. He weighed up the odds of a quick escape and discounted them immediately. Without turning around, without daring to breathe, he opened the fridge door and peered inside.

The dog growled again, and Christian reached in for the bacon. He allowed himself to exhale as it hit the floor. The dog's claws scrabbled quickly and there followed the sounds of a hungry pooch lapping up the offering. Still without turning, he grabbed a block of cheese from the fridge, unhooked the keys and edged over to the window.

He was halfway out when the lapping stopped and the growling started again. Christian made it to the BMW, threw himself inside, and slammed the door as an Alsatian leapt at the window, slavering down the glass as it barked. The keys wouldn't go in the ignition, and just when he thought the dog was going to break the window, the key hit home and the engine screamed. So much for a silent exit. He turned left and booted the throttle.

The cuffs rattled against the steering wheel, and he breathed a sigh as the road opened out. He headed towards Leeds, wondering if Alice's body had been discovered yet.

Chapter Fifty-Two

Wednesday 24th June

Eddie said goodbye to Ros outside the station. It was rush-hour, car horns and loud music spoilt the mood; okay, they spoilt *his* mood. Ros's mood was nothing worth cherishing. Her eyes were downcast and she hadn't smiled all afternoon. "You okay?"

"I'm fine. Gotta go."

He watched her pull out into the traffic, feeling bad but not knowing why. Eddie waited for her car to disappear and then set off home.

Forty minutes later, he parked his car and walked across the road, heading for Booze King, hand already reaching for his wallet, mouth already watering.

It had been a strange day, but not, he would later reflect, as strange as tomorrow would be, and not half as life threatening either.

Back at the office, he and Ros had completed the DNA mini-sequencing from the old blood on the passenger seat and from the cigarette lighter. They'd plugged in the laptops and at one o'clock, auto-upload would send all the information and all the electronic evidence across to Wakefield HQ and onto the DNA database. They'd emailed the images to studio. And the fingerprints and the palm prints were in the store, ready for transport tomorrow morning to the bureau at Bishopgarth. Even Jeffery had taken an interest, peering over Eddie's shoulder as he did the mundane computer work, listening intently as he told of the fingermarks and DNA and whom he suspected of depositing them.

Stuart stared from across the office. Eddie ignored him.

Eddie had the power, at least for now, to let issues like Stuart and McHue slide right off his back as though he were shit-proof. He had the power because he had the knowledge, *this* knowledge. The sun was shining on Eddie Collins, and he inflated his chest because he not only knew who owned the car, but he thought he knew who was driving it when… anyway, he thought he knew. Unfortunately for Eddie, he wasn't shy of sharing that information.

The only thing worrying him now, as he carried the bottle to the wired booth to pay, staring at the fuzz-eyed kid behind the counter who told him to look into the camera, was that he might be suspended or even out of the job before the fingerprint and DNA results were back and his suspicions confirmed.

But what would he do if he got that information first?

He paid for the booze and the automatic door allowed him to exit into the smog that glowed in Wakefield city centre's bright sunlight. He dodged between buses and taxis and made it across the street, picturing the moment when he would blow the bastard's brains out, scalp him, and take his remains to Jilly for verification of a mission well done. But it wouldn't bring Sam back. It wouldn't even stop her going to see Freaks Inc.

"It's not going to work out, Eddie," he said as he let himself into the dirty foyer. And that's when he realised why Ros had been so downbeat. Talking about moving back in with Jilly like that. "Idiot."

But back to the conundrum in hand: job versus no job. As he mounted the steps, his mind worked at the problem with the efficiency of a brick telescope. And then he stopped. There was a noise like a man cutting wood with a blunt saw echoing around the stairwell. Quietly, he climbed the steps and peered towards the figure slumped against the wall outside his door. Mick.

Eddie placed the bottle on the steps and silently opened the door to his flat, lifting it so the hinges wouldn't squeak. He was back moments later, and dribbled warm water from a cup into Mick's lap, biting his lip as Mick groaned.

Having replaced the cup and locked the door, he crept down the first flight of steps, picked up the bottle and collapsed on the stairs, fist in his mouth, eyes screwed up, laughing silently. Eventually, Eddie composed himself, looked straight ahead and started up the stairs again. "Hiya, Mick," he called. "Mick!"

Mick's eyes opened, and eventually focused on Eddie as he scrambled to his feet, brushing dust from his trousers.

"Looked like you were fast asleep there, mate."

"What? No, I was…" Mick looked through Eddie and became quite still.

"You okay?"

"What? Yes, yeah, yeah," he avoiding Eddie's eyes, mind elsewhere. "Just resting my eyes." He almost looked startled.

Eddie threw the door open. It squeaked, and the two men walked into the smell; one as though his piles were painful today.

"How's your day been?" Eddie asked.

"Wet."

"Pardon?"

"I said what."

"I asked how your day was."

Mick slipped his coat off, paused and pulled it back on again. He sat by the window but curiously didn't throw a leg over the arm of the chair today.

"As good as that, eh?"

"Listen, you pour the drinks," he handed over a bottle of Caribbean Rum, "and I'll be back in a second."

"You sure you're okay? You look like you've shit yourself. Or pissed yourself even."

On his way out of the room, Mick stopped dead. He turned to face Eddie. Eddie could take no more, and he broke down laughing until his lungs hurt and his cheeks ached.

"Very funny. Oh yes, very funny." Mick put his hands on his hips, nodded. "Yeah, go on, laugh at a man with a weak bladder, why don't you."

Eddie paused, looked up.

"You'll see; it'll happen to you one day."

Eddie fell over, holding his stomach.

* * *

"Sure you don't want to borrow some of my boxers?"

"Believe me, I would rather shove wasps up my arse. But I appreciate the offer."

"Where have you left your old pair?"

"Huh?"

"Your grots, where are they? In your coat pocket?"

Mick shook his head.

Eddie squinted. "You've left them on my bathroom floor—"

"Well, where else could—"

"That is disgusting. I don't want your skiddies in my bathroom! I'll get a bag and you can go and get them. And don't tell me which part of the floor they were on; I don't want to know. Okay?"

* * *

"Any news from Farrier's nail scrapings?"

"Got a file DNA profile."

271

"Really?"

Eddie nodded, "But he's not on file, sorry."

"Bugger."

"He will be, eventually."

"I interviewed Sir George Deacon yesterday."

"Bet that was a thrill."

"It was."

"For him, I meant." Eddie leaned forward, grabbed the rum and refilled his glass, smoke curling up his face, stinging his eyes. "Is this what you wanted to tell me yesterday?"

"What?"

"You were going to tell me something, and then you changed your mind."

"We were discussing Jilly. But Deacon," he winked, "I fooled him. I've got even more against him. Now I *know* he had something to do with Lincoln Farrier's death."

"This should be interesting."

"I told him that the old guy was murdered, *murdered*, mind."

"You said in your article he was killed, so what's the revelation?"

"He said he hated gun crime."

Eddie stopped mid-sip, eyebrows raised, and looked across the smoky room at the dishevelled creature lounging in the chair, shirt hanging out, whiskers getting longer by the minute. "He said that?"

Mick nodded solemnly.

"Ah, but he's the Justice Secretary. All kinds of info will get back to him."

"Why anything about an old geezer he claimed initially not to know?"

The thought took a while to permeate Eddie's mind, but when it did, he realised just what a revelation this was. "This could sink him. You know that, don't you?"

"It's no good in isolation, though. I need much more than that."

"To do what? Bring him down?"

"Yes."

"But why?"

"I don't like him anymore."

"Why not let the police handle it?"

Mick looked shocked at Eddie. "I'm an investigative journalist, you prick. We do our own investigating, that's why they call us—"

"If Deacon's behind it, they'll—"

"You're about to insult my intelligence again, aren't you? I can tell, you know. Forensic evidence is wonderful stuff, I grant you; but it can be manipulated, and if you think for one minute any of it would implicate Deacon, then you're one naïve little puppy.

"And that's where I come in handy." Mick swung his leg off the arm of the chair, lit a cigarette and rested his elbows on his knees as he leaned forward to make his point. "The Rules are a great piece of legislation – look at Margy Bolton; she said she wouldn't have killed all those poor kids if she knew the death penalty was up an' running. It's a great deterrent, and it works. And if it can reduce killings then I'm all for it. You know I am."

"I feel a 'but' coming on."

"But, he stinks. He is scum; I knew it for sure yesterday, though I've suspected it for years. He is corrupt, and if he's corrupt, he's a hypocrite because he's broken his own fucking rules and suffered no punishment. He probably should be on a Rule 300 by now!"

"You've heard of the Teflon man."

"Turn him over and he's just an ordinary frying pan underneath. I have bits of info on him, and when I get it all, he'd better watch out because I'll blow him out of the water."

"You feel really strongly about this, don't you?"

"What gave it away?" Mick gulped, "The Rules are good – if *everyone* abides by them. No exceptions, not even by their creator. Because there can be no flaws in them; once a flaw is discovered, all faith in them is lost and every time someone is executed, there will be an outcry. The decision, and so the punishment, is unsafe."

"So how are you going to prove this revelation?"

"Any ideas?"

"Nope."

"Me neither. But when I eventually do nail him, he'll be the one looking down the barrel of a gun."

"If you're allowed to run with it."

"It's the ultimate exclusive. It'll be *The Yorkshire Echo's* biggest story this century. It'll propel our name worldwide. It'll end up with the government on trial for corruption. It may well see the introduction of a new PM, or at least of a tightening of legislation. And, my forensic friend, it will secure my job, if I should choose to remain there, until I'm so old that I piss myself every day!"

"My news is equally astounding, my journalistic jerk."

"Didn't know you had any news."

"You wouldn't, since you're a selfish bastard and I couldn't get a word in edgeways."

"Go on then, hotshot."

"I examined a car today." He sat back and smiled.

"That was five words, and they were all equally boring."

"The car that killed my Sammy."

Smoke drifted up Mick's yellow fingers. "You want to begin that again, now that I'm listening?"

"I examined a green Jaguar. They recovered it from Great Preston yesterday. Been there a while, judging by all the dust."

"That's good news." Mick's tone was respectful. "I hope you get the bastard." He emptied the glass, was about to swallow it and get a refill.

"It belongs to Henry Deacon."

Mick spat rum across the room, gagged and coughed until his voice was as thin as a balloon ready to pop.

"It PNCs back to him, though he claimed it was stolen from him back in May. No sign of anyone else having driven it, certainly no sign of more than one person ever getting into the thing. No fibres on any seat other than the driver's."

"What else?"

"Curiously, there was a singed shirt sleeve poking out the fuel filler pipe."

"He tried to burn it?"

Eddie nodded, lit his own cigarette. "He used the cigar lighter to try and get the sleeve started but it didn't work." He looked out the corner of his eye, and said, "It was an Oxford & Hunt shirt."

"They're about eighty quid a pop."

"Precisely, my dear Watson."

"Who knows about it?"

"The office. Plus I put my report on the computer; sent my photos over to studio and my DNA to the bureau. Why?"

"Let me explain: Little Deacon is son of Big Deacon. If Big Deacon gets upset, people usually die. Small point, but it's worth bearing in mind."

"I work for the police, not a bunch of criminal informants."

Mick looked askance. "Let me see, 'police' and 'criminal informants'... No, I'm struggling to find a difference there."

"What I want to know from you is what are you going to do about Henry Deacon?"

"Me?"

Eddie nodded.

"Why me?"

"Because he's the son of a corrupt politician, and so might be able to help with *your* enquiries. And I want to see if he'll admit to killing my boy."

"Why—" Mick stopped himself.

"Because if I go near him, I will kill him. Twice. And I think that might be illegal."

"Leave it with me. I'll get you some answers."

Chapter Fifty-Three

Thursday 25th June

– One –

He closed the car door softly, patted the bulges in his pockets and set off walking for the office, keeping an eye out but trying to look natural. It was one-thirty in the morning, the air was clear, the darkness abrupt, almost captivating. But Stuart paid it no attention. Stuart had other things on his mind. He had parked his car a hundred yards away from the office, careful not to be seen.

His mind imagined the look on Eddie's face when he found his presents – or rather when Jeffery found the presents. It would finish Eddie; no more snide comments, no more rivalry, no more jibes about failing the CRFP. Stuart's smile withered. No more remarks about his hair or his appearance. The smile died; a grimace lived in its grave.

And there it was, the CSI office, at the far end of the yard. Stuart quickened his pace, checking, making sure he was alone.

– Two –

"This is going to take hours."

"Henry, shut up. We've only been here ten minutes and already you're pissing me off. Do you think I want to be here?"

Henry sighed.

"If it wasn't for your dad, I wouldn't be. 'Do the job right', he said. 'See it through to the end', he said. Well, here I am, seeing it through to the fucking end; so cut your whining and keep searching."

"Yeah, but—"

"Shut up. Last time I tell you."

Henry was still shaking. He searched through the green books, CID6, they said on the front. These were the CSIs report books. All he had to do was find the one relating to the Jag, and they could take things from there. But he was shaking because he was inside a police building, illegally, and despite his father's insistence that he attend, it could land him in even more trouble. Tampering with evidence, he believed, was considered fairly serious. "What are we going to do about the computer records?"

"The what?" Sirius straightened.

"These books contain nothing more than basic notes of jobs they've done: details of a burglary, several reference numbers, boxes for stats. That's it. There's no mention of the exam they carried out; surely there should be."

Sirius looked deflated. "We're fucked. Actually, you're fucked. If any evidence has left this office, electronically or physically, you've had it. And if they use computers…"

"What?"

Sirius strode over to the dark far end of the office. He stood before a large bank of green and red LEDs, some flashing, others constant. "Laptops."

"Shit."

"Precisely. This is where they keep their detailed notes, and you can bet your arse they upload everything when their shift is over."

"But they might not. They might save everything until the weekend or… they may only keep examination notes—"

"They'll have all their DNA software on them. Betcha."

"But we could still try to locate the physical evidence."

"How long do you think we've got, exactly? It'll take longer than we have. The only thing we can do is—"

"Shush." Henry froze. "I think someone's coming."

"In here, quick."

– Three –

Stuart selected the Yale key and turned the lock. He stood in the small foyer, drinks dispenser to his right, health and safety notices fluttering on the board directly in front of him, and next to it, another poster, this one prepared by studio; its title was *Your Morley CSI Staff*, and there were unflattering pictures of the whole mob, with Stuart on the top row and beneath him, Eddie Collins. Strange that he should be able to see them at all. "Why are the lights on?"

He pulled his jacket tight around his chest and edged forward, peering around the corner into the main office. "Hello?"

He strode into the office and realised everything was not as it should have been. Scattered around the desks were CID6 books. Stuart felt vulnerable and even pulling his jacket tight around him didn't alleviate the feeling. He licked his lips and walked further into the office.

"Fuck, we've been burgled." His first impulse was to run and get a police officer, but he couldn't. How would he answer their first question: *what were you doing here?* And this new situation made Stuart's mission all the more complicated. *But if the office has been burgled,* he reasoned, *they'll pull up the CCTV that covers this building.* It would cover the burglars coming in, for sure, but it would also cover him coming in too!

He was about to walk over to Eddie's desk and slip one of the half-empty bottles inside when he heard it. A noise from Jeffery's office. Stuart's heart tripped. What was *he* doing here at this time of night?

He gulped and knocked on Jeffery's door, no other excuse coming to mind except that he couldn't sleep and thought he'd catch up on some work.

There was no reply to the knocking, so Stuart pushed the door open. His greasy smile was fully developed as he looked right into the tiny dark hole that was the barrel of a gun.

* * *

"Did you ever pick the wrong time to poke your nose in here."

Henry checked the foyer, made sure there was no one else in tow, then he came into the main office, legs shaking, and stood at Sirius's side.

Sirius asked, "Who are you?"

The man edged backwards, raising his hands, unable to take his gaze from the gun pointing at his chest. He stuttered, mumbled a name. "Stuart, my name's Stuart, I'm sorry I disturbed you, I didn't mean to, I couldn't sleep, I'll go, I'll—"

"Be quiet." Henry stepped forward, gun also raised, trying to take command of an impossible situation, trying to impress Sirius perhaps.

"Why the hell have you brought that? Put it away," Sirius's voice grated.

But Henry was in no mood for being told off. In his mind, all the SAS "training" he practised in his youth flowed through his veins right now, and at last, he came face to face with the enemy, and he had that enemy shaking. It gave him a buzz, but he felt nauseous too.

He wasn't a natural as Sirius was; it was forced, his arm shook, his voice shook. "What are you doing here?"

"I… I couldn't sleep. I just thought… who are you?"

"Never mind who we are," Henry shouted.

"I know…" Stuart blinked rapidly, pointed. "You're Henry Deacon."

"Fucking great!" Henry waved the gun furiously like a demented spoilt kid who has just been told no.

"Shut up," Sirius said. "Put that away."

"But he's—"

"Shut up!"

Henry still felt sick; all this SAS stuff began to feel like a kid reliving his dreams when he considered the mess he was in. And on top of that, he felt anger at Sirius undermining him in front of this whimpering man. His stomach flipped.

Sirius was calm. "Now, Stuart, what are you doing here?"

"My– I'm…"

"Take it easy, no one's going to hurt you. Tell me why you are here."

Stuart backed up more. "I work here, I'm a CSI. What do you want?"

"We ask the fucking questions," Henry said.

Sirius ground his teeth and said politely, "Please let me handle this."

"Yeah, but—"

"Last chance. Be quiet."

"Sirius, you can't—"

Sirius turned at the waist and slapped him hard across the cheek. Henry's eyes were slits, his mouth a narrow pink line. He felt like ramming his gun in Sirius's face and pulling the fucking trigger until nothing came out but a dry click. He was so close. Then he realised something fundamental. He had signed Stuart's death warrant.

Sirius let the gun slap against his leg. "Come on, Stuart; tell me what you are doing here."

"Seriously, I couldn't sleep. Thought I'd catch up. Paperwork." Stuart's eyes didn't blink. There was a chatter on his white teeth. "Please," he looked at Henry, "put your gun down, I'm no threat."

"Don't tell me to lower my gun."

"Please—"

"What happens to the evidence you collect through the course of a day, Stuart?"

"Lower your gun."

"Answer the damned question!" Henry barked.

"Calm down," Sirius said.

"Please, put your gun away."

"Answer him."

"I'm afraid of—"

"Just tell me what happens, Stuart."

"I can't," Stuart's hands went to his face as he shrieked, "please put—"

"Put the damned gun down, man," Sirius said.

"I won't. He's the enemy, I can't—"

"Enemy?"

"I'm not; I won't hurt, just please, put…"

"Put it down!"

Stuart screamed, walked forward. "I just want—"

"Stay back!" Henry shouted.

"Put it down, man. You, stand still!"

Stuart walked.

"Stand fucking still!"

Stuart stood still. His hands were at his contorted face, eyes pleading, sobs pulling at his shoulders. And then his hands flew from his face, and he made a grab for Henry's gun.

"No!" Sirius shouted.

After the bang, Stuart's tearful face whipped backwards, taking his entire body off its feet. His body hit the floor with a thud, and after the echo fled, there was silence. And then Henry discharged a second round into Stuart's chest.

Henry breathed out and stood quite still, shaking arm outstretched, a faint wisp of grey smoke twisted into the air. *Is that how it feels?* was Henry's first thought. His second thought was how to keep the vomit off his clothes. He crouched, hand still curled around the weapon and he threw up right there on the floor.

For the moment, Sirius was silent.

* * *

Though control was soon back at the helm, fury took charge and Sirius pointed the pistol at Henry's rocking head, ready to have done with the whole business. Instead, he holstered his weapon and took a handful of Henry's hair. "What the fuck did you do that for?"

Henry wrestled with more vomit in his throat. "He was going to run."

"No, he wasn't, he was going to try and make you put the fucking gun down, which is what you should have done!"

"He knew my name. He knew *your* name."

"Thanks to you, you fucking moron." Sirius thrust Henry's face forward, overcame the feeble resistance and kept pushing until it met vomit.

Henry resisted and then surrendered. Sirius only let go when Henry began crying. Vomit dripped from his chin as he stood up, leaning heavily against a desk. His quivering lip made Sirius want to punch him. "What kind of man are you? Man enough to kill someone but you can't handle the feeling that comes later?" Sirius stepped up a little closer. "Go and get cleaned up, you arsehole."

Henry hurried into the foyer but before he turned the corner, heading for the washroom, he stopped. "You're not going to tell my father, are you?"

"Clean up. We'll talk later."

The moment Sirius heard running water; he dialled Sir George's private line.

* * *

One sentence from Sir George's angry conversation sat on top of Sirius's pile of thoughts. Over and again, it repeated itself: "What's to stop them re-examining the Jaguar?"

So all this was for nothing. Destroy the physical evidence, and the CSIs would go back to the Jaguar and try again. They might not get everything they got at the first attempt, but it would still be enough to put a name to the driver. There was enough to hang him. Or shoot him, as was today's preference. The mobile phone, for one thing. They could reassemble it, using spare parts to get the information from it. No problem.

It was clear that Sirius and Sir George had reached that crucial stage in helping Henry stay out of the courts: the end.

Henry walked back in like a kicked dog. His head was down and he'd brought a handful of paper towels that he constantly rubbed his face with. He was a wreck. Sirius shook his head, looked back at the faceless body. "We have to leave before someone else comes along."

Henry binned the paper towel and started for the door.

"Wait." He watched the bin lid flip back and forth. "We can't just walk away. They'll go over this place in fine detail and they'll eventually discover who was here, and they might even lock you up before the week is out. We have to cover our tracks."

"Right," was all he said. Then, "What do you want me to do?"

"Look around for something flammable. But not diesel, okay?"

For ten minutes they searched and found nothing except a crate of de-icer for the CSI van windows.

"You're going to have to find a garage and buy a can of fuel."

Henry looked upset again. "Why me?"

"Okay, I'll go. You stay here and guard the body."

"No, no," pleaded Henry. "Okay, I'll go, I'll go."

Henry had reached the foyer door when Sirius called him back. "No need for the petrol, look here."

By the side of the computers, in a red painted metal box, were nylon aerosol cans full of something called MLPD spray. Neither of them had any idea what it was, but there were warning triangles stuck all over them, and a bank of foam fire extinguishers on wall hooks next to it.

Sirius handed Henry four cans and took the remaining four himself. They started from the furthest corner of the office and discharged the yellowish liquid on the carpet and onto desks and onto anything that would burn. The CID6 books, the stack of stationery, the wooden shelves of stats and then into the storeroom. The air grew heavy; a fine mist floated in the air, and when concentrated like this, the smell was overpowering, made their eyes water. But they continued, spraying the body thoroughly, until they reached the foyer.

Henry took a step outside to make sure everything was quiet, and then he gave Sirius a nod.

"Give it five minutes to settle."

"What?" Henry said. "Why wait, I thought we were in a hurry."

"If you strike a match in there now while that stuff is floating around, it'll blow you out of your designer shoes. We wait. Then, you can have the honour of striking the match."

"Oh, no, I'm not doing that."

"You killed some poor bastard tonight; you can go some way to putting it to rest. Do not argue. I warn you."

Henry's lip curled again and his eyes fell in resignation.

Sirius whispered, "Keep the door open or the windows will blow out. We're after a fire, not an explosion." Then he disappeared back inside the building.

"Where are you going now?"

Within a minute he was back, a rolled-up piece of printer paper and cigarette lighter in hand. "I've wedged one of those cans against the desk. It's spraying the last of its stuff right now. Light the paper, walk in and throw it towards the aerosol. Don't wait to see if it catches, because it won't warn you, it'll just burn your eyeballs out of your dumb head, just throw it towards the spray and run like hell. Right?"

"Couldn't you—"

Sirius slapped him. "I told you, no arguing. Here," he handed him the paper. "When you come out of here, you'll be frantic, so there," he pointed to the far fence, the gate closed but unlocked, "is where you're running to."

"Where're you going to be?"

"Right beside you. I'll hold the gate open, you just run. Now go."

With evident nerves, Henry took the wad of paper, and it lit at the first attempt. He shuffled into the foyer. Sirius could hear the can hissing and then saw Henry disappear around the corner. He felt like closing and locking the door, trapping the fool inside where he'd witness his own cremation, but decided to stick to the plan; there was no point leaving the arsehole at the scene of his own crime. He had only a moment to contemplate Sir George's final words before there was a loud whoosh, followed by a wave of heat, before Henry bounded around the corner, eyes wide, arms pumping furiously.

The office turned orange instantly, and as they ran, a kind of exhilaration filled Sirius, and when some of the windows finally blew out because of the extreme pressure, he howled with laughter.

Chapter Fifty-Four

Thursday 25th June

Mick put away his phone, stunned by Eddie's words. It stank of arson; no way was it an accident. He hoped, for Eddie's sake, that it put all this McHue shit into perspective from his bosses' point of view, and that they left him alone to get on with the job.

He slid the phone away and stared through the windscreen, wondering who would want to set fire to— Mick smiled. He knew the answer already, and it all added weight to his method of questioning.

How would he compare to Old Man Deacon?

Wigton Lane was wide. Even the grass verges were palatial, like second lawns. When the driveways were full, the occupants positioned their surplus cars (all prestige models) at the perfectly square pavement's edge. They were arranged in this manner along the frequently scrubbed gutters as a show of status – a middle-class pissing contest.

This was Alwoodley; a grand neighbourhood reserved for those with equally grand salaries, or for those of a more creative self-employed nature, some of whom probably operated perfectly legally. Solicitors lived around here, accountants, architects, and the doctors, and even the odd politician's son.

But right now, parked outside a swish detached bungalow, Mick's old Ford Focus stood out among the Bentleys and the Rollers and Jags like a fresh turd on a banqueting table. Mick smiled, relishing the thought. He locked the car door – couldn't be too careful – and peered through the black wrought-iron gates outside Deacon's bungalow. He marvelled at the gardens, the mature trees enveloping a stubby driveway, and gawped at the size of the hardwood conservatory sticking out at the side like a leftover from an Ideal Home exhibition. It was big enough to have its own eco-system.

There was a new Audi on the drive, R8 badge across the back.

Mick went to adjust his tie, then remembered he wasn't wearing one; it was in a bin somewhere back at the office. He pressed a chrome buzzer set into one of the stone pillars at the side of the driveway, and gazed into the mini-camera at its side.

"Hello?"

"Oh good morning, Mr Deacon. My name's—"

"Thanks but I don't buy at the door."

"I have some news." Mick waited, clicking his fingers.

"Go on."

"Not out here, Mr Deacon. You never know who's listening."

There was a pause where Mick had enough time to wonder if he'd blown it, and then the gates rolled back on tracks hidden behind the stone wall. He tipped a wink to the camera, and began walking. Every reporter dreams of a scoop. Mick had the spoon in his hand.

The solid wood front door opened before he was even at the step. A face that belonged on the other side of death peered out at him. Mick froze. He was famed for disliking dead bodies, and one just answered the fucking door. "You're not the butler, are you?"

"What do you want? I'm very busy." It was Deacon. It was just…

Mick didn't recognise him. His eyes were dead: they had no sparkle in them despite the morning's brightness. The skin surrounding them was dark, loose; the teeth yellow; hair a mess. "Can I come in?"

"Who the hell are you?"

Mick struggled with his jacket, hands patting pockets, searching for some business cards. "My name's Mick Lyndon. I work for *The Yorkshire Echo*, and I wondered…"

"No comment to whatever it is you're about to ask." The door began to close.

"They found your Jag."

The door paused. Mick's heart pummelled.

"Go on." Deacon's face reappeared but showed no surprise.

"Not out here." Risky, but worth a shot.

* * *

If he'd spoken to Old Man Deacon like that, he could have expected a busted lip. And that told Mick something about this kid. He was weak. Might have his own business, but according to the old man, it was on its way to the liquidators at an astonishing speed. Henry Deacon was still a little boy.

He sat in a leather seat in a lounge so opulent it was rude. The blue velvet curtains were pulled against the sunlight, and there were three, no, four standard lamps burning around the room. Some kind of weird LED chandelier suspended from the ceiling complemented the modern ensemble. Rich, deep rugs were scattered around the oak floor. There was a large TV on the wall, big enough to make a cinema happy, and a small but expensive stereo on a crystal-topped table.

"You stink of alcohol." Henry passed him a cup of very dark coffee.

"Thanks. For the drink, I mean. I'm allowed to stink of booze if I want, but I appreciate the warning."

"That wasn't the warning. This is." Henry took a seat directly facing him, hands together, tired eyes prominent, glaring at him. "If you've come here to threaten or to blackmail…"

Mick sipped his coffee.

"Well," he wagged a finger, "just be warned."

"Oh, I am, I am. And no, I haven't come for any of those things, but like I say, thanks for the warning."

"Then, Mr Lynton, why have you come here?"

"I told you, they found your Jaguar."

"That's what they're paid to do, isn't it? And why you? Are they sending reporters out now instead of uniformed officers? I bet they could make quite a saving."

"Not on my salary." Mick's face glowed with humour – this was his kind of setting. "That's quite a burn you have there."

Henry tried to pull his shirt sleeve over it. "I really am very busy."

"Doing what? You look as though you've just got up."

"None of your business."

"Mind my asking how you came by it? The burn?"

"It's not a burn, and yes, I do mind."

"I'm sorry, I meant no offence." He looked at the burn again. "It is a burn though, isn't it?"

"It's an injury I sustained while trying to keep possession of my Jaguar."

"Bet you're pleased to have it back?"

"It belongs to the insurance company now."

"How do you feel about it; the car, I mean, being stolen from you at gunpoint?"

"It was stolen from me at knifepoint."

"But how do you feel about it?"

"Use your imagination, Mr Lyndal. Now, if you'll—"

"That car killed two people the day it was stolen from you."

Henry's pause was longer than mere surprise. He was calculating. "Nonsense."

Waste of a pause, Mick thought. "Oh yes it did. I have friends in the right places, you see. Forensic friends."

Henry flinched.

"Have the police visited you yet?"

"Obviously not, since I didn't know the car had been recovered."

"Well, this'll be good practice for you. Mind if I smoke?"

"No, you may not smoke." Henry stood, hovering over Mick as though it might incline him to leave sooner. It didn't work. "Mr Lyndsay, tell me why you're here or get out."

Mick sipped. "You look very nervous to me, Mr Deacon. Not that I'm insinuating any connection with the murders."

"Murders?"

"That's what it's called if you run people over and leave them for dead."

Henry folded his arms; lips tight.

"They can put you on a Rule Three for that. They can kill you for it."

"As you said, Mr Lyndley—"

"Lyndon. Mr *Lyndon.* Just call me Mick."

"As you said, I had no connection—"

"I wouldn't cast aspersions, Mr Deacon." Mick paused. "I'll let the evidence do that."

"I want you to leave."

Mick looked up. "I spoke with your father on Tuesday."

Henry's eyes widened slightly.

"He mentioned you, and your business. Things not going too well, I understand."

"Things are just fine, now if you'll—"

"Nice shirt you're wearing."

Henry reached out and grabbed Mick by the sleeve. Mick looked at Henry. Henry let go and sighed as though he'd lost the war as well as the battle.

"Is it an Oxford & Hunt? Always liked those."

Henry closed his eyes. "Yes, it's an Oxford. Now, please leave."

"It'll come out, that you killed the man on Leeds Road, and that little boy on Westbury Avenue. The man was Peter Archer. He was thirty-eight, had two grown up daughters. And the kid was called Sam. Not quite twelve years old." Mick watched. "It will come out, Henry."

"Get. Out."

"You were driving that Jaguar that day, at that time. They recovered your broken mobile phone, the one you smashed. All they have to do is find out when it was last used, who you called at what specific time, and… Bingo!"

Henry's top lip shone with new sweat. "Someone else could have used my phone and then—"

"But what about the woman?"

"What woman?"

"The one on the bus. She saw you throw Mr Archer under it. She recognised you through the side window of your car."

"Gotcha, Mr Lynon. The side windows of my car are blacked out, she couldn't have seen me."

"Then it *was* you?"

"I never said that. I said…" He paced the floor, his hands began flapping around.

Mick let him rant. An innocent man really *would* have thrown him out by now, or threatened to ring the police if they disliked him as much as Henry seemed to dislike him. Henry was… afraid.

"I meant that she couldn't have seen whoever was driving my car."

"And then there's the shirt."

"What shirt?"

Mick stood. Stepped forward. "The piece of burnt shirt hanging out of the filler pipe."

"I don't know what you're talking about." Henry pointed to the door. "Now get out, before I call the police."

Mick stood his ground, eye to eye with Henry Deacon. "Call them, I insist. We can wrap this whole matter up here and now." Mick smiled. "Make a great story." He began walking out of the lounge. "Did you get help burning the car or did you do it yourself?"

Henry followed. "Where're you going? You can't go through there."

"Who helped you?"

"Stop it."

"Think of me as the one who's trying to find the truth, Henry; the genuine truth. When the police get a hold of you after I tell them about the female witness, they won't be so easy on you. They have quotas to fulfil."

"Nonsense."

"Maybe you think they'd go easy on you, mislay some evidence, get you off the hook, that kind of thing; you're the son of our Justice Secretary. Wouldn't look good if you went to the slaughterhouse, would it?"

"What do you want?" Deacon closed his eyes.

Mick froze; just on the threshold from the hallway to what he thought might be Henry's bedroom. There were no footsteps behind him; he knew Henry stood there like a lame animal waiting to be shot. He relished the moment and praised the gods for giving him this job.

He opened the door and discovered the room was a bathroom. Very neat, polished tiles, Jacuzzi bath the size of a small pool, two sinks, bidet, even palms in the corner by the bay window. Looked like it belonged in Florida. Mick closed the door.

He straightened his face, turned, and looked at Henry's slumped shoulders. His hands had gone back inside his pockets. A good sign, that. Mick stepped across the hallway, opened another door and sure enough, it was Henry's bedroom. Big TV hanging on one wall, abstract prints splashed the one opposite, the one where a huge super-king-size bed sprawled. The third wall, opposite a pair of mirrored French doors that presumably gave out onto a private patio, was wardrobe space and there was a door too, probably to the en-suite. "Mind if I sit in here?"

Henry tagged along in a slovenly manner.

Mick stood in the centre of the massive room. Slowly he turned, taking it all in. Next to the French doors was a cream leather sofa and Mick chose to conduct his interview there. "Mind if I help myself to a drink?" He didn't wait for an answer, just took a crystal tumbler from the mahogany table next to the sofa and poured a generous quantity of what he hoped might be whisky. "Want one?"

Henry shook his head.

"Sit down, Henry. Don't mind if I call you Henry?" The bed was made. Or it hadn't been slept in last night. It would explain the tiredness.

Henry sat on the bed, eyes creeping to the void beneath the wardrobes, the flap still open, exposing the darkness underneath.

Mick followed his gaze, wondered what was so interesting under there, and wondered why the flap should be open at all. It was wasted space covered by a fixed valance. Usually. Unless you planned to store something under there. Was it Henry's drug store?

He placed the tumbler on the occasional table just inside the French doors, and fumbled inside his jacket pocket.

There was a click.

He brought out a dictaphone.

"I told you, I'm not giving interviews."

"Good. This isn't an interview. This," he put the dictaphone down, "is switched off. See? The things we'll be talking about will not be on any record. You may speak freely to me."

Henry folded his arms.

"I have the name and address of that woman, don't forget. She swears blind she saw you in the car when those awful things happened. She's a good witness too. Teacher. She'll look great on a witness stand."

"If that's the case, why haven't you passed her details on to the police?"

"Who says I haven't?"

"Because you wouldn't be here now. The police would be."

"I haven't passed her details on to them. Yet. And I suppose you're wondering why she didn't go to them in the first place?"

"Go on."

"We pay better."

Henry nodded, a smile of understanding passing across his lips. "Go on, Mr Lynford."

"*Mick*, Henry. Please call me Mick." He sipped the liquor, appeared happy with the aftertaste and proceeded. "You sure I couldn't smoke?"

"Christ's sake." Henry rolled off the bed and slid the French door open a couple of feet. Light belched into the room.

"Very kind." He pulled out his cigarettes then fumbled the lighter and dropped it. "Clumsy me." He got on his knees and made a slow grab for it, eyes roaming as he did so.

"What do you want to know?"

Mick retrieved the lighter. There was nothing of note beneath the wardrobe that he could see from this angle. "I don't want you in trouble. Seriously, I don't. Please, though, just be straight with me and then I'll be out of your hair and you can get on with whatever it was you were doing."

"Is it about my father? Because if it is—"

"Do you know the name Lincoln Farrier?"

Henry shook his head.

"Thought not. Lovely bloke, seventy-eight years old. He died a week ago. Someone shot him with his own World War Two antique. Can you imagine that? How awful."

Henry shrugged.

"He'd visited your father on the day he was shot."

"I'm still listening."

"Your father killed him."

"Wouldn't have thought so. My father's fingers are always spotless."

Mick struggled to conceal his surprise at Henry's blasé attitude. If someone accused *his* father of murder, Mick would have hit them, after picking his chin up off the floor. Not Henry. Henry sat there checking over his nails. "Then who dirties their fingers on his behalf?"

Henry shrugged again.

"One last time before I have to begin threatening you again. And I do hate threats, they're so ungentlemanly, don't you think?"

"Listen, I think we've exhausted our charitable conversation."

"Did you know that part of Morley Police Station burned down in the early hours of today?" Mick watched.

Henry looked away. "No. And I don't fucking care."

"The part that caught fire was the CSI office. That's the place where all these forensic-types work from. You know the ones, they go to murder scenes and burglaries and the like, and they find evidence. Clues. Can you imagine it! The place that houses evidence is burned down? How absurd, you'd think they would have a shit-hot kind of fire prevention system in place to protect all that sensitive evidence, wouldn't you?"

"Is this leading somewhere?"

Mick sipped his drink, flicked ash through the French window and said, "It does have a shit-hot fire prevention system. The foam sprinklers came on almost immediately and put the thing out," he waved an arm, "squat. Just like that."

Henry sat up.

Mick could see his cheeks throbbing as he ground his teeth. "Good, eh? So all that lovely evidence will still be intact."

"So how does this relate to me?"

Mick smiled. "Well, when you came home last night, sorry, this morning, did you notice a blue Ford Focus parked at the end of your street?"

"No." Henry shuffled on the bed, "I didn't come back here at any time this morning. I was in my bed from around midnight."

"Strange. That blue Ford Focus belongs to me. I was sitting in it. I had my camera with me. It's a beauty, one of those long range digital things that takes wonderful—"

"Okay, okay, get to the point!"

"The point is, the police will pop round and ask some questions, since that building houses evidence against you. But without hard evidence of your involvement with the arson, they'll soon be on their way again. After all, they can't force you to give your fingerprints to compare with those they will find at the scene. And since Sir George has protected you from ever having a police record, the fingerprints from the scene will mean nothing because you're not on file. But if I were to… help them, perhaps giving them the information I have, they might try a little harder. I'm not sure, but I think if they have a named suspect for a job they can insist you give fingerprints and DNA. Even your dad might not be able to lend you a hand. See what I mean?"

Henry stood up, straightened his trousers and fixed himself a drink. And while he did, Mick had that warm feeling inside that comes only from being able to tell lies based upon a hunch so slender that it was transparent. And subsequently being proved correct.

"Let's assume you're right, Mr Lyndon, how do I know you won't carry out your threat anyway?"

"Henry," Mick's eyes looked earnest, "I am interested only in Lincoln Farrier's murder. I assure you. I'm not interested in the bloody CSI office, and I certainly don't give a flying shit about Mr Archer on Leeds Road."

"Then why say you have friends on the forensics team?"

"Because I do, sort of. I used to go out with a girl from the labs in Wetherby. Shame though, she was married—"

"Let me make myself clear. I'll offer you the information you need, Mr Lyndon, but if anything 'leaks' out, I will have you killed."

"But—"

"I've listened to your threats. Now have you listened to mine? Do you understand?"

"Why not have me killed anyway?" It was a thought that speared Mick's mind as soon as the words 'I'll have you killed' fell out of Henry's bloodless lips.

"I have my reasons, Mick Lyndon of *The Yorkshire Echo*. You'll be of use to me."

"I will?"

"You think you're the only one to benefit from this little meeting?"

"I have to admit it, I thought I was." Mick was on the defensive now; he prayed he wasn't in over his head. He was a hero, it was true. But only inside his own mind.

"Do we have a bargain?"

Mick nodded. "You can trust me."

Henry gulped the liquor, refilled and paced the bedroom. "His name is Sirius; that's all I know; don't know if it's his first name or his last name, whatever. He's the one who carries out my father's dictates. And if what you're saying is correct, about this old chap visiting my father on the day he died, then that's where I would be looking."

"How do you know this Sirius man?"

Henry stopped pacing. "Because he's the one my father sent to help me sort out the Jaguar and then burn the CSI building."

Mick showed huge restraint; he almost fell off the sofa. Instead, he drained his glass, looked indifferent. He pictured the front page, the meetings with Rochester. He coughed, lit another cigarette and then asked, "I'm curious to know how he's going to get you out of this mess if it does escalate. I mean, I have solemnly promised not to tell the police about your involvement, and I will stick by my word, Henry; but if they find out through the course of their own investigations, what will he do to help you then?"

The question brought a smile to Henry Deacon's pale face. He sat back on the bed, sipped his drink. "There will be no more help."

"Surely, he can't let you…"

"Die? As you said, they'd take great pleasure in executing me; a Home Office bullet can cost more than *one* life. But it would never get that far."

"You saying your old man would fly you out?"

Henry laughed. "He'll have me killed. But he won't wait until the full story comes out."

Mick puffed furiously on the cigarette until it burned his lips. "Forgive my asking this, but if he's so determined to keep you out of the press and out of the slaughterhouse, because he's worried about his career, then…" Mick stopped. Even though Henry Deacon was a walking turd, he found his tact had abandoned him.

"Why didn't he kill me earlier?"

"Well, yes."

"Because I blackmailed him."

"With what?"

"Right now, I can look forward to a swift departure, but if I gave out my secret before I died, and especially to a member of the press, my departure may be elongated somewhat."

"Shit," Mick slurred the word. "You say, *'before you died'*? What do you mean by that?"

"I have things to say, but I daren't say them while I'm alive."

"Then, how will—"

"Search for them. I'm sure if anyone can find my secret, Mr Lyndon, it will be you."

"Is this the 'use' you have for me?"

Chapter Fifty-Five

Thursday 25th June

Eddie pressed end, put the phone away. He knew from their conversation last night that Mick would be paying Deacon Junior a visit this morning, and had wondered if news of the arson might interest him.

He stood at Ros's side looking at the state of their building. The side windows had blown out where the small storeroom and exhibits lockers were. The rest of the building appeared not too badly damaged; warped gutters, charring to the entrance door, melted UPVC window frames, smoke staining above them, cracked glass in some of the others, and even the drinks dispenser in the foyer had melted.

Steam, or maybe the last tendrils of smoke, curled out of the windows and was dragged away by the breeze.

"Hope you didn't have anything of a personal nature in there." Jeffery strode towards them from the main building, clipboard in hand, frustration glowing on his face.

"What time did it happen?" Eddie asked. "Did the upload happen?"

"Don't know, and don't know."

"What about our physical evidence, you checked on it yet?"

"Don't want to examine the Jaguar again," sighed Ros.

"The shirt sleeve," Eddie said. "And the DNA, we've lost it all."

Jeffery's clipboard flopped against the side of his leg. "Done a full inventory, everything is still there, no damage at all."

"Really?"

"No, not fucking really!"

"Can we go in?"

Jeffery looked from Ros to the building. "No one's going in there until a surveyor's checked it out."

"Then what?"

"Then we get suited up, go and see what caused it. I've got a fire investigator on the way. And someone's coming from the lab too." He looked directly at Eddie, "Evidence in the store is last on the list."

"Who's doing the work with you?"

"I called over Aadi from Bradford."

"I want to do it," Eddie said.

"Forget it, I have—"

"Look, it's our stuff in there—"

Jeffery pointed his clipboard at Eddie, "Don't question me again. I'm short of people, I have jobs coming out of my ears and I don't have time to fanny about looking after your ego."

"I'll bet you let Stuart in there."

Jeffery backed off. "Stuart hasn't shown up yet."

"Christ," Eddie said, "that's a first. Has he rung in sick? Maybe he's dead."

"Enough." Jeffery pulled a bundle of paper from the clipboard and handed it to Ros. "We had a murder came in early this morning. You're both on that. You'll need fresh laptops, so I've included requisition slips in there for new ones—"

"What about configurations?"

"Taken care of, Eddie. Go draw them from Bishopgarth. Here are your van keys, they're the spares from the main building."

"And our cameras and kit?"

"You pick up one camera from studio while you're getting your laptops and all the kit you need is at Unit 41, put aside, and ready for you to collect."

Ros rolled up the paper and began walking to the main building.

Jeffery took hold of Eddie by the arm. "How are you feeling? You okay with this?"

"Aw, you *do* care about my ego."

Jeffery just stared.

"Can't see a problem," Eddie shrugged.

"Good, because your meeting with HoD is due out of the blocks first thing Monday morning." Jeffery offered a faint smile, turned and left.

* * *

They collected their kit, and travelled through to Wakefield to pick up the laptops and camera.

Eddie bit his nails as they drove back from Wakefield into Leeds and towards the scene. He was thinking about what Mick said last night, and how he planned to visit Henry Deacon today, hoping to scrape some information out of him concerning Lincoln Farrier's death and Sir George's possible involvement.

What he hoped for more than anything else, was some information about Henry's Jaguar. He wanted to see if anything slipped out, or even if the man admitted killing Sam and that guy on Leeds Road.

And if he *did* admit it?

Well, if he admitted it, then Henry Deacon wouldn't be troubling anyone for too much longer. It was a promise he made to Sam. And to himself.

And then his phone rang. He looked across at Ros, who glanced at him, a questioning look on her face. "Jilly," he said.

"Go on and answer it, promise I won't listen."

He selected audio and then okay. Jilly spoke: "You okay to talk, Eddie?"

"Yeah, go ahead."

"About the other day," she began. "I said some things that I shouldn't have said. Look, I want you to move back in. There. I said it. No strings attached."

"You'd be happy living with an alky then?"

Ros shook her head.

"Not really. But I want you back."

"Right."

"Put your phone on video; I like to see what you look like."

Eddie closed his eyes. This was getting silly. It wasn't Jilly speaking; it was a woman whose mind had gone to slush.

"Eddie?"

"Okay, okay." He pressed the button, and she smiled at him.

"How are you?"

Everyone is suddenly concerned for me today. And how am *I feeling? I'm feeling pissed off, that's how I'm feeling. I know who killed my boy but I'm going to have to kill him before he can destroy the evidence I have against him. My boss is pushing me through the doors of the nearest Job Centre; I have a colleague who's out to sabotage me, and my wife is batshit crazy.*

"Everything's fine." He stared down at the screen. "You?"

"When are you moving your stuff back in?"

"Work is taking up a lot of time, but I'll make it as soon as I can."

"Pop round sometime, I can give you the new keys so you can bring your stuff over even if I'm not in."

"You're always in, Jilly."

"Not these days."

He was about to ask where she went, but Ros was pulling the van up to the scene cordon. "Okay, Jilly, gotta go now, I've just arrived at a scene."

"Oh," she said, "I thought you were in the van by yourself, pulled up on a hard shoulder or something. Who's out with you?"

"It's Ros, you know Ros."

Jilly said nothing for a second or two, then, "Oh, Ros. Yeah. Okay, speak soon." She hung up.

Eddie flipped the screen closed. "Great. Can't wait." He saw Ros smile just the tiniest amount. He smiled too.

Chapter Fifty-Six

Thursday 25th June

The cobbled street of Back Eshald Place was rammed with police vehicles. It was a bright day, but clouds in the western sky looked bruised and angry. Nearby, youths sat on swings in a ruined playground cum alfresco drugs shop; they watched, laughing at the police every now and then.

Nearer to him were a smaller, quieter group of onlookers, some, noted Eddie, with digital cameras. And at the furthest cordon, television media had gathered, their vans with satellite antennae parked neatly in a row, newscasters and crewmembers frantically rigging up in case they missed something juicy. "Why are they here?" Eddie climbed from the van. Today there were more killings in Leeds than in the entire county twenty years ago. They were nothing spectacular anymore, barely news fodder at all.

A suited figure walked briskly towards them. As he neared, he thrust out a hand at Eddie and said, "Morning, DCI Benson, Holbeck CID." His eyes never ventured near Ros, who stood with her arms folded.

"Eddie Collins, CSI." Eddie shook hands.

"Right, Eddie, this is what we've got—"

"This is Ros," Eddie said, "Ros Banford."

"Ros." Benson nodded, returned his attention to Eddie. "We've got a dead girl at the foot of some cellar stairs, looks like she's lost a lot of blood, can't say where from just yet."

"House been searched?" Ros asked.

"Yeah, all clear."

"Have they searched the cellar?"

"I told them to keep away from it till you got here. If you want—"

"No," Eddie said, "we'll go in and have a look first. If we find someone, don't worry, we'll shout."

"Any idea who she is?"

Benson shrugged. "Not yet. This lot here," he motioned to those closest to the fence, "think it was being used as a squat."

"What's the report from your search crew; what's it like in there?"

"It's being lived in, alright. They found drugs paraphernalia in what used to be the lounge, some kind of slow water filter, other bits and bobs. No signs of life upstairs, though."

"Right," Eddie turned to Ros, "shall we make a start?"

"Let's," she said, "don't much like being filmed for posterity."

Ten minutes later, suited up, Eddie and Ros approached the house.

"So who's Benson? You heard of him before?"

Eddie said, "He's from Wakefield CID. Been over here a month or so. He has a bad reputation so I try to stay out of his way when I can."

They entered the house through a warped tin door, torches in hand, new camera slung around Eddie's neck. Even through the masks, they could smell dampness and the familiar undercurrent of blood and drugs, shot through with a tinge of death. They stood in the kitchen, the tiled floor here at the very entrance to the house too coarse, too damaged to be of any value for footwear marks.

Forward a few paces and to their right was the rough cellar door. On the floor nearby were droplets of blood; in and around them were several footwear marks. And in the doorway between the kitchen and the lounge lay a hammer. Even without artificial light, they could see blood and hair sticking into it.

"Give the floor some oblique, Ros," said Eddie, "see if we can't detect a few."

Ros crouched, focused the torch beam into a long thin tube of light, and cast it slowly back and forth in an arc. It showed up all manner of goodies on the floor, curly hairs, crumbs, pieces of food, a layer of recently disturbed dust: footwear impressions. "Yep," she said, "plenty to go at."

"Let's clear the kitchen floor first so we have somewhere to stash our gear."

They did, using a combination of oblique light and white fingerprint powder. Outside the common path of foot traffic, where the dust had had a chance to accumulate, torchlight picked out good quality footwear impressions, and Ros lifted them using sheets of black gelatine rolled out onto the floor. And for those marks that were within the common path, and that responded well to white globular powder, she lifted using transparent adhesive sheets.

They scanned and powdered the floor; and the further into the kitchen they got, away from the deep scars made by the metal door, the better the quality. They were rewarded with seven footwear marks, all of reasonable value, detail in abundance. Most were Arrows, the favoured boot of police officers, but Nike and Reebok made an appearance, and one that neither had seen before. It was more of a shoe, like a deck shoe, certainly nothing that any self-respecting youth of today would be seen wearing. It raised their spirits and now they had cleared the kitchen floor, except for the marks in blood and the hammer, they had access further into the scene.

Eddie scanned the lounge floor while Ros filled in the orange Criminal Justice Act labels to verify the footwear marks they had recovered, turning each one into a specific exhibit recorded in her paperwork - referred to as her CID6. She drew a plan of the kitchen floor, took rough measurements and then plotted the location of the footwear lifts on the plan.

"No decent ones in here." Eddie stood, gripped the small of his back and then massaged his right leg.

Ros joined him at the lounge threshold. "Look," she said, her voice muffled by the mask, "a smashed doll. I wonder if they had kids in here?"

"And the drugs stuff too. But the floor is shit; we won't get any footwear in here."

Ros made a test. She used the ESLA electro-static device to try and lift the dust surrounding a footwear mark she had planted, but the floor was too badly damaged to give any detail. Then, she tried a black gel lift; still nothing. "Right," she said, "forget the lounge floor, waste of time."

Eddie walked in, suit crinkling as he moved.

Ros joined him, stared around at the crumbling wreck that used to be someone's home. "Do you fancy doing the body and I'll concentrate on all the crap in here?"

"How could I refuse such an offer?"

"Thought you'd say that."

"But let's clear the blood on the kitchen floor first."

"Okay, but photography's yours," she compromised, "I'll do the reagent and swabbing. Fair enough?"

The blood had no direction – other than straight down. It hadn't been deflected by an object, hadn't been flung or cast-off by an implement, hadn't arrived here from another place at high velocity. This was nothing more dramatic than drops of blood that had hit the floor and fanned into star shapes; some of them had pooled together within a five-inch radius.

Eddie photographed it, and the partial footwear marks in it, with and without a scale alongside, all in relation to the cellar door. Then, after Ros swabbed the blood, to prove it belonged to the girl (they were never going to be lucky enough for it to belong to an injured offender), he retook his earlier shots and took them for a third time after she applied a dark blue reagent, gentian violet, which brought out and enhanced lots of additional detail the naked eye couldn't pick up.

This process highlighted two footwear marks in what they presumed to be the girl's blood. A Nike Air, and a small part of the deck shoe.

The trouble with the reagent was that it highlighted proteins, which was how it managed to develop the detail in the bloody footwear mark. But because this was a kitchen, old blood from meat, juice from burgers, even spilt milk glowed when Ros cast ultraviolet light over it. Discerning what was relevant and what was abstract would be the footwear bureau's job. Thankfully.

Eddie peered down the cellar steps. The twisted body lay three-quarters of the way down them, crumpled like the doll in the lounge. Eddie stood over her, looking at the waste of life. The first thing he noticed were the Reebok trainers she was wearing. So that left the deck shoe and the Nike Air as possible suspects' footwear.

The walls were a mixture of whitewash and bare brick; flakes of white damp clung to them like desiccated cobwebs, so there was nothing to be gained by getting the chemical boys from the Fingerprint Development Laboratory involved.

He stood on the gritty stone steps and despite the nagging throb in his leg, crouched and inspected the girl. She was between twenty and twenty-five, slim, almost wasted, blonde with petite features; good-looking. Good-looking apart from the neat stab wound in her chest that had oozed sufficient blood to cover her chest and part of her neck. Doubtless beneath her there would be more, congealed, pooled. Slug food. Eddie shuddered.

"What did you die for, eh?" The blood on her chest had trickled to where it was now: across her right shoulder, and formed a little pool in the niche of her collarbone. This is where the murder happened, no doubt, but it started up there; Eddie looked back up the stairs. She was stabbed up there, hence the blood on the kitchen floor, and then hurled or fell down here where the final shallow beats of a dying heart cast its fluid.

The needle marks on her exposed arms proffered some background, and the darkness beneath her half-open eyes, stark against the pallid quality of her skin, suggested that drugs played a big part in her life. But did they play a big part in her death? Another feature to catch Eddie's eye, was the thread protruding from the nails of her right hand, like a symbol, a sign pointing to the killer? It was golden, like the one nestling in the slash mark on her T-shirt, wafting away in a breeze too light for Eddie to feel.

Working in the confined space of a cellar stairwell proved difficult for him. Not only was the corpse upside down and the exposed areas of skin he needed to tape, furthest from him, but working constantly in his own shadow, cast by the lighting rigs at the top of the stairs, was just plain annoying. He'd photographed the body an hour ago, and now he planned to make his way past her with a tapings kit, and head-and-hands bags, ready to begin sealing her away until she reached the mortuary.

Eddie used a pair of sterile tweezers to recover the golden threads, and found another couple under the nails of her clenched fist. They came away easily, indicating that they hadn't been there for too long before her death. He placed the threads into small paper wraps, and then sealed them away into tamper-evident evidence bags, already signed and dated. He opened the tapings kit to pull from her exposed skin any stray fibres, any contact evidence, any trace evidence that was too fine for the eye to see, and too delicate to risk losing it in transit to the mortuary.

A six-inch strip of sterile tape lifted invisible evidence from her bare forearms. He used more for her face, noting how strange it seemed when the tape lifted her part-open eyelids from the eyeball. And again, how strange when her forehead distorted, as he pulled the tape off, and how she never flinched when a clutch of eyebrow hair came away too. He taped her hands, her feet, and that part of her upper chest not contaminated by blood.

"How are we going to get her out?"

The light from the kitchen dimmed, and Eddie looked up to see Ros's silhouette against the lighting rig. "Christ knows. Tell you what, if you've done with the floor up there, we could lay the body bag there and bring her to it instead of the other way around. No way can we package her here."

"I'll go and get one. Back in a mo."

When the full force of the light returned to the stairwell, he returned his attention to the corpse. He slid the acetates, with individual tapes adhering to them, into a pre-recorded evidence bag, laid them a couple of steps above her bent knees and ripped away the seal of a head-and-hands kit.

"What's your name, kid?" He slid the largest bag over her head, pulled it down so it squashed her nose, made her eyebrows appear heavy like a bank robber wearing tights. He tied the bag off, reached up and bagged her hands. And then each foot. The knuckles of her right hand were scuffed, probably as they skidded down the wall there. But they were small, petite even. They were a kid's hands.

Eddie licked his lips, felt the coarse fibres of his mask against his dry tongue. He sweated, and sure enough, he could hear Brandypuke Farm calling to him as his gloved hands trembled. He brought his mind back to the dead girl looking up at him with her creamy eyes.

He remembered Sir George Deacon's mesmerising words in his House of Commons speech. "If you want to kill serious crime, you have to kill serious criminals."

Eddie found himself staring at her; noting tiny details like the fine spray of blood on her cheeks, and the fine hairs growing around her temples giving her that wispy, romantic gypsy look. She was a sweet-looking kid.

He was getting in too deep, could feel it. The shakes were booze-influenced, but the dampness in his eyes was compassion. And he wondered why. He'd always remained detached. After all, it was a stranger's body, and so it was a job, a piece of meat. Overtime. But the hair, the wispy, gypsy look, it was… She was a kid, for fuck's sake!

Eddie turned away from her, scraped a plastic sleeve across his eyes and breathed through his mouth into the cool darkness of a stranger's cellar.

The Maglite beat away the blackness, but the smell of damp was strong. Mixed with it, overpowering it was wood oil, linseed, maybe. The remains of a candle sat just beyond the stairs and then he shone his light higher, towards the back of the room.

"Well, I'll be fucked." Eddie walked towards the easel. There was a plastic sheet suspended above. Across its white surface were curtains of dust, and of course, more webs. He shone the torch light across it and saw recent disturbance, the smears from three fingers where someone had lifted this sheet. There was nothing to see beneath it though, just the naked wood of the easel.

Above him and slightly to the left, was a bare bulb, small enough to be a vehicle bulb, and from it ran a skinny flex that bypassed a haphazard collection of old drawers and cupboards and connected with a huge black battery on the floor. This was a studio, a palace among the ruins, and Eddie felt a prickle of pride for the dead girl's ambition.

He felt sorry for her, the artist who died on some cold stone steps in a derelict house. "Who killed you?" Eddie put his gloved hands on hips and into his mind came the word: *boyfriend*. "Ah, right. The boyfriend did it, in the cellar with a letter opener. It's all clear to me now." But it wasn't clear – and despite his attempts at throwing humour at the problem, it came back as two-dimensional, like a slap in the face. "Sorry," he whispered.

To his right was a small open wooden door with a web blocking the entrance and a spider the size of a child's fist hanging there, almost daring him to enter. Well, Eddie dared. Grit crunched underfoot, and his scene suit crackled like a packet of crisps as he approached what used to be a coal chute. Now, it was some kind of store and as the spider disappeared into the upper reaches of its world, Eddie ducked beneath its web and entered its lair.

It wasn't long before he found something.

Black bin bags covered two rows of… of what? If you removed all the cupboard doors from a kitchen, and put each one into a black dustbin liner, and stacked them edge on it would look just like this. He pulled aside a torn corner from one of them and his gloved fingertips touched something with a texture. Eddie held the torch up, peered inside the tear and saw it was an oil painting.

"Hats off to you, my dear." He pulled the plastic away from several others and they too were paintings. Rather lavish paintings. And then he saw a scrawl, a name signed in black paint. He closed in, opened the plastic a little wider and read the name: "Ledger." And on the next, "C. Ledger." Same on the next three, and then, "Christian." Christian? It was a man's name, an old man's name too, not much heard of these days.

Eddie poured himself into the snippets of the paintings; wondered about the artist, what he was doing now, if he was alive, and then it hit him: if these were painted by a male, who the hell was she? "I take it all back," he said, "Hats *on* to you." He was busy constructing the dead girl and the artist when he heard the grate of a metal clad door above him, heard Ros call out.

"You finished down there?" Ros asked.

"You want me to come up?"

"Yes, please."

That wasn't Ros. That was Benson. What the hell did *he* want? Eddie peeled himself away from the paintings and headed for the stairs.

Refusing to give the body a second glance this time, Eddie stepped over it and emerged into the kitchen. "What's up?" he looked at Ros. "Is the food here? I'm starving." *And if you could manage without me for half an hour I could sure as hell use a little rum or vodka.*

"No food." This from DCI Benson.

"It's gone lunch time. We're hungry, could do with a break."

Benson shrugged. "So sue me."

Eddie's mood darkened, and off came the gloves. Literally.

"What're you doing?"

"I'm going to get some bloody food."

"You can't leave a scene!"

Eddie peeled off his suit and stepped outside onto the path. "So sue me."

Ros followed, watching Benson's cheeks flush as though he'd just been airbrushed a fetching shade of crimson, and hid her smile at Eddie's bluntness.

Benson stepped next to Eddie. He was a bulldog; short and stocky, flat nose, face like someone played cricket with it. Eyes an untrustworthy translucent green. Eddie didn't find his face or his manner at all appealing. "You get your fucking arse back to work." Benson smiled. "Or I will personally throw you down those stairs myself. And then I'll submit a report to your Department Head. I'm sure you'd appreciate that, Eddie, wouldn't you?"

Eddie tried to step away from Benson, but he had a nauseating magnetism that kept him on the spot. And he couldn't look away either.

"Am I okay to go for sandwiches?" Ros asked.

"I'm warning you, Eddie. I need a quick result from this job. We're aiming for the first Rule Three direct from a scene."

"Forgive me for sounding like a dick, but what are you talking about?"

"We know who she is."

306

"Yeah?" Eddie found a hint of bravery, closed the gap down.

"Hey come on, you two—"

"And we know who her boyfriend is, too."

"Ten quid if you can tell me what they called their doll."

Benson grabbed Eddie's wrist. His eyes narrowed and he squeezed, digging his thumb into the carpal tunnel. Eddie breathed in, held it and tried to retreat. He couldn't.

"DCI Benson—"

"Shut it, woman!"

Ros did.

"Don't fuck around with me. We have a hunch that Christian Ledger is her killer. She is Alice Sedgewick, a misper from four years ago. A girl with mental health problems. An absconder from Juniper Hill."

Eddie raised an eyebrow, not in admiration of the information, but making a subconscious connection between her mental health problems and Benson himself – a sleight of hand insult that Benson wasn't slow on noticing. He squeezed hard enough to draw a whimper from Eddie, and more concern from Ros. She came closer, rested her hand on Benson's. She was about to speak when he abruptly turned to her. "Go get sandwiches. He doesn't mind which type."

"But—"

"You want me to write it down for you, love?"

Ros was about to launch into him when he beat her to it again. "Fuck off, girl, before I snap your boyfriend's wrist. Okay?" He tightened his thumb into the flesh. Eddie yelped this time.

Ros backed away. "I'll be back soon, Eddie," she said.

"Ros," Eddie called, a prickle in his voice.

"What?"

"No mustard on mine."

Ros laughed and even Eddie giggled a bit before Benson stopped him.

"Alright, alright! Pack it in." Eddie tried to pull free but Benson was keeping hold of Eddie's attention. "Get the fuck off me before I punch you in the knackers."

"That'd look good on the report."

"Not as good as you'll look holding one of your nuts in your hand and watching the other roll away down the path." Eddie nodded sincerely. "You know about my situation. So let go before I put you in hospital and turn you into a non-man."

Benson seemed to consider this, relaxed his grip and then let go.

Eddie stood back from Benson and massaged his wrist as pins and needles leaked in with the returning blood supply. "You are a spiny bastard, aren't you?"

"I like to get results."

"Yeah, the prehistoric way."

"If it worked for my forebears…"

"You didn't have forebears; you were grown in a beaker."

Benson made to step forward.

Eddie smiled. "Tell me about this Rule Three guy."

Chapter Fifty-Seven

Thursday 25th June

Christian left Leeds, and headed out towards Bradford, taking the back roads where he knew the likelihood of ANPR cameras was less. The Wellborne district was a scrap-man's version of heaven. If you were not rich, and if your car was on its last legs, here was a place where automotive miracles happened. Toleman Road ran parallel with the main A650 and the closer it got into Bradford town centre, the richer it appeared; independent dealers began a mile away from the town centre, then franchised dealers and finally, for the remaining half mile or so, the main dealers.

The closer into Bradford he drove, the more frequent were the vidiscreens. He nearly swallowed his heart when he caught sight of his own face with his name below it. *How did they get my name?* he wondered. "I'm not known to the police at that address, how did they link me—" The words dried up as he suddenly realised how they connected him with Alice: through his paintings, he always signed his paintings. And that meant… "They've taken them. Bastards!"

Christian was at the beginning of Toleman Road, the down-at-heel end where the common guy went for repairs, for part-worn tyres, and for dodgy MoT certificates to keep the old banger on the road for another year.

He pulled off the road, took a gravel track and followed it to a large wide-open pair of faded blue wooden doors. Inside, dull fluorescent tubes illuminated people who worked on cars well outside this neighbourhood's price range. Showers of sparks from grinders, the rattle of air tools and the constant groan of an air compressor.

His heart raced as he wondered how you brokered a deal with…

From the workshop, a man wearing red oil-smeared overalls walked towards him, cigarette dangling from his lower lip, smoke floating over his shoulder.

Christian wound down the window, and tucked his right arm out of sight down by the side of his seat.

"Help you?" The man's eyes hovered on Christian's bloody, matted hair, the dirt in his skin, the dried blood soaked into his T-shirt.

"It's done just over 6,000." Christian patted the steering wheel. "Not a mark on it."

The man stood back; he looked from the front of the car to the rear, and then took a slow walk around it. All the time, Christian sat there praying to get out of here alive. A couple of workers stood in the doorway, watching the BMW and the scruffy geezer sitting behind the wheel.

"I'll give you a thousand for it."

"It's worth over forty."

The man laughed at him. "Not round here, mate."

"Thousand and a legal car," Christian said.

"Five hundred and a legal car."

"Seven-fifty and a legal car."

The man eventually nodded and began to turn away again.

"And I need your help too." Christian brought his right arm into view. The cuff rattled.

* * *

The floor was plain dirt, in one corner was a four-poster car ramp with a red Toyota pickup in the air. Toolboxes and benches with racks of tyres next to them made up the far wall, and above them, a mezzanine floor bulged with body panels and exhaust systems. In the background, a tiny office with Goodyear posters under a cracked window spilled music into the dusty air through an open doorway.

Christian stood next to a metal workbench, the cuff on his right hand clamped firmly into a vice. A group of mechanics gathered around to watch the fun, laughing, smoking, coffees in hand, while one youth uncoiled a hosepipe from a tyre rim bolted to the wall, and another plugged in an angle grinder complete with a slitting disc.

"What happened to you, man? Look like you just stepped out of a war."

This got another wave of laughter from the easily amused mechanics. "Druggies beat me," Christian whispered. Some of them nodded knowingly, others seemed to know he was walking on the wrong side of the law, seemed to understand that fights with dealers were an occupational hazard, but at least he didn't moan about it, which was in his favour, and they had a little respect in their eyes.

He looked up from his wrist in time to see the BMW disappear up another dirt track behind the garage.

"My name's Sid. Do you trust me?"

Christian looked back to the man who had struck the deal; he was holding the grinder, oily thumb resting on the button, ready to go. The kid turned on the tap and stood tight up to Christian with the water trained on the handcuff loop, and he added a strip of steel between the cuff and Christian's wrist to prevent the sparks burning his skin. Christian smiled at Sid, "No, not really."

Sid laughed and the grinder howled into life.

* * *

Christian parked the old Nissan by the kerb and checked the sign outside the shop. Top Cutz. He locked the car, entered the shop and looked around. There were three staff, all huddled around a small television in the corner. On the floor were mounds of cut hair, some swept into a corner, most just left by the three chairs, and in the air a strong odour like thinners. In one of the chairs sat an old lady with strips of silver foil stuck to her head.

One of the women looked over from the TV, and Christian said, "Sid sent me."

Chapter Fifty-Eight

Thursday 25th June

"His name's Christian Ledger. Waster." Benson stepped back into the shade of the kitchen. Eddie followed. "He's been shacking up with Alice for about four years. He's a thief and he's a burglar. We pulled him only yesterday for shoplifting in some fancy art and crafts shop in town."

They walked through into the lounge, gazed at the ceiling with no plaster, at the cardboard box with dolls' clothes in it. Eddie stared at the lottery card. And then he squatted to look at the hammer. There was blood streaked up the head, hair caught in it. "But how do you know he killed her?"

"It's obvious."

"Enlighten me."

"It's strange that *you* should be working this scene."

Eddie stood. "I can't stand the tension. Do tell."

"It's because of you that we know who he is. Evidence you found at a burglary scene matches Ledger. He gave us a phoney address, but when he jumped bail this morning, his picture hit the vidiscreens and… well, there's nothing like waving a carrot in the public's face to bring them out of the fucking woodwork. Ten minutes later, we had a call. Then we had this address."

"Now I feel depressed."

"Need a snort of the hard stuff?"

Eddie glared at him. "You offering?"

"What have you got so far?"

"Apart from hunger pains and a DCI who won't piss off and let me work?"

"Come Monday, the only work you'll be doing is street cleaning."

"Just make sure you don't step in front of my cart, Benson." Eddie headed for the door. Then he stopped, turned. "How do you know about…"

"Your clumsiness? Your drunkenness?" Benson grinned, "I have friends."

"Now that *is* a shock."

"He's up for a Rule Three, Eddie. Better tell me what you've got."

"Hold on." Eddie came back to Benson. "You can't put someone on a Rule Three when you have no evidence. Whatever happened to innocent until—"

"Don't bore me. These two lived as recluses. She's dead, right? Who does that leave, Einstein?"

"You still need evidence."

"That's what I'm asking for. What have you got?"

"Footwear marks in blood so far."

"What make?"

"Nike Air, it looks like. And some kind of a shoe."

"Good, you found Nike Air at the burglary and that's what we have from the cells."

"Doesn't prove he killed her. There were other foot—"

"It proves he was here. That's enough to haul his arse in and start asking some pretty big questions."

No argument there from Eddie, but, "How can you advertise him as Rule Three? He might not have killed her."

"I think he did. Anyway," Benson turned to leave, "we post him as provisional Rule Three. That way, we don't get vigilantes knocking him off. When we get him in, he coughs to killing Alice."

That explained the press – pre-ordered no doubt by Benson himself. "Why don't you get it; he might not have killed her."

"He'll cough. Don't you worry. Now, find me some more evidence." Benson stopped by the front door. "And Eddie, don't take too long with the lunch. Oh, and no booze, okay?"

The words sliced him, just as they were meant to. He was about to go outside, have a cigarette and wait for Ros, when his mobile rang. It was Mick.

Chapter Fifty-Nine

Thursday 25th June

– One –

Mick buzzed. This was better than alcohol, and several times better than sex; even real sex, with another person. This was what he had waited for and he acknowledged it as the pinnacle of his career to date. He walked approximately six inches above the carpet, and for the first time in a decade, wasn't thinking too hard about his next drink.

He rode the escalator to the first floor and then slid his card through the reader, allowing his entry into the staff-only sections of *The Yorkshire Echo* building. It was two o'clock and the office was frantic – as usual – with people running around desks, negotiating deals, securing space, others not bothering to run, just shouting to their colleagues. Computers hummed, telephones rang, and the air conditioning droned. He glided right through it, oblivious.

Today, Rochester would offer him a blowjob, performed personally, would buy him a shop-full of ties and give him a raise. He reached the door, took a deep breath and knocked.

Nothing. He knocked again, smile prepared. Nothing.

Mick opened the door and stepped inside. Rochester sat behind his desk, glanced up at Mick and thrust out a hand, holding it there as his eyes flitted around the room, not seeing anything, but he was obviously listening hard. Mick stopped dead, mid-step, mouth half-forming the first important sentence of his years at this newspaper. He could hear a hissing, and then noticed Rochester pressing something silver deeper into one ear.

At last, Rochester said goodbye, pressed a button and stood, pulling his jacket from a hook on the wall by his large desk.

"Mr Rochester?"

"Mick, I have to go," he flicked an arm, looked at his watch, "I'm late already."

"But, Mr Rochester, this is the story of the century."

Rochester put his coat on, face expressionless, ignorance apparent.

Mick stared. "Excuse me!"

"It will keep until tomorrow; I have a meeting and then dinner this evening."

"Please, sir; this won't take long—"

"*Tomorrow*, Mick." Rochester almost ran around the desk, hooked his briefcase and was on top of Mick, almost pushing him out of the door. "Come on, move, man." He barged Mick out of the way and set off across the main office.

Mick watched him disappearing through *advertising*, past *electronic space*, through *classifieds*… and then decided he was worth a thousand times more than any dinner. He wasn't just some washed-up old hack; he was a man with talent and he was going to make sure Rochester considered himself lucky to have him on staff. "Rochester. Stop!"

It worked.

Just as Rochester turned to see who dared shout him like that, Mick set off after him. The office buzz stopped as quickly as a bluebottle under a rolled-up newspaper. Everyone stared as Mick chased Rochester down.

"Hope this is good." Rochester looked not at all amused.

"Bet your arse it is." Mick offered no subservience, no 'sir' this time. This time, Mick was king of the dung heap. "I need to talk to you in private."

"I told you—"

"You don't get it, do you? This isn't me asking about a paisley tie or begging you for a pay rise or pleading for another chance—"

Rochester turned red. "Get *on*—"

"Remember me telling you how The Rules were…" he looked around. A thousand eyes peered at him. "We need to talk privately; this is bigger than anything this paper has handled before." There was intrigue in Rochester's eyes. "This is that world exclusive I promised you."

"Farrier?"

"Not just him," he whispered, "it goes into Whitehall. It goes into the Justice Ministry." Mick paused. "Now do I have your fucking attention?"

Rochester pressed the button on the wire dangling from his ear. "Tony, hold the car would you. I'll be along shortly."

* * *

Mick made sure the office door was closed as Rochester retook his seat. "You have my attention. Use it wisely."

He did, for almost half an hour. For the first five minutes, Rochester fidgeted in his chair and stole glances at his watch, but soon became absorbed, and forgot about the time completely. And Mick could tell how seriously Rochester was taking his story because his jaw opened fractionally with each new sentence until it was wide enough to cram the barrel of a WW2 handgun neatly inside. Without chipping teeth.

"You used to support The Rules wholeheartedly."

"I still do, but not while Deacon controls them."

Rochester scratched his chin, "This changes our stance too. I need to work on what implications that will have for the rest of us."

For a moment, Mick was dismayed, "Don't bring this argument down to pounds, shillings and pence."

"What?"

"It means more… this whole story means more than revenue, and it's not about being a good bedfellow to the government."

It took Rochester a moment to grasp Mick's meaning. "I'm not in this for the money. This is my newspaper, the biggest in the group, and it has never bent over for an easy life. We get news, we print it."

Rochester was enthralled enough to propose devoting two days' front headlines to the story, and enlisting the help of *The Sunday Echo* for the observers' points of view, and any further information Mick and the researchers could pull from the archives. He listened to Mick's recorder twice through, made notes and then contacted his secretary to email a part transcript to the sub-editor with details of the proposed coverage and space needed for Mick's main story.

There were editorials to prepare, straw polls to conduct… Rochester worked himself into a frenzy and Mick thanked God for the courage to bluff Henry Deacon. His mind flitted to the secret Henry mentioned.

"Take Suzanne Child as your number two," he told Mick. "Treat her well and teach her the ropes."

Mick blinked as though he were coming round from a bout of unconsciousness. "Okay," was all he could say.

He left the office an hour and ten minutes after stepping in there, his scuffed shoes licked to a brilliant shine by Rochester's tongue.

– Two –

The stairs to the first floor ran directly out of the lounge, and they creaked underfoot. Ros peered out of the hole in the rear bedroom window at the vehicles parked on the cobbled street below. Beyond them was a field of sorts where the drug barons hung out on the swings, drinking lager and cider. Ros thought of Eddie and wondered how he was getting on without an alcohol top-up.

"Hold on…" She leaned closer to the broken glass, saw the lone figure walking through her scene and was about to shout when she recognised the slight limp. Eddie? He carried his scene suit in his hand and waved to someone further up the street. Ros craned her neck and just made out the shape of a man standing by a dark blue car, door open. "Mick," she whispered.

Ros leaned through the broken window. "Eddie?" He walked on, never even broke stride or glanced over his shoulder. "Where the hell are you going?" Eddie reached the waiting car. She tore a hole in her scene suit, searched inside for her trouser pocket for her mobile phone and dialled. He answered after three rings. "Eddie," she said, "where the hell are you?"

"I'll be back soon. Hold the fort for me, would ya?" And then he rang off.

– Three –

"I've walked out on a murder scene for this, I've left Ros on her own, I could get into…"

Mick smiled across the roof. "…a shit-load of trouble?"

"Yeah." Eddie sounded deflated again.

But Mick had refused to talk about it until they were safely ensconced in Eddie's flat. By which time Eddie was ready to throttle him.

Mick slammed the flat door behind him and Eddie wasted no time getting acquainted with the rum he'd bought yesterday, swigging straight from the bottle. "You gonna tell me what's so urgent?"

"First, I'm going to get us a couple of glasses; we may be alcoholics, but we are not without decorum!"

Each sat in his customary seat, cigarette in one hand, glass of dark rum in the other. "This had better be good; I abandoned a major scene for this, and I abandoned Ros."

Mick solemnly nodded. "It goes all the way to the top."

"Will you stop talking in riddles and get on with it? I'm losing patience."

"I *know* who was driving Deacon's Jag when it killed Sam."

They stared at each other. The rum tasted like nothing to Eddie. He gulped the liquor on autopilot; he could have been drinking water for the effect it had on him, or petrol for all he cared. "You went to see him? And?" Eddie held the glass and held his breath.

"It *was* him," was all Mick said.

Eddie inhaled on his cigarette so violently that the filter collapsed and burned his lips. "Fuck!" He crushed the cigarette into his fist, and let it fall to the floor where he dragged a foot across the smouldering embers. "I think I've dropped the biggest bollock in my life."

"Who have you hit this time?"

"I blabbed it round the office. I found all this evidence in the car and I blabbed 'cause I knew that no one other than the regular driver had driven it. I just *knew* it. And I was giddy."

"Don't worry who you blabbed to, it won't make the slightest difference after what I found out."

Eddie eyed Mick, not sure if he wanted to know.

"When I saw Henry Deacon today, I played the old two dictaphone trick on him. He told me everything."

"Christ's sake, Mick. *What* did he tell you?"

"Listen to this." Mick drained his glass, laid the dictaphone on the table, and pressed play.

Eddie heard Mick's voice, muffled as the machine had moved around inside his jacket pocket.

The machine played, and Mick's voice said, "*Strange. That blue Ford Focus belongs to me. I was sitting in it. I had my camera with me. It's a beauty, one of those long range digital things that take wonderful—*"

"*Okay, okay, get to the point!*"

"Hold on, let me wind it forward a bit." Mick's voice came through the tiny speaker, "*Even your dad might not be able to lend you a hand. See what I mean?*"

There was a considerable pause before, "*Let's assume you're right, Mr Lyndon, how do I know you won't carry out your threat anyway?*"

At those words, Eddie looked across at Mick, raised his eyebrows. "This is Henry Deacon?"

Mick nodded.

"Henry, I am interested only in Lincoln Farrier's murder. I assure you. I'm not interested in the bloody CSI office, and I certainly don't give a flying shit about Mr Archer on Leeds Road."

Eddie looked up; Mick waved a hand. "Just words, that's all. Now listen."

Eddie did listen. He listened while Mick lied about having a girlfriend on the forensics team. He listened to Henry Deacon threaten Mick, and he listened as Mick asked, *"How do you know this Sirius man?"*

"Because he's the one my father sent to help me sort out the Jaguar and then burn the CSI building."

Mick pressed stop.

For a long time, Eddie said nothing. He relaxed back into his chair as though recently satisfied by a large Sunday lunch, reached for his cigarettes, and cried.

– Four –

"He said it all with no feeling. Like he ran over a fucking hedgehog or something. Has he no feelings?"

"He has feelings alright, but only for himself."

"Bastard!"

"Though I have to say, for a man under pressure, he was remarkably subdued, no real evidence of nerves."

"You a doctor now?"

"Eddie, don't get shitty with me. There's more to come yet, and it'll explain what I mean about the pressure he's under."

"What did you mean about your car and some camera?"

"It was a cheap bluff and he bought it like his dad buys policemen. He burned your office, him and that Sirius bloke. Easy as tickling a trout."

Eddie sank further into a depression and his eyes were drawn to the corner of the room where the seldom used vacuum cleaner lurked. It laughed at him. "I can't understand why he fired the CSI building. I mean, I know it was to try and destroy evidence, but if he's wise enough to find out which CSI from which office examined the Jaguar, you'd think he'd be wise enough to know we upload our DNA and fingerprints over to the relevant…"

"What's wrong?" Mick sat forward.

"What time did he set the fire?"

"Not sure, why?"

"Everything is uploaded at one o'clock."

"What about all your physical evidence, like the shirt sleeve?"

Eddie shrugged. "Won't know until Jeffery's checked the store room."

"You shouldn't worry; it'll still come bouncing back on him."

"Do you really think he'll face Rule Three? I don't. The scene I went to today, the one you dragged me away from, already has a provisional Rule Three suspect."

"So?"

"They advertised a man's identity before we even found anything, All they had was a name, just a man who *could* have done it. Deacon has gone well over the top; he's forcing coppers into a competition; now no one cares if the guilty are caught and punished, they only care that *someone's* caught and punished. It keeps the number-crunchers happy."

"No, you're wrong, Eddie. If the system fails, the public will revolt against The Rules—"

"Bollocks! Who's to know if the system fails? Do you think they'll publish their mistakes in your paper? I don't. This guy they're broadcasting now, this Christian Ledger, he might have been out of the house while someone killed the girl, and he'll go down for it. Who's going to stand up for *him*?" Eddie fell silent, the exertion of the argument caused his chest to heave and he eagerly reached for another cigarette, flexing his right hand after the burn from the previous one. "Get me a top-up, will ya."

Mick refilled their glasses, sat back down.

"And what did he mean by his threat to have you killed? You mix with the most unsavoury characters."

"And you don't?"

Eddie thought of Benson, nodded his agreement.

"He means that if I go to press with this he's going to see I end my days propping up the M1 extension."

"He won't do that."

"How do you know?"

"They're not building an M1 extension."

Mick squinted at Eddie.

"What're you going to do?"

"I've already done it."

"Done what, Mick?"

Mick tilted his head to one side; gave a half smile.

"What? Are you mad?"

"I suppose I am." He laughed out smoke puffs that added to the layers of smoke hanging around the room. "I gave him my word that I wouldn't tell the police, didn't mention that I'd print the story though. But it's going out over a few days, not all at once." He laughed, and then it fell quiet. "I think he was serious though, so if I go missing one day, I'd appreciate it if you could have a quick scout around for me."

"Why did you write the story now? It could have waited till this had calmed down a bit, surely?"

"This is England; things don't calm down anymore, they merely return to simmer. And anyway, the longer I waited the less chance I had of it remaining an exclusive."

"You've opened up a right one there, you have. I don't know the man, but he sounded pretty firm when he threatened you."

"I've no doubt that he'll consider coming after me."

"There's something you're not telling me, isn't there?"

"Sir George Deacon is about to add his son's name to Sirius's to-do list."

"You are shitting me."

"And, strange at it sounds, I think Henry sort of trusts me. The fool. He knows he's about to die and he's holding back a present for me. It's one of the reasons I went ahead with the story now, I think Henry Deacon needs this little old journo." Mick leaned forward, pressed play again. "Listen to this."

Mick's voice again. *"You saying your old man would fly you out?"*

"He'll have me killed. But he won't wait until the full story comes out."

"Forgive my asking this, but if he's so determined to keep you out of the press and out of the slaughterhouse, because he's worried about his career, then…"

"Why didn't he kill me earlier?"

"Well, yes."

"Because I blackmailed him."

"With what?"

"Right now, I can look forward to a swift departure, but if I gave out my secret before I died, I suspect my departure may be elongated somewhat."

"Shit. You say, 'before you died'? What do you mean by that?"

"I have things to say, but I daren't say them while I'm alive."

"Then, how will—"

321

"Search for them. I'm sure if anyone can find my secret, Mr Lyndon, it will be you."

"Is this the 'use' you have for me?"

Mick turned the machine off, stared at Eddie.

"I can't believe it." Eddie's face showed shock. "His own father is going to have him killed?"

"He values his career, does our Sir George."

"So do you."

"Keeps me in this," Mick tipped the glass at Eddie.

"And you thought he was an angel."

"I always knew he was a slimy bastard, I said The Rules were an excellent idea. I still do think that, in principle. That's why I always supported them, and that's why I knew Sir George would see me. And that's why I'm going to be the one to bring the fucker to his knees."

"So what do you think his little secret is?"

Mick shrugged. "I have no idea. But I can't wait till he's dead; I'll do some real digging then."

"If you've published your story already, you might not have long to wait."

Mick smiled, tipped his glass to Eddie and whispered in a mischievous voice, "That's what I'm hoping for."

Chapter Sixty

Thursday 25th June

The surveyor had tutted like a plumber giving a quote. It took almost an hour before he finished and presented Jeffery with a *Proceed with caution.*

As the surveyor's vehicle trundled off site, the fire investigator's vehicle trundled on. It was gone within five minutes. Jeffery had not been quite so polite this time, but promised that if he found anything noteworthy, he would call them back.

His team consisted of three people. Any more would be counterproductive, since Morley CSI office was tiny; and now, with blackened and melted furniture, the twisted carcasses of lockers, and a floor-wide tangle of wires, he deemed it a health and safety hazard.

Before lunch, Jeffery had liaised with a dour young woman called Anne, the input from the Forensic Science Service.

Work began in earnest after lunch. Dressed in scene suits, steel-reinforced wellington boots and hard hats, Jeffery, Aadi, and Anne had cleared the main entrance of fallen notice boards, and sifted the charred remains for signs of accelerants. They had pulled out hunks of melted furniture, successfully removed the twisted lockers from just inside the main office, and trimmed back the lengths of wires that hung from the ceiling like garrottes ready for the careless.

Each time they triumphed with a little progress, Aadi photographed it. They meticulously worked through the scene, trowelling aside sodden debris until they cleared a large patch on the office carpet, aiming towards the far side of the office where the chargers, uploading stations and exhibit stores were. The expanse of carpet revealed two things to them. Firstly, a large blackened section neatly outlined against the relatively unburnt surrounding area.

"This is deliberate." Jeffery stood with his hands on his hips. "Pool burning. And the rest of the carpet's surface is singed. Vapour?"

Anne nodded her agreement, and Aadi approached with camera and nylon bag ready to take the obligatory sample.

Nearly two hours after this initial find, the carpet revealed its second and rather more significant "exhibit".

Jeffery was half way through his latest cup of tea, wondering why there were the remains of so many CID6 books everywhere, when he spat out a mouthful and promptly dropped the cup. He scrambled across the damp floor, pointing. "There's a hand!" Anne and Aadi watched in shock as he reached the desk, dropped to his knees and pulled aside a melted chair to reveal a charred set of fingers, and a thumb that had cracked open at the base. He could see red muscle and a slice of yellow fat gaping at him.

The colour in Jeffery's face leached away. "Stuart," he whispered. But if Jeffery thought *this* was a revelation, then Stuart had one last thing for him to marvel at.

* * *

"Leave him where he is till I get back." Clearly upset, Jeffery scurried from the building, and returned ten minutes later with DI Taylor. The light had diminished, and a breeze scooted through the office, lifting black ash. It fluttered around like dead snow, settling everywhere, even on Stuart's grilled face like a final indignation.

"Sure it's him?"

Jeffery nodded. "Ninety-nine per cent."

Taylor stared mesmerised at the body. "What was he doing here?" he asked no one in particular. "Right, treat it as a suspicious, and get him out soon as you can. I'll jack up a forensic PM for later tonight, but you keep me posted on your progress, Jeff."

Jeffery hated being called Jeff, but it suddenly seemed unimportant after the chill realisation that a colleague was dead. *Jeff* was like *sky* and *doorknob*: ordinary. "I will," he said, "we'll work all night if we have to." He looked at Aadi and then at Anne, and received no negativity from either.

Taylor stood alone with his thoughts for just a moment longer before turning for the exit.

Jeffery asked, "Who's going to give the death warning?"

Taylor's head slumped. "Confirm it's him." He walked away.

Jeffery gave the nod and Aadi got to work with the camera. And that was fine because it allowed him time to replay a memory that was only a few days old. It had been sunny, and there were voices, two of them, male voices, angry. And then he saw them: Eddie Collins – the superhero – and him, Stuart, the one nobody liked. He saw Stuart walk away, with that smug grin on his face, the one reserved for deliberate provocation, and he heard Eddie Collins mumble something. And the first time Jeffery heard that mumble, it slid by him as harmlessly as *Jeff* or *sky* or *doorknob*, but then he rewound it and listened again, and some of the threat in his voice made Jeffery take notice, like snapping awake during a bad dream. And now, as the careful excavation around Stuart's body began, the words he recalled, combined with the tone, made Jeffery shudder.

I'm gonna kill you, Stuart.

An hour later, they had freed the warped desk from two plastic chairs that seemed determined to hold on to their friend as long as possible. The desk was now outside in the twilight, lit by battery-powered lamps and guarded by a PCSO. Back in here, Aadi took a series of photographs to show Stuart's semi-prone position more clearly.

His head and shoulders and one hand had blistered under the radiated heat, while the valiant desk had protected his torso, the other arm, and his legs. They were relatively unmarked, though covered in a layer of ash and soot.

Jeffery knelt at Stuart's side brushing away the soot, and that was when Stuart gave up his best exhibit yet for them all to marvel at. "Jesus." He sank back to the floor. Aadi and Anne crept closer, bringing with them one standard lamp each to further illuminate the gruesome mess that was once Stuart.

Most of the skin on Stuart's face had peeled away and the rest had blistered or flaked off in sheets to reveal a light grey skull with cracks across its surface. And the fat from his neck had run in tiny rivulets down to soak the sweater and drip into the ashes on the floor.

In the centre of his chest, charred and flaking, was a pool of black blood. With gloved hands, Jeffery slid Stuart's sweater up revealing his abdomen and chest. "He's been shot." His voice was little more than a whisper and Jeffery felt strangely emotional right now. Jobs where one excavated a body from a fatal fire scene were wholly unpleasant. But he'd never excavated a colleague from a fatal fire scene until now. This job transcended distinct lines that had always remained so far apart.

He considered two things. Firstly, he wondered if he should vomit about now. It seemed fitting considering the circumstances; and secondly he wondered if he should step aside and let someone more detached take over the scene.

"He's taken one through the head as well, Jeffery," Aadi pointed.

Between the eyes and about an inch upward was a small hole with radiating cracks. He pulled the sweater back down, and then gently swung the body to the side but thankfully, there was no exit wound.

"We need those bullets," Anne said. "Let's get him out of here, and then we can search properly."

As he laid Stuart back down again, Jeffery noticed the bulge in Stuart's jacket pocket. It was a half-bottle of brandy. And he found another in the other pocket. He stared at them for a full minute, wondering what they were doing in Stuart's pocket here in the CSI office. And no matter how hard he tried, he could not get away from the possibility that Eddie planted them there.

Jeffery put the bottles down on a table that he had brought in, on which rested his notepad, and empty cups. "Photos please, Aadi. And see if there are any shop labels on them, price tags or what have you."

"Will do."

"And then fingerprint them."

"Okay."

"And then unscrew the caps and swab the rims. Please."

Aadi nodded and got to work.

"And I want decanted samples too."

Anne looked at Jeffery. "We should get the body out—"

"Stuart; his name's Stuart."

Anne nodded in deference, though there was a little worry in her eyes too because it was *always* a body, it was *never* "Stuart". "We need to begin looking for shell cases."

Jeffery nodded. "I'll get the undertakers here." He left the building and made the arrangements. And then he made a call to Ros. Part of him wanted to warn her in case she came back here and saw Stuart; he didn't want her shocked as he had been, but part of him wanted to hear her reaction, to listen for glee in her voice. She and Eddie were close, and if Eddie had mentioned anything to her about retribution, he had a good chance of hearing it in Ros's voice.

* * *

Jeffery fidgeted with a fresh pair of nitrile gloves. "No matter how hard I try, I can't get away from the possibility that Eddie planted them there."

"Eddie?" asked Taylor.

"Collins."

326

Taylor peered into the CSI office foyer and then turned to make sure the PCSO wasn't earwigging. "Why the hell would he do that?"

Jeffery paused, unsure of whether to continue with his theory; because that's all it was, just a theory. "Eddie has a drinking problem. Everyone knows about it. He and Stuart were enemies—"

"Why?"

"Only yesterday Stuart found a bottle of brandy in Eddie's drawer and brought it to my attention. I reprimanded Eddie."

"You're saying Eddie shot him, and then planted the bottles on him?"

Jeffery threw his arms out to his sides. "It's a message for me; Eddie's saying the first bottle was a plant, and here Stuart is trying to do the same again."

"But—"

"They hated each other."

"Any fingerprints on the bottles?"

Jeffery sighed. "Clean."

Taylor shook his head, "I can't take it all in, Jeff. Stuart being shot, booze 'planted' in his pockets and then—"

"I could understand it if it happened in that sequence: Eddie shoots Stuart, plants the bottles, and then fires the building to cover his tracks. But I still fail to understand two things: where would Eddie get a gun from, and what were they both doing here at that hour of the night?"

Taylor turned to walk away. "I need his address."

"There's one more thing."

Without turning, Taylor said, "There can't possibly be any more."

"I heard him say he was going to kill Stuart."

"Jeffery," Anne called from the main office. The rustling of her scene suit preceded her entrance into the foyer. She was carrying something small held aloft on the end of a cotton swab.

Jeffery peered at the brass shell casing.

"9mm," she said. "Federal."

Chapter Sixty-One

Thursday 25th June

– One –

The lounge was totally bare; the smashed doll was in an evidence bag waiting for the exhibits officer to collect it along with the blood-stained hammer, the cigarettes, the lottery card.

The body was at the mortuary.

Ros faced the dark rectangle of the cellar entrance. The smell was strange; like oil, thick, clingy. Curiosity prodded her and she stepped towards it. It was the only room she hadn't visited yet.

As she descended, her stomach fluttered at the thought of Benson coming by to see how they were doing. What if he did; what if Jeffery did? What could she possibly say about Eddie's absence? "Stupid man."

Ros noticed a structure in the centre of the room. It was an easel, and the plastic sheet suspended above it had waves of dust in its creases. This dust was right across its surface, except for two places at the front edge, as though someone had recently lifted it to examine whatever was beneath. But there *was* nothing beneath it; a glance at the sides would tell you that.

And that in itself was curious. Why lift the sheet if there was nothing to see? It wouldn't have been Eddie, he would have crouched too – look first, touch only if necessary. Ros inspected the fingermarks and discerned valuable detail in the dust. "Robbery?"

And then she paid the easel close attention, noted how its feet were not in their original place, how they had left slip marks in the dust on the floor.

Her torchlight caught the bulb directly over the plastic sheet and she followed its wire up to the ceiling and along, deeper into the cellar, past a part-collapsed chest of drawers containing paints, brushes and spatulas and on to the large battery on the floor in the far corner. Then her attention moved to the rest of the room. The torch pushed aside the shadows and revealed a small doorway.

She walked to the door, peered inside through the web that dangled there like a sentinel ready to attack those who dared enter.

She could see plastic bin bags covering the paintings that Eddie had seen.

Crouching, she entered the small room. There were a dozen or more, some with the bags pulled partway back, and it was to these she carefully edged her way. Ros dared not look up for fear of what might be dangling over her. She swallowed and bent to the paintings.

She held her breath, teetering on her tiptoes. She leaned forward and stretched out a gloved hand.

"Ros."

She jumped. Her foot slipped and she fell against the wall. The torch fell and Ros screamed.

"You okay in there?"

Someone shone a light as a spider fell onto her face. She screamed again and writhed about on the floor, kicking, frantically slapping herself down, the crackling of her suit flooded her ears. The torchlight grew larger and Benson poked his head through the doorway as Ros calmed and reached for her own torch. "Don't ever do that again! Imbecile!"

Benson backed out again. "Wrong time of the month?"

"I don't usually swear," Ros shouted, "but just fuck off!"

"No need to get tense."

Ros growled and continued her search for the damned spider. Her torch traced her scene suit, then the floor and then the walls. She followed the rotten doorframe upwards until…

"Anyway, you can wrap it up now. We're out of here."

"I– we haven't finished yet."

"Whatever you've got will be enough. We know who did it—"

"You can't close a scene down till we've finished, we might lose—"

"I'm not posting men here all bleeding night just so you two can confirm what we already know. The exhibits officer's collected all the crap you found already and now it's time to ship out."

"But—"

"You've got half an hour. If you're not ready, you're on your own."

"And I'm telling you—"

"*Don't* tell me how to do my fucking job, woman." He crouched in the doorway. "If you needed more time, then you shouldn't have spent so long on lunch." He half-smiled. "Where's your boyfriend? I want to let him know."

"Alright, alright. I'll go tell him." Ros glared at him, snatched her hood down.

Benson checked his watch. "You've got until seven and then—"

"We're on our own, I know." She watched his torch-lit silhouette disappear towards the stairs and then heard the grit beneath his feet as he climbed them. "Bastard."

It was smeared against her chest. She shuddered at the sight of long black legs and the squashed grape of its thorax that had spilled a smear of green-yellow liquid two inches long. She closed her eyes and cursed Eddie.

When she opened them again, she was staring at a white bundle up between the doorframe and the crumbling brick above it. It was clean. It was fresh.

– Two –

He still didn't answer. "Damned phones!" She had twenty-six minutes before the police left. Not even two people could accomplish all she had to do and get packed up in twenty-six minutes. "Might've had a chance though," she whispered. And then her eyes narrowed. "If he's gone drinking…"

Ros made her mind up to do it anyway. And she also made her mind up to kick Eddie's arse until he had to shit out of his mouth for leaving her like this. She crawled from the alcove, dragged the paintings out and lugged them up the stairs. It took three trips just to get them in the kitchen and by the time she'd carried the camera back downstairs, she had sweat trickling down her back and could see bubbles of it floating around inside her gloves.

She took location shots of the easel and the plastic sheet, and shot eight exposures of the fingermarks in dust, using oblique lighting to capture the ridge detail. Putting her dreaded hood back up, she crept into the alcove, taking further shots along the way. Once inside, she crouched, spun on her toes and photographed the clean white bundle up there by the corner of the doorframe.

Two minutes to isolation. She could already hear engines outside. She bit her lip and moved on, grabbing a clear tamper-proof evidence bag, and rammed the bundle of cash inside.

Shouts from outside, more engines, and then a strange kind of silence.

Ros stuffed the cash into the camera case, grabbed the torch and climbed the stairs again.

Now came the part she dreaded: walking to the van to get evidence sacks for the tarp and, "Shit," she cursed again, "what about the easel?" It would keep until tomorrow when she could return with a colleague. A colleague who wouldn't desert her. Right now, she was jittery and didn't need to be here. Jeffery would hear about Benson pulling the plug on her though, leaving her vulnerable in the Leeds equivalent of Beirut. But as she opened the van doors, it dawned on her: she couldn't say anything to Jeffery without dropping Eddie in it.

She yanked her old gloves off, dried her hands and put on a fresh pair, grabbed the evidence sacks and locked the van. Without making it obvious, she looked around. The youths, boisterous, drunk, high, were still there, and it appeared their number had grown. Her stride quickened and despite the shouts and whistles coming her way, she kept her head forward and matched her stride to the speed of her rushing heart.

Back in the cellar, the plastic sheet came down easier than she thought it would, and once she'd marked its upper surface with an indelible pen, she packaged it inside an evidence bag. Above her, the kitchen door grated across the floor. She froze, mouth open, eyes wide.

Was it Eddie, come back to finish up?

No, it wasn't Eddie.

– Three –

Christian steered the Nissan out of the neighbourhood. He saw police cars heading towards his old house and realised this wasn't the dream beginning of a new life for him, it was the death of his old one.

He drove through the outskirts of Leeds and saw the vidiscreen on a supermarket wall. The face of a Rule Three villain scrolled off the screen, and a new one took its place. His own. Christian Ledger, it said, Rule Two Infringement. They'd given him a number as well: 1313. *Contact Crimestoppers and claim your reward. This space is sponsored by Tesco, Every Little Helps.*

So now he was a wanted felon. And for what? For stealing a tube of burnt umber. And for burglary. His eyes were so drawn to the face, and to the word reward, that he didn't see the police car in his rear-view mirror.

The blue lights blazed at him.

Somewhere inside, his heart shrivelled to a walnut and almost stopped beating, not because of the fear of finally being hauled in by the police but because of the sudden attack of regret; he had wasted his talent. He could have been–

The police car drove past him, its blue lights slapped the side of his car and the siren screamed as the car approached a junction a hundred yards away.

The walnut kicked once, kicked again, and then resumed a steady rhythm somewhere near his bowel.

For a wonderful moment, Christian dared to hope that he could take off from here, maybe go far south into Cornwall, or far north to the highlands of Scotland and begin all over again. He could take on a new name, to go with his new, shortened and dyed hair, maybe put a couple of earrings in and a nose stud or something, anything to prevent people from making a connection between him and number 1313.

Chapter Sixty-Two

Thursday 25th June

– One –

Eddie kicked the empty bottle, and put the phone down and staggered to the kitchen. He felt guilty about leaving Ros like that. But he'd tried to ring three times, left a message the last time, expressing how bad he felt, and that he'd make it up to her. He promised to treat her better from now on. He liked her, and had no right to trample her like that.

It was a little after eight on Thursday night and Eddie crammed buttered bread into his mouth, and swallowed black coffee as though he wasn't going to drink for a week. An hour passed before normality returned to his world. He stared at Mick, pleased that he was at last staying in focus. "There are three stages, I think, to being a pisshead." Crumbs clung to his wrinkled shirt.

"Is this *Wisdom According to Collins?*"

"Sobriety," he said, "is smack in the middle. Inebriation is above it, and hangover or withdrawal, whatever you want to call it, is below. See?"

"How profound." Mick stubbed out his cigarette, dumped it in the kitchen bin, and rested his backside against the sink, arms folded, waiting for the next morsel of divinity.

"When I wake up in the morning, regardless of whether I've had a drink the night before—"

"You've always had a drink the night before."

Eddie was working on his balance, and he reckoned in another half an hour he'd have it cracked for sure. "Fair point. Anyway, when I wake up in the morning, I have to drink just to get to sobriety. Does that happen to you?"

"I keep a bottle at the side of my bed. When I wake up, my friend, I'm already sober."

Eddie nodded, finding the idea most agreeable. "You ever thought about quitting? The booze, I mean." From here, he could see the empty rum bottle in the lounge.

Mick poured another coffee, took Eddie's mug and refilled it.

"After what we just put away, you should be pissed, and I have to say it's annoying that you're not."

"I am. But I control it better. You're still a beginner. I've been like this most of my adult life and my kidneys are old hands at railroading the poison. I am one of life's perpetual pissheads. I cannot go an hour without something. Well, if I do, I start to feel groggy—"

"Hungover, the stage below sobriety."

"Whatever, Frankenstein."

"You mean Einstein."

"I know what I mean. And the answer is of course I tried," Mick said. "I try every day of my stinking life because every day of my stinking life I think this'll be the last one. I think my kidneys, good as they are, will just say 'fuck you' and shut up shop. Or my ticker will resign and I'll hit the pavement like an alcohol balloon. I always think to myself, *Mick, when you get a moment to have a word with yourself about this, you are going to have to convince yourself that it's probably doing you no good at all. Could even be harming you.*"

Eddie laughed.

"But I never get the chance to have that conversation. I think I avoid myself."

"I try to stop, too. But I enjoy it." And then Eddie noticed his trembling hand. "Well, I used to enjoy it. Now it's a habit and whenever I find myself getting low, I drink because it stops me getting lower. It gives me stability. And they're right; it does help you forget." Mick nodded his agreement, and Eddie's eyes sank towards the floor and he contemplated breaking the news.

This could be it; this could cause them to go their separate ways.

Mick never questioned Eddie's desperation to get back to sobriety so quickly. But the odd look in his eyes told Eddie that maybe he knew already.

Eddie asked, "Fancy a drive?"

"Where?"

"I'll tell you on the way."

– Two –

They had driven around Wakefield for twenty-five minutes and Mick was getting naffed off with him, but Eddie couldn't muster the courage to ask him outright. He mentally challenged his friendship with Mick, and each time he practised asking the question, Mick slammed on the brakes and kicked him out of the car. He was worried. But some things in life are worth ending your life for, he repeated to himself.

"Out with it." Mick pulled the car up quickly without indicating. The car behind swerved, tyres slipping on the wet road, horn blaring. Mick turned his head to Eddie and asked, "It's Henry Deacon, isn't it?"

Eddie paused. "Do you think I'm a tit?"

Mick stroked his chin, and Eddie could hear the bristles scrape against his hands.

"No need to give it so much thought."

"You have every right, Eddie. I don't blame you at all, not one bit. But what's done can't be undone, poor Sam is still dead, and afterwards, he still would be. And I know you can't put a value on something like this, but do think it's worth it? Really?"

For a long time Eddie said nothing, noticed the spits of rain falling on the screen, join with others and in the dazzling light of approaching cars, watched them trickle downwards before the wipers obliterated them. At last, he said, "You keep a bottle at the side of your bed and have a swig or two through the small hours until daylight comes and you take a couple of gulps before your breakfast and after your shower. And before you set off for work, it's like a bolster to have a cupful?"

"You been spying on me?"

"It's like that with me and my kid. Has been for weeks. Except during the night, I don't sip gracefully, I gulp bucketfuls of his memory, and I cry. There's no wailing, no sobbing. Just tears. I do that all night, like a drip-feed only in reverse. And in the morning the tears stop. But the thoughts don't. After my breakfast I take a bath in those thoughts, I lather myself up with hatred." Eddie looked forward through the screen, the pearls of rain out of focus, the streetlamps sharp yet hazy. "Sound like a prick, don't I?"

"You sound like a grieving father who wants…" Mick stopped.

Eddie looked at him. "Don't *you* be afraid to say it too. I think it all day and all night and, hell, *I'm* still afraid to say it."

"Comes down to trust, my friend."

"I trust you. Ever since—"

"Ever since the first nightmare?"

"In one." Eddie looked hopefully at Mick. "You up for it?"

– Three –

There was a phone ringing somewhere and she wished to God that someone would answer it. Her eyes flickered, and opened.

It was approaching twilight, and she was still in the damp terraced house where that girl's body was found. And worst of all, she was alone. Ros's eyes grew wide and along with the pain in her head came the memory of why she was here. She'd been examining the scene alone, and while she was packing up, there was a noise from up in the kitchen, and foolishly she had come up the cellar steps.

The noise had stopped by then, and she thought the wind had picked up while she was below ground, and it had chased rubbish into the kitchen, or it was pulling at the plastic bags on the paintings and then…

The phone was still ringing.

She fished it out of her trouser pocket and glared at the screen. It flashed up a name: Jeffery. "Hi, Jeffery," she pulled down her facemask.

"Ros—"

"There's no need to worry—"

"I'm sure you're doing a great job, but that's not why I'm calling."

"What's up?" She rubbed her eyes, felt a little further towards the back of her head. Her fingers came away with blood on them.

"I have some bad news."

"I not in the mood for bad news."

"We found a burnt body in the office."

She held her breath. She'd seen enough bodies to fill a decent sized graveyard, bodies didn't worry her. But what did was the solemnity in his voice as though it was personal. "Go on."

"Is Eddie there with you?"

"Who is it, Jeffery?"

* * *

Ros called Eddie four times but he didn't pick up. Maybe it was just a poor signal. She sat on the bottom step watching a spider ensnare a small fly in one of its myriad webs. At first they thought Stuart had started the fire for some reason, though they couldn't understand him even being there. Jeffery had told her about the bottles of liquor they found in his pockets. Obviously Eddie's name had come straight to Jeffery's mind, and if she was honest, it had come straight to hers too.

Were they saying Eddie had knocked Stuart out and planted the bottles as an elaborate double bluff before setting the place on fire? But that was preposterous! The whole scene was wrong because it meant that Stuart and Eddie had met at the office when neither of them was scheduled to be there. And it meant Eddie had the bottles with him to plant on Stuart, which meant it was all premeditated. But why would they choose to meet? They wouldn't. They loathed each other.

And then Ros remembered what Eddie had said at the garage while they examined the Jaguar. Something about a bullet hole in Stuart's face.

When quizzed, Jeffery had given no further information. Everyone who worked there was a potential suspect to a murder. But Eddie more so than anyone else.

Her immediate relief at never having to endure Stuart's rancour again was tempered with a sense of guilt at her own callousness, and that life was just a case of working your way through a list of bad news.

She stood and leaned against the crumbling wall but her head banged, her neck ached, and her knees clicked. And now she was freezing; the sweat inside her plastic suit and nitrile gloves had cooled and soaked into her clothes, and every time she moved it was like lying down in a puddle.

It was nine-forty. She had been unconscious for almost three hours, and it felt like it. Trembling, she looked around for the torch, but remembered it had been down in the cellar and turned on. "Flat by now."

The camera! *Shit, no, please don't let that have been stolen, I have all the evidence in there, and there was also the money from above the doorframe.* She felt around the floor, kicked the camera bag, opened the zip, felt the bulge of the camera and the tamper-proof bag with the roll of cash inside it.

And then she checked around for the paintings she had propped against the wall. Only two left. Fourteen stolen? Fifteen? "Bastards!"

Ros found the van keys, slung the camera bag over her shoulder and then screamed as though she'd been shot.

"Hello."

Ros fell backwards as the youth opened the metal door.

"Yo, don't worry. Everything's cool, sis."

Chapter Sixty-Three

Thursday 25th June

– One –

"How do you feel?"

Eddie peered through the windscreen at the front of the bungalow and the big white car on the drive. He could see a six-foot wire fence at both sides of the property disappearing towards the back before the shrubs and trees blocked his view. "How do we get inside?"

"Don't know." Mick's tone was flat, lacking conviction now they'd travelled all the way out here to Alwoodley.

Great, Eddie thought. "You know you don't have to take part. I'd never ask you to do…"

Mick stared at him. "I know that, you think I don't know that. Well, I do, okay. But I want to hear from you what you're going to do once you get in there."

"Depends if he's home."

"His car's on the drive, let's assume he's home. What are you going to do?"

There was silence for a long time. The second hand on the dashboard clock was the only noise, and Mick moving in his seat. Then Eddie farted. Mick opened Eddie's window and turned on the fan.

"You haven't answered my question."

"Ah, you noticed."

"I noticed."

"Thought the fart would do."

"Alas, no. Do try again."

"I want to ask him questions—"

"What kind of questions?"

"You wanted me to answer you, so shut up while I try and deliver."

"Carry on."

"I want to know what it felt like to run down another human being. I mean, I've hit a small dog before and it made me shake like hell afterwards, you know, the shock?"

"What happened?"

"What? I took it to a vet. Broken legs and fractured pelvis."

"Did it live?"

Eddie breathed loudly. "Does it matter, I'm trying to make a point here and you're asking about the fucking dog!"

"Sorry!"

"It lived! It still lives on a farm in North Yorkshire, it's called Rex, it has a pension and its very own kennel. He's old now, and he's deaf in one ear, but he lives life to the full. Every Christmas both of his sons bring presents like socks and miniature bottles of whisky. His master shares the traditional drumstick and sage and onion stuffing. He can't chase the cat around the Christmas tree anymore because of an ingrowing hangnail, but at least they have fun—"

Mick slammed the car door, and Eddie did likewise, following Mick at a slower pace, but one he could maintain without falling over sideways. "Wait," he called. "I'm sorry; I didn't mean to take the piss."

"What?"

"Okay I meant to take the piss, you were annoying me—"

"Why're you going in there?"

"I want to know how—"

"*Why* are you going in there?"

"I want to know why—"

"Why the *fuck* are you going in there!"

"I want to kill him!"

They stared at each other, panting.

Even from here, they could hear the second hand in the car ticking. Nothing moved in this affluent neighbourhood.

"That's all I wanted to know." Mick took a long blink.

Eddie swallowed. "So now you do. What are you going to do about it?"

"Nothing."

"You don't feel the urge to…"

Mick put his hands in his trouser pockets. "I'm not going to the police. And frankly, I'm more than a little pissed off at you for thinking that of me."

Eddie's eyes hit the pavement.

"But I understand you asking. I would have asked it too."

"You don't have to take part, Mick."

"But I'm allowed to if I want?"

Eddie nodded, "Of course. I must admit though, I'm not prepared for it."

"Obviously. If you were, you'd have gloves and those white suits and whatever else."

"But I'll be asking him first; I really do have questions for him."

"Just a warning, Eddie, don't try to make him feel guilty by telling him Sammy's past, or what he was doing that day, or how well he was doing in school. It won't work on him. He has no emotion. All it'll do is make him angry."

"Good. I'd like him to be angry."

They went back to the car and pulled the carpet mats up out of the front footwells, locked the doors and walked around the block, away from Henry Deacon's bungalow, coming around the back of the property and through the trees and bushes of a dark woodland nearly fifteen minutes later. The lights were on but they saw no shadows against the curtains. It looked good as far as not being detected was concerned.

He had thought of this moment maybe twice an hour every hour of every day of every week since the day his life changed. And that was a lot of thoughts. And in most of them, he was killing the driver. Be it a street kid with no future or a doctor who worked diligently in an accident and emergency unit, he would kill the driver with anything to hand or with anything his imagination told him to bring – from a hairbrush to a vacuum cleaner, from a kitchen knife to a chainsaw.

He'd put doctors and junkies in the driver's seat, but never a politician's son. A very important politician's son too. There was something justifiable in a poetic if not ironic sense, in letting the public have him. They would kill him through the courts. "Do you think the courts would kill him if we handed over the evidence?"

"Seems as though you don't have too much evidence left to hand over since your office burned down."

"Yeah we do. Anyway, we still have the car; we could always try examining it again if the upload failed."

"You're more naïve than I took you for. He is Deacon's boy; he belongs under Daddy's wing. And there he shall remain until Sir George decides otherwise. There is no way Henry will face a Home Office bullet. Sir George would not allow it. Think of the shame."

"Then let's not kill him, Mick. Let's…"

"You want to kidnap him now? What?"

"I just—"

"You can't do it, can you?" Mick's voice was a raspy whisper. "Just wait till you get in there, Eddie. Wait till you see the arrogant twat, and then decide whether you can do it or not."

"I thought it would do more harm to let justice run its course."

Mick shrugged. "I say again, there will be no Home Office bullet."

It was Eddie's turn to stare. "I thought you had it all rigged up? Henry's walking the tightrope, and Deacon is below chewing his fingernails down to the elbows."

"It's rigged up ready to hit the presses. But once Sir George gets a whiff of the story, he'll try to suppress it, and then he'll try to discredit those of us who would broadcast it."

"And if he can't—"

"I shudder to think." Mick lit a cigarette, exhaled so that a cloud of smoke rose from the bank. "But it's up to you. Your call."

Eddie was torn between ripping the bastard's head off, because revenge was a wonderful therapy and he could say to the NY cap that he had done what he'd promised to do, and letting Henry suffer in jail until he died of old age. He gave Mick the nod. Mick flicked the cigarette up the bank and into the darkness of the low shrubs. "Sure?"

"Let's go."

– Two –

There were five of them. They all crammed into the tiny kitchen to see what was so interesting. Ros backed away as far as she could, pulling the camera bag close to her chest, and noted how badly she was shaking. All it needed was for one of them to be especially high, especially bored or especially randy, and just a little brave, and within thirty minutes she'd be a changed woman.

"What do you want?"

The leader stepped forward; his dirty woollen hat displayed the Nike tick. He smelled her perfume and smiled. "Don't want owt," he said. "We saw your lot leave, but you was still here. Having plod around is bad for business. Word gets around, see?"

Ros's head throbbed. Her tongue was a small rectangle of desert sand and her watering eyes stung as though she'd used an onion-based eye bath. She glanced at her phone's battery; it also showed three missed calls and a voice message.

"You gonna fuck off and let us get on?" Nike-man said. One youth stepped outside, followed by a second who pushed the first down the steps and laughed about it. Another stared at her as he took a cigarette from behind his ear, nipped it between his brown teeth. Then he pulled out a snub-nosed gun that glowed in the dregs of red sunlight slanting in through the open door.

Ros stared back at Nike-man with his gold chain around his neck matching the one around his wrist, with his trendy tracksuit matching his trendy trainers as though he was a remodelled Usain Bolt.

He was lowlife, but even lowlifes occasionally made it big. This was his chance. He stepped closer.

"I'm just about done, thanks." *Thanks?* "Said I'd be back about now and they'll be wondering where I am." Out flew a nervous laugh, the sign of a woman telling a lie. The gunman aimed at her. She held her breath and thought about Eddie and what a bastard he was and how she would never talk to him again and how she would always hate him if she ever got out of this and wondered how he could walk away and allow this to happen.

He pulled the trigger. There was a click, and a pathetic flame lit his cigarette. She sighed the breath out.

"Look like shit there, sis. Got blood in yo hair."

She touched the swelling that was now barely hidden by her hair. "Banged my head, that's all." She smiled and in a swift movement, grabbed the remaining evidence bags, looking up all the time, waiting for them to kick out or push her to the floor. "You didn't see someone else come in here after the police left?"

The Nike-man shook his head, but druggy number two said, "Yeah; small white dude, fat. Snooker player's waistcoat."

"Can you remember what he was driving?"

"Don't know. But he was carrying something under his arms, like them there." With a pair of smoking fingers, he pointed to the paintings on the kitchen floor.

"You want me ta carry them?" Nike-man nodded at the plastic-wrapped paintings.

"Would you mind?"

* * *

When Ros sat in her van with the doors locked and the interior lamp turned out, she cried. She hadn't even taken off her dirty sweaty scene suit; content to worry about such comforts when she finally got the bloody hell out of here.

– Three –

Eddie's bravado shone like the chrome on a Harley D.

They threw the rubber car mats across the top of the fence. When Mick had said, "Wait until you get in there and see the arrogant bastard" Eddie became scared.

He could imagine Henry Deacon giving out the big come-on, and he could imagine himself obliging. He could see the anger rising inside him, and he could see himself charging at Deacon and he could see himself becoming a murderer before tonight was out. Once Eddie Collins got angry, there was no stopping him until it ran its course; might as well try slowing down a steam train by thinking about it really hard.

That's what scared him. If Deacon was placid, displayed sorrow at Sammy's death, Eddie would simply go home with his tail between his legs and wrap the vacuum cleaner cord tightly around his neck.

Mick leapt the fence first and Eddie swallowed his fear and followed. In silence they sneaked like a couple of burglars around the back of Henry Deacon's bungalow to the conservatory. "Stay here." Mick skulked off into the darkness.

That darkness disappeared as Mick triggered a security light at the far side of the conservatory. Eddie heard him curse and then saw him running back. "There's a window open."

"Great."

"Come on, let's get on with it."

"Right behind you." Eddie came out of the darkness and into the light. He could see speckles of illuminated rain landing on Mick's hurrying shape. And as the open window came into sight, the security light blinked out and the rain fell invisibly again, Eddie wondered if this was the worst decision he had ever made.

The white plastic window frame was a grubby grey in a darkness that was almost total. Mick looked at Eddie. "What about alarms?"

"Won't have it set if he's in, will he?" Eddie said. "And the car mats are still there if the place is zoned, we'll be long gone before the police arrive."

"Wish we'd worn gloves."

"But we didn't!" It was almost a shout and in the stillness of the night it was very loud. Only the sound of rain falling on shrubbery and onto the conservatory roof came to his ears. Eddie stared at Mick, working himself up for the confrontation he'd dreamed of. "Come on, I'll help you through."

"Okay," Mick said, not moving from in front of Eddie's face, "but I expect to see your ugly arse right behind me."

He nodded, "I'll be there." As Mick opened the window further and leaned in, Eddie's fear of what he might do melted, and suddenly became appealing. Eddie listened for alarms. He knew that Mick wanted Henry Deacon dead just as much as he did. Only for different reasons. But that didn't matter. They wanted Deacon dead; *that* mattered. And what Mick knew when tonight became tomorrow, he would take to the grave with him. Eddie peered left and right and then followed Mick through the window.

The house was quiet. Eddie crouched down, and he listened for a whole minute. They were in a carpeted hallway. Dark, except for a bar of light coming from beneath a door at the far end of the hallway some fifteen yards away.

"That'll be the lounge," Mick whispered.

Eddie nodded in the darkness.

And then Mick was gone, creeping towards the light. Eddie followed; his hand lightly skimming the wall. Mick was a barely perceived shadow and only when Eddie's outstretched hand touched him, did he stop.

Mick listened at a doorway on his right. "Bedroom," he whispered. It appeared darker than the others on the hallway because it was open. Wide open. Only darkness in there. After a moment, Mick pulled away and crept towards the lounge. Eddie followed but slower, more cautiously, aware of the chances of another door opening suddenly, aware they might face a battle, aware someone might already know of their presence. Hell, the police could be parked outside already.

Eddie needn't have worried. The police were still twelve minutes away.

He saw Mick's head turn sideways as he placed an ear to the lounge door. Eddie crouched. Watched. Mick twisted the doorknob. Inside the lounge, the lamps were on and there was a muted glow from the artificial fire in the artificial hearth. Apart from that, the place looked like it had just been built, furnished, and locked up.

Except for a coffee or tea stain on the fawn carpet by the leather chair, nothing was out of place; everything appeared to be perfectly arranged by a setsquare.

Eddie stood in the expansive lounge with his hands on his hips and did a 360 turn. There were shadows, but they were transparent enough to yield everything. And there was no person here. "Now where?"

Mick's lips were a tight grey line, eyes squinting in frustration. He shrugged.

Eddie let out a breath, and his shoulders slumped. "I'd psyched myself up," he whispered. "I was gonna kill—"

"Keep a lid on it. Start looking."

"Looking? What for?"

"Dunno," Mick said. "But he has a secret he's desperate to share with me. And I'd hate to let him down."

"Hold on, hold on." Eddie pulled Mick around by the shoulders. "I came here for a specific task. I came here to get even for my kid. I didn't come here looking for a fucking secret. I didn't come here to *steal*."

"What?" Mick faced Eddie full on. "Murder was fine, but you're a bit unsure about burglary?"

"That's about right."

"And what about me? I came here to give you support, and now you don't need that support—"

"Then I may as well be of some use?"

Mick stomped out of the lounge, opening doors up and down the hallway, and any caution he once displayed had blown away on the wind.

Eddie folded his arms and stared after Mick's prancing shadow. "And what happens," he whispered, "if Henry pops out of the fucking gym or snooker room and catches you rifling through his underwear drawer?"

"Then we go back to plan A."

Eddie blinked, "Oh yeah." He walked up the hallway and turned into the darkest room of all, into Henry Deacon's bedroom.

"Arsehole," Mick said.

"Arsehole, yourself." Only a minute ago, Eddie was ready to rip heads off, and it took a while for that fury to dissipate into a cold anti-climax and a dull frustration. He understood that frustration precisely. It yielded recklessness, a need to attract fate, a need to attract Henry Deacon.

And then he turned the bedroom light on and stood quite still. "Shit," he whispered.

– Four –

Ros locked the door and yawned until tears were squeezed out between her eyelashes. Three hours she'd been here in the Normanton CSI office writing up the notes on her new laptop and plugging it into the mainframe ready for the upload at one o'clock. She booked all her exhibits into the store and the freezer, copied the photographs, and began to cry. And then she grew angry for allowing the emotion to show itself. "Damn you, Eddie."

The place was deserted.

She headed back to Morley where she briefly stared at the twisted wreckage of furniture outside the office door. She signed out, collected her car, and headed home. A police car sped past her, blue lights flicking, but no sirens. She wondered where it was going at this hour.

Ros closed her house door behind her and shuddered a long hollow sigh into the shadows. She hung her bag on the coat hook and snatched the mail and newspaper from the floor. The mail was junk, it never made it further than the recycling bin, but the newspaper, the late edition of *The Yorkshire Echo*, caught her attention. She didn't breathe for the next two minutes as she read.

The Yorkshire Echo. 25th June

One rule for them and The Third Rule for us

By Michael Lyndon

On Friday, the 29th May, the reckless killing of two people in the Wakefield village of Outwood baffled police. One, 38-year-old Peter Archer, a father of three, was thrown under the wheels of a bus on the main Leeds Road.

Passers-by were distraught at the sight. They reported seeing a green Jaguar speeding off from the scene.

The second was a 12-year-old boy. Sam Collins recovered an errant football on Westbury Avenue in the village when he was struck and killed by the same green Jaguar.

The deaths of these two people have shredded the lives of their families, but despite intensive investigations, the police have no one in custody.

The Yorkshire Echo has discovered the driver's identity. The driver was Henry Deacon, son of our Justice Secretary, Sir George Deacon, and we have the proof.

We have to ask that if Henry is proved to be the driver by the police investigation, will he face the same fate that a normal member of the public would? Would he face a Rule Three execution?

How coincidental then, that around midnight last night, Wednesday 24th June, the Morley Police Station's CSI office succumbed to what is believed to be a vicious arson attack that gutted the building. Police are refusing to comment, but a source believes the fire was a deliberate attempt to destroy evidence recovered from the recently found Jaguar.

– Five –

The patrol car hurtled down Wigton Lane. With only a slight squeal of brakes, it pulled up outside a large bungalow. Both officers alighted and climbed the fence at the front.

A hundred metres further down the street, a man watched from his hire car.

Chapter Sixty-Four

Thursday 25th June

– One –

"Now what?"

"Come and see this." Eddie stood in the bedroom, his heart rattling at the bars of his ribcage, trying to break out before the adrenaline blew it up.

Mick came up behind him. "Fuuuck."

"That sums it up." Eddie crept up to the body, keeping an eye out for signs of a trap and for possible forensic evidence; evidence he didn't want to destroy or contaminate. No matter how disparate he and "work" were right now, he couldn't suppress his eye for detail.

"Aw, shit, I hate—"

"Keep a lid on it, Mick; it won't fucking bite you."

"I know, but—"

He turned. "And don't you dare throw up!"

Mick shrank back towards the door.

Henry Deacon looked like a marionette that had been abandoned half way through a show. Around his chubby neck was a black leather belt, and in the same way a tree trunk will eventually grow around the barbed wire stapled to it, so the belt similarly disappeared into the loose skin of Henry Deacon's throat with such pressure as to force his bloated tongue out between his lips. The other end of the belt was tied to the wardrobe's clothes rail. There were no clothes hanging on it; seemed Henry had more storage space than clothes anyhow.

Deacon's hands rested submissively on his thighs.

"Is he dead?" Mick asked without daring to look.

"Are you dead, Henry?"

"Not the time for funnies."

"You deal with it your own way; this works fine for me. Death makes me laugh. Well, *his* does." But it didn't. It was just the humour trigger going onto automatic every time he stood before a human body. None of it was funny. But he couldn't help it, *wouldn't* help it; it kept the mind-monster away. Start taking shit like this seriously and they'd refer you to a shrink within a month. He'd seen it happen.

For now, he had a body. A fresh body. Henry Deacon's body. "Autoeroticism."

"In English."

Eddie moved around the body, avoiding the porn magazines that were spread out on the floor between and around Deacon's open legs. His lower clothing was scattered across the bedroom floor, and his hands were shiny, his legs, groin, and shrivelled penis too. A bottle of baby oil just by his right buttock, slowly dripped into the carpet. "They get horny," he said quietly, "and they strangle themselves—"

"What?"

"They asphyxiate themselves. It happens all the time."

"Well, I've never heard of it."

"So?"

"Go on."

"It's reckoned that the ultimate orgasm occurs just as you're blacking out. But sometimes they black out too quick, and by then it's too late. They strangle themselves."

"Shame. In his case, I mean."

"Shame we didn't get to kill him, you mean."

"How long, do you think?"

"How long's he been dead?" Eddie shrugged, looked at the face. "See the blood and mucus leaking out of the nose? In all the hangings I've ever been to, that usually takes an hour or so to begin." He reached out, touched Deacon on the chest, near his armpit. "Still fairly warm, too." And then he pinched Henry's sleeve and lifted his arm. "No rigor yet." He looked up at Mick, "This happened recently," he shrugged, "between an hour and two hours ago. Approximately."

Mick shrank back. "You're disgusting. I don't know how—"

Eddie smiled, "Did you shake his hand when you saw him earlier?"

"No. Why?"

"Would it have bothered you?"

"Don't think so."

"So what's changed?"

"What's changed? He's fucking dead!"

"So he's even less likely to hurt you, don't you think."

"Bugs. He's riddled with death, bacteria…"

"You only need to worry about shit like that when a body's infested or putrid. He ain't going to hurt you now."

Mick ventured around the wardrobe, arms folded tightly into his chest. "I need a drink."

"Not here, mate. They'll—"

"I know, I know! I was only saying, that's all." He stepped closer, top lip curling with revulsion. "Why on earth would you want to…"

Eddie put his hands in his jeans pockets and stared almost with sadness at Deacon's corpse. What puzzled him was this: "If he was under the amount of pressure you said he was, why—"

"Why would he be thinking about sex?"

"You'd be thinking about running, you might even be thinking about turning yourself in, maybe going to church if you were that way inclined—"

"Or killing yourself."

Eddie looked at Mick. "But how could you get horny enough to do it this way with everything going on around you? You'd drink yourself under and load your system with sleeping pills. I can't imagine that anyone with so few happy choices would be able to think erotically at all."

"Does it matter?"

"Well, yeah it does, actually. I wanted to do it."

"I know." And then Mick came nearer, was brave enough to bend at the waist and look at Deacon a little more closely. "You thinking what I'm thinking?"

"He was murdered. But if he was, they did a good job. I mean, on the face of it, it's a suicide."

"The timing alone suggests it's not."

"You and me know that. But would the police?"

"If they read my newspaper they will," he smiled. "Anyway, I ask again; does it matter?"

"Depends," Eddie swallowed, "whether you care about the man-made justice system or whether you simply care about natural justice."

"Yeah, he got what was coming to him."

Eddie didn't look up for a response. "And what about the murderer? He's now out there ordering himself a latte and a digestive at one of these trendy late-night coffee houses. Is *that* right?"

"Two-faced git. If we'd been here two hours ago, you would now be the man ordering a latte."

"I would not!"

"Why?"

"I prefer espresso."

Mick shook his head.

"You're right. I'm two-faced. But only because *I* wanted to do it. I've been cheated. My kid has been cheated out of his justice."

"I can honestly say I have never stood over a human body and discussed the rights and wrongs of justice before. You are one hell of a conversationalist, Eddie Collins."

And then he surprised himself. The body was just that, a body, meat, nothing. But even that rationality didn't stop him swinging his foot into the dead man's face with enough force to snap the clothes rail and send it slumping to the floor.

Mick looked at him and shook his head. "Feel better?"

"Is this the beginning of a lecture?"

Mick shrugged. "I just don't see the point."

"You don't have to."

"I think it was a stupid thing—"

"I don't care what you think."

"What good is—"

Eddie grabbed Mick by the collar of his grubby shirt and pushed him backwards into the bedroom wall. Mick looked up at Eddie, and Eddie glared down at Mick.

"I'm sorry," Mick whispered.

Eddie relaxed his grip, blinked as though recovering from a bout of amnesia. He let Mick go and walked away. Mick stayed there a moment, glued to the wall, and then he started breathing again, smoothed his shirt and tried to regain some of his lost composure.

"Mick, I'm—"

"It's okay."

"I'm sorry."

"I said it's fine." Mick strode into the centre of the room. "Help me find it."

"Find what?"

"The secret he wanted me to have."

"Will it be a box with *secret* stamped on it?"

"Yes. And it'll have flashing lights on it too."

"Righto." Eddie pulled open the bottom drawer next to Henry's bed, took it right out and peered into the void. Nothing. He replaced the drawer and walked around to the other side of the bed.

Mick crouched in front of the wardrobe by the French doors, the one he'd tried to see beneath earlier today, the one with a gap beneath it large enough to slide a hand into.

353

"Nothing here," Eddie said. He looked up and saw Mick on his stomach. "Enlighten me."

"You got a torch?"

Eddie patted his trousers. "Funny you should say that…"

"There's something under here."

Eddie dropped to the floor at the other side of Deacon's body. "I'm not seeing any flashing lights."

Mick swept his arm into the void beneath the wardrobe.

Eddie followed suit along his part of the wardrobe. His fingers brushed something hard.

"Aha," Mick said. "What's this?"

Eddie's fingertips swept again. Whatever it was, was heavy and just outside comfortable grip.

– Two –

"I hate these 10-15s." Wiseman struggled over the gate; one of those fancy electric things with an intercom set into the wall. "You never know what idiot is farting about inside."

"Hey, yeah, there's probably a gang o' junkies, high as a kite, waitin' in the lounge or the kitchen, householder dead, throat slit for his cash, and then the lookout spots a couple o' dumb coppers waltzing up the garden path, nudges his friend—"

"Aw, stop it, Pricey; I hate you trying to wind me up."

"And they laugh, sharpening their knives, taking bets on who kills 'em both."

Wiseman landed on the drive and punched the air out of his lungs.

Price seemed to float down, gracefully continuing his stealthy walk as though he'd just stepped off a kerb.

"Do you think we should get a dog?" Wiseman rubbed the stab vest that covered his generous gut.

"I find cats are more independent, but—"

"Oh cut the shit, just for once, will ya!" Wiseman trotted alongside, and asked Price, "Should we? I'm serious, at least we should wait till the others get here. Come on, Pricey."

Price stopped and faced his partner. He held a finger across his lips. "Shush. Please. If there are burglars in there, you'll scare them away. If there are burglars in there, pull your gun, you're allowed to, you know that, don't you? And if by some miracle there *are* burglars in there, I'll buy you a fucking pizza—"

"But—"

"With any topping you want. Now, piss off down there and check the doors and windows, and I'll check round the back and meet you by the conservatory. Okay?"

"But—"

"With a gaff this size, don't you think they'll have a really complicated alarm system?"

Wiseman nodded.

"Has it sounded?"

Wiseman shook his head.

"Exactly. It's a false call, good intent."

Reluctantly, Wiseman walked away fidgeting with his holster.

– Three –

Eddie's fingertips brushed it again.

"Hey, look at this," he pulled an A4 envelope out into the room.

Eddie pulled his hand out from beneath the wardrobe, massaging his shoulder before the cramp came on properly. "What you got?"

Mick's face drained of colour. "Now I really do need a drink." He held the envelope out, turned it to face Eddie.

Eddie's eyes widened. "True to his word."

"We have to get out of here." Mick got to his feet and even from seven or eight feet away, Eddie could see him shaking.

"Just a minute." With renewed effort, Eddie plunged his hand back into the darkness beneath the wardrobe. His fingertips caught it, grabbed it and dragged it forward. And when he curled his fingers around it, he knew he should have stayed home and watched something shit on TV. "Christ."

"A gun!" Mick backed up to the velvet curtains by the chaise longue. "Put it back, Eddie, quick."

"What? Piss off," he said. "It's now got my DNA all over it."

"Nonsense, you only just touched it."

Eddie half-smiled, "It's DNA, Mick. It's not the ten-second food-fell-on-the-floor rule, you know."

"You can't take—" Mick backed into the chaise, and sat down with a jarring thud. He felt a draught against his cheek, nudged the curtain aside and saw that the French doors were ajar. "Quick," he said, "out this way."

"Wish we'd come *in* that way—"

"Run, Eddie."

Eddie took a last look at the man who killed his boy and made for the door. Mick already had the curtain open and the door wide. They stepped back into the open air, drizzle cooling their faces and saw a police officer standing less than twenty yards away. "Run," shouted Mick.

"Oi," shouted the officer. "Stop there or else I'll fire!"

Eddie glanced back to see the officer groping for his gun.

The officer saw Eddie's gun and dropped his own.

"Pricey!" The officer picked up his gun and jogged after the two intruders. "Pricey," he yelled again. A security light came on and blinded him just as he fired. Two panes of glass in the conservatory exploded.

They swore simultaneously, ducking their heads as the shot rang out. Eddie felt fragments of glass fall into his hair as he rounded the far side, heading for the fence with the car mats draped over the top.

Eddie panicked; his sprint slowed to a hobble as he searched the weapon for the safety catch. He felt a small lever unlock and totally forgot about the really important lever beneath his right index finger. The rear of the conservatory lit up in an orange brilliance that only registered as a gunshot when the explosion accompanying it filled his ears, and only registered as a gunshot from his own gun when the recoil nearly broke his thumb. "Bollocks!"

Behind them, as they scrabbled over the fence, two voices shouted. In the far distance, sirens grew nearer very quickly. Eddie and Mick did their best impersonation of a sprint up the slick embankment and ran, Eddie with pains in his chest and Mick with pains in his legs, across a wooded crown and towards the road.

"When we reach the road, walk casually as if nothing's happened."

Eddie thought about that for a moment and then burst out laughing.

– Four –

Sirius watched Eddie Collins walking with his usual slight limp across to the Ford Focus. Courtesy of DCI Benson, it had taken merely twenty minutes to find out who the car belonged to: Michael Lyndon, the journalist who was very pro-Rules and very pro-Deacon. Sirius had a feeling loyalties were changing in Lyndon's mind.

Preceding Collins by a pace or two was a man Sirius had seen before, the man who owned the Ford, and the man who had partaken of Sir George's whisky before now. Sirius squinted, trying to see what Mick Lyndon had left Henry's house with. Looked like an envelope, A4 size. The phone on the dashboard blinked and vibrated. Sirius answered.

"Well?"

"As planned, Sir George. He was with a friend though."

"Who?"

"Michael Lyndon. They got away from the house but I'm sure they were clearly seen." He closed his eyes, waited for the response. And when it finally came, it was measured, calm.

"Michael Lyndon and Eddie Collins." There was considerable thought behind Deacon's distracted voice. "Make the necessary arrangements. For both of them."

"Sir." He didn't tell Deacon of the envelope, there was no need to get him anxious. An anxious Sir George usually spelled trouble for him; and anyway, he'd just been given all the permission he needed to find the envelope and make Deacon aware of how good a man he had in Sirius.

"Have you seen the newspaper tonight, Sirius?"

"Negative, sir."

"It makes interesting reading. The headline, written by our friend Mr Lyndon, captures the imagination. It seems a local police building burned down last night. It housed lots of forensic evidence."

"Destroyed?"

"Whether it or any evidence was destroyed or not, seems to have been overlooked in the article. Of further interest is this: *Henry Deacon's Jaguar was found and examined yesterday. Is there a link?* asks the report. Michael Lyndon is beyond useful now. Is this getting through to you, Sirius? This man is bad news for both of us."

"Sir, I think I know what you—"

"For instance; would you know if that particular building was overlooked by CCTV?"

Sirius grimaced. He held his breath.

"It is," Deacon said. "Very good quality too."

Sirius closed his eyes. "Do you know where—"

"An outside contractor takes care of all West Yorkshire Police estate monitoring. I called in some favours. They were very expensive favours."

"Thank—"

"Don't let me down."

The line went dead.

Chapter Sixty-Five

– One –

Mick drove out of the neighbourhood, and forty minutes later arrived in one of the busiest parts of Wakefield he could find.

"Where to?"

"Pub."

"I'm not leaving this in the car." He flicked the envelope. "And I'm not taking it into a pub either. It'd be just my luck to get mugged."

"This the big secret you were hoping for?"

"Why else would it have my name and address on it?" He drew the car to a halt in a petrol station.

A hire car followed at a discreet distance, its occupant on the phone.

"Where're you going?" Eddie asked.

"Just look after that," he pointed to the envelope. "Don't open it."

Eddie thought back to Henry's bedroom. And the mind-monster seized its opportunity to come and converse. How strange a feeling it was to have the chance of revenge snatched away like that. Empty. Robbed. Relieved?

But at least this way, no one could accuse him of murder.

Did that copper recognise you, do you think? Maybe they could *accuse you of murder.*

And then he smiled: *this is the age of The Rules,* he thought, *they don't make mistakes anymore.*

He looked at Mick's envelope. It had his name and address written neatly in black ink. Not Mick, but Michael. How formal. And then his address: 1 The Coach Road, Kirk Steeple, Wakefield. It sounded grand, much too grand for someone like Mick. *Bet it's a shit-tip,* Eddie thought, *that's why he never invites me over there.*

Mick came back with two packs of cigarettes and a newspaper. He slammed the door and asked, "Know anyone who drives a brand-new Vauxhall Insignia?"

Eddie began to turn.

"Don't look round!"

"Why, why?"

"There's one parked thirty yards up the road, one man inside, trying not to look as though he was looking at us. I think it's been following us a while."

"Oh bollocks."

"That'll be a 'no' then."

"Police?"

Mick shook his head and pulled back out onto the road.

"So where are we going?"

"It rules out anywhere I know; can't drive to yours, can't drive to mine."

"Pull up over there," Eddie pointed to the pub called Charlotte's Lodge a hundred yards away on their right. Mick brought the car to a halt. "Okay," Eddie said, "just get out, take that with you, lock the car and we walk nice and slowly into the pub like we're off for a pint. Okay?"

"I want to open it."

"Just do it, Mick."

"Right. Then what?"

– Two –

Sirius grew nervous. He tapped the steering wheel, eyes constantly flicking between the old Ford Focus parked outside the pub, and the dash-mounted phone. "You ever been had?" he said to himself. He took the keys from the ignition and was about to open the door when the damned phone got to him first. It was Deacon.

"Well?"

"Sir George, they've parked up, gone into a pub—"

"When?"

"I'm just on my way in—"

"When!"

Sirius closed his eyes. "About ten minutes ago."

There was a long pause before Deacon finally spoke; anger seeped through the cracks in his calm voice. "Follow them. When you—"

"I was just about—"

"Get me a conclusion to this!"

– Three –

Thursday evenings in Wakefield were always busy. It was *the* local party night; where all the clubs and pubs were full, where the restaurants and street cafés did good business, where the roads throbbed with revellers dressed for a night out, most already drunk and the rest getting there.

Northgate was slow, heaving with taxis, with buses, with police vehicles stationary at intersections watching the crowds. It was loud, the squeal of brakes, the sounds of horns, sirens, of music beating the bodywork of the local boy racers' cars, of thudding bass breaking free of the bulging nightclubs, the shouting, singing and the laughter of youth.

Brook Street was just as busy as Northgate had been; traffic was manic and its noise was an uncomfortable cacophony for Eddie, and his head boomed as he climbed into the taxi's back seat. Mick shouted Eddie's address at the driver and then sank into his seat with a sigh. Eddie peered out of his window, watching Wakefield become blurred, watching for a Vauxhall Insignia, and seeing nothing but Henry Deacon's lolling head.

– Four –

It was a little after eleven-thirty when the phone interrupted Benson. He was gazing at the ceiling of his car, enraptured, eyes flickering, head spilling from side to side, groans dripping from his lips as she worked on him, a dark scruffy shape moving rhythmically in the soft glow of the dash lights.

He was almost there when the phone ruined it all. The woman lifted her head, the beginnings of a smirk on her dampened lips. He slapped her.

"The fuck wa' that for?"

"Get out."

"Money first."

The phone continued to upset Benson as he reached into a dashboard storage unit and brought out a twenty. "Be back tomorrow night, same time."

She snatched the money, opened the door and was absorbed by the darkness as Benson pressed the button beneath *Accept?*

"This had better be good."

"It's me, Sirius. I need an address ASAP."

"Another one? What the fuck do you think I am?"

"You were right about Collins going to Henry Deacon's house."

"And?"

"I need his address."

– Five –

It was late evening when Christian cruised down the road leading to the old terraced house. It was quiet, dark. There was no one around acting suspiciously, no police. He drove in ever-decreasing circles, plucking up courage, wondering if he could park outside and get into the cellar and out with his paintings – provided they were still there. He thought he could. The Nissan had a full tank of petrol, enough to get him four hundred miles away; enough time to plan some kind of intermediate future.

What about Sirius, and that fat guy, Henry?

Christian parked outside his old home. Call it instinct, call it cowardice, but he sat there with the heater on and pretended the pain in his shoulder was all in his mind. He looked towards the part-open door clad by a rusting corrugated sheet. It would take five minutes to nip in and–

Movement dragged his eyes up to the rear-view mirror. A man walking a young dog, one of those things that constantly jumped at its master. He engaged gear and let the car roll forward, missing his paintings already, but knowing he would never see them again.

Chapter Sixty-Six

Friday 26th June

– One –

The concrete stairs had never seemed so hard to climb before. Mick panted alongside him, head down, rasp in his throat, legs more a hindrance than a help. With the door locked behind them, Eddie pulled *The Yorkshire Echo* from his letterbox. He looked at Mick, looked down at the envelope in his hand and regretted being here. "If that arsehole was following us—"

"Fix a drink, no one followed us."

"The Vauxhall—"

"I'll fix it myself if you're gonna whine." Mick threw the envelope on his chair, then slunk into the kitchen. There was the sound of glasses chinking and Eddie strode to the window, swallowing apprehension. "Check out the front page," Mick called from in the kitchen.

He peered out through the dirt-smeared net curtains at the grimy street below where groups of drunken youths headed downtown towards the nightclubs. Not one of them could walk in a straight line, not one of them could stagger in silence either. "Pissheads." He watched them weave between buses and taxis, laughing and shouting at nothing, as inebriated people did. He watched normal people eating in a civilised way in the Chinese restaurant over the road, and felt envious of them. Mick set the glasses on the table.

"Not sure I like this." Eddie slipped out of his jacket, downed the gin and poured another. He read the newspaper headline: *One rule for them and The Third Rule for us.*

"Catchy line, eh?"

"Sum it up for me; my life may be shorter than I think."

"I told the world of the CSI building fire, and how it conveniently went up in flames the same day evidence of Henry Deacon's murderous activities was locked up inside."

"Let me guess, you continued by saying that certain high-ranking members of the government have seen to it their wayward offspring are protected against the Slaughter House?"

"My editor practically had my cock out when he read it."

The Third Rule

"Who's following us?"

Mick lit a cigarette, shrugged almost absently and sank into his chair, fingers tearing at the envelope's seal.

"Who killed Henry Deacon?"

"Sirius." Mick flicked ash, strained for his glass and emptied it.

"We've just turned ourselves into bait, haven't we?" Eddie looked out the window again, then turned back and faced Mick. "Sirius?"

"George Deacon's muscle," Mick said.

Eddie searched Mick's face for a clue to what was on that paper. "Come on, we gotta go."

"One minute." Mick studied the sheet, and then looked up, forehead furrowed. "A crossword puzzle."

Eddie nodded thoughtfully. "Oh, that helps."

Mick passed it over while he read aloud the accompanying sheet. "It's from Henry Deacon, *You're lucky I met you when I did, Mr Lyndon; I was going to forward this to Akhbar Shunian at* The Times. *But now… well, maybe you're unlucky. Watch your back.*' Shit, do I feel lucky."

"Yeah, you should do the lottery this week."

G	R	I	D	A	E	R	E	R	U	O	Y	F	I	E
M	A	S	T	I	P	H	R	T	E	G	S	N	T	O
I	K	E	M	D	A	H	N	R	E	H	T	A	F	Y
I	P	R	R	I	I	S	N	D	C	E	E	L	E	L
T	S	I	R	H	C	D	E	L	L	D	I	K	S	U
T	W	O	A	H	R	S	D	I	R	N	O	A	A	I
E	R	I	F	T	E	S	D	D	N	A	O	C	O	S
F	N	O	B	Y	S	M	P	O	H	T	I	T	E	S
P	T	A	E	R	G	O	E	H	T	R	E	H	T	A
R	F	E	F	D	M	N	U	E	D	T	T	E	R	R
R	O	F	E	A	C	A	E	P	N	I	T	S	E	R
O	C	F	K	E	L	M	O	E	O	V	K	I	O	G
T	I	L	E	H	T	G	U	N	I	L	L	I	K	R
T	T	W	O	Y	W	O	E	B	R	E	S	L	T	T
I	T	N	E	D	I	C	C	A	N	A	S	A	C	K

Eddie whispered, "Ever had that feeling that something infinite – isn't?"

"Life, you mean?"

"This is getting seriously heavy. And I'm seriously shitting myself."

"I have to check my emails." Mick pulled out his mobile phone.

"Good idea. You check your email while I write the obituary."

"Bingo!"

"Life's one big game today, isn't it?"

"It's a time-delay email." Mick looked at Eddie, who stared back, face blank. "It's sent automatically to its destination unless the sender enters a password every hour, day, week, whatever you want, to prevent it going."

"He knew he was toast, didn't he?"

"Quick, grab a pen."

"A pen? You're the fucking journalist."

"Please."

"You're not taking this seriously."

– Two –

Sirius parked in a side street near Eddie Collins's address. Benson had come through for him again.

He walked briskly to the end of the road and turned a corner, only fifty yards from the address, and tried to maintain a discreet but healthy pace along the main road, busy with drunk and loud people.

– Three –

Eddie and Mick made it down to the darkness of the foyer below the flat, and stopped at the glazed front door. "When's all this going to end? We can't run forever."

Mick shrugged. "Once we find out what's going on and who's to blame for it all—"

"Deacon's to blame."

"I know! But we need proof."

"That's cheered me up no end. I hope you're good at puzzles."

"We need somewhere safe…" Mick peered out of the window and into the throng of people outside. "Sirius," Mick said. "How the hell did he—"

"Back door!"

Eddie turned and ran through the foyer past the stairs, seemingly heading straight into blackness. He blundered his way through an invisible fire escape, and a brief wedge of orange light from the back yard leaked in and showed Mick the way. Above the doorframe was a smashed fire exit sign.

Mick slammed the door closed behind them.

They were in a small yard, enclosed by a glass-topped brick wall, and a pair of wooden gates that gave out onto a cobbled street behind Eddie's flat. Beyond the wall, a streetlamp spewed the ghastly orange light they'd seen from the foyer. To their right was the carpet of moss created by Eddie's broken toilet overflow, and it provided them with a noise like an urban waterfall, a drone to take away the eerie silence.

Mick was still trying to work out where in the yard of industrial wheelie bins, of rolls and folds of dead carpets and hundreds of their cardboard centre tubes, he should hide. "Here," whispered Eddie, "over here!"

"Where, I can't see a fucking—"

"Sssshhh!"

* * *

Sirius silently mounted the top step and peered at the wooden door of flat number 2. He placed an ear against it and listened. Then took out his sidearm.

* * *

"We should go over the gates," Mick whispered.

"No chance. Now shush, he could come out any second."

With a creak, the fire door opened.

Eddie held his breath, peered between the wall and the back of an industrial wheelie bin, something the size of a small skip, and could just make out the shape of a man threading his way deeper into the yard.

Behind them, and constantly splashing them, was the overflow waterfall. Eddie edged around the side of the wheelie bin and crouched as he peered around its front.

Sirius stopped and turned.

Eddie's eyes froze.

"I can't see, where is—"

Eddie nudged Mick in the face with his elbow, then drew the weapon from his inside pocket.

"What the fuck—"

Eddie stared a warning at Mick, and then turned back towards Sirius. But Sirius was gone.

If Eddie could have seen that Sirius was standing at the other of side of the wheelie bin, he would not have chosen that particular second to stand up. Sirius had his weapon drawn and was searching for signs of recent disturbance in a place that was full of recent disturbance.

Luckily for Eddie, the waterfall cloaked his gasp. And he was further blessed with luck. He peered over the crown of the wheelie bin and stood there with his mouth wide open. If the light had been stronger, it would have been possible to see his heart beating like crazy in the back of his throat. And that's when he thought Sirius *had* seen him.

But he hadn't; it was the moment that Sirius's phone began to ring. As he pulled it from his jacket pocket, his face illuminated by the screen, Eddie slowly sank back down, hoping like hell that Mick would keep his mouth quiet.

"What?" Sirius said.

Eddie leaned forward, trying to catch the conversation over the waterfall that now worked against him.

"Who's on a provisional Rule Three?"

Eddie listened.

"For what? You serious?" He laughed for a moment, and then said, "He's not here. Okay, give me her address. I'm gonna have to bring more men in. Now I gotta find him before your lot do."

Sirius replaced the phone and then thudded back to the fire exit, leaving Eddie feeling momentarily relieved, but ultimately afraid.

– Four –

"How much longer we gonna stay here?"

Eddie shrugged.

"There could be rats in here. Diseased rats. We could catch tuberculosis. Or worse."

"He was talking about me, wasn't he?"

"They carry rabies too."

"How can I…"

"Vermin. Horrible things."

"The copper at Henry's. He must've clocked me."

"I'm gonna scrub myself with Domestos when I get home."

"Do you think he was talking about me?"

"Well I hope to Christ he wasn't talking about me!"

"Some fucking friend you are," Eddie whispered.

"On a provisional Rule Three? Nah, don't think so. You have to kill someone for that. And we haven't killed—"

"Henry's dead, remember."

"I know!" Mick paused, then said, "Whatever happened to your faith in forensic science?"

"People have a habit of reading it wrong."

"So that's where the Review Panel comes in."

"Okay, you win. I have no faith in The Rules or how they're administered. Happy now?"

"And I thought it would be true justice. But it's open to the same corruption that's always been there."

"After your headline tonight, he'll be after both of us, so it doesn't matter which one of us is on a Rule Three, we're both dead."

"Whose address do you think he just asked for?"

"Got to be Jilly's," Eddie said. "This is my address; Jilly's was my last address. Makes sense."

"You should warn her."

Eddie shook his head, "No need. He'll soon realise I'm not there and leave."

"Hope you're right."

"He's working with the police, though, getting information from them at least."

After a moment, Mick groaned. "This is getting too hot for me—"

"Too hot!"

"Ssshhhh, Christ's sake!"

"It began to get warm the minute we entered Henry Deacon's house—"

"Oh no, it was already on a gentle simmer back then; it began to get warm when you found incriminating evidence on Henry's Jaguar."

Eddie flicked the envelope in Mick's hand, "Well, it'll reach boiling point if there's any more revelations in there."

"I'm hungry, I'm thirsty and—"

Eddie stood up and pushed the wheelie bin aside.

"What are you doing?"

"We've left it long enough. He's gone now for sure—"

"And if he hasn't?" Mick stood, and even over the sound of the waterfall, Eddie could hear his knees clicking in protest.

"Then we'll find out which one of us is on a Rule Three."

"I get the feeling that Sirius won't allow a court case, Eddie. Henry Deacon didn't get one."

"How comforting."

Mick put a hand on Eddie's shoulder, gently turned him around to face him. He nodded at the gun still in Eddie's hand. "What you still doing with that thing?" he whispered.

Eddie slipped the weapon out of sight, into the inside pocket of his jacket. And now the orange glow of the streetlamp picked out the bulge in his jacket, highlighted it and shouted *I gotta gun!* "I was going to dump it."

"You're not Bruce Willis, Eddie."

"With all this shit happening—"

"You feel safer, right?"

"Yes I do. And don't mock me; so far as I can tell we are outside the law. At least one of us is already on a Rule Three, so by carrying this, we have nothing to lose…"

"I hope you know what you're doing." Mick stepped out into the yard, and cautiously moved closer to the fire exit. "And I hope you know how to use it."

Chapter Sixty-Seven

Friday 26th June

– One –

It was a roadshow outside Henry Deacon's bungalow, even though it was two o'clock in the morning. There were no sirens, but there was sufficient noise from police radios, from car and van doors slamming, from police dogs barking and even from the force helicopter, to keep bedroom lights on, and curtains twitching, to keep smokers planted on their doorsteps in dressing gowns, watching the circus.

At each side of the immediate scene, a police van blocked the road, blue lights piercing the night.

From the helicopter, the perimeter of Henry's bungalow and the expansive grounds in which it sat must have appeared like an extravagant dot-to-dot, with the reflective uniforms of PCSOs strung together every twenty-five yards, forming a daisy chain in the darkness.

The darkness was being punched back as large diesel-driven lighting rigs were erected in the grounds of the bungalow itself, but also to the back where the chain link fence was, and even one in the woodland beyond.

Two distinct factors governed the extent of scene protection around Henry's house. Firstly, it was a firearms job, something that always provoked an increased level of activity within the police service; one didn't want to be working a firearms scene only to be confronted with the armed criminal sticking a muzzle in the side of your neck – not good for morale. And gun crime was still deemed serious enough that extra efforts would be made to protect the integrity of any evidence. And secondly, the place in question was the house of a prominent government minister's son, which brought its own set of protocols.

Somehow, the media had become aware of police activity at Henry's house, and their satellite outside broadcasting vehicles were already parking up, sure to belch pools of their own light into the scene.

Jeffery stood by one of the generators with the total manpower of the overnight CSI department for West Yorkshire Police – both of them. The trio were joined by DI Taylor. And with him came the first responding officers.

Taylor asked Jeffery, "Slept much?"

"I don't even know what day it is."

Taylor chuckled politely, and nodded to the officers. "Tell him what you told me."

"Me and Pricey were sent here after an anonymous call saying this place was being burgled—"

"And we came in that way—"

"Hold on," Jeffery said. "Names please."

"Price and Wiseman."

"And what time did you get here?"

Price pulled out his notebook, flicked through pages and said, "23:50."

"Right, carry on."

"We came in from the roadside," Wiseman began, "and we split up. Pricey went around the back and I continued coming this way. I got to about there." He pointed to a spot occupied by another generator that was on the driveway near a white Audi, thirty yards or so before the sliding French doors of Henry's bedroom. "And I seen these two men come out of the sliding door—"

"Was it already open?" Taylor asked.

Wiseman looked from his DI to Jeffery and across to Price as if hoping one of them could help him out a little. No one did.

"Carry on," shrugged Jeffery.

"And so these two men came out, saw me and began running towards the rear of the property. It kind of took me by surprise 'cause to be honest I wasn't expecting anything other than a false call good intent—"

"Fast forward a bit," Taylor said.

"Oh yeah... well I shouted, and they started running, so I began running too, getting my gun out and shouting a warning." He looked at Taylor, acutely aware of the policy surrounding un-holstering side arms. "And I got to the corner there just this side of the conservatory and that's when the security light came on. Blinded me. I could make out both shapes still running up towards the grass. One of them might even have been at the fence by this time. Anyway—"

"They shot at him," Price said.

"No, no, it wasn't like that, boss," Wiseman said in a hurry. "I saw the one nearest to me stop, and he was kind of fidgeting, and that's when I saw a flash, I don't think he was shooting *at* me, I think it more or less just went off."

"He was on the grass?"

"Yeah… few yards onto it I'd say."

Taylor asked, "Did you go inside?"

Wiseman looked at the ground.

Price looked away.

"I needed the bathroom, sir."

Price sniggered, and Taylor shook his head at both of them.

"Did you discharge your weapon?" asked one of the CSIs.

"What? In the bathroom?"

Jeffery closed his eyes. "No, prior to you visiting the bathroom; as you were giving chase."

"Yes, the broken glass… it's what I hit. Sorry, sir."

Taylor turned to them. "You'll need to surrender your weapon."

"Already done, sir."

"Okay, good; go Code Eight, contact your sergeant and write your books up. I'll want your statements for the IPCC before you go off duty."

Price and Wiseman nodded at the inspector then turned and walked away; Pricey elbowed Wiseman in the ribs and laughed at him.

Taylor whispered, "You know we got a taped confession from him, don't you?"

Jeffery looked blank. "Taped confession from whom about what?"

"Him, Deacon. Confessed to killing Peter Archer and that nipper, Sam Collins."

"No," Jeffery said, thinking about Eddie. "I didn't know."

"Got it via *The Yorkshire Echo*." He smiled. "*They* don't have laws to abide by." Then, to Jeffery and the two CSIs, "You got everything you need?"

"Think so," Jeffery said, looking skywards. "Wonder if it's—"

"Yes, it is going to rain," Taylor said, walking away. "I got a meeting to get to. Ministerial liaison officer and a man from SO19."

"SO19?"

Taylor only nodded, turned and carried on walking, waving as he went.

"Keep him out of my scene!"

Jeffery looked at the CSIs, "Get suited up." Then he stood tapping his lip for a while as he thought more about Eddie Collins.

– Two –

Back in the darkness of the foyer, Mick continued to peer through the weathered glass and out into the street. Eddie came down the steps and stood beside him. "He kicked the door in. Caused at least sixty pence worth of damage. Bastard."

"We need transport." Mick waved the envelope at Eddie. "I have to get back home and decode this thing."

Eddie nodded to the window. "It clear out there?"

"Who knows?"

Eddie opened the door. "Let's go get your car." They stepped out and crossed the road, watching all the time, expecting Sirius to leap out at them, expecting to see him following. But, aside from the revellers, there was nothing, no one.

"I think we should walk. I want to be stone cold sober."

Eddie laughed. "Jesus, I never heard you say that before."

"I never felt so scared before."

Eddie's smile soon faded; though he'd felt the gravity of the situation back in his foyer, it kept escaping him so that he was once more just a pissed-up Eddie Collins with a shitty life to worry about. But now he had the government following him, and the government wanted him dead.

Had someone offered him death only a few days ago when the vacuum cleaner was climbing the other side of his door, he would have bought the would-be killer a drink and even passed up the chance of a last request. But now they'd denied him that choice. They were going to kill him whether he liked it or not, and that made him determined to live.

In silence, they walked out of town and into the relative seclusion of the back roads leading towards the *Charlotte's Lodge* pub. They were never confronted by gunmen, they were never challenged, they never heard any footsteps behind them, but all that didn't stop Eddie shaking; in fact, the very absence of any threat made him more cautious. And it was this heightened sense of caution that caused him to stop dead in his tracks less than 200 yards from Mick's old Ford Focus.

"Hey," he whispered, as Mick continued along the footpath.

Mick looked around and walked back. "What's up?"

"I got a bad feeling about this."

Mick snorted, put a hand over his mouth.

"What? What's so funny?"

"Let's see," he laughed, "we bust in on a dead guy, almost get shot by pursuing police officers, get followed by a fucking hitman, almost get caught by him, and you have a bad feeling about a peaceful walk to my car?" He dipped into his pocket and brought out a packet of cigarettes. "You are priceless, Eddie."

Eddie took a cigarette, lit it and said, "It's been too easy. That Sirius fella wants us and he tried very hard to get us; he's not going to leave us alone, mate." He dragged on the cigarette. "He's going to hope we step right back in that car of yours where he can nail both of us at the same time."

"So what do we do?"

"I'll bet you a tenner there's some geezer with a bent nose and a Glock sitting in a car on the petrol station forecourt watching your car. And his job is to—"

"To stop us driving…"

Eddie was shaking his head. "His job is to let us drive away, to follow us. See where we go. He's going to want that envelope first, and then who knows what he'll do to us, but he won't set us free."

Mick slouched against the wall. "Now what? What about *your* car?"

"Same deal. Too risky."

"Taxi?"

"Thursday night in Wakefield?"

"Okay, so now what? Steal one?"

– Three –

"You know how you said you were bad news and that I should stay away from you?"

Eddie looked awkward. "I did say that, didn't I."

Ros turned in her seat. "I should've listened to that advice."

"But you didn't," he said, "you came—"

"Like whistling a dog, eh?"

"I didn't mean it like that. I meant you came and I'm so damn grateful."

"You treat me like shit, Eddie. In fact, on a good day you treat me like your cleaning lady, or your assistant, or your fucking sister!"

Eddie looked at her, shocked.

"It's well after midnight, I feel like shit, and I want to be in bed asleep, not ferrying two drunks around. We have work in the morning."

"Henry Deacon is dead."

"But I wouldn't go in if I were you. If I were you, I'd catch a train to a very remote place and lay low for a few years."

"Why?" He looked at her as though she knew something of his adventures of today.

"You are a first-class bastard, Eddie. And you know what; I only came out here tonight to tell you that to your lousy face."

He sat there, mouth open. "I thought you were my friend."

"Really? After you ran off and left me in that house by myself?"

"I tried to call—"

"Fuck you, and fuck your piss-arsed friend there too."

He stared at her.

"Now get out."

"What?"

"Get out!"

Eddie reached for the door handle, opened the door. "You serious?"

"Out."

Eddie stepped out of the car and didn't even get a chance to close the door before she set off, wheels spinning, engine screaming, and the passenger door slammed closed all by itself. Mick flicked away his cigarette and walked to Eddie. Together they watched her tail-lights grow dimmer.

"She's not keen on the idea, is she?"

"I think we're gonna have to get a taxi after all."

The brake lights came on. Then the reversing lights. Eddie and Mick looked at each other as she drew the car alongside. The window wound down.

"Get in, Eddie." The window wound back up again.

Eddie climbed back in, and Mick took out another cigarette. "I'll er, I'll just wait here, shall I?"

Eddie closed the car door and looked across at Ros. She had been crying; she was obviously close to tears now, blocked nose, red eyes. He could see a hanky sticking out of her sleeve.

"I'm so sorry, Ros."

"They all left me; the uniforms, CID… all of them. You'd abandoned me."

"Oh, Ros, no."

"I'm okay now. I was knocked out—"

"What!"

"There were paintings there. I had them in the kitchen ready to leave." She turned so Eddie could see the dried blood in her hair. "When I came round, they'd gone. And a group of junkies showed up."

"Oh Jesus, Ros." He instinctively reached out, but she pulled away from him. "I'm so sorry; I wish—"

"I'm okay, no thanks to you. But it could have turned out very different. And that's what hurts me the most. I run around after you, I treat you very well, and you... you treat me badly, you don't give me a second thought, because you're too busy with him..." She trailed off, and for a moment, was silent. "Deacon is dead?"

Eddie nodded.

"How do you know?"

"Because I went to kill him. And someone beat me to it."

Ros was quiet for a long time, immobile too, just staring first at Eddie, and then straight ahead through the windscreen. "Is that why you left the scene?"

"I'll understand if you never want to see me again."

"Jeffery rang after you abandoned me."

"Mick has proof that—"

"Stuart is dead."

"What?" It was his turn to be silent for a while. "Our Stuart?"

She nodded. "They found his body in the burnt-out CSI building."

"Jesus, this is a night of surprises." Eddie studied the dashboard for some time, trying to let it all sink in. Then he gasped and punched the dashboard. "You think I killed him, don't you?"

"Why would—"

"I mentioned Henry Deacon was dead and that I was going to kill *him*, and you put two and two together."

"Would you have killed him? If he'd been still alive I mean."

Eddie's fingers fidgeted. "Part of me says yes, and the other part... I didn't kill Stuart, Ros. I hated him, but I couldn't have killed him."

"You have proof that Henry killed Sam? The office is gutted, remember, not much direct evidence left I suppose."

"A recorded full and frank confession."

"And that's why he's dead?"

"We think he was being silenced, yeah."

"So what's all this about?" She shrugged, palms outwards. "Why am I your taxi?"

"We were followed. My flat door has been kicked in—"

"Ah, I get it." She nodded in Mick's direction, "It's because of his headline, isn't it?"

"It probably didn't help."

Ros wound down the window. "Get in, Mick." Then, to Eddie, "Where're we going?"

– Four –

As requested, Ros drove along the road where they'd dumped Mick's car. Eddie had been correct, there was a car parked on the edge of the garage forecourt, a lone male in the driver's seat, elbow resting on the windowsill. A hundred yards further along, Eddie and Mick sat up in their seats. "There's someone watching it, alright," Ros said. "I'll drive by your flat."

"This is bigger than I thought," Mick said. "I wonder how many people Deacon has on this case now?"

Ros drove up Northgate, and the two men sank down in their seats again, Mick just peeking his head above the windowsill.

"One plain car, and one police car there," he said. "Copper standing in the foyer too."

"Jesus," Eddie whispered.

As she passed by, Ros looked up into Eddie's window. "There's someone in your flat, Eddie, probably searching it."

"I hope they find the remote control."

"So the Rule Three that Sirius mentioned in the back yard, is you."

"Great, I got the police *and* Deacon's mob after me."

"Who's Sirius? And what was he saying?"

Eddie was about to answer when his mobile phone rang. "Now what?" He pulled it from his jacket pocket. "It's Jeffery."

"Don't answer it. He wants to know where you are."

Eddie stared at the screen, heart pummelling. He wondered just how much more bad news he was expected to take. The car passed The Booze King, and he looked at it longingly as the phone rang off.

"How do you manage to get in shit so deep?" Ros asked, and when the phone in her car rang, the speaker made them all jump. "Okay, quiet." She hit 'talk' and said, "Hello."

"Hello, Ros," Jeffery's voice crackled over the speaker.

"Jeffery? Is that you?"

"Yes… Are you in your car?"

Eddie looked across at her, saw her take a breath, gripping the wheel, psyching herself up.

"Just on my way back from my sister's. Why, what's up?"

"Have you seen Eddie this evening?"

"Eddie? No, why? What's happened? Is he okay?"

There was silence from the speaker.

"Jeffery?"

"If you see him, you need to get in touch with me as a matter of urgency."

"Aw no, something happened to Jilly?"

"He's on a provisional Rule Three."

Eddie closed his eyes.

"What on earth for?"

"They think… we think he may have had an involvement with Stuart's death."

Eddie's eyes sprang wide open, and for a moment, he wanted to scream into the mic that he had no involvement, repeat *no involvement* with Stuart's death. But he had a feeling who had.

Mick's mouth fell open.

"You're kidding, right? Eddie would never—"

"Ros, please, if you see him, ring me." Jeffery ended the call and Ros just drove on autopilot. Eddie's face was utterly devoid of emotion because shock sat there hogging the limelight and refused to move over. Mick, in the back seat, cradled the envelope, hoping it would provide an exit route for all these troubles.

"Stuart?" Mick asked. "*The* Stuart?"

"Why would they think I killed him?"

"You hated him, remember?"

"Ros, everyone hated him."

"Yeah, but you two had a special relationship."

"Did I miss a meeting?" Mick sat forward.

Eddie turned, "They found his body in the burnt-out CSI building."

"No," Mick slumped back in his seat. "This is getting too much."

"Tell me about it."

"I wonder if you can be put on a Rule Three twice?" Mick disappeared into thought, and then suddenly surfaced again. "Someone ought to let Suzanne Child know."

Ros flicked a glance at him, "Who's she?"

"My apprentice. Good kid. And no doubt Rochester will send her to Deacon's press conference later this morning."

"How do you know he's having a conference?"

"He'll jack up a conference as soon as Henry's death hits the airwaves; he'll want to weep a little on camera, say how sorry he is for Henry's crimes, and how he has suffered as a father. He'll distance himself from Henry quick as he can."

"Fucking politicians," Eddie said.

"It's an ideal time to dishonour him and his family name." Mick stared at Ros, could see her half looking at him as she drove. "Just need someone to ring Suzanne," he said, "maybe spill the beans anonymously."

Chapter Sixty-Eight

Friday 26th June

– One –

"You never told me there was a phase two, Eddie. Did you conveniently forget that part?"

"I'll leave you two alone." Mick climbed from Ros's car, closed the door and looked for something to lean against as he lit a cigarette.

"I'm sorry," he said. "This was the first chance I had to tell you."

"You're playing with fire, and I just want you to know, no fuck it, I *have* to let you know that it's going to end up killing you. And I don't want that to happen. You're into this thing too deep and if what you said is true, then you're not going to be alive much longer." She squeezed the bridge of her nose, purposefully avoided looking at him. "I don't want that to happen. I always wanted you to get back with Jilly; I always wanted you two to work it out and to get back to normal again…"

"Normal? With Jilly?"

"But I think I've grown selfish recently, because I don't want that anymore. I don't want you to get back with Jilly, because I know what she's like now, and she's not healthy for you." She stared out of her window.

Eddie could see her chin trembling. She was hitching breath as though fighting back tears or sobs or both. And even when he was mixed up in murders and all manner of bad things, she was still helping him, she was still lying for him, and he felt like crying too.

He reached over to her and pulled her across to him, and that's when she could hold the tears no longer.

– Two –

"Prime Minister?"

"Come in, sit down, George." Sterling Young took off his glasses, threw them across the papers he was busy with. Then he stared at Deacon. "My father was a sheep farmer. Did I ever tell you that?"

"I think it's common knowledge."

"At its height, we had over 3,000 head of sheep on two farms. We had a couple of managers, eight shepherds and around fourteen sheepdogs." He paused as if recollecting old memories. "It was a lot to handle. Everything had to run like clockwork; everyone had to get along, and everything had to work."

Deacon sat still, watching the old man. He knew precisely what this was; Sterling Young never called to see someone at this hour without an agenda, without facts and figures, without cause. This was a lecture and Deacon clasped his trembling hands tightly in his lap and let it run its course.

"We had three bitches. We kept them to produce our dogs, and if we were lucky we turned a profit on them. Always plenty of call for a good collie." Sterling smiled at Deacon but there was no friendship in his eyes. "Father was good with animals, loved them; very fond of dogs. But like everything else, they had to work; they had to pay their way.

"When I was young, I don't know, five or six maybe, one of the bitches dropped a litter, and among that litter one dog stood out, and that damned thing was a beautiful dog; very placid. I took an unusual liking to it, decided to keep it for my own. You'd think with a thousand acres of land, there would be sufficient room for one pet."

Deacon smiled.

"As it grew, we discovered it was blind. It was broken, George, it was no good for its intended purpose. When I asked my father if I could keep him as a pet, he refused, saying no one gets a free ride; if it doesn't work, it isn't worth keeping. Father shot him.

"And though I never really forgave him, I understood his rationale. No point having everyone pick up his slack." Sterling turned directly to Deacon. "I believe you have similar issues to deal with, George. I urge a swift resolution."

* * *

Deacon dragged a hand down the white whiskers on his troubled face. This was all going horribly wrong. It should have been so easy: declare Collins as a Rule Three miscreant, wanted for the murder of a colleague and for arson, and kill him before he could be arrested. Keep his dirty little secrets a secret, shut him up for good, but someone had messed up, and that someone was Sirius – again. A man who couldn't work out how to spell Stephen!

"Justine!" he called again, louder this time.

The door opened, and Justine entered his office looking slightly bedraggled, hair awry, eyes not quite as pin-sharp as they usually were, brushing crumbs from the side of her mouth. "Sir?"

"How's the speech coming along?"

"Almost done."

Deacon nodded. And Collins was only 25 per cent of his problem at what, nearly one in the morning. Another quarter of his problem was a drunken reporter called Mick Lyndon and his turncoat rag *The Yorkshire Echo*. "Get Thomas Gordon out of his pit and down here pronto." Justine nodded. "And then I want Sirius. I don't care what he's doing, get him to call me."

"Sir." Justine was almost back outside Deacon's office.

"And, Justine?"

"Sir?" she said without turning.

"Would you bring me a cup of tea, and something to eat?"

"Sir."

– Three –

Mick leaned against a wall in Ros's home town of Normanton and watched the village closing its eyes for the night. The last of the lights on this quiet road went out and the only movement came from the clouds coming in from the west. The wind had begun without him even noticing and still they sat there in the car, only now, so far as he could see, they weren't sitting quite as far apart as before.

Either way, Mick thought as he peered at his watch, at nearly one in the morning, he wished they'd hurry the fuck up because he had lots to do and a deadline to meet. He tapped his foot.

* * *

"They'll kill you when they find you, Eddie."

Eddie breathed the scent of her hair as she rested her chin on his chest. He held her as best he could; clumsily, but with affection. "I know," was all he could think of saying.

"I blame him."

"Mick?"

She nodded.

"Why?"

382

"He's been nothing but trouble for you since you hooked up with him."

"Maybe. But now he's the only one who can get me out of trouble. We have to decode whatever's in that envelope."

"Fingers crossed."

"I'll have the car back by seven at the latest. Promise."

"Don't promise. Just try. If not, ring me so I can get a taxi; I can't be late for work, I have arguments to start." Ros opened her door and climbed out. She split her house keys off the keyring and tossed the ignition key back to him. "Please be careful." She walked away without looking back.

Eddie climbed into the driver's seat, moved it back on its runners and watched Ros close the front door.

Mick took his place beside him. "Come on, mate."

– Four –

Ros turned the bedroom light off and walked to the window, peeled back the curtains and watched her car drive away into the darkness.

There was a kind of permanence to it that petrified her yet comforted her. The feeling said she would see neither her car nor the man driving it again. They had him cornered. They had him on trumped up charges and he was as good as dead. And that was the trouble; if this had happened a year ago, she would call her boss, she would call friends in CID, correct the error, adjust the mistake, and allow Eddie to put across his point of view.

Now things were very different. This had become a scary world to live in. If they made an error, the chances of them correcting it were minute because it was easier to have a man killed by the Home Office and score a hit with the public than it was to back down and remove his details from the vidiscreens.

And the Home Office wouldn't acknowledge an error anyway. The Rules were king; they were infallible. One might think that they would go all out to make sure they *were* infallible, to guarantee the public's faith in them.

Bollocks.

Any system was only as good as the people running it. And the people running this system were blind and they were greedy.

Ros lay awake, staring at the ceiling and wondered how they could get away with making such fundamental errors. Well she wouldn't allow it.

– Five –

"Where you taking me?"

"I like my privacy."

"Privacy is good, but this is delving into recluse territory."

Mick laughed, and pointed at something in the distance, half way up a hillside and surrounded by a black smudge of trees. "That's the farmer who owns my place. He gets a hundred and fifty a week, I get total peace and quiet – everyone's happy."

"This isn't the address on the envelope."

"Ah, you spotted that, you sharp-eyed bastard. That's my mother's place; I need a mailing address, but not here. Only me, the farmer, and now you know about this place."

Ros's Renault bounced up the rutted track and Eddie pulled the handbrake on alongside a break in the bushes, killed the engine and listened to the sound of total silence with wonderful clarity. "You'd never know it was here unless you knew it was here," he laughed.

"It's as well hidden as you can get without it being a cave." Mick ducked beneath low branches and Eddie followed him, but still couldn't see where they were going, such was the acute darkness and the surreal camouflage enjoyed by this place. Mick had told him it was a two-storey cottage covered entirely by creepers, with a small front and back garden entirely overgrown and surrounded by woodland.

Mick closed the door after them (it was missing a letterbox, Eddie noticed), and then opened another into the lounge. He flicked on a light and Eddie squinted.

"For such a slob, you got a nice place." Eddie looked around. The uneven floor was carpeted, and upon it stood a two-seater cloth couch, a small but modern TV on a glass stand, a bureau and some bookshelves. Tucked away in a corner was a healthily stocked drinks cabinet. And that was all. "You know what," Eddie stared at the drinks cabinet and the wonderful array of whiskies and vodkas on offer.

"What?"

"For the first time in months—"

"You don't want a drink?"

"How did you guess?"

"Me neither. I just want to get this sewn up. If I get pissed now, I am going to die, absolutely no doubt about it."

"Live first, drink yourself to death later?"

"In one, mate. Through there is the kitchen: white coffee, no sugar. I'm going to make a start. I'll be upstairs."

– Six –

As the first tinges of light tickled the eastern sky, Jeffery had a rough handle on the scene.

They had erected three tents. There was a normal tent over the grassed area, where they found a shiny 9mm Federal shell casing.

The second and third tents were lean-to affairs designed to protect doorways and windows from the elements, one over a wide-open window into the hallway of the house, a possible entry point for the offenders, and the second over the French door that gave straight out onto the driveway and gardens from the bedroom.

Jeffery had assigned jobs to his two CSIs. Linda Wilkinson was on her knees right now, carefully digging away the grass on the banking, searching for the bullet, which had probably, barring deflections, penetrated to a depth of just over a metre – she would be there for some time, sifting each shovelful, looking for something dull and grey about the size of a pea.

Initially, they had found what could have been the entry hole, carefully trimmed the grass from around it with a pair of scissors to get a better look, to judge more carefully if they were even in the right area. And then, using a trajectory rod, they were able to determine that yes, this was a straight and parallel hole directly into the earth that seemed to stop, or veer off to the side, about 100cm down. Linda had carefully photographed the X, Y, and Z axes of the rod, and had been able to determine that the firer had indeed fired directly into the grass banking. Luckily for Wiseman.

Jessica Mulberry, the CSI dragged across from Bradford to help out, had conducted photography from the conservatory right up to the grass banking, and onwards to the fence where some old rubber mats lay across the topmost wire. A fringe of weeds and a congregation of dead flora on both sides of the fence had prevented them getting any kind of useable footwear evidence – the ground beneath the plants had yielded nothing more than indentations, two pairs on either side of the fence.

And the mats looked like abused mats from any junk car: a coating of cigarette ash covered most of the surface. They had worn smooth in their centres, but not smooth enough to proffer any visible ridge detail. Jessica had labelled and collected them, packaging them carefully for the chemical treatment labs later that day. She had concluded the examination of the fence site by photographing the now naked fence, and by taping for fibres along the top of the fence to a yard either side of where the mats had rested.

The operational support unit would search the woodland during daylight hours. Jeffery guessed that Jessica had moved on to the next point of his instructions to her. She was to take samples of glass from the smashed conservatory windows, hoping to link fragments of that glass with any found later in the offender's clothing, all adding to the proof that he was there when the glass exploded. On its own perhaps, it would not be conclusive proof, since glass in any modern frame is not unique, but it would add weight to the prosecution.

And after she had done that, Jessica was to fingerprint the open window at the end of the long hallway.

Jeffery stood at the opposite end of that hallway, just outside the kitchen. He was dressed in full scene suit and overshoes, DNA mask and hair net, Nikon dangling on a strap around his somewhat slumped shoulders, hands on hips, looking and thinking; the trait of a good examiner. The hallway was carpeted, so of no use for footwear impressions, but he made a mental note to have a control sample of it removed for any future comparison.

Behind him, in the kitchen, a trail of metal stepping plates led to where he now stood. The kitchen floor was smooth oak and would yield good footwear impressions. For now, he stood on the hall carpet, having photographed the entry to the house from the front door, into and out of the kitchen, and lounge, and now he found himself in the hallway, wondering at the course of events that had brought the whole team here.

He swivelled left, facing the open bedroom door.

Using the tip of a double-gloved finger, he pushed the door right at the very top, near the edge, until it opened another ten inches and then came to a halt. Jeffery sidled into the room, feeling the draught from the open French door cooling the sweat on his face. It brought with it the odour of urine from the dead body slumped half inside a wardrobe on the other side of the door. He entered the room fully, stopped after a couple of yards and turned to face the dead body of Henry Deacon.

Henry's face looked bloated, dark in the creases of his skin and pale on the cheeks and forehead. Blood and mucus had escaped his nostrils and made a trail down towards his mouth; another similar trail headed for his ear straight across the cheek. A sheer opaqueness covered his half-open eyes and killed the sparkle, the crystal quality of a living eye, turning it from a pathway into the soul into a barrier of utter emptiness.

That wasn't the first thing Jeffery noticed. Henry's semi-nakedness was; the trousers and underwear abandoned further into the bedroom. And this image was closely linked to the next feature – that of the belt around his neck, puckering up the skin there like the drawstring on a bag.

On the face of it, just another autoerotic death.

But, this was different for many reasons.

The resting place of his body now certainly wasn't the position in which he died. Lividity, the settling of blood in the body's lowest points, yet not at the point of contact with the ground or with the wardrobe – where the blood cannot squeeze into – meant Henry had moved after his death and during the early stages of lividity. The change of direction of the blood and mucus on Henry's face confirmed it. An amazing feat for a dead man.

Jeffery reached into the camera bag and pulled out an infrared thermometer, and took readings from several non-reflective surfaces in the room: the carpet, the curtains, the bed. They all reported an ambient temperature of 14°C. Then he turned the thermometer onto Henry, in the abdomen, then the head. A healthy body operates around 37°C, and after death, in non-extreme surroundings, it will lose a degree or so per hour until it reaches the ambient temperature where it will then stabilise. The abdomen read 30°C, the head 29 – but that was to be expected because of the head's larger surface area.

He took hold of Henry's left arm and tried to move it. He couldn't; it was as though the entire body was made up of one piece of wax. "Rigor."

The magazines around Henry's body appeared to have been placed there after death, rather than while Henry was alive and still enjoying them. And also curious was how new they all were. Not a crease or a tear anywhere on the glossy covers.

He used a little aluminium powder and a new squirrel-hair brush, and immediately fingermarks became visible on the cover of the first magazine he examined. And that was good, until the next stroke of his brush, when a leather glove mark appeared, complete with seam stitching. Same on the next magazine, and the next; also more glove marks on the pages that were open. Jeffery looked at Henry, and Henry's hands were bare.

Chapter Sixty-Nine

Friday 26th June

– One –

Eddie carried two mugs of coffee into the room, where he found Mick sitting in an old green leather and wooden office chair before a large desk that ran the length of the window wall. On the walls were clippings from Mick's published stories, pictures of news events before he became an old hack. And there were even silver-framed awards from newspapers and press agencies, handshakes at gala events, black-tie awards and prestigious dinners.

Mick knew his stuff, and had been around long enough to know when he was on the verge of something big. Only this something big was razor-edged: one side would kill them both, and the other would see the collapse of a high-ranking British minister and all the laws he supported.

Mick had changed out of his sweaty and grimy shirt, and had replaced it with a red checked shirt over a T-shirt, and a pair of light blue jeans.

"You look like James Dean." Eddie set the coffee on the desk next to a computer screen that showed nothing more grand than a crossword puzzle.

Mick moved the mouse, concentrating on the screen. "You look like a prick," he said absently.

"Thanks."

"Welcome."

"That the thing you showed me in the flat?"

"Yeah, this is what was in the envelope. I scanned it in, but it's just a puzzle, a box full of letters."

G	R	I	D	A	E	R	E	R	U	O	Y	F	I	E
M	A	S	T	I	P	H	R	T	E	G	S	N	T	O
I	K	E	M	D	A	H	N	R	E	H	T	A	F	Y
I	P	R	R	I	I	S	N	D	C	E	E	L	E	L
T	S	I	R	H	C	D	E	L	L	D	I	K	S	U
T	W	O	A	H	R	S	D	I	R	N	O	A	A	I
E	R	I	F	T	E	S	D	D	N	A	O	C	O	S
F	N	O	B	Y	S	M	P	O	H	T	I	T	E	S
P	T	A	E	R	G	O	E	H	T	R	E	H	T	A
R	F	E	F	D	M	N	U	E	D	T	T	E	R	R
R	O	F	E	A	C	A	E	P	N	I	T	S	E	R
O	C	F	K	E	L	M	O	E	O	V	K	I	O	G
T	I	L	E	H	T	G	U	N	I	L	L	I	K	R
T	T	W	O	Y	W	O	E	B	R	E	S	L	T	T
I	T	N	E	D	I	C	C	A	N	A	S	A	C	K

"So what're we supposed to do with it?"

"And this," Mick clicked his mouse, "was in the time-delay email that Henry sent me."

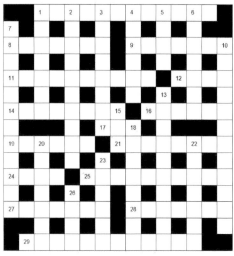

"Oh good," Eddie said, confused. "I guess there's a message in there somewhere."

"You'd think so, but I'm at a loss as to where it's supposed to be."

"Can you overlay one on top of the other?"

It took Mick twenty-five minutes and used most of his vocabulary of swear words, but eventually he managed it.

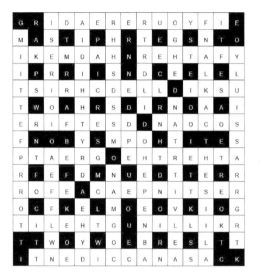

"IDAE," Eddie said. "What the hell's that? Or backwards, "EADI."

"No, no, I get it now, I get it." Mick pulled his chair forward, and Eddie leaned in over his shoulder. "Take just the letters in the blacked-out bits." He reached for a pen, snatched an envelope and began writing. "Read them out to me; left to right, top to bottom."

When they'd finished, they had a string of letters that initially made no sense at all. "You can see why he went to such lengths, it still makes—"

"Wait. It does, look." Mick picked out the words from the string of letters, split them using a slash and suddenly it *did* made sense, suddenly it made perfect sense.

Great/preston/Prince/Edward/road/Nob/Shite/Off/
Mud/track/lookout/tower/stick

"Well, it more or less makes sense. Great Preston, half an hour away. Prince Edward Road, that's…"

* * *

"…no problem," Mick said, trying to read the map by the car's interior light.

"We on Prince Edward Road now?"

"Have been for half a mile or so."

"So what the hell's Nob Shite Off?"

"I was hoping we'd just come across it."

But they didn't. They went as far as the next T-junction but hadn't seen anything referring to Nob Shite. "Okay, let's turn around and do it from this end."

It was twenty past one in the morning. Both had rumbling stomachs, both had a healthy growth of stubble and both were looking for something neither had any real hope of achieving: freedom from something they'd been sucked into, unlikely ever to be spat out of again.

By half past one, the headlamps picked out the first drizzle of what promised to be a heavy rainfall, the glossy road shining back at them in between encroaching hedgerows and treacherous bends. Eddie slowed right down, finding his way cautiously. When Mick shouted, "There!" Eddie hit the brakes, locked the car up and the back end swung around and collided with the hedge.

"Bollocks!" Eddie climbed out and slammed the door in frustration. He went to inspect the damage and Mick went to inspect the road sign.

"I found it, we're here."

Eddie stood upright, "Where the hell's 'here'?" He looked along the headlamp's beam and saw nothing but green hedgerows and a thin strip of slippery asphalt.

"Nob Shite Off." Mick pointed to a faded rusty sign slowly being swallowed by the bushes. All he could actually see was OFF, but when he followed the hedge line there was a slight gap and several broken branches and twigs on the ground. "Here," he approached the gap and could see the ever-decreasing arch of foliage that had tried to keep Henry Deacon's secret a secret.

"Jesus," Eddie joined him, "we'll never get the car up there."

"Have to, can't leave it here. Either someone will slam into it, or if we're being followed…"

"Okay, come on."

Eddie swung the car round, thankful there was no apparent damage, and aimed for the centre of the archway. The car slipped into a claustrophobically dark tunnel, and branches, some freshly snapped, scratched down the sides of the car and long grass pulled at the underside as he gently edged forward.

"I hope she's got enough money for a spray job."

Eddie glanced at Mick, "Don't. I feel bad enough as it is."

"What did she say to you? If you don't mind my asking."

Eddie kept driving, and half a minute or so passed before the scraping and scratching receded, before he needed the wipers again, and they broke through into what appeared to be a wide featureless access lane.

"She said we're gonna die." Eddie felt the wheels slip, felt the car being pulled along by deep ruts before it found a potholed lane.

"You two optimists were made for each other."

They were travelling a slight incline and it wasn't long before the headlights picked out a building up ahead. Eddie stopped the car twenty yards before it and together they climbed out.

All this tumult and danger, this fight against a murderous government was the source of a new-found enhancement of Eddie's squalid life. The image of Ros nestling into his neck, the smell of her hair and the warmth he shared with her, it was all thanks to the Third Rule, and however short his life had become since Henry Deacon killed his son, then at least he was grateful that it now had a little colour around the monotone edges – Imminent Death had forced her hand, and even if they never saw each other again… well, maybe that was a thought not worth thinking.

"We're never going to find his bleeding lookout tower in this." The rain came heavier as if listening to Eddie.

Mick pulled out a torch from his jacket, and then pulled his jacket collar up.

"Didn't pack any sandwiches when you packed the torch, did you?"

"No."

"Coffee?"

"No."

"Bugger."

They walked over the dirt, past the dilapidated building and towards what they hoped would be a summit, somewhere high that could give them a clue as to where Henry's tower may be.

"Why couldn't he have played in a fucking tree house like a normal kid?"

It turned out there *was* a summit of sorts, and luckily for them, Mick happened to be shining his torch at the grey earth, marvelling at how it was turning from dusty dirt to slick mud before their eyes. And then the earth disappeared.

Both men stood on the edge of the great opencast mine, and when Mick shone the torch straight down, the beam just disappeared.

"Okay, we're not high enough. I can't see anything."

They scanned all around but the only thing coming back at them in the torchlight was the steadily falling rain. Mick turned it off, and surprisingly things improved; they could make out the dark valley they had just walked up, black embankments either side receding into various tones of dark grey. With their backs to the opencast, either side was different; to their left was the sheer face of a slag mound that travelled upwards almost forever until the slightly lighter sky showed them its silhouette. To their right however, was a lane that gave way to one of the valley sides and, without speaking, they elected to travel this way.

"You know you're on a Rule Three?"

"I had forgotten, but appreciate the reminder, cheers."

"I could stop it," Mick said.

Eddie stood still for a moment. "How?"

"I ask Rochester to bring forward the publishing schedule for the juicy bits that Henry gave me."

"Have it transcribed so the entire country will read that he fired the CSI building?"

Mick nodded through the rain.

"I can see two problems with that."

"You really are a pessimistic bastard. I thought you'd be grateful."

Eddie walked on, his limp growing more pronounced.

"So go on then, what problems? We already did a forensic match on the voice, it's definitely Henry Deacon. We have independent corroboration that the recording hasn't been tampered with—"

"First," Eddie shouted back over his shoulder, "it's big of Henry to admit firing the building, but that doesn't prove he killed Stuart."

"And they can't prove that *you* killed him either."

"Seems to me that's where convenient justice comes to life… they already got me on a Rule Three so I'm betting they'll want proof not that I *did* it, but proof that I *didn't*. I'm on a public death list, mate, won't be easy to get me off it."

"But he said—"

"I know what he said, Mick, but they reckon they already have the killer."

"You're full of shit."

Eddie staggered down the lane.

"And what's the second good reason I shouldn't go public now?"

Eddie stopped again and waited for Mick to catch up. "Having a headline claiming that Henry killed Archer and Sam is one thing, but if you claim he tried to evade justice by altering evidence, *with* government help, I guarantee you free admission to a very private death list."

– Two –

The phone on Deacon's desk buzzed. He picked up. "Yes?"

"Sir," Justine said, "I have Thomas Gordon on the phone."

"I wanted him here—"

"He's in Scotland, sir."

Deacon closed his eyes for a moment, made an effort to take a deep breath and failed half way through. "Put him on." The line clicked. "Thomas?" he said.

"Sir George. How can I help you?"

"I want an injunction taking out against a local newspaper in Yorkshire and its affiliated national edition."

"When?"

"When? Now!"

There was a pause on the other end of the phone long enough for Deacon to wonder if the line had been cut.

"Three days. Minimum. Depending on—"

"Don't give me three days, Thomas, I want it doing before the morning edition hits the streets."

"Impossible! The morning editions will be printed by now, probably already in transit."

"You're a lawyer, dammit, stop them."

"Cannot be done. And the online versions will be available soon anyway. You may be able to get one in time for tomorrow's edition, but no chance for today's. Sorry."

"Put the wheels in motion. And use as much grease as you need."

"What's it about? And what newspaper is it?"

"It's *The Yorkshire Echo*—"

"We're off to a bad start already then; Alan Rochester is the editor, and he's an old bulldog—"

"Then get a wolf on the job—"

"Who has access to Media Corporation's lawyers… they play rough and can delay—"

"Thomas. Stop there." Deacon leaned back against the cold leather of his chair and squeezed the bridge of his nose. "I want the stories they're about to run killed. Dead."

"On what grounds?"

"National security."

"You'll need to be more specific, that's a huge umbrella."

"Specific. Right. We have a drunken journalist and a drunken police employee running around the fucking country making stories up about my family and about the policies concerning the new Criminal Justice Act, which may bring it into disrepute, and which may damage my reputation and the government's reputation beyond repair."

"Don't worry about reputation, we have tough libel laws."

"Fuck the libel laws, Thomas; I don't want it even reaching the courts! Once it's in the public domain it will never go away; even when I'm vindicated, my career and The Rules will be in tatters."

There was another considerable silence before, "I'll get someone to visit Rochester in a few hours; maybe we can lean on him a little."

"Make it happen, Thomas. I can cover this morning's headlines if I must, but God knows what's coming my way tomorrow."

Deacon put down the phone, clasped his hands before him, and finished off the deep breath he'd promised himself.

– Three –

With the smell of freshly rained upon dust in the air, they walked in silence, slipping and tripping along the treacherous lane with feet made twice as wide and twice as heavy with clinging grey mud. Eventually, a compound came into view, blocked by metal gates that had perished over time. Mick took out his torch, and with ease they forced aside the corroded chain link fence at the gates' side and climbed through, a gusting wind at their backs. Soon they were walking not on slippery grey muddy earth, but on slippery concrete.

Ahead, the carcasses of abandoned machinery stood open to the elements like rows of slain giants and all they could hear was wind whistling among them, and incessant rain beating them.

"Up there." Eddie pointed into the near distance. Silhouetted against the lighter sky was what looked like a Second World War aircraft control tower. It was a cold concrete structure high enough to have a pretty good view of the compound, and probably most of the opencast too. A plethora of other eerily dark buildings seemed to spread out to one side of the tower. Eddie rammed his wet hands deep into his wet pockets and trudged on towards the tower of dreams.

* * *

The door banged shut after them, and even Mick's torchlight seemed reluctant to be here, its light as meagre as a candle flame. Wind rushed along the concrete staircase beside them, adding to the chill in their wet clothes. Outside in the dark yard, a door banged incessantly.

Mick's torchlight picked out the stairs and the debris crowded onto them, and then they were on a landing of sorts with doors left and right, all open, all willing to give up their innards to a curious eye. But none of them contained anything of note, just bare floors, massive spiders' webs, smashed windows, and utter darkness.

Their footfalls echoed in this chasm that had stood abandoned perhaps thirty years. In one or two of the rooms, they found very old empty lager cans, discarded porn magazines, cigarette ends, even a couple of uninviting blankets complete with rat droppings. But nothing pertaining as yet to any kind of stick.

"How are we going to find a stick in here?" Eddie pushed open the door to a small toilet block. "It could be anywhere."

"I know. But what else can we do? Keep looking."

"I have no idea what we're looking *for* though. Why send us out here for a fucking—"

"Stick. Yes, I know. But maybe it's a hollow stick, contains some important documents, maybe the stick is pointing to something, I don't know, mate, just keep looking."

And keep looking they did. Through a warped wooden door, with the remnants of smashed glass inside a rotten frame, they entered the main part of the tower. Glassless windows peered out into a mess of turbulent clouds, and the rain flew in, propelled by a chill wind directly into Eddie's eyes as he stood squinting out into the night, observing the black hole of the opencast some 200 yards away, and closer, the dead diesel and water tanks on a light grey concrete hard-standing. The door out there continued to bang.

"He's been here, alright." Mick shone his torch at the narrow strip of wall between the windows and the door they'd just entered through. Scratched into the remains of the damp plaster were the words *Henry Deacon* and a date below them read: *24/8/94*. "Scruffy little bastard."

"I'm not seeing a stick."

And then they both turned, almost simultaneously, towards each other, as though an idea had at last shared itself with them, and both said, "*Memory* stick!"

"But that's even worse," Eddie said, "They're tiny. I was imagining a two-foot length of wood, dammit. But a memory stick, Jesus, we could be here all night."

"Think about it though, what other clues has he given us?"

Eddie folded his arms. "Well, this could be interesting."

"I'm thinking aloud here. Feel free to join in at any time."

"What a prick that guy was. I mean, we're looking for something the size a of a fucking matchbox in a—"

"Where would *you* hide it?"

"Me?"

"We've got to think like him."

"You mean go back to the car and run some people down?"

"If you were him, where would you hide it?"

"Behind a picture in the kitchen! I don't know, but I wouldn't—"

"If you *had* to hide it here, where would you hide it? It would need to be out of sight of any kids who came here—"

"It'd need to be waterproof," Eddie said.

"Right."

"Maybe higher than your average kid to keep it out of reach."

Mick shone the torch slowly around the room, shoulder high and above, looking for loose plaster, missing bricks or the like. Almost imperceptibly, the beam had grown fainter, yellower.

"There." Eddie pointed to the electrical conduit running between the light switch and a scattering of five or six ceiling lights. "Run the torch along its length."

Mick approached the switch, looked doubtfully at Eddie.

"Seriously; it's metal, it's big enough… wait, shine your torch up there." Eddie pointed to the dark stain of a junction box on the ceiling. Mick brought his light up, and they could see it was a shallow metal circular box attached to the ceiling. It had three tubular conduits leading away from it; its cover was a flat circular disc, rusty as hell and screwed to the box very loosely. And although the screw heads were also rusty, their threads were still a shiny silver, as though they had been recently unscrewed. Mick looked at Eddie; raised eyebrows said he could be on to something.

Eddie reached up but the rusty screws were just out of reach.

Chapter Seventy

Friday 26th June

– One –

Under the cover of darkness, Christian decided to go south after all. There were moments during his four-hour stretch at the wheel where he almost felt happy, where his injured shoulder had settled to a tolerable throb. There were moments when he forgot about Alice, and even the loss of his paintings temporarily left him alone too.

The hum of the tyres on the road made him drowsy. The stereo didn't work, and the window didn't open. So his tiredness grew, amplified until he was only seeing glimpses of the road between bouts of eye-rolling drowsiness.

Up ahead on the M5 was Sedgemoor services. His dream of getting all the way to the remotest part of Cornwall in one journey was proving too much. Almost without thinking, he slid his right hand across the steering wheel and flicked the indicator stalk down. Moments later he shut off the engine in the darkest corner of the car park he could find. Through the screen, and over the top of a hedge, he could see the silhouette of black trees against the mid-blue of the night sky. He took a long drink of water, climbed into the back seat, and was asleep in less than a minute.

– Two –

"Hurry up," Mick said, "the fucking torch is dying."

They scavenged around the room for something screwdriver-shaped, and came up empty. And then Eddie stood up, wiped grimy fingers down his trousers and looked at the window. "Here, bring your candle over."

Eddie tiptoed to the rotten window frame and when Mick arrived with the torch, he saw the perfect tool. He grasped the wood, and shards of glass broke free; the larger pieces fell outside, but the wind hurled the sharp, powdery bits into their faces.

"Nice," Mick said, spitting glass. "I'm no mechanical genius here, but I suspect the window frame may be a tad too large to fit into the screw's slot. Just an observation."

Squinting, Eddie yanked the frame, twisting it top and bottom until the spongy wood released the top hinge. He grabbed the frame at the top, eyes fully shut now, and twisted it out and down until the window broke free of its frame. Eddie hauled it inside and got upwind.

"Okay, shine your light, need to see if we can get the hinges off."

Mick played the light at both hinges just as it faded and went out. "Fuck."

"Timing is just wonderful."

The room ceased to exist; all that did exist to them now was the noise of the wind and the stinging of the rain. "Well, at least we can get to work now."

"Using a fucking window frame?"

"Watch and learn, watch and learn." Eddie shuffled into the centre of the room. "Get your lighter out, up near the junction box."

"This I have to see."

"Me too, or else we'll be here all night."

With wet fingers, Mick fumbled his lighter from his pocket, thumbed the flint. Nothing happened. No spark. "It's wet through."

"You're taking the piss."

"Yes I'm taking the piss, Eddie. I thought it would be fun to spend the night in a wind tunnel, freezing cold, starving, needing a shit, needing a drink, striking a dead lighter so you could work your magic on a junction box with a *fucking window frame!*"

"You're upset, aren't you? Don't deny it, I can read the signs."

"Stop it, Eddie, I'm not in the mood."

"Reach into my left jacket pocket, there's a push-button lighter in there. No flint, just piezoelectric quartz. Modern technology, it's called."

Mick held the tiny light as high as he could, shielding the flame from the gusting wind long enough for Eddie to locate the edge of one of the seized hinges into the slot of a screw in the junction box lid.

The flame blew out several times, the hinge parted company with the slot just as many times, with progress being tediously slow. They had managed maybe two full turns of one of the screws. And then the flame blew out and no amount of furious button-pressing could coax it back into the life, the wind was too strong, the rain too persistent.

Eddie screamed and threw the window frame aside, the remaining glass broke and joined the rest of the debris somewhere in the corner. "My arms are killing me."

"Why's it so tight to unscrew? The threads look brand new."

"Stupid tosser got it cross-threaded. And instead of taking the screw out and starting again, he just tightened it and tightened it."

"Now what?"

Eddie shrugged. "Can't believe this," he muttered, and crunched his way over to the window. "What time is it?"

"Half four," Mick said. "I need food, Eddie. I'm gonna fall over soon."

"Settle down for half an hour or so, and all will become clear."

"What you talking about?"

"It'll be dawn soon," he said, peering into the eastern sky. "And then we won't need a torch." He stared to roughly the spot he thought Mick was, "I ought to just smash the thing to bits. It'd only take one or two good blows and the whole junction box would come down."

"Not worth the risk of damaging the memory stick."

"I have an LED torch on my phone."

"I thought I asked you to turn it off!"

"I did turn it off, just saying, that's all."

"Can't risk it."

"It would take a minute, two at the most."

"Think about it. They think you killed Stuart and they've been all over your flat like a bad case of mould, so they're looking hard for you."

"Not hard enough to warrant checking cell phone masts."

"You think? Course they will, you're a Rule Three bad guy, and they'll want you quick. This is all about drive-through justice now, Eddie. They want results and quick, they're not so bothered about quality, they just want results.

"They already know Henry Deacon is dead and no doubt your forensic buddies will have found our fingerprints in his house by now so we'll be in the frame for topping him too."

Eddie shook his head, "No we won't; he was dead hours before we got to him."

"If someone like your friend Benson is leading that enquiry, do you think that little fact will get in his way? You said yourself people interpret things how they want." Mick rubbed a sleeve across his leaking nose. "Anyway, we can't prove we were only in Deacon's house ten minutes."

Eddie sighed.

"If they catch us now, we'll be railroaded straight through court, a very brief Review Panel hearing and our feet won't touch the fucking floor on our way to the slaughterhouse. Seven days from now, we'll be cooling in the ground in some graveyard somewhere." Mick touched the nearest wall, made sure it wasn't wet, then turned and slowly slid down it into a crumpled position. Hands on his knees, he waited. "Maybe we wouldn't even see a courtroom either. We're very bad men, and if the police or someone else thought we were dangerous…"

Eddie turned back to the window, bared his wet face to the wind, and watched the sky. "I'm fucking freezing."

"We already went to press with doubts over the Jag and the CSI building burning down. Deacon knows we're not on his side anymore; he's after both of us. And logically, if he's after us, he'll want to silence us permanently."

Eddie turned into the room, his back to the wind now.

"So no, I don't think we can risk turning the phones back on even for a minute."

"I've never been hunted before," Eddie whispered. "Kind of weird."

"Only kind of?"

"It's not how I imagined it to be."

"You *imagined* being hunted?" Mick laughed.

"Well you know, it's one of those things. You watch an action film or you read an espionage book, and you imagine what it would be like. Well, I did anyway."

"And how did you imagine it to be?"

"I thought I'd be fine, because the guy I just watched on the screen or the fella in the book always was. But it's not really like that, is it? I couldn't survive for long. Especially if they have technology on their side too. I'm absolutely knackered, struggling to keep my eyes open. I'm hungry, thirsty—"

"Scared?"

Eddie was silent for a moment. "Yep, I'm scared too. Part of me wants to walk into Holbeck nick and just reason it out with Benson or Taylor or whoever. That part of me says all this is ridiculous, it's just a misunderstanding, it's just a misinterpretation of forensic evidence and it can easily be explained away. And when I've done that, Benson or Taylor will look a bit sheepish, hold out their hand and offer an apology and we'll all carry on as though nothing has happened," Eddie laughed.

Mick didn't laugh. "Then you really should be scared. I don't know what's on that thing up there in the ceiling, but even the stuff I already have is enough to end Deacon's career. Some of it, like Henry being worried his old man would kill him, isn't really printable because it's conjecture unless we find some hard facts at Henry's scene. But make no mistake here: if Deacon suspects I have any kind of damaging info on him or reads my story in the paper, it'll be a straight battle between him and me. And that battle has already begun."

"You could take him out of the equation with what you know; he won't have the power—"

"Don't be so naïve about politicians, Eddie. Even when they're out of the job, they are fierce, and none more so than Deacon, he's the king of retribution. And so in answer to the question you haven't yet asked of me, I am scared too. Scared shitless, in fact.

"I have enough ammunition to do irreparable damage to him and his misadministration of The Rules. And hopefully enough up there in the ceiling to bury the fucker. And I will too, given the chance."

"What if he offered you immunity for all the info you have?"

Mick shook his head. "I've been doing this shit for twenty-odd years. Some of my work has been quite good; some of it earned me awards. And sometimes I've come across a story that makes the hairs on my neck stand up. I've finished my copy and sent it to the editor and thought 'this is it, this is the one'. But it never really has been. Oh, there have been ground-breaking stories, hard-hitting stories about criminals in Eastern Europe or paedophile rings in Scotland… whatever. But none of them has had the potential that this has. And trust me, mate, these stories land in a journo's lap once in his entire life if he's extremely lucky." Mick straightened his back. "I'd never agree to any terms or immunity he'd offer. Never."

"Even if agreeing could save your life?"

"And what a life to save, eh?" He looked across at Eddie; the fact that he could now actually see him quite clearly passed him by. "The story is everything and everything is the story."

"Come on," Eddie said, "let's get you your story."

Eddie retrieved the smashed window frame, positioned the seized hinge upright and carried it to the junction box. It wavered several times, but at last Eddie managed to engage the edge of the hinge in the screw's slot and began turning around. Only half a turn later the screw leaned sideways and fell out. Then the disc swung aside and something slid to its edge, teetered, and then fell on to the wet concrete floor.

Mick retrieved it quickly enough, and stood with the object of their quest wrapped in a self-seal plastic bag. Both stared at it in awe as though discovering some priceless relic.

* * *

At almost five in the morning Mick placed the memory stick reverentially as deep as it would go into the inside pocket of his saturated summer jacket and closed the zip, patted the bulge and headed for the door.

Once out in the yard among the hulks of dead machines, Eddie shielded his face against the rain and trudged through the grey mud towards the black gates he could see in the distance, maybe quarter of a mile away. The light of the new day was thin and the world was a mass of varying degrees of greyness lacking definition and solidity, a lot like his life, he thought. "How sure are you they can't find your cottage?"

From behind, Mick shivered, pulled up his collar and entered the same field of mud they'd exited three and a half hours earlier. "I'm not sure of anything. Like I said, only the farmer knows I live there, and he doesn't know who I am anyhow; he doesn't know I've got the government's future in my pocket."

"And ours."

Mick laughed, but it sounded like the groan of a horror-movie door.

"Okay, just thinking things through; how secure is your email?"

"We use re-routers to try and lose capturing devices. Until now it wasn't the government we were avoiding; it was other newspapers and television broadcasters. They often claim a story is their own exclusive when really they stole it from the ether. So all our emails are encrypted. Take them months to crack it."

"I mean, would it be wiser to go straight to your office?"

Now Mick did laugh, "Oh no, no, no. I wouldn't make it through the front door before I was bundled into some car and taken away and shot and left in a ditch."

"Nice thought."

"I'm taking as few chances as I can."

"Sounds like you've had experience of this shit before."

"Unless you're reporting on the local school's gala it pays to take precautions."

Eddie approached the chain link fence. "But you mean to tell me that all you correspondents live in isolated cottages—"

"Listen, I work in crime, so I probe into—"

"I get that, but even so, it's extreme. You use a different mailing address…"

Mick stepped through the hole in the fence followed by Eddie, and they trudged through a list of discomforts towards a distant summit that still hid in the shadows. "I worked in other countries earlier in my career," he began, "Eastern European ones. I was a special correspondent. I had a flair in those days for searching out news that no one was aware of… not unlike this kind of shit, I suppose.

"They put you out there for several reasons: maybe you're good with foreigners, can be empathetic towards them, can build up contacts with the local police; or you've got a keen interest in that country or a specialism within it; or they want you out of the way. I don't know," he shrugged, "maybe there's someone with better connections who wants your current job in *this* country, whatever. Anyhow, I was over there whether I liked it or not. And I was over there ad infinitum too."

"You really know how to piss people off, don't you?"

"Who said I was out there as punishment?"

"Is that what *I* was to you, a 'contact'?"

"I won't lie, Eddie, that's exactly what you were in the early days. I needed a forensic slant on some of the stories I wrote, something different from the usual police angle. But I grew fond of you and it developed into a rather nice friendship I think. Didn't it?"

"Go on."

"I was there for five years, had become well known and well liked. I was turning in good work, and then I got married to a local girl, so I sort of 'belonged'."

"Didn't know you were married."

"Lots you don't know about me."

They crested the summit and less than a minute later, they could see the roof of Ros's car.

"So what happened? Why did you come back to the UK alone?"

"Let's just say we weren't together for very long."

"That's women, mate, very fickle."

"She was murdered."

Eddie stopped, turned in the mud and waited a second for Mick to catch up. "I didn't know, Mick. I'm sorry."

Mick shrugged walked on past Eddie towards the car. "It's history."

Eddie caught up and walked by Mick's side. Through the rain, he whispered, "Is that why—"

"Barely had a sober day since." He smiled across at Eddie. "And I don't want to start now," he grinned. "When this shit is over, if it doesn't go well, I want to die pissed out of my tree."

"Now I understand…"

"Most people don't, Eddie. But I really think you do."

"I meant the seclusion and the postal address stuff."

"Oh that. I went a little OTT on the security stuff, I didn't think they would follow me from over there, but I like to sleep soundly."

"It's better than a flat over a fucking carpet shop."

"We'll see." Mick veered off the track, waved a hand, "I got to pee."

Eddie trudged on a few paces and then took out his phone, and pressed the on button. It seemed the decent thing to do, just to send Ros a quick message, one word, that's all, so she wouldn't be late for work.

He looked at the keypad, typed one word and pressed send. When the little envelope on the screen fluttered away into the distance, he pressed off. *There, no harm done and everyone's happy.*

Chapter Seventy-One

Friday 26th June

– One –

The alarm brought Ros back from a sleep so shallow that her eyes were barely closed. She pulled aside the curtains, saw the empty parking slot outside her gate and sighed. Maybe she should wait for him, maybe he would be here any minute. It was six-thirty. He had thirty minutes left.

She was about to take a breath and become Strong Ros, the one she'd always been when she visited Eddie. It required skill and determination; it required self-belief so that Eddie didn't see her quaking inside her shoes. She got ready to inhale when her mobile phone buzzed and startled her.

It was him, it was Eddie. A text message. 'Sorry.'

She dropped the phone and headed straight for the shower. Strong Ros was nowhere to be seen; Timid Ros closed the bathroom door. On the one hand, she was relieved he was still okay, and not to mention pleasantly surprised that he had the courtesy to let her know, but on the other hand, she was sad he was still battling with his ordeal. She wondered why he was sorry though: that he still had her car; that he was going to be late? Or was he sorry that he wasn't going to spend the rest of his life with her after all, because the rest of his life was only about an hour or so long?

– Two –

From thirty yards away the scratches along the roof and down the sides of the car stood out proud; there was foliage protruding like a tongue from under the front bumper, more stuck behind the wiper blades and embedded into the joints of the wing mirrors. "She is going to kill me."

Exhausted, cold and soaked through, Mick sat in the passenger seat while Eddie scraped away as much mud as possible from his shoes before he collapsed behind the wheel and started the engine. "Get the fucking heater on, quick," he said, "before my fingers fall off."

Eddie engaged first gear and turned the car round, wheel-spinning most of the way, until it successfully pointed downhill.

The roads heading out of Great Preston were empty. The rain gathered strength, and the wind hurled rain at the car with enough intensity to slow Eddie down. The car veered and rocked but after forty minutes of steady progress, they made it onto the busier main roads heading north towards a discreet village called Aberford. Neither spoke throughout the journey, each content to dwell upon his own thoughts.

Mick was playing his plan through his mind, from walking in through the front door to shaking hands with Rochester in the office in a week or maybe even two, depending upon how the news was received and what the authorities chose to do with it. Sometimes, the wheels moved slowly, but when public concern was a major priority, they were jet-propelled.

There was always the possibility that he would never see Rochester again; a freak accident perhaps, a blatant killing, or an unexplained disappearance were all equally plausible. *And if that was the case,* he thought, *then so be it, so long as my work reaches the public.*

The information Henry Deacon had given him would make Michael Lyndon famous as the one who told the story, entwined with the famous Sir George Deacon like Woodward and Bernstein entwined with Watergate, a kind of notoriety. And he wondered what treasure the little waterproofed parcel in his inside pocket held; must be something big to go to all that trouble hiding it. And there was a tinge of honour creeping into Mick's mind as he thought of Henry choosing him, Mick Lyndon, to tell that story. Yes, there was pride there.

* * *

Eddie too drew out a plan, though his was considerably shorter. He figured the cottage was as safe a place as any right now. Once the stories were out, his biggest concern would be skipping work and avoiding a Rule Two infringement for assaulting McHue.

He began thinking of Ros, and wondered if they had a future together. And that's when he smiled at the thought of Sam, his little fellow, his mate, his son. And the smile went away.

"Park it up there under the trees." Mick pointed to a rough track to the south of his cottage that went nowhere, simply ended between the trunks of two trees. "If they get lucky with a sweep."

"Helicopter won't be flying in this weather." But he parked it there anyway, because if Eddie was going to get any luck at all, it would be of the bad variety.

* * *

"Won't be long and you'll be a free man," Mick said as they walked into the hallway. "Shoes."

Eddie slipped his shoes off. "I always was a free man." Mud plastered the lower part of his jeans and had crusted on the inside right up to the knees, drying out and flaking off in lumps. He pulled off his socks, and marvelled at his pure white wrinkled feet.

"You know what I mean."

Eddie threw his wet jacket on the floor next to a cold radiator and then unbuttoned his jeans and rolled them off his legs. "You got a shower in this dump?"

"Washing machine and drier in the kitchen, feed the vent pipe out through the window otherwise the place'll steam up; shower upstairs, towels in the airing cupboard. Fix me a drink first, would ya?"

"Coffee?"

Mick stopped halfway through yanking his jacket off, raised his eyebrows, and continued when he was sure that Eddie got the message.

"I'm not having one."

"What?"

"I feel okay without. My *y*-axis is flat-lined."

Mick stared blankly at him.

Eddie walked through into the kitchen, laughing, leaving wet footprints on the dark quarry tiles, found the washing machine and dumped all his clothes in. He was about to remove his boxers.

"Whoa, boy. I *so* do not want my whisky served to me by a naked man, thank you very much."

Eddie laughed, walked back into the lounge and poured a generous measure.

"If you feel okay without, it begs the question of your alcoholism in the first place."

Eddie stood before Mick with a generous tumbler of neat whisky and, sniffing it briefly, he smiled at him. "I'm good, thanks." Then he walked back into the kitchen, rolling his boxers down as he went, and laughing as he imagined the grimace on Mick's face.

"Please don't turn around…"

Eddie laughed again; the mood was lightening.

"…but seriously, I'm amazed that a week ago you had signs of alcoholic poisoning, and here you are now without so much as a single withdrawal symptom."

He slammed the washing machine door, turned the dial and listened to the machine filling with water. He turned–

"Hey," Mick looked away quickly.

"Sorry," Eddie said and walked behind the door. "I have a headache, but that's all," he shrugged. "I can't explain it; I'm just not bothered about booze. For the first time in months."

"Amazing," Mick walked up the stone stairs, treading lightly on the carpet, almost silently.

– Three –

Ros sipped tea. She turned on the television just as the background picture of George and Henry Deacon blinked off the screen behind the shoulder of a happy smiley broadcaster with too much make-up on and whose breasts seemed determined to break free of the blouse that struggled to hold them. There was a banner scrolling across the bottom of the screen, just below the errant breasts, but all she could see before it changed to an advert for Robinson's Barley Water, was the single word: Deacon. This was part of Channel 5's breakfast news show dedicated to Rule Three "stars". It was a gimmick, when it should have been about a successful new justice system rooting out the worst people in society and elimin–

The plain red wall over the broadcaster's shoulder changed into the evil-looking face of a dangerous criminal. Christian Ledger stared right back at her.

"…and last for today is 1313, Christian Ledger, a twenty-eight-year-old male from West Yorkshire. Mr Ledger is a convicted burglar with a history of violence towards his victims. Yesterday he became wanted for the murder of his twenty-four-year-old girlfriend Alice Sedgewick who was found stabbed to death in their squat in Leeds. Ledger's notoriety was further increased as he became the first person in the UK to gain provisional Rule Three status from his own crime *scene, such was the confidence of West Yorkshire homicide detectives in his guilt; and, said a West Yorkshire Police spokesperson, it's demonstrative of the level of commitment the police have in making The Rules work, and work quickly, which all helps to allay the fears of the general public..."*

Ros blinked, and then shook her head. "Bullshit," she whispered. Really, what was the point of scene examination at all? They may as well pick a name out of a hat. "Incompetent!"

She turned off the television and stared at the blank screen, feeling angry, grinding her teeth. She delved inside her handbag, took out her phone, and flicked through the contacts. She pressed CALL.

"Holbeck CID, DC Cooper."

"Coop, it's Ros from CSI." She could hear laughter and banter in the background.

"Hey, Ros, how's—"

"Is DI Taylor there?"

"A minute."

She heard Coop's hand cover the phone, and in a muffled voice heard him call out, 'Boss!' Coop took his hand away and said, "He's here, Ros."

"Thanks."

"DI Taylor."

"Sir, it's Ros from CSI."

"Hello, Ros."

"I just saw Christian Ledger advertised as a Rule Three."

"Number 1313, I think—"

She could hear the humour in his voice, "He's innocent! He shouldn't be on a Rule Three at all."

"Ledger is one of Tom Benson's jobs; you'll have to take it up with him."

"He won't listen; he said he wanted Ledger before I'd even finished the scene."

"I'm sure once he has all the evidence—"

"He'll go right ahead and ignore it. He wants the glory of—"

"Ros, you'll have to speak to him about it—"

"He won't *listen.*" Even Ros detected the desperate tone in her voice, trying to convince someone of something they have absolutely no inclination to hear.

Taylor's voice sank to a whisper, "If any evidence comes to light that shows Ledger as innocent, DCI Benson will listen, because once the Review Panel sees it, Ledger will be released and Benson will be in serious trouble. And he's wise enough to know that, Ros."

"And what if that evidence is never recorded? What happens if the Review Panel don't get to know about—"

"Ros."

"They'll kill an innocent man, and keep a murderer on the streets. It's not all about stats, Alan. At some point we're going to have to bring justice into the equation." Her heart pummelled, she gripped the phone tightly enough to hurt her hand, and in a trembling voice was begging for the freedom of a man she had never even met… and losing.

"Ros," Taylor said gently, "I appreciate your concerns, but I'm not the one you should be bringing them to. I think DCI Benson knows how the law works and you have nothing to be concerned about."

"But—"

"Have you seen Eddie today?"

Ros stopped, dumbfounded. How could someone of Taylor's stature ignore her; he'd always sought her opinion at scenes, had always sought her expertise when something special came up. Now he was blanking her as though she was interfering with something that wasn't her business. And worse than cutting her off, was the abrupt change of subject.

"Ros?"

Ros pressed END and threw the phone. It hit the chair and bounced onto the floor.

* * *

Composure was hard to come by when the world was falling into chaos all around her. Ros felt as though she were swimming against an inevitable tide that was strong enough to convince her for a moment that *she* had got things all wrong.

There was no way she could sleep at night knowing government-sponsored bullets were killing the wrong people for the sake of conveyor belt justice.

She snatched the phone off the carpet just as the damn thing rang. She shrieked and almost dropped it again. The number on the display was "unknown". She breathed deeply, and pressed okay. "Hello," she said.

"Ros, it's Alan Taylor again."

"Hello." There was no noise in the background this time, so she guessed he'd returned to his office to make this call.

"We seem to have been cut off." He waited for her response, but Ros said nothing. "I have to ask again if you've heard from Eddie recently."

"No," she said, almost confidently, "I haven't heard from him."

"Let me just remind you that if you do hear from him, you must get in touch with us."

Us? *Us?* Why us? Did Taylor view her current situation differently from her previous situation? Was she one of *them* now, one of those outsiders, maybe even one of those dangerous people who consort with criminals! "I will," she said quietly.

"Okay, that's good," he said. "You spoken to Jeffery?"

"Jeffery? No, why, should I have?"

"You know he's been working Henry Deacon's scene all night?"

She thought he was going to ask her to stand in and finish off the scene because Jeffery was exhausted, or perhaps there was a secondary scene needed looking at or–

"We think Eddie had something to do with his death."

"With Henry Deacon's death?"

"It's just a possibility. But he was definitely there, Ros."

"Eddie was there? How do you know that?"

"We found his fingerprints. Climbing-in marks in a hall window frame."

Ros closed her eyes, couldn't think of anything to say that would help Eddie. So she kept quiet.

"And there's more, Ros."

"What more?"

"He's chosen to arm himself."

"Haha, Eddie? You know how much he hates guns."

"He fired the weapon when two officers gave chase."

Her eyes were wide now. *Why didn't Eddie mention this?*

"He fired it into the earth, maybe a warning shot, maybe a misfire, who knows."

"Oh my God. I don't believe it."

"Believe it, Ros. And there's one more thing you should know before you consider not letting me know if he contacts you."

"I already said I would."

"I know what you said, Ros. But let me leave you with this."

"With what?"

"We found the bullet and the shell casing. Five o'clock this morning, a bleary-eyed scientist at ballistics checked them out. Both are a perfect match for those we found at your office, at Stuart's scene."

Ros's mouth fell open, and nothing other than a squeak came out. Eventually her mouth closed, and her eyes blinked as ridiculous tears fell onto the arm of her work sweater. "Stuart was *shot*?"

"It's true, Ros. And despite your lack of confidence in Tom Benson, you know how thorough *I* am about evidence."

Ros hung up and she stared at the phone. Then her eyes fell on yesterday's copy of *The Yorkshire Echo*.

Chapter Seventy-Two

Friday 26th June

– One –

After an hour or so, the heat inside the car had dissipated. And for most of the night, Christian had been cold; not cold enough to awaken fully, but cold enough to keep his sleep shallow and fitful. And only now, as he realised the back of his eyelids were pale orange instead of the black he was used to, did he begin to surface into what he thought would be his first real day of freedom.

The sun was full up over the horizon, piercing shards of light through the trees and the hedgerow right in through the windscreen. The delicate sound of bells from St George's church half a mile away in Easton-in-Gordano, was a crisp contrast to the dull rumble of traffic on the M5 a hundred or so yards behind him. But the rumble was growing, and in another hour, it would be a loud enough roar to drown out St George's voice.

* * *

"He's mine," a woman said.

"I saw him first!"

"I heard you actually gotta touch 'em afore it counts. Like a game o' tig."

The officer holding the M16 turned and eyed the crowd. "You go anywhere near and I'll have you locked up."

"I'm only telling you what I heard."

"And I'm tellin' you this ain't a game, and if you go anywhere—"

"Here," the woman said, "what they doing?"

The officer turned away from the small crowd as a colleague crept up to the side of the silver Nissan Micra. His weapon was extended, his steps were slow and deliberate, and his eyes never strayed from the vehicle.

"What's he doing?" the woman asked.

"He's gonna tig him," someone replied. The crowd giggled.

* * *

There was a light tap against the window. And he thought he heard someone laughing. Christian opened his eyes and peered upwards, straight into the barrel of a gun. Above it, an Avon and Somerset police officer smiled down at him and Christian's world of dreams exploded into a universe of cruel nightmares.

The officer motioned to the door and Christian groaned as the pains in his leg, his shoulder, head, and his bust lip, and his broken nose, attacked him simultaneously. He grabbed at the side of the driver's seat and pushed it forward. The first tears fell as he reached for the door handle and the cold morning air leaked into the car as freedom leaked away. As he climbed out, he saw they'd parked a large four-by-four police car right up to the rear bumper of the Micra, just in case he had any thoughts about driving out of here. And nearby was a crowd of maybe ten or fifteen people, gawping at his every move.

Once out, the officer spoke to him calmly, asked him to raise his arms, place his hands on the roof of the car and spread his legs. "I can't," he said. "I have a broken collar bone."

"You taking the piss?"

"No. Really. I promise I'm not armed and I won't resist, I just can't raise my—" And then the officer was patting him down, taking no care of his damaged shoulder or his mashed ear, or the scratches running up his back from the gravel. All he could do was wince. And then they started.

"He's mine, you know."

"What you on about, I made the call!"

"Alright, calm down."

"What's happening?" Christian asked the officer who was now going through his jeans pockets.

"I'm searching you, dummy."

"No, I mean—"

"Oi, back behind the cordon, now!"

"He's mine and you gotta touch him—"

"Get back!"

"I ain't lettin' her—"

And then they were on him. Christian turned to the officer who had been searching through his pockets, and saw the shock on his face. Half a dozen people in a frenzy, most of them women, knocked him aside and grabbed and yanked Christian's hair, pulling his clothes. Christian screamed as someone pulled his arm and a bolt of white pain from his shoulder crashed into his brain.

The crowd was growing, and Christian hit the ground before the police could regain control. Through their shuffling, mad legs, he could see other people running towards them. It didn't matter to the crowd, who just wanted to lay claim to him, that he was on the floor, screaming in agony; they continued to pull him, smack him on the head, drag him by the clothes, or even kick him. He heard shouts of jubilation erupt from each of them in turn, and then shouts of frustration, then screams of their own, screams of pain as the petty violence began.

He heard the officer request back-up.

Christian saw four pairs of black shiny boots, but they were massively outnumbered by the training shoes, the business shoes, the high heels, all jostling, all fighting. It turned chaotic, and then, when someone grabbed his left arm and began to pull him upright, he blacked out.

– Two –

Whitehall is a myriad of rooms joined by corridors as complex and intricate as the veins in a human body. Behind the doors of those rooms, secrets as complex and intricate as the lies inside a politician's head are formulated, rearranged, tidied up ready for presentation. Inside Room G23, Deacon squared things inside his own head, ready for presentation.

Justine Patterson, Deacon's aide, nodded at him from across the room. "Ready?" she asked, about to open the door.

"Where's the pepper?"

In the crowded press room adjoining Deacon's antechamber, television cameras were crammed against the back wall and journalists gently elbowed a little writing space with their neighbours, and photographers flanked the centre spread of chairs. The muted chatter of the gathered journalists – carefully selected by Justine – awaited the greatest show of the week. So far.

One noticeable absentee from the seated crowd was Mick Lyndon; his absence from such an announcement by the politician central to his own speciality didn't go unnoticed. Mick's protégée, Suzanne Child, fielded questions about Mick from journalists with nothing more than a shrug, but as the representative of *The Yorkshire Echo*, she found it appropriate to remove her smile of good fortune and replace it with a sombre grimace of concern.

The low rumble of chatter ceased as the door of Room G23 swung open and Deacon filled the doorframe for a moment. He looked around the room, took a deep breath and then walked to the lectern, head forward, arms swinging like he was some kind of sergeant major, or maybe like the old man who will not crumble in the face of absurdly horrid news. Justine silently pushed the door to and remained inside the room, peering out into the press conference.

Deacon gripped the lectern, looked up and around the room. Cameras clicked, and he let them take their pictures before clearing his throat. They would be focusing on his red eyes, the ones that had seemingly cried all night, they'd notice the slight greyness of his cheeks; but the resolute manner in which he held himself was still there.

"My friends," he began, "I want to thank you all for coming here this morning at such short notice." Deacon's voice had a feathery edge, an unsteadiness never heard before; this was a man struggling to keep it together.

"Last night I was brought news that no father could ever wish to hear. My son, Henry, was found by the police dead at his home in Leeds." Deacon swallowed hard and appraised the shocked, silent faces of the crowd. He blinked, and a single tear dropped onto the lectern. Cameras flashed, feeding on the moment: something poignant for the front pages perhaps. "You'll forgive me if I keep this brief; not only am I feeling unwell, but Henry's death is under police investigation.

"I am told he was found just before midnight, alone in his house; the circumstances surrounding his passing are not yet known.

"You will no doubt be aware that Henry chose to live a life not modelled around my own Christian values, and as a consequence, was not," he paused, "always in the public gaze for the right reasons. In two separate incidents, Henry's motor car collided with and, I'm desperately sorry to say, fatally wounded a man and a young boy."

At this point, Deacon could maintain the eye contact no longer, instead dropping his gaze to the lectern, shoulders hunched, knuckles white as he struggled to maintain a grip. Fifty-seven seconds elapsed before he took a huge breath, looked up, cleared his throat, and resumed. "I feel desperately sorry for the families of those two victims, and I pray for them constantly.

"Though not yet conclusive, forensic examination of Henry's car cannot rule him out as being the driver at the time of both tragic collisions. It seems reasonable to me that Henry was overcome by guilt for his recklessness and chose not to let justice take its course."

A murmur spread quickly around the room, and Deacon watched it pass from person to person before quashing it with a polite cough. "Like any other citizen of the United Kingdom, Henry would have faced swift justice under the new Criminal Justice Act and it is likely he would have been the subject of a Rule Three directive. I don't want to prejudice the police investigation, but this seems the most likely of outcomes to me."

Suzanne Child, audio recorder thrust towards the lectern, stood up. Eyes swivelled towards her, cameras moved on their mounts, Deacon stared down at her, and Justine Patterson looked from the doorway of G23 with concern on her face.

"Sir George, Suzanne Child, *The Yorkshire Echo*—"

"No questions today," Justine said from the doorway.

But Suzanne chose to ignore her. "On behalf of all my colleagues here, may I thank you for having the strength to speak with us this morning." She remained standing.

Deacon eyed her with suspicion, and then mellowed slightly, taking the gesture at face value. "I believe there would be much speculation circulating very quickly had I not, Miss Child. And I also wanted it known, difficult for me though it is, that Henry would have been granted no special treatment because of my position." He focused on Suzanne. "It is very important that the, ah, execution of this legislation is seen to be impartial."

"Thank you, sir. A building housing the forensic evidence from your son's car was set on fire in the small hours of yesterday morning..." Rumbling and gasps came from her colleagues, one man even reached up and gently grasped her elbow, but Suzanne pulled it free, kept her eye on Deacon. Justine Patterson walked briskly into the room.

"Do you know if Henry had anything to do with the fire? Instead of feeling guilty, he actually tried to evade justice." Suzanne watched Deacon.

Justine said, "That will be all for today, ladies and—"

"Perhaps you're aware that the body of a police employee was found in the same building?"

The mumbling in the crowd ceased immediately; cameras flitted between her and Deacon, watching his face turn from the ashen grey of a grieving father to the scalding red fury of an accused man, of a man whose family name had just been thoroughly trashed.

Justine took Deacon by the arm, surprised him, and brought him back to where he should be inside his mind, like an actor picking up the cue and finally going with it. He brought his handkerchief to his eyes and sobbed, allowed himself to be ushered from the room, hunched over like a wounded man.

The door to G23 closed loudly, and the room burst into explosions of activity, of people clambering for the exit, of others gripping mobile phones to their ears, replaying his words on recorders. Throughout it all, Suzanne Child stood quite motionless, and smiled to herself.

* * *

Justine slammed the door with the heel of her shoe and Deacon shook himself free and threw the handkerchief angrily at the wall. "Get me something to get this bastard pepper out of my eyes. Now!"

– Three –

Sirius wasn't allowed to feel tired. He did, of course, but he refused to let it affect him; he subconsciously promised his body all the sleep it could handle when this shit was over. For the time being though, he had to remain alert. Not only because he feared Deacon's wrath; but because he wanted the job to end well to protect his professional pride – despite the error with the old man's suicide note. And once the job *had* ended, Sirius vowed to look for a new, more stable employer.

He'd been greedy; the need for wrapping this up quickly had clouded his judgement. It turned out that he couldn't do it all alone, and had wasted over five hours before he'd brought in a small team to help.

On the passenger seat, the radio beeped once, and a green LED blinked. "Six," a voice said.

Sirius reached over and picked it up. "Go ahead."

"Triangulation results from Collins's phone came through."

"Coordinates?"

"496 743 to 532 789."

Sirius unfolded the map, scanned it for the coordinates and looked confused.

Those coordinates showed an area approximately 400 square miles, mostly uninhabited, three small villages at the outer ends of the coordinates: Allerton Bywater, Kippax, and Garforth. But in the centre was nothing. And then he saw it: in the middle of all the villages was Great Preston, the place he'd visited with Henry Deacon. The Ordnance Survey map showed a large crater in the earth, something like an, "Opencast mine. What the fuck was he doing there?" He clicked the button, "Six?"

"Go ahead."

"Try for air support."

"Already did, they say the weather is outside safety parameters."

"What about the number he sent the message to? Who owns it?"

"It's a pay-as-you-go number, unregistered."

"Out," Sirius said. Now he was getting nervous. Mick Lyndon and Eddie Collins had been to Henry Deacon's house last night, had walked neatly into the trap and were running from the police. But they'd left Henry's house with something, an A4 envelope. And now they had been to the place where Henry had abandoned the Jaguar. Sirius failed to make a connection between the two events.

What was it Henry had said about the opencast? He'd played there as a kid, had his first shag there... so what? Sirius punched the steering wheel, and then grimaced at the pain in his hand from the stab wound.

It was obvious that Henry had seen the opencast as an adventure playground, probably knew it quite well, felt happy there, trusted it. It would make an ideal place to hide something valuable. But what? What would you hide in an old opencast mine that you wouldn't hide in your home, or in your bank?

And how were they getting around?

Sirius picked up the radio again, clicked the button. "Five?"

"Five, go ahead."

"Update."

"No change. Collins's car still here, Lyndon's car still outside the pub, and no one's been near the flat."

He sighed, clicked the button again, "Two?"

"Go ahead."

"Update."

"No change, Jilly Collins hasn't left the house all night, car still here."

"Fuck!" Sirius screamed inside the car. "Six?"

"Six."

"Wakefield taxi companies, see if anyone went to Great Preston overnight."

"Copy, will take a while."

"Just do it!" Sirius threw the radio onto the seat and stared straight through the rain-sodden windscreen at the old woman's house. "Fuck it," he said and climbed out.

He ran across Coach Road in Kirk Steeple, raindrops bouncing off its grey surface, rivulets coursing along the gutters. He ran up the garden path and knocked on the door. He knocked again before it opened a fraction and stopped on the chain. "Mrs Lyndon?" he asked.

"Yes, dear."

"Can I come in?" He glanced skyward.

"Who are you?"

"My name is Davies; I work at *The Yorkshire Echo*."

The door closed and then the old lady opened it fully, letting Sirius into the house. "Thank you," he said, water dripping from his face.

"Oh, dear, you're all wet."

"Have you seen Mick, Mrs Lyndon?"

"Michael? No, not for a while, dear."

"He hasn't been at work, and we're getting a little worried for him. This is his registered address."

"Oh yes, he puts this address on all his forms and such," she said. "But he moved out years ago, set up in a cottage somewhere. He said he likes his privacy, not that he didn't get privacy here, I mean, he had his own room and I never went in, except for Fridays, because I like to clean through on Fridays—"

"Do you know where his cottage is?"

Mrs Lyndon became quiet, stared down at the "welcome" mat, then slowly up the wall and across to Sirius. She shook her head, "No, dear. I never asked and he never told me."

"Do you have his number?"

"Is he alright?"

"We're trying to find out. Do you have his phone number, Mrs Lyndon?"

"Oh yes," she beamed, "I have his number. Won't you come through?" She turned her back and led him into the parlour. "Would you like some tea, dear, I have biscuits too," she said, "but they're only plain digestives. I used to like the milk ones, but they made—"

"No thanks, just his phone number please."

She shuffled to the telephone table, a low thing covered with a sheet of red velvet. An old-fashioned beige phone occupied most of the table, but next to it was an indexed folder. "He never answers me, though; he always calls me because I can never get through to him when I try." She moved the little slider down to the letter *M*, hit the button and the lid sprang up and revealed only one entry in a sloping hand: *Michael*.

Sirius peered down at the entry.

"Do you have a piece of paper? I have a pen here, see."

"No, thank you, Mrs Lyndon, I'll remember it."

"If you're sure," she said. "I used to have a memory like that, but now I'm afraid…"

Sirius stepped back out into the rain, pulled his collar up and ran back to the car. The number she had for Mick belonged to *The Yorkshire Echo* switchboard.

Chapter Seventy-Three

Friday 26th June

– One –

Christian came to in a white-painted cubicle. At one end was a light blue door, and at the other a light blue curtain. Sitting on a plastic chair, and leaning forward to stare at his mobile phone was a police officer; and next to him was a cart with medical dressings on its three stainless steel shelves.

There was noise outside the curtain, hushed voices, keyboards being given a thorough workout, the sound of trolleys being pushed around.

From here, he could see the officer's watch, a large face with red digital figures proclaimed it was 09:46 nine-forty-six. He had been unconscious for two and a half hours.

Christian's shoulder still throbbed, only now his arm was constricted by a padded sling that crossed behind his neck and forced his shoulders back. His ear too felt different, it felt clean but the hearing was muffled by a gauze. The worst pain was in his nose; couldn't smell a thing through it, and he was forced to breathe through his mouth. His tongue licked lips that felt foreign to him. And then he realised his top lip had a stitch in it.

Before he could close his eyes again, the officer looked up, saw Christian's open eyes and smiled. "Looks like my cushy number for today just woke up, eh?"

An hour later, Christian's surroundings were a whole lot more depressing. The walls were grey brick, the door was grey steel. He lay upon a blue vinyl pad, and his good hand scrunched up a green blanket.

His newly purchased clothes were in a clear bag inside a locker somewhere. For now he wore a dark tracksuit with bright orange lines down the sleeves and down the sides of the legs. A large orange P filled the chest. He wore a pair of bright orange plimsolls.

Christian's eyes flicked to the door as a steel peephole slid down and an eye filled the small round space. The peephole slammed shut and the levers inside the door clapped loud like a private thunder. The door swung open. Bright light from the corridor made him blink, and then a pair of silhouettes reduced the glare. "Right, boy," one of the men said, "coffee and a bacon butty. How's that sound?"

Christian grunted.

"How's the clavicle?"

"The what?"

"Shoulder. How's the shoulder?"

"Painful."

"Get used to it, boy. In three hours, you'll be back in West Yorkshire. They're looking forward to your return. I'll bring that bacon, eh?" He slammed the door, but Christian could hear them talking as they ambled up the echoing corridor.

"How did they catch him?"

"Put it this way, there's a little old lady in Bradford who'll never have to raid her pension money to pay for another blue rinse as long as she lives."

Christian closed his eyes.

– Two –

She couldn't work it out. She'd been up this corridor a million times, nodded to officers as they passed by, raised her eyebrows in a silent *hello* to people from CID with whom she had worked on a million cases. But her palms were sweating.

And when she reached his door, Ros found her fingers trembling as she made a fist to knock. She swallowed, drew her no-nonsense stare from somewhere deep, and rapped.

Within a few seconds the door was almost ripped from the frame as Benson opened it. His bulk was intimidating, but her stare remained strong. His glare made her feel uncomfortable, as though she were about to ask for an undeserved wage rise.

"What?"

"Sir, I just wanted a quick word."

"Busy. Go away." Benson slammed the door, and Ros blinked a long blink. The no-nonsense stare departed quickly and in its place was a lump of humiliation and defeat about the size of a fist.

* * *

Benson slammed his office door and for a moment, he gazed at his reflection in the mirror on the wall. His eyes had darkened, his hair seemed to be receding even further and the hair that was left was greyer and thinner than he remembered. "Happens to us all," he whispered.

From his desk drawer he took out a shaver and began making himself a little more presentable. Today was going to be a good day, he could tell. The shaver buzzed and his mind hummed with music from the police band as he walked towards the smiling chief constable. He could see the gathering of press jostling for a better position, flashes erupting as the chief shook his hand. Both men turned to the press and gave them a duo of perfect smiles.

Benson bared his teeth into the mirror, noticed their yellowing and the stains on them, the blackness between them down at the gum line. He made a note to get to the dentist soon as he could.

The audience, in the ballroom at HQ, applauded long and hard, and toward the end of that applause, there were whistles and cheers. All at once, Benson felt his cheeks flush. And now the smile wasn't forced anymore, it was natural and the sparkle was back in his eye, and the chief leaned in and whispered congratulations. *"You have rejuvenated West Yorkshire Police,"* he said.

And the smile was still there as he studied himself in the mirror. He didn't want it to fade away, it felt good and it felt refreshing, and for the first time in thirty years of hard slog police work, he felt justified in having a smile at all.

All he needed was for Christian Ledger to take a bullet and everything would be as nature intended, the scales of justice would be a little more in favour of the public, and another piece of shit would be off the streets; West Yorkshire Police would again look good. The whole *country* would look good!

* * *

And she *had* gone away. Well, twenty yards at most. Inside her head, she cursed herself for being so easily intimidated.

Ros headed right back to Benson's office, and by the time she got there her chest was heaving with hot breath and below the smooth skin of her cheeks, her teeth ground away menacingly. This time she did not knock, this time she marched straight in and it was she who slammed the door.

Benson was standing before a large mirror, preening himself. He was pulling down the eyelid under his right eye and staring at its redness. He never flinched when Ros burst in. She stared at him angrily. "Don't ever be so rude to me again."

Benson blinked a couple of times to reseat the eyelid and then he began laughing at her. He turned and continued laughing.

The fire in Ros's chest lessened somewhat and her grinding teeth quietened.

"Rude?"

"Yes, rude."

His laughing eased into a smirk, and he said, "Get the fuck out of my office, girl, before I kick your sorry arse out of here."

"How dare—"

"Now *that* was rude."

"You are a dinosaur."

"You're going to have me in tears if you keep calling me names. I have a very delicate side."

"I need to talk with you."

Benson took up his seat and leaned forward, fingers laced on the desk blotter. "Sit down, Rose. You've got three minutes."

"I've got as long as it bloody well takes, and you know my name is Ros, so stop it with the cute remarks."

"You know who you're talking to?"

"An arsehole."

Benson's eyebrows rose at that, and he leaned back, folded his arms.

Ros sat, cleared her throat. "Christian Ledger has been arrested in Bristol."

"So my sergeant wasn't lying to me!"

"Will you please be serious?"

"At the risk of being rude to you again, you have done your duty, you have done it well, and I appreciate it. Now piss off and leave the rest of it to me."

"You're making a mistake."

"The man is a criminal, Ros. I am not making a mistake."

"He's a burglar, not a murderer."

"Ergo, he is a criminal."

Ros stared at him. "You think that's sufficient? You're allowed to try a man and then kill him for something he didn't do?"

"He did do it; I told you that at the scene. And I don't give a sideways fuck if you have a different opinion—"

"It's not an opinion, it's a fact."

"What have you got? What fact have you got that says to me the man did not kill Alice Sedgewick?"

Ros leaned forward, "I have fingerprints on the easel in the cellar that do not match Christian Ledger, I have fingerprints on a roll of cash from the cellar that do not match Christian Ledger."

"No! Aw shucks," Benson said. "Why didn't you tell me sooner? Who do they belong to?"

"We don't know yet."

"Okay, I'm not getting that warm fuzzy feeling yet."

"We found golden threads on Alice's body at the stab site."

Benson shrugged.

"After you *abandoned* me at the scene, I was assaulted. I was knocked unconscious," Benson's eyes narrowed, "and when I woke up, some of the paintings from the cellar had gone."

"Right?"

"There's a motive there."

"There's also a field full of junkies about fifty yards from that squat. They'll have the paintings."

Ros shook her head, "No, they helped me to my van with the rest of the paintings and my kit. They were okay."

"Let me get this straight: you're sticking up for the drug-dealers who knocked you unconscious and stole most of the paintings, and you're sticking up for the guy who murdered his girlfriend and threw her down a flight of stone steps?" He stared at her. "I have to ask, are you in the right job?"

"Damned right I am. I look at evidence, I evaluate its meaning and I draw conclusions from it. Whereas you look at circumstance and randomly point a gun at the first person who walks into the room."

Benson laughed, "Okay, Ros, touché." And then his face became the same menacing block of granite she had seen at the door only minutes ago. "Get this into your horse-shit mind. I am here to lock up the bad guys, and trust me, I *will* lock them up. I couldn't care less what the government does with them after that, but The Rules are an excellent piece of legislation, which makes a fucking change.

"They give me the ability to really clean the crap off our streets for ever, instead of giving them a five-star cell for a few weeks and then turning them loose with a fresh set of burgling skills and new contacts to offload stolen goods onto.

"I don't give a shit if Christian Ledger killed her or not if I'm honest, because he's good for it, he's scum, and he doesn't deserve to breathe English air... he's a criminal; and in a week's time he'll be a dead criminal, and he will never again break into someone's house, blind them with a flashgun and steal from them.

"And he will never even get the *opportunity* to kill anyone. The only thing out of all this that I feel sorrow about is that I'm not supposed to thank him for killing a whacked-out junkie whore. I must remember to do that, by the way."

Ros shook her head. "I can't believe what you just said—"

"Enjoy replaying it inside your head, because I'm not going to repeat it."

"You're so far up your own arse that you think it's fine to play judge, jury and executioner."

Benson shrugged, then nodded. "I don't have a problem with that. I do what people like you could never do: I catch bad people. I'm not interested if they have a good streak or not, I couldn't give a shit if they once helped granny across the road, or they bandaged a Labrador's bleeding paw; if they commit a crime, I'm taking them away from people who've had to deal with them year in year out for generations.

"People like you have governed what happens to people like him since the beginning of the last century, and look at what a shit state you've left England in, look at how grannies and kiddies daren't go out after dark, look at how the drugs culture has bred armed gangs and killed thousands of bright youths every year by fucking up their minds or making them shoot each other. Your lot have bollocksed it up for years. Now move over, it's my turn to put things right."

Ros sat there, stunned. Her eyes had widened throughout his speech, and her jaw, instead of grinding away, had slackened and her mouth had fallen open slightly. She couldn't believe what she was hearing. It was as she had suspected back at Alice's scene, but to have it confirmed in such graphic detail... she shook her head, still absorbing the lunacy of it all, and from a man who commanded enormous power. She was genuinely now more afraid than when she'd set out for work this morning.

This morning she had pondered the future of England under such ill-executed laws, and fear was the resultant emotion that seeped out. But now the seepage was more of a gush.

"Shocked?" Benson arched his fingers, smiled at her.

Ros blinked out of her shallow trance and looked around the room, feeling trapped.

"And guess what?" He stood and leaned forward towards her. "I'm going after your boyfriend next."

– Three –

"I think it went beautifully." Rochester stared at her and he could see she was beaming inside, just like the others before her had. A tinge of nostalgia made him smile; he'd been just like her when he started out twenty-five years ago, bristling with enthusiasm, unstoppable, belligerent even. And it's the way Mick Lyndon had started out here too, and if he'd managed to stay dry, he could be on top of the world right now, instead of climbing his way back up from base camp.

"Did you see the look on his face?" She was almost dancing around his office.

She was an infectious breath of fresh air, and he loved it. "I replayed it more than once," he said. "And I know how keen you are, Suzanne, but learn the ropes first; this job is like potholing without a light, and even worse, potholing without a sense of touch. You need to develop an instinct, an acute awareness of a story and of the dangers it can present."

Suzanne calmed slightly, and even bowed her head in deference.

"I don't want to kill your enthusiasm," he went on, "just be careful. This isn't reporting on the new footpath on Main Street, it's delving into people's lives and that's when they get defensive—"

"If they have something to hide."

Rochester considered this. "Yes, if they have something to hide, that's true. But suppose they don't? Suppose you're well off the mark, and they find out you've been delving into their bank accounts or you're following the spouse to try and get a lead? That kind of stuff would aggravate even a saint."

She nodded.

"Okay," he said, "I'm moving you up a level; you're officially Mick Lyndon's second now."

Suzanne gulped a large breath and no matter how hard she struggled, could not help smiling. "Just need to know where he is," she said.

Rochester was about to comment on that, when the office door opened. He looked across at a bearded man, "Craig?"

"Two men in reception for you. On government business, they say."

"Who are they?"

"A Benjamin Teal, and the other fellow seems to be a deaf mute. You want me to get a meeting room ready?"

"Show them up."

Craig nodded, closed the door.

Suzanne said, "I better give you some privacy."

"Pull up a chair. You are my witness."

"Why do you need a witness?"

"I need lots of witnesses. Whatever they want, it's bad news for us."

Five minutes later, Craig admitted two strangers into Rochester's office, then left them to it. Rochester stood and extended a hand. The lead man shook, a warm and firm shake, and the other guy, the deaf mute, stood by the door, hands folded before him as though he were chanting a silent prayer.

"Mr...?" Rochester asked the Asian man.

"Benjamin Teal, pleased to meet you, Mr Rochester." He looked at Suzanne, "Ah, Miss Child, good to see you here."

Suzanne flushed at her notoriety, and merely nodded.

"And who's your companion?"

Teal glanced over his shoulder. "I have a terrible sense of direction; he's here to make sure I don't get lost." There was no humour in his eyes.

Rochester gestured to a seat. "Now, what can I do for you?"

"I'm a lawyer for the Justice Ministry. And I'm here to help you."

"An inside story perhaps?"

"Not that kind of help." Teal reached inside his suit pocket and brought out an envelope, which he handed directly to Rochester. "It's a request from the ministry," he said. "We're rather hoping you'll defer any future comment on the ministry or the recently introduced act—"

"No." He placed the envelope, unopened, onto his desk, and leaned forward, staring at Teal. "This is a prelude to a gagging order, isn't it?"

"Well—"

"Get the gagging order, and then we'll talk. I'll have my lawyer come along too, so you two can get embroiled in all that legal jargon."

"Ah. I was hoping it wouldn't come to that; you see, the ministry thought it had a rather special relationship with *The Echo*, thought you may like to cooperate without the use of coercion."

"We went all out to help you introduce The Rules, Mr Teal, and you bent over backwards to accommodate us then, as I recall. Now that we're seeing one or two things happen that shouldn't, and we want to provide the public with an unbiased opinion, which is what we did for The Rules, you're putting a block on us?"

"Well, we were hoping that you'd hold off with any news concerning the late Henry Deacon. Obviously this is a hard time for Sir George, so we'd appreciate his name being kept out of the press for a short time too, to help him come to terms with his loss, to help him regain his… his composure, as it were.

"And concerning the new act, there are always situations and scenarios that the draughtsmen cannot foresee; and so…" He faded into a *you know what I mean* smile.

"Teething problems shouldn't be a worry to the ministry; no one is perfect, but surely you want the press there to assure the public that even though there are problems, you're working your way through them for the future of the country and for the future of justice? You want the learning process to be transparent?"

"Our discussion is at an end, Mr Rochester. I urge you to read that document. It clarifies for you the order with which we are serving you, it helps you understand the differences between the old appeal process and the new one now afforded you."

"Which is?"

"There isn't one." Teal stood, made no effort to shake hands this time, merely turned and headed for the deaf mute. "It also outlines some of the consequences should you choose not to cooperate. I bid you good day." He opened the door and exited with the deaf mute, without looking back and without attempting to close the door behind him.

"They can't do that," Suzanne said.

"One minute." Rochester reached under his chair and flicked a discreet switch.

"You were taping them?" she asked.

"Videoing them," he said, "I never take chances with officials anymore. And there is another lesson for you, Suzanne. Each one is subservient to their master's whim. Even if that whim is illegal."

"They can't take away a right of appeal; that's why it's called a '*right*'."

"Never mind that now," Rochester said. "Find out for me all you can about those two clowns. And then find out where Mick Lyndon is."

Chapter Seventy-Four

Friday 26th June

– One –

Benson read the notes. He was busy editing the disclosure file for Christian Ledger's lawyer. There were certain things in it that might be better left out; for instance the unidentified fingerprints on the roll of cash. They could belong to anyone, they were probably there innocently as the result of a business transaction, or maybe the cash was Ledger's last stock of booty from some poor burglary victim. No doubt the prints belonged to some honest secretary or hard-working mechanic; either way they weren't on file, so whomever the cash belonged to was not a criminal. To include the prints would serve only to add a layer of uncertainty to a sound prosecution case.

Benson's mobile phone rang. He looked at it for several seconds, saw the familiar number and knew it was Sirius wanting yet another favour. Reluctantly, he answered, "What's up, Sirius?"

"Do you know if Eddie Collins has any close friends at work?"

"Yeah, I'm his fucking Arrange-a-Date advisor."

"Come on, Benson. I need this—"

"Really? I got you his number, I found out his—"

"And I'm grateful, but this could prove very beneficial to us, to you, in fact."

"How's that then?"

"I don't need him; I need his friend, Mick Lyndon. And if I can get to him, it'll protect the government… and the government can be really generous."

"You seen my fucking salary?"

"Please, Benson."

Benson paused a moment. "It so happens that there is someone, a woman called Ros Banford. That's all I know about her, I'm not finding out where she lives for you, and I'm not getting her phone—"

"Thanks, Benson. I'll be in touch." The phone went dead.

"I'm sure you will. Twat."

– Two –

"What are you doing, Ros?"

She looked up from the paperwork. There was a questioning look on Chris's face.

"I'm busy."

"We're all busy." He looked around at the others in the office. They didn't seem particularly happy right now. "There are major scenes running left, right and centre, and we need all hands on deck just to keep up with the volume crime jobs."

"I realise that," she said, "but I'm still busy."

"What are you working on?" Chris was a CSI with whom she had never really worked before; he was standing in while Jeffery caught up with some sleep, he was the guy who acted up when a senior CSI was on leave or was absent through illness, like a supply teacher in a school. "Maybe I can get you some time later, or even get you some help?"

Ros tried counting to ten but only made it to five.

"Ros?"

"I don't need time later, thanks. I need time right now, and I need to be left alone to get on with it." She stared at him. He meandered back to his desk, and then she noticed the rest of the team in the makeshift office looking across at her.

"Okay," he said. "But I have to let Jeffery know when he gets back."

"Fine." Ros went back to the post-mortem report of Alice Sedgewick, and heard the others tutting, banging their equipment around, and then she heard them leaving, one by one, and eventually she was able to concentrate.

The report was nothing out of the ordinary for someone who lived on drugs. The toxicology section was spiked with chemical names that said she was a long-term addict; she was malnourished, and suffered from the early signs of heart disease. She died as a direct result of a single stab wound to the upper right ventricle, and died quickly, judging by the small amount of blood pumped into her chest cavity.

And of course, there was the question of the golden-coloured fibres in the clothing around the wound and under her fingernails.

Chris stood against the wall, arms folded, staring at her.

She sighed and put the paper down. "You want to help?"

He sat opposite her. "What you working on?"

"Trying to stop a young lad from being sentenced to death for something he didn't do."

Chris shrugged, "Isn't that what IRP and CPS are for?"

"And it's what the senior investigating officer is for too, but we're talking about Benson here, and all he wants is a line through this thing, and another tally on his wall."

"But if there's evidence—"

"There is! But he won't disclose it because it keeps the prosecution case straightforward and gives the defence nowhere to go. And at 800 quid an hour, the IRP don't want barristers running around for longer than it takes to hold a two-day trial."

Chris took a deep breath. "World's gone to shit."

"Glad you said that, I thought I was going insane."

"Run it by me."

"Christian Ledger, artist, very *good* artist by the way, and a burglar. He's a recluse. Steals to fund his painting, steals to fund his girlfriend's drug habit. She too is a recluse – or *was* a recluse. Anyway, we think she left the house at some point because there was a lottery ticket with her prints on it. She's found half way down the cellar steps, dead from a single stab wound to the chest."

"Right."

"Me and Eddie examined her scene, but Eddie had to leave half way through, and Benson pulled the scene guard off before I'd finished."

"He did what?"

She waved aside his concerns. "Never mind. We found unidentified prints on an easel in the cellar, and more on a fresh bundle of cash tucked away in the cellar door frame. Also, there were about twenty paintings in a little alcove in the cellar. When we first got there, six were missing, judging by the marks they left in the dust."

"Christian could have been selling them."

She shook her head. "Why burgle if your paintings sell?"

"Can't be overheads, living in a squat."

"No overheads anyhow; he might buy canvas, but he steals the paint. And don't forget, his prints weren't on the cash anyway."

"*She* was selling the art then, hiding the cash in the cellar."

Ros shook her head, "No, *her* prints weren't on the cash either."

"So that suggests someone came into the cellar and took them. Which means the thief paid her for the art." And then he thought about it, "Which sort of makes him not a thief, doesn't it?"

"No way."

"Why not?"

"Because how many art thieves just happen to travel past a derelict squat and nip inside hoping an artist lives there?"

"True," he mumbled.

"I'd brought all the paintings up from the cellar ready to leave when someone attacked me and stole them—"

"Jesus, Ros. Did you report it?"

"Please can we just get on with this?"

Chris shook his head, "Christ, I can't believe you, Ros. How—"

"Please?"

He shrugged.

"And there's something more. When I came to and found the rest of the paintings missing, there were some local drug-dealers in the kitchen—"

"You fucking what?"

Ros laughed. "Sorry," she said. "Your face was a picture."

"Did they—"

"No, no, no, they didn't harm me and they didn't steal the paintings. But they said they'd seen a man walking up the lane, carrying bin bags that could have had paintings inside them. No description other than he was wearing a snooker player's waistcoat."

"Now it's making sense. She sells his art to a dealer. The dealer brings her home, takes more art and leaves a token payment. And when she gets greedy, he kills her and just takes what he can carry."

"Then *we* show up—"

"And he waits; gets his opportunity to clear the place out when you're on your own."

She thought about it. "It's a good theory. It covers her leaving the house to buy the lottery ticket, it covers the money, the unidentified prints, the unidentified footwear marks in her blood in the kitchen, and I suppose it accounts for the golden threads."

"What golden threads?"

"We found golden threads under Alice's nails, and on her clothes at the puncture site."

"From the snooker player's waistcoat?"

"That's what I think, yes."

"And Benson ignored all this?"

She only looked at him.

"That man's incredible."

"We had them looked at, these golden threads, and it's called Kreinik, or Japan thread. It's not metal based so it doesn't tarnish during use, but it's very delicate, can't wash it regularly. It's less than half a millimetre thick."

"You know," Chris said, deep in thought, "I have to wonder where the Christian chap is during all this."

"Oh, don't you start!"

"I'm not taking Benson's side, I'm just wondering, that's all."

Ros dropped her pen on the desk and rubbed her tired eyes. "I have no idea. There was a hammer in the lounge with his blood all over it. Draw your own conclusions."

Chris scratched his chin. Then he got up, took the Yellow Pages from a shelf. "Let's find out where the greatest concentration of art dealers is."

"Got to be Leeds city centre."

– Three –

Sirius had parked near Ros Banford's home in Normanton for half an hour. Nothing. No movement at all.

And now he was parked in the town centre, his thoughts shattered by a vidiscreen.

It flashed the faces of wanted people, their names and numbers and the Crimestoppers number, all in a deep red. These were regularly interspersed with news of those the police had captured; same photo, blue name and number beneath them, blue Crimestoppers number too – no doubt something psychological about it.

Sirius stared at the screen, waiting it for it to cycle through the mug-shots. He'd seen it once, just a glimpse before it moved along to the next criminal. Seven minutes went by before his face came up on screen again, blue writing below proclaimed, 'In Custody: Christian Ledger'.

He stared at the face; a face he knew very well. But the last time he saw that face, it was a red mess and it was disappearing over the edge of an opencast mine. Sirius went cold.

– Four –

By the time they had sorted out the helicopter, Christian was exhausted again. For some reason, they'd landed at some South Yorkshire Police building, and he was driven to West Yorkshire by a pair of traffic cars. The further north he travelled, the worse the weather became; gusting winds and strong rain.

According to the clock on the wall behind the desk sergeant, it was three-fifty. Had his plan worked successfully, Christian would have been eating along the seafront in Penzance, a pint of lager by his side and a view to die for. He looked around the Bridewell, and to his surprise, he found that he still had a view to die for… in a much more literal sense.

Two armed officers stood within four feet of him, his wrists were cuffed. As well as the sergeant's bored face, Christian stared into the black hole of a Shelby Industries video camera, his own personal documenter of his demise. Unlike Holbeck, this wasn't so much a conveyor line of miscreants; Christian was treated a little more special this time, his own piece of desk and only one sergeant to stare at, no noise from other offenders.

"Name?"

Christian looked from the camera back to the sergeant. The sergeant waited a few seconds, then looked up from his keyboard, sighed.

"Name?" he asked again.

And there was the choice. Answer and get it over with, or keep quiet and let them struggle.

"Longer this takes, worse it looks for you. Longer it takes, more annoyed people are with you, less likely to get cream in your coffee, more likely to get powdered milk. Making sense?"

"Christian Ledger."

The sergeant didn't even bother to smile at the victory. This was routine to him, a hundred times a day, not even worthy of a mealtime bragging session with the wife anymore.

"Date of birth?"

The booking-in procedure swallowed another twenty-two minutes of Christian's life, and then a medical examination another thirty-seven. The file that followed Christian around from room to room grew thicker by the minute. And then, at last, two detention officers and two armed police officers marched him into a carpeted corridor. Rows of wooden doors on the right, and above each door, a green and a red lamp. Some lamps were green, most were red.

The small entourage stopped outside a door with a green lamp above it. The label on the door read D43.4. The lead DO opened the door, and nodded at Christian, "Okay." He moved aside, allowing Christian and an armed officer access.

Around the periphery of the room was an inch-thick black alarm tape with a red LED strip running through its centre. Sound-deadening tiles covered the walls and ceiling, just a couple of tiles missing to accommodate a pair of video cameras; one pointing at the interviewers and one at the interviewee.

"Sit down, Christian," one of the two suits sitting at the other side of the desk said, shuffling papers into a new order, barely looking up.

Christian sat and rested his cuffed hands on the desk. The armed officer took up position on a bench to his right. On the wall above the desk, was some kind of comms panel, with "D43.4" scribbled on it in black marker. And above that, a digital clock threw minutes away at an alarming rate.

Eventually, one of the suits looked up, cleared his throat. "Everything we say and do is being video recorded. There is no *stop* or *start* button, it's on all the time. Okay?"

Christian nodded.

"Would you like a drink, Christian?"

"Yes please."

"What would you like?"

"White coffee, no sugar, please."

The suit nearest the wall pressed a button on the panel and said, "Refreshments, please."

The speaker in the panel hissed, "Go ahead."

"Two white coffees without sugar, one black coffee without sugar." He paused, looked past his colleague towards the armed officer, who evidently shook his head. "That's all, thank you."

"Okay." The hiss from the panel ended and the suit returned his attention to Christian.

"I am Detective Constable Ian Webster, this is Detective Chief Inspector Benson, and over there is an authorised firearms officer, collar number 7322. Is that clear?"

Christian nodded.

"Please speak your answers."

"Clear."

"Good. I shall run through the preliminaries, by which time our drinks and your solicitor should have arrived. You need to stop me if any of the details are incorrect; that is very important, okay?"

"Yes."

DC Webster read from several sheets on the desk before him. His voice was monotone, as familiar to this business as had been the desk sergeant. "Your name is Christian Ledger, you are a white male aged twenty-eight, date of birth 24th May 1987, and whose primary residence is England, United Kingdom, and whose primary language is English. You have no dependants and no known next of kin. You have been certified as physically and mentally capable of being interviewed as stipulated under the Administration of Justice Act 2012.

"Your personal items and effects have been seized under the Police and Criminal Evidence Act 1984 and are securely lodged here at West Yorkshire Police Leeds Bridewell in locker C176. Cash money to the value of 487 pounds was among your belongings, and under the Administration of Justice Act 2012, an amount not greater than fifty per cent, that being 243 pounds and fifty pence, has been confiscated as part payment of compulsory legal advice and representation. The balance is repayable by yourself or your estate as detailed in the above act should you be subsequently found guilty of the charges against you; a leaflet explaining this payment is offered to you now."

He slid the leaflet across the desk until it touched the cuffs. Its title was: *Helping to Pay Your Debt to Society*. Christian stared as Webster read without looking up. Webster's eyes followed row upon row of text on countless sheets of paper. Benson was emotionless. Cold eyes stared right at him, making him look away instantly. When Christian dared to sneak another glance, he was still staring.

Webster continued to read.

"You were cautioned by officers in Bristol—"

Just then, Benson's mobile phone rang. "Excuse me," Benson stood and left the room.

"DCI Benson exits the room," Webster said, not breaking stride from his monotone voice.

* * *

Benson stepped into the corridor and answered his phone. "Sirius," he said, pulling the door closed. "I'm busy—"

"I know you are. Christian Ledger, right?"

"How do you know that?"

"Is this a secure line?"

"What is this about?"

"I want you to let him go."

"What the fuck are you—"

"I have business with him."

"He's here, he's mine, and I'm gonna see him dead."

"As I said, I have business with him." There was a pause as Sirius licked his dry lips. He whispered, "Set him free, *I* need to deal with him."

A DO with a tray of drinks walked along the corridor, his leather shoes squeaking. He smiled at Benson, and Benson ignored him, waited until he'd disappeared into the interview room.

"Tough. I did shitloads of work for you, risked my neck getting you info, without so much as a thanks. You had your chance and you fucked it up, this whole thing is unravelling for you and whoever you work for. Time for me to take a large step back out of your limelight."

* * *

"Okay, stop there," Christian said as Benson was half way through closing the interview room door. The name he heard sent a shiver riding down the deep scratches on Christian's spine.

The wall clock said it was 15:42.

Webster looked up from his notes with the disappointment of a man stopped in full flow. "What's up?"

"Never mind." Christian stared at the cuffs and felt the throb in his shoulder.

"Under the Offences against the Person Act 1984, you have been arrested for the murder of Alice Sedgewick on Tuesday 23rd June of this year. You do not have to say anything. However—"

There was a knock at the door. It squeaked open and the DO entered with a tray of Styrofoam cups. "Detention Officer 546 enters the room with refreshments."

DO 546 set the tray down.

"Can you take his cuffs off now?"

The DO nodded, slid a bunch of keys from a pouch and leaned over Christian. There was a strong smell of sweat as he extended his arms and fiddled with the cuffs.

Chapter Seventy-Five

Friday 26th June

– One –

There were twenty-four art shops listed within the nine square miles of Leeds city centre. Of them, thirteen could be discounted as art and craft materials shops, and four others had closed down since the directory had been issued.

Ros and Chris parked the van in Millgarth Police Station, close to the central bus station, since they figured that's where Alice would have begun her great adventure. They scanned the map for the closest shop on the list, and began walking, ignoring those who stared at them in their uniform.

Away in the distance, they could hear the demos in full swing up by the Town Hall; the loudhailers thundering all day were a regular thing, even in the rain.

They arrived at the first shop less than ten minutes later, and peered in through the window. There were prints on hole-board display walls, birthday and Christmas cards, balloons and even fancy-dress clothes on two central rails. At the far end was a pair of middle-aged women engrossed in chatting, pointing to the magazine on the counter before them.

They walked on, and Chris looked again at the map. The next shop was completely different. They again looked in through the window at shelves of fine art. There were no price tags visible.

"If you have to ask, you can't afford it," Chris said, and opened the door. Classical and contemporary art lined the walls and there were mobile shelf units scattered around the wide-open store with more draped across them, chrome and glass everywhere, parquet floors that gleamed. "May I help you?" An elderly gentleman appeared from behind a counter of sorts, more like an island made of opaque glass with chrome adornments.

"Do you buy art?" Chris asked.

"I have to buy art, sir, in order to sell it."

"If I walked in with a painting," Ros said, "would you offer to buy it?"

"Ah no, not really." He shuffled closer. "I mean it would have to be an extraordinary piece, and it would have to have a paper trail. I could not commit to buying anything without proof of ownership."

"Have you been approached in the last two weeks or so by a young woman trying to sell you some paintings? She might have said that her boyfriend painted them?"

"What might she look like? I see quite a few young ladies."

"Scruffy, five nine, very thin—"

"Blonde," he said. "Drug addict too? I told her to leave."

"When was this?"

"Tuesday, as I recall." His head tilted to one side, "What's she done?"

"You've been a great help, sir, thank you very much."

"Oh please. I'm interested in what she's done—"

"She's dead," Ros said. "Murdered."

The man covered his shocked mouth with a hand. "Oh, my. I'm dreadfully sorry."

– Two –

Benson could hear the desperation growing in Sirius's voice. And he loved it.

"How would you like to get your hands on Eddie Collins?"

Benson blinked. "You know where he is?"

"Getting there."

"Whoopee."

"He'll be in the bag soon, and he's yours if you set the kid free."

Benson's eyes were unfocused though his mind ran at light speed. It would be a catch worth two Christian Ledgers. Not only the status it would afford him, also the effect it would have on the public's perception of him and of the force as a whole – not afraid to bring your own to justice, or kill him while trying.

It was tempting.

But getting the kid off would be a massive task. He had built the case against Christian inside his head, as he always did, could repudiate any mitigating evidence or circumstance. It had worked on Ros this morning, and it would work for him again. He could undo it all if he had to; he could begin to set Christian Ledger free in an afternoon of form-filling. Easy. All he had to do was call Ros's evidence, turn it around and make it work in Ledger's favour. And when he'd done that, CPS would throw the case out, and if by any chance they didn't, then the Independent Review Panel would for sure.

How, though, would it make him look if he "lost" the case against Ledger? It would mean Ledger would be back on the street – a known Rule Two burglar – and it also meant there was a genuine murderer out there still to have his collar felt. It was a tough decision.

"See what I can do," he said to Sirius. "Call me back in an hour." Benson checked his watch, it was 3.45. He shut the phone off, slid it into his jacket pocket and walked back over the stains in the carpet and past the flaking pipe work towards D43.4 just as a DO escorting a man in a suit and carrying a briefcase, approached him. The door was ajar and so the DO waved the man inside, turned and walked away again.

* * *

From the corridor outside, Christian could hear voices, shoes patting on the carpet as they approached. Benson and another guy entered the interview room. Webster looked up and nodded at Benson, said, "DO 546 exits the room, DCI Benson enters the room along with?"

Benson retook his seat, and resumed his glare at Christian. The new suit placed a briefcase on the floor and sat heavily next to Christian. "My name is Anthony Cruickshank, I am the legal representative of…" He pulled a sheaf of papers from the briefcase, glanced at the cover, and said, "Christian Legger."

"Ledger," Benson corrected. "His name is Christian Ledger."

"Oh, beg your pardon." Cruickshank corrected his notes with a chrome pen, then checked his watch. "Shall we say three-thirty?"

"No, we'll say three-fifty, because it is three-fifty."

Christian closed his eyes, he was not hopeful.

"Gentlemen," Webster said, "we have run through the preliminaries, and a copy of this and any interview tape will be made available to you, Mr Cruickshank. So shall we begin?"

Cruickshank nodded. Christian's heart rate bucked and his head sank lower.

Benson leaned forward. "Tell me why you killed Alice Sedgewick."

"I already said I didn't kill her."

"You were there when she died."

Christian shook his head. "I wasn't."

Benson looked at Cruickshank. "You have the pre-interview disclosure document. You know we have scientific evidence that puts Mr Ledger there at the time of her death."

"What evidence?" Christian asked.

"Your footwear mark in Miss Sedgewick's blood," Webster said.

"Explain to me how it got there."

Christian stared from Webster to Benson, and then across to Cruickshank. "I don't know."

Benson placed his hands on the desk and smiled at Christian. "Shall I tell you how it all happened?"

"I didn't kill her." There was a tinge of desperation in Christian's eyes now.

"You kept Alice as a... partner, let's say. You supplied her with enough drugs to keep her compliant, to enact your every wish—"

"No, I—"

"But one day, Saturday last, she had run out of the drugs you had made her reliant upon. She was angry with you, maybe even a little crazy, judging by the doll you gave her as a, I don't know, as a comforter. She was mad at you, you had a row, a heated row where you punched her in the face; she picked up the hammer and tried to hit you with it—"

"She did—"

"And maybe she was aiming at your head, but you were a little too fast for her, and you ducked away just in time. But you weren't quite fast enough and the hammer tore open your ear, and fractured your collar bone. Your blood was all over the hammer head."

"It wasn't like that."

"Now it was your turn to be angry, even angrier than you already were. Now you went to the kitchen, took out a knife—"

"No!"

"And she followed you. And there, at the top of the cellar steps, you stabbed her once to the upper abdomen. One stab, in here," Benson swept aside his tie and pointed with a stubby index finger right into his sternum. "She died fairly quickly, the pathologist said. And this part I'm not sure of, so maybe you can guide me. I don't know if she just fell to the floor and you shoved her down the steps, or maybe she didn't even make it to the floor. You stabbed her, held

448

her close maybe, and then as you looked into her dying eyes, you simply... pushed."

"That's not what happened."

"Which bit?"

"All of it."

"All of it?" Benson glared.

"The hammer bit is true. I mean, she went for me."

"You kept her as a private sex slave, high on drugs."

"No. She was a user when I met her; I was trying to wean her off—"

"You bought drugs to keep her docile."

"She hit me with a hammer. I left. When I came back, she was dead."

"Wow," Benson said. "How long were you gone?"

"I don't know; twenty minutes maybe."

"That's incredible. You have a bust up with a drugged-up girl, and leave after she assaulted you. And then came back, not full of thoughts of retribution, but ready to forgive and patch things up?"

"No, that's—"

"And miraculously, someone had been into the squat in those twenty minutes and finished the job for you."

"I said it didn't—"

"Mr Ledger," Benson said.

"DCI Benson," Cruickshank said. "Take some of the pressure off my client, please. Your pontificating is giving him no opportunity to reply."

Benson stared at Cruickshank. Cruickshank continued to look at Benson. "Carry on, Mr Ledger, my apologies for interrupting you."

"I was very protective of her, didn't like her leaving the house because it was unsafe outside."

Benson smiled.

"And I found out that she *had* been leaving the house, and not only that, she had been selling my paintings, and she'd been... she'd shown some of the local youths her breasts for money to buy drugs with."

"Ah, so we have an explanation as to where the missing paintings are. Do you know who she sold them to?"

Christian shook his head. "No. So yes, I was mad as hell with her. We argued, she hit me with the hammer and I slapped her face. In that order." He waited for a challenge, but none came. "I left the house, meaning to leave altogether. Instead, I went to a pharmacy, got something for my ear and came back. I was going to tell her we were finished, that I was leaving…"

"But?"

Christian's head was down, and all three observers saw the teardrop hit the table, and could make out his wobbling chin. When he looked up more tears crested his lower eyelids and streaked down his cheeks. "I found her slumped halfway down the cellar steps. And there was blood in the kitchen."

"And then what did you do?" Webster asked.

"I left. I ran away."

Benson suggested, "Not the actions of someone who is innocent, Mr Ledger."

"I ran because there was no way the police would have believed me."

"You surprise me," Benson smirked.

"So you found out that she was prostituting herself. How did that make you feel?"

"I already said. It made me very angry. Can I have some painkillers please?"

"And you needed to get away?" Benson asked.

"Yes."

"But how could you? You were flat broke, you have no job, you have no benefits that we can see."

"You know how I got my money." Christian glared at Benson.

Benson looked across at Cruickshank, his eyebrows raised in a question.

Cruickshank nodded.

"You are a convicted burglar and a shoplifter, Mr Ledger."

"Yes."

"So you had plenty of money. The last burglary that we know of, netted you five hundred pounds. And is the 480-something pounds we found on you the remainder of that five hundred?"

"No."

"No. No way could that last you what, a week, ten days?" Benson leaned forward again, and his voice was little more than a whisper as he said, "The money you have on you now, Mr Ledger, is money from the paintings you yourself sold, isn't it?"

Christian looked at him, confused. "No, I have never sold a single painting."

Benson leaned back, smiling at Cruickshank and Christian. He had him in an airlock, no chance of getting out. There was no way a jury or even the IRP would let him go. And this was the make or break part for Benson. If he wanted to help Sirius by setting the kid free, this was the point at which he would volunteer Cruickshank further disclosable evidence, those fingerprints on the roll of cash in the cellar, the gold threads and the other bits and pieces that Ros had mentioned this morning. It wasn't concrete by any means, but it would be enough to cast doubt on the prosecution. And that evidence would rupture Benson's case.

The video cameras caught nearly three minutes of inactivity and of absolute silence as Benson mulled the dilemma over. Webster looked across at him. "Boss," he said.

The temptation was Eddie Collins. And only Eddie Collins. But he reckoned he could nail him soon all by himself anyway. He had a choice right now: provide the evidence that would free this kid and help Sirius, or keep it back and nail the kid, and nail Collins later by himself.

"Gentlemen," he said. "Shall we have a break?"

"I don't want a break."

In all his years of doing this, a prisoner had never told him he didn't want a break.

"You say these cameras record continuously?"

"Yes," Benson said.

"With sound?

"With sound. Why?"

"Good quality sound, is it?"

"You pissing me about?" Benson stood.

"I wanna make a deal." Christian looked Benson in the eye, sharp and crisp, no blinking, no movement.

"I don't do deals with murderers."

"First, I'm not a murderer. Second, play the tape from 3.42. Listen very, *very* carefully, and then tell me you don't want to do a deal."

"Get him back to his cell." Benson headed for the door, Webster pushed the intercom button, and Cruickshank looked plain confused.

Christian uttered one word as Benson passed by. "Sirius."

Benson stopped. He swivelled on the balls of his feet, and said to Webster, "Cancel the DO." Then he sat, took a sheet of plain paper from the file, took his pen from his jacket pocket, and stared across at Christian. "Well?"

"What is Sirius?" Cruickshank asked.

Christian said, "Sirius is a who. A very nasty *who*. A *who* that knows Mr Benson." Christian looked directly at Benson.

"Whoa," Webster said. "You can't bring in a third party—"

"Does he feature in your own case, Christian?"

Doubt crossed Christian's eyes; he paused and looked across at Cruickshank.

"If he has no direct bearing on your own case, however small, it will not be taken into account."

"He features very heavily," Christian nodded. "Now can I please have some fucking painkillers?"

– Three –

"Six."

"Go ahead," Sirius said.

"Ros Banford owns a dark Renault Clio."

He waited for more, almost began biting his nails. "And?"

"Not reported as stolen. It has a tracker fitted so I've begun the activation process. Should know the results soon."

"Keep me posted soon as you know."

"Will do. Out."

Chapter Seventy-Six

Friday 26th June

"When I left my house, I headed over towards Burley, hoping to steal a car."

"You're not helping yourself," Cruickshank said.

Christian ignored him. "I managed it, too, on Turner Avenue, an old Escort. I'd just about got it started when I was grabbed from behind and had a pair of cuffs slapped on my wrist." He held out his right hand so Benson could see the bruising. "I fought him off pretty good and got rolling, just wanting to be out of the city and away from these cops. I thought they were police," he said, "but I later found out they weren't."

"Go on."

"I only made it fifty yards before they rammed me off the road. Then this one, this Sirius—"

"How did you know his name?" Webster asked.

"I'll get to that." Christian looked back to Benson and continued. "So this Sirius guy opens my door and smashes my face into the steering wheel, really goes OTT, even for a copper. I must've lost consciousness because I woke up in the rear footwell of their hire car, which turned out to be a Ford D-Max."

"Not hearing anything worthy of a deal yet." Benson dropped his pen by the paper, and folded his arms.

"The two men up front got talking while we were driving. I got the impression they didn't like each other. Then it dawned on me who one of them was. His name was Henry Deacon." Christian watched Benson and Webster, saw their pupils dilate slightly. He nodded to himself, and carried on. "Heard Sirius – that's what Henry Deacon called him – I heard Sirius taking the mick out of Henry for trying to burn a diesel car, not sure what all the fuss was about, but that's what he said, and this Henry fellow was trying to defend himself. It turns out that's what they wanted *me* for; they were going to sit me in the car, beat me up some more, get me to bleed on the controls and the seat belt, they said, and then take me away and kill me." Christian paused, and asked, "May I stand?"

Benson eyed him for a moment, then nodded.

Christian stood, turned his back on Benson and Webster and lifted his T-shirt all the way up to the shoulders. "The scratches your nurse made notes of, they were caused by Henry and Sirius dragging me out of their rental car and across the gravel to this green Jag."

"Okay, we see them. Sit down."

"So far we haven't heard anything—"

"You will, please, be patient," Christian looked to Webster. "Sirius said he was employed by Sir George to clean up mess in times of national security, or something like that. That he was tying up a loose end, and then he asked Henry what his secret was.

"Oh, and then he said if he messed him about again he'd use his own toy gun to turn his head inside out."

"How do you know this Sirius, Mr Benson?" Cruickshank asked.

"Professional acquaintance from another department."

"Thank you."

Benson picked up his pen. "What else, or is that it?"

"More to come," Christian said, "And this is where it gets real juicy."

"I'm waiting."

"Henry said to Sirius, 'you did that old fellow. The old man from Methley. You used his own gun and blew his brains all over his cottage walls'. Then Sirius was really pissed off at Henry, and he says, 'If you mention a word of it to anyone, I'll give you the slowest death I can think of.'" Christian blinked, looked between Webster and Benson.

"You have any proof of any of this?" Webster asked.

"Proof? How could I make up something like that? I don't even know what old fellow they were talking about – that's your job. But the cars… check with the guy whose car I stole, he saw it all, I remember seeing him in the rear-view mirror, running down the street in a string vest with a coat over the top, shouting and waving his arms. And then there's the Jag, you lot recovered it just in the nick of time too, another five minutes and I'd have been dead."

"So where's the car now?"

"What, the Jag?"

"No, the hire car."

"The place where the Jag was parked was a quarry or something. Sirius left me inside while he went to get Henry. He thought I was still unconscious. I tried to get out but ended up rolling it off the edge and into the quarry. It'll still be there."

Benson sat still for a moment, then looked across to Webster and nodded before standing and leaving the room. Webster pressed the intercom and asked for a DO. Cruickshank collected his papers, stuffed them into his briefcase and stood. He nodded at Christian, said he'd be back shortly and left.

Christian looked across to Webster. "So was that any help to you?"

"Don't know. Mr Benson has gone to try and verify some of your story. But I don't see how it helps you out with Alice's murder."

* * *

There was only one thing out of Christian Ledger's story that really made him sit up and take notice, and that was the story of the old guy. And Benson knew exactly which old guy Christian had been talking about.

He had been the SIO on that case. And they had always known it was murder, ever since one of the CSIs pointed out that the alleged suicide note had the name "Stephen" spelt incorrectly. This was Lincoln Farrier, and there was no way on God's green earth he would ever spell his son's name incorrectly; it had been almost laughable.

With speed, Benson barged into the inspector's office, nodded a brief greeting at the officer behind the desk, and picked up the phone. He dialled and listened. "It's Benson. You have a task to do, and I need it doing faster than you've ever done anything before, even it means you getting your arse into a traffic car and driving up to the labs yourself."

* * *

Benson had only just exited the inspector's office and taken a breath when his mobile phone rang. He stared at the number, wondering what to do. Eventually, he accepted the call. "Sirius."

"Well?"

"Where's Eddie Collins?"

"Shacked up with his journo pal in a cottage near Aberford."

"When are you going for him?"

"I'll be there within the hour if I push it. You coming along?"

"What's the address?"

"Marsh Cottage, Greengates Farm, Aberford."

"I won't be able to get there for maybe an hour and a half. You going to keep Collins for me?"

"Yep. You gonna let the kid go?"

"Can't."

"Why not, why can't you?"

Benson held the phone away from his ear. "He's saying some shit about you and some other guy abducting him." He tutted. "Now I've got to look into that bollocks as well, as if I haven't got enough to do!"

"What's he saying? I can work you round it."

Benson smiled, closed his eyes. No denial from Sirius whatsoever.

* * *

Benson sat down next to Webster, gave him the nod.

"Interview recommenced at 1628. Present are DCI Benson, Christian Ledger, Christian's lawyer, Mr Cruickshank, AFO 7322, and myself, DC Webster."

"Did you have a chance to verify what I told you?" Christian asked.

"I have spoken with the man called Sirius, yes." Benson watched the kid's eyes, full of hope. He was leaning forward, desperate to hear good news, but Benson was about to kill him stone dead. "It's all refutable; most of it is hearsay, which your lawyer will tell you, is inadmissible."

"That's bollocks!"

"He claims to know nothing of any car theft except that of his own. He said he was driving along Turner Avenue slowly because of the heavy rain when someone pulled out from the kerb in an old Escort. He couldn't avoid hitting the car, he shunted it quite hard he says, and the Escort lost control and it hit a wall at the foot of the street. He then got out of the car to see if the driver was alright. The car thief punched him in the stomach and then stole *his* car and left him alone in the middle of the street."

Christian's mouth opened, and he stared wide-eyed at the table. "That's bollocks," he whispered. Then he looked up. "What about the owner, the string vest guy, he can vouch for me."

Benson shook his head, "A police officer is on his way there now to verify the statement he originally gave—"

"He's paid him off, hasn't he? Mr String Vest is gonna have a shiny new car outside his house and ten grand in the bank if he alters that statement. You know it! How can you sit there—"

"Christian," Webster said.

"The rest," Benson continued, "is not admissible in your own defence, which is what we're here for."

"Wait, wait, *I* punched *him* in the stomach?"

Benson nodded.

"No other contact?"

"He didn't mention any."

"He didn't cuff me, I suppose."

"Nope."

"Okay, okay. Will you allow me to show you something?"

"What?"

"I have to stand up and reach down. Is that okay?"

The AFO sat up straight, and Benson nodded again.

Christian stood slowly. He raised his right foot and placed it on the chair he'd been sitting on. Then he rolled up the leg of his police-issue jogging bottoms. He pulled off the plimsoll from his right foot, rolled down the sock, and slipped it off. From inside it, he pulled out a shard of plastic. "This is a part of the interior lamp from the Escort." He placed it on the table. "This Sirius guy punched me as I was trying to get the Escort started. He tried to punch me again, and I held this right where his fist was heading. It stabbed him in the back of his right hand. You can still see his blood on it."

"You kept that this whole time?" Webster was astonished.

Christian nodded. "I figured I might need it for protection. Turns out I was right, wasn't I?"

"How did you get it past all the searches?"

"Luck."

Benson stared with incredulity at the lad. And with a little admiration too.

"That proves there was contact between us. And that proves my story is true. And if I'm telling you the truth about this, then I'm telling you the truth about the other stuff, too."

Cruickshank's eyes closed momentarily, and then he spoke to his client. "Christian," he said, "that's all well and good, but it's a totally separate issue, it has no bearing on your own case whatsoever."

"What?"

"It's inadmissible."

Benson stood and left the room.

"Wait!"

He closed the door and walked fast along the corridor. He could still hear the kid screaming when he passed through the double doors at the end.

Chapter Seventy-Seven

Friday 26th June

– One –

The last shop on the list was a fifteen-minute walk away. Leeds was growing hotter, the crowds heavier, the shoppers more eager, and the chanting from the Town Hall even more fervent. Ros could see why everything appeared more turbulent than before. Approaching from the railway station was a line of police officers, leading a noisy march towards the law courts, a mere two blocks away from the Town Hall. "Come on," she said, "I don't want to be around when they clash."

They hurried down The Headrow for another hundred yards, carried along by rushing people, when Chris pulled Ros's sleeve. They had found it. The last shop on the list. "Doesn't look much like an art shop," Ros shouted.

"It's full of junk, sells everything in here by the looks."

A small bell tinkled when they opened the door of Dunfield Arts. A large fat man wearing a cravat stepped into view from behind a counter where a kettle was boiling. "Yes?"

Ros ducked out of the way to a side wall where she pretended to be interested in an antique globe held in position by a cast iron pivot.

Chris ambled towards the man, engaged him in a muffled conversation.

She saw a small sticker on the iron pivot that proclaimed "made in China". And then there were the cult classics of skulls and medieval swords and shields, followed by a glass cabinet in which were dragons of all types, made from coloured glass and pottery and cast iron. No paintings, she noted. Plenty of prints, but not one original painting.

Ros turned and saw Chris heading up the centre of the shop towards her, a disgruntled look on his face. "Come on," he said. "Waste of time."

They stood outside Dunfield Arts.

"Now what?"

– Two –

Sirius pushed the car as hard as he dared on the slick road. His face was cast into a solid, determined block, betraying no emotion, rarely blinking, just concentrating on the road, and imagining how all this would end. He didn't know what big secret Mick Lyndon had; he only knew that he and his pisshead buddy Eddie Collins had left Henry's house with an A4 envelope, and wished he'd taken it from them. Sirius had searched Henry's house as best he could in the short time he had available and had come up blank. But *they* had found it inside fifteen minutes. They had been to the old opencast mine at Great Preston too; why? What was there for them?

It had been Henry's playground as a kid, it was where he dumped the Jag, and logically it was where he would hide anything of a sensitive nature. What was it?

They had evaded him for eighteen hours, plenty of time to familiarise themselves with whatever revelation was in that damned envelope, and make their plans.

And what of the end game? *His* end game consisted of locating the cottage and dispatching both men as quickly as possible; saving Collins for Benson was always going to be a non-starter. Then find that envelope and discover their secret. *Henry's* secret.

He told Benson it would take him an hour to get there. That, of course, was a lie. It would take him forty minutes. It was vital he got there alone because he felt sure Benson wouldn't agree with killing Mick Lyndon. So far *his* only crime was breaking into Henry Deacon's house.

On the other hand, killing Eddie Collins would be fine; he was on a Rule Three for murder. The forensic team would eventually work out that Collins and Lyndon couldn't have killed Henry. For some reason they had arrived late, allowing the body to cool and begin entering the rigor stage. So it was important to silence both of them, not only for Deacon's sake, but for his own too.

Benson said it would take him ninety minutes to get there, which was also a lie, he assumed, so he could be there to make sure Sirius didn't do anything illegal. So he had twenty minutes, maybe thirty. He pushed the car a little harder.

– Three –

Eddie made himself a strong black coffee. He took it black because the milk wasn't exactly fresh anymore. He sipped, then stared out of the kitchen window, leaning against the earthenware sink, gazing into the foliage beyond the wavy glass in the rotting sash window frame. Beyond the foliage was a narrow path running between thick trees before disappearing around a curve. He could see nothing left or right other than more trees.

Today was a day to celebrate: he had successfully removed himself from alcoholism and had absolutely no idea how he had managed it. Certainly, there was no effort on his part. It had just happened, or rather, the craving just never presented itself. And when he'd poured the whisky for Mick, it had neither attracted nor revolted him; he simply wasn't bothered by it anymore. And as Mick had said, it posed the question whether he'd ever really been hooked in the first place. Well yes, of course he had been. He stashed it everywhere, he spent hundreds on the stuff, he made himself ill with it and still he drank more. So how could he just stop?

Eddie shrugged as if to answer his own question, but whatever, it was wonderful not being a slave to it anymore. And today was a wonderful day for another reason: Mick was going to make sure Eddie Collins kept his life. And for someone who had thought so much about getting rid of his life, it was a blessing that his attempts so far had failed.

Of course, the one reason he'd always wanted to kill himself was Sam. That thought made his brow crease as he pondered on it for a while. And then he remembered Jilly's Freak, the one who told him to stop drinking. No, no, he refused to accept any of that stuff. It was all bollocks, and he should stop dwelling on it right now.

That guilt at having killed Sam was still there, and it was something that would never leave. But he didn't want it to leave; he wanted it to stab him in these quiet moments. Because Sam couldn't have any quiet moments with his own thoughts anymore.

"Eddie!"

Eddie's eyes widened, and then he was running, the towel he wore flared around his legs like a flag furling, and then he was taking the stairs two at a time. "What?" he yelled as he entered Mick's study.

Mick sat in his chair with a mixture of happiness and horror painted across his already reddening face. In his hand he held a glass of whisky.

"What?" Eddie said again, panting.

"I made you a copy of this." He threw Eddie a memory stick. "Make sure you look after it."

"Why, what's on it?"

"It's an audio file," he said. "Grab that chair."

Eddie kept tight hold of it, meaning to stuff it into his jeans pocket when they had dried. He pulled a foldaway wooden chair from the side of the room, and sat next to Mick.

"We thought all the other stuff we had from Henry was top drawer stuff, didn't we?"

Eddie nodded. "So what's this then?"

"The other stuff about Sirius killing Lincoln Farrier on the same day he left Deacon's surgery, the fact that Henry thought his dad was going to kill him, and then, surprise-surprise, Henry died—"

"Yeah, come on then!"

"That stuff alone would sink Deacon."

Eddie stared at Mick.

He pointed to the audio file on the computer screen, "This stuff will sink The Rules." Mick swivelled in his chair. "Whatever happens, *please* make sure you keep a tight hold on that memory stick." Mick prodded "play" on his keyboard. "Listen to this."

– Four –

Benson had taken his time with the preparations. The coordinates that Sirius gave him belonged to a farm way out in the sticks. A quarter of a mile from the farm was a lone cottage and that's where he thought Mick Lyndon and Eddie Collins would be. Would put money on it. He checked Google, zoomed in as far as the image would allow. There was a definite path to the front of the building, and so far as he could see, there was no such path to the rear. Simple, one way in and one way out. And there was only one access road, a narrow driveway that split from the farm track which itself had split from a normal rural road only wide enough for one vehicle at a time.

Before he searched Google, he tasked the Bridewell inspector with getting him a traffic car; it would provide the fastest means of getting there.

Hopefully before Sirius did.

He'd tried X-99 again in the hope it was permitted to fly, but they'd refused again. The weather front, they had said, would intensify over the next hour.

And then he'd enquired with division if there was any chance of back-up meeting him there, or at least being en route. No, was the answer; too busy with the marches in Leeds town centre for one, and intel had suggested tension was running high. They were predicting nothing short of a riot this evening around the Town Hall and court buildings. They would send someone if any paired unit came free.

So, he was on his own. He had an armed traffic officer and a fast car, had borrowed two sets of cuffs and a bulletproof vest. When the front counter called to say the car had arrived, Benson ran from the building and slammed the door after him. He told the driver the address, and then punched in the postcode into the satnav. With blue lights and sirens clearing the way ahead, he hoped to annihilate the sat nav's estimated arrival time of fifty-seven minutes.

– Five –

"I don't get it," Eddie said.

"What's not to get?"

"Why don't you just send what you've got? Why do you have to fuck around writing a story first?"

"It's my job, you prick."

"Hold on, hold on. I know it's your job, and powdering windows in Middleton is my job, but look! I'm not powdering windows in Middleton, because sending this shit off is far more important right now."

Mick shook his head. "So?"

"Look, get it in the bank first. Send all the stuff raw, naked. Make sure he has it, and then you can fanny about putting fancy words to it."

"We're safe here, Eddie."

Eddie sighed. "You really think so?"

Mick nodded. "Safe as anywhere."

"Exactly, so it's not safe. Nowhere is safe. I don't get you, I don't get how we can be on the run all night, not using our own cars for fear of being caught, and now we've *got* the stuff, you're content to sit here and type pretty words when they're still hunting us!"

"Look—"

"What's got into you?"

"I'm a reporter—"

"And tomorrow you'll be a dead fucking reporter!"

"Shut the fuck up and listen." Mick rasped a hand down his tired face. "I already told you, this is what I do, and I already told you that this kind of story might hit an old hack like me once in twenty lifetimes. And yes, I know staying here is a risk, but being anywhere is a risk. At least here, there are only us and farmer Giles who know it. I have my computer—"

"I know all that. What I don't understand is why you don't send…" Then Eddie sat back in his chair, clicked his fingers and pointed at Mick. "You don't want it stolen by a colleague, do you?"

Mick shifted in his chair.

"You're prepared to risk everything, and I don't mean your shitty life here, I mean everything we've found out. You're prepared to put all that at risk, leaving me on a Rule Three into the bargain, just so Clark fucking Kent doesn't get your Fleet Street Prick of the Year award!" Eddie stared at Mick, veins standing out on his neck, and when Mick looked out of the window, with rain beating hard on it, he reached over and took a cigarette from Mick's packet, lit it and said, "Why?"

"Tell you what, I'll put my story to the audio file, won't take me long to transcribe it, then mould a story round it, then I'll send it off, and I'll send off all the other stuff raw and naked, as you say. Good enough?"

Eddie puffed angrily. He nodded. "We're going to have to stay hidden until this shit goes public."

"I know. So are you happy to lay low here till it's over with?"

Eddie thought about it, and came to the only sensible conclusion he could. "If you snore, I'll smash your face in."

"You could take Ros's car back."

"I don't want to leave you alone." He was serious too; Mick would become engrossed in his story and forget to send the rest. More to the point, Mick would become engrossed in his story and forget to send the rest before Sirius found him. He stubbed out the cigarette. "So I guess I'll have to put up with your flatulence a while longer."

Mick looked at Eddie with his yellow eyes. "I just thought this might be your last chance to be with your lady."

Chapter Seventy-Eight

Friday 26th June

Sirius rounded the corner, wipers on full speed, foot on the brake pedal, and he saw the sign to the farm, jerked the steering wheel and left the road for the mud and stone track leading up a hill to a farm perched on a summit maybe four hundred yards away.

He killed the lights and brought the car to a crawl in the greyness of a premature twilight. He saw the ruts of a track on the right and the car bounced into them, splashing water into the nettles. Cautiously, he followed the track, and it gradually opened out, the nettles receded and he was in a more substantial lane, creeping forward, wipers still flicking water from the screen.

Sirius craned forward and saw a dark Renault Clio on the stub of a lane to his right, and up ahead spotted one golden-coloured light through the dark foliage of a wall of trees. He brought the car to a stop, switched off the engine and listened to the rain beating on the roof, watched the scene before him disappear into an aquatic avalanche on his screen.

The interior light shone comparatively brightly as he opened the door. He pushed it closed, and ran through the rain toward the cottage, unheard over the noise of the wind tearing at the trees as he hurried forward.

* * *

Mick sat at his desk, a cigarette burning in the ashtray to the left of his keyboard, his head resting intermittently in his hands between long hard stares at the screen and sips of whisky. Rain slammed like a million grains of sand against his windowpane, ran down it in rivulets. He looked at his words, not happy that he'd accurately caught the atmosphere of the words on the tape. He'd done the transcript, which he implanted into the body of text, but he could improve it. Of course, he could say bollocks to it and just hit *send*, or he could make it perfect just as Rochester had wanted. This after all, could put him undeniably in the crime correspondent's seat, could even elevate the paper to a new plateau.

He stubbed out the cigarette, lit another and listened to the trees screaming against the wind.

* * *

Eddie lay fully clothed and wide awake on Mick's bed. Until an hour ago he'd been the most tired human being on the planet. But the tiredness had gone now, like hunger will go if you ignore it long enough. He watched the rain on the window, listened to the wind screeching through the gap at the bottom of the ill-fitting sash.

The rain grew an edge as though it wasn't rain at all, but something more like sleet. The pane of glass didn't so much hum anymore; it sounded like a hundred people drumming their fingernails against it. It was almost hypnotic.

And then the snow came, and suddenly Eddie felt cold. And the dampness in his hair felt very uncomfortable and he shivered. His breath burst out of his ever-open mouth as he ran along the wet grass. And the howl of vehicles on the motorway a hundred yards away was deafening; plumes of misty white water hung in the air, capturing the falling snow.

The figure stopped by the fence and turned abruptly, and Eddie felt huge and powerful, utterly in control of the situation. He was gonna nail this fucker for what he just did.

Eddie's run became a jog and then, in the snowy mud, became a slow walk. Twenty yards away from the black-clad youth, he took his final step, breath exhausting hot over his cheek. He resisted the urge to lean forward, palms on knees as he regained his composure. That would be a sign of weakness, but he was Eddie Collins and by God, he was not weak. "Gimme the fucking bag."

The kid, instead of appearing afraid, smiled at Eddie. Eddie couldn't quite grasp why. The kid should have been in the region of desperate, trying to negotiate his way out. But there was no fear at all.

* * *

"Fucking weather!" Benson screamed. "Can't this thing go any quicker?"

The traffic officer looked across to him. "No."

Benson banged the side window with a fist. "How much longer?"

"Sat nav says thirteen minutes."

* * *

Mick swallowed the last of his whisky, belched, and enjoyed the burning sensation in his throat. He stared at the computer screen and lit up another cigarette. He was much happier. The big event was just right, pitched perfectly, he thought. It was a shame the disclaimer spoilt it a little, but it was necessary, "this information has been passed on to the police in its entirety", and added extra weight, he supposed. Not that it really needed extra weight; this was heavy enough by itself. He allowed himself a little chuckle, and then he dragged all the other information into one folder, along with the "heavy" on his screen, and opened up his encrypted email.

* * *

Rain was running down the wall, settling in one long puddle against the side of the building but Sirius never noticed how wet his feet were as he crept along to the open rear window. The noise engulfing him was enormous; the rain on the trees, the trees rattling and groaning in the wind.

He neared the window, saw a small white vent pipe poking through, and crouched beneath it, trying to listen for sounds in the room beyond. There were none so far as he could tell. Sirius allowed himself a very brief peek into the room, quickly scanning it from one wall to the next. It was empty. Sixteen seconds later, he was standing next to the warm drier using a nearby towel to get the water off his face and hands, trying to get a better grip on the gun. He flicked off the safety catch.

The cottage was substantially built, an old worker's cottage that was designed to be robust, something that would need little maintenance, something that would be there as long as the main farm house, solid right the way through with no sign of wooden floors, but instead great flags of Yorkshire stone.

He crossed the kitchen, past the huge old iron Rangemaster, and peered through the crack in the door into a small lounge. Grey light grudgingly seeped in through a window partly concealed by the windswept ivy outside. The room was empty, and so he edged right into the hallway. It was almost black in here; the front door was windowless, solid wood but old and flaky, rotten at its lower edge.

He walked softly up the hallway towards it. It was locked with a Yale. Good, but the frame was holed with painted-over woodworm. To his right, the stone stairs with a strip of red and black patterned carpet running along their centre wound at a shallow angle upwards towards the faint glow of artificial light.

Standing at the foot of the stairs, he listened for voices or signs of movement. There were none, so he looked around the corner up the stairs and began his slow ascent, listening all the time, watching the light grow steadily brighter.

And then he heard it, the sound of fingers prodding at a keyboard, the irregular pattering of a two-fingered typist. Sirius didn't know what Mick Lyndon was writing, but it signified unfinished work at least, so there was still time. Yet again he cursed Henry Deacon, and questioned Sir George's decision not to kill Henry when they first had the chance and the inclination.

His only real concern at this moment was Eddie Collins. He felt certain he was still in the cottage too – who in their right mind would be out in this weather? - but where was he if he wasn't downstairs? In the toilet? Sleeping in another room? In the same room as Mick?

He was three steps from the top and he ducked down hoping to see something of use under the part-open door of the room with the light on, but the carpet and undulating floor prevented him seeing anything. At least the typing continued, in its stuttering fashion. He could smell tobacco smoke, and mixed with it was whisky. Mick would be hard at work, mind focused on the task in hand, oblivious to his surroundings, used to the dull drumming of the rain and screeching wind. Sirius could let off a party-popper and he probably wouldn't notice.

He stood on the landing, and scanned the surroundings. To his left was Mick's study, well lit, target sitting in an old green leather chair, hunched over a keyboard, cigarette and whisky easily to hand. To his right was a short landing, two doors off it, one left one right, both doors open. One a bedroom and one a bathroom.

The typing stopped.

He returned his attention to Mick and watched him take a last mouthful of whisky. Sirius stepped silently into the room and looked at the computer screen.

His eyes widened.

Chapter Seventy-Nine

Friday 26th June

– One –

They walked slowly and dejectedly down the remainder of The Headrow towards Millgarth Police Station. There were people rushing by them up the hill, heading for the growing noise near Park Lane and the Town Hall. Some of those rushing carried furled banners and looked intent upon creating trouble. Ros stepped aside to let them pass, made it obvious to them that she wanted no trouble, and for the first time today, she wished she were not in uniform. The T-shirt with the force crest on it drew more and more attention so she walked along with her arms folded across her breasts, trying to cover it up. The police radio and her Maglite dangling from her belt were things she could do nothing about.

"Let's hurry up and get the hell out of here," she said to Chris.

Chris walked faster, Ros following close behind him, when suddenly he stopped and she walked right into him. "Sorry," she said.

He was looking to his right into a shop window. She followed his gaze and then stared up at the sign over the door: Bookman Antiques. They swapped glances. "This looks promising," she said, and they went inside.

Chris caught her up and took a gentle hold of her arm. She turned and saw the concern in his face. He whispered, "We could be in trouble if it's him. If he recognises you—"

"Should be fine, I had my mask on and hood up."

"Sure?"

She nodded and he closed the door behind them.

Their boots squeaked as together they walked across the floorboards looking around at the cramped little space that was filled with everything from globes to clocks, wicker furniture, carved oak furniture, candelabras, and stuffed animals. Shelf upon shelf of dusty old books with spines two inches wide and their titles embossed in gold. The ceiling was a latticework of cast iron hooks, from which hung a thousand lamps and lights and crystal chandeliers that cast a million rainbows on the walls. And on those walls were paintings;

hundreds of them crammed into the tightest spots, more resting on pianos, on tables of all descriptions, leaning against walls.

On the far wall was something quite extraordinary. Ros and Chris felt drawn to it, as though pulled there by some kind of gravity, some kind of magnetism.

From beneath an archway draped with beads, a small rotund man with spectacles poised on the end of his nose watched them. He wore a golden-coloured waistcoat.

They stood before the most wonderful paintings they had ever seen. Each of the twelve pictures was two feet square, and framed in either gilt or silver. And they spoke to them, the pictures *spoke* to them; they held them in a trance for they were created in layers and in each layer was an image that complemented those above and below it, until the viewer understood the entire work from the foreground right to the horizon.

In each corner, a white label adhered to the frame, or inserted between the canvas and the frame, proclaimed the price. Not one was below three thousand pounds. Each label seemed to obscure the flourish of the painter's name.

Ros nudged Chris, and he looked to the left at a further painting. This one was huge by comparison and it was the grand master over all the others. This one depicted a stunningly beautiful woodland nymph gazing skyward, a light mist surrounding her and a myriad of forest creatures who stared alongside her up into the heavens. A pair of large opaque wings drifted down to the grass, and she wore a delicate smile that complemented her crying eyes. It was unfinished, but in the bottom right corner, was a dark squiggle.

Ros moved closer, and she bent to see the artist's signature. She gasped: *Christian Ledger.*

"May I be of some assistance?"

– Two –

Eddie swallowed, looked around. They were both trapped, and then Eddie saw it for the first time. The kid was laughing because he was far, far stronger than any version of Eddie Collins had ever been. The gun in his hand provided him with infinite power. Suddenly Eddie felt very weak indeed. Suddenly Eddie felt like he should have ignored the screaming woman and continued driving home, maybe put on some Floyd to take away the tedium of the journey.

Instead he was facing down a robber who wasn't a robber at all, he was a would-be killer. And the person to grant him that status, to permit membership of that illustrious club, was Eddie Collins. This wasn't a stranger that he was reading about in the paper, or some poor bastard on the TV news who had left behind a grieving wife and three young children. It was him, Eddie Collins. And he wouldn't get a chance to feel sorry for the guy and his family, because he would be dead.

The end.

Dead.

The kid stopped laughing. He aimed the gun and shot Eddie.

Eddie blinked. So it was real after all. He felt the impact, like a tug, like someone had taken some fur-lined pincers and just gently pulled on the skin on the inside of his leg. There was no immediate sharp pain, just the tug. And then a kind of dull throb that was a little disconcerting. Eddie looked at the kid. The kid wasn't smiling. The gun was still outstretched. The throb became a definite pain. He had been hit, and it now began to hurt a little. No, it began to hurt a lot. And then a strange sensation; his leg began to grow warm, at least on the outside.

But on the inside it grew cool, like he'd been sitting on it too long and the circulation had stopped. He looked down.

Water dropped from his hair and from his nose, he could see the droplets falling, and they just disappeared as they hit the white snow. Except the snow wasn't white. The snow was red. Around his foot the snow was turning red.

And quite suddenly, he was on his back looking into the sky. His face was exposed to the snow, and it stung his cheek and the wind was biting so cold, and his mind grew cooler, and a hollow feeling spread over him, and he raised a hand and it was red too, and it was shiny, and from it droplets of blood fell, and from it steam rose. And it was the strangest of feelings. And then he whimpered because he was frightened and then he screamed because now it fucking hurt.

He moved his face downward a little, could see the tips of his toes, and over the tips of his toes he could see the kid standing only a couple of yards away. The kid pointed the gun at him again.

And then he felt light-headed, just as you do on the cusp of being drunk, except there was another less pleasant feeling that came with this; he had an awful sensation deep inside his chest, as the new

472

hollowness expanded. And then he was struggling to keep his eyes open.

He looked back at the kid, made himself stare into the face of the bastard who was going to make his wife a widow and his Sammy fatherless. And it was that thought alone, nothing to do with inherent fear of dying, it was his family that made him sit up. He swooned again, but stuck with it. In his lap, blood pooled, his groin was shining with it, deep enough that you couldn't see his trousers anymore. There was a pulse to it, slow and regular, a little fountain of blood spurted outwards into the snow, and it reminded him of garden sprinklers in summer time. *That's a fucking artery,* he thought. *Blood pattern analysis.*

It ran between his legs, and steam whipped from it carried by the wind along with its curious mortuary smell.

Well, this was no good, and Eddie was having none of it. "You fuckin' coward, gimme the bag," he slurred, glaring at the kid. He tried to stand, but couldn't raise the energy to do more than put a hand into the snow. He was shaking now. He grabbed a handful of snowy mud and he chucked it towards the kid. It missed, it never even went in the kid's direction, but it was all he could do, that and the glare and mutter the words, "You fuckin' coward."

* * *

Sirius brought the gun up, and coughed.

Mick Lyndon turned around. His face remained emotionless as his right index finger hovered above the "Enter" button.

Sirius shot Mick through the front of the head.

Chapter Eighty

Friday 26th June

The kid raised the gun and aimed directly into Eddie's face. Eddie bared his teeth and growled, wide-eyed, and then there was a shot.

Eddie fell backwards, face once again turned to the sky, arms outstretched like a snow angel bleeding to death. Snowflakes fell on his cheeks and into his closed eyes, melted and ran into his ears.

He heard the throng of the traffic.

But how could you hear anything if you're dead?

His eyes flickered open and the image of a police officer's outstretched arm, hand holding a Glock, vanished into the cracked ceiling in Mick's bedroom.

Eddie was wet with sweat. His eyes darted around the room; his hand touched his groin, and came away dry – no blood. But even if it hadn't been for the loud crack he just heard, he would have sensed something was wrong, like a nagging that told him to get his sorry arse in gear. He reached across to Mick's bedside table, grabbed Henry's gun and edged off the bed.

Three paces brought him into the hallway and he could see right into Mick's study. And he froze. He stared. Sweat dripped into his eyes and he scrubbed it away with his sleeve. Rain beat against the landing window and Eddie walked forward, damp feet on the carpet, determination on his face, and a tremor in his hands.

He was in Mick's room and Mick was lying awkwardly, twisted somehow between his chair and the desk, right arm hanging limp. And there was Sirius, the same guy who had been in his flat, who had followed them into the back yard, the same man who had spoken into the phone less than a yard from him. He had his back turned, he was reading the computer screen and then he was bending, searching for something. He snapped a memory stick from the USB port and turned.

Eddie stuck the gun in his face.

Silence. Utter silence.

He stared into Sirius's eyes. They were cold, emotionless, just-doing-my-job eyes. They had no fear in them. They had nothing in them. And it was this lack of reaction that stoked the fires in Eddie's chest. He breathed hard through clenched teeth, and he squeezed on the trigger, felt the metal resist his skin; and then he wondered about the no going back thing. He wondered how it would feel to kill someone, because once they're dead, they don't come back and let you make a different choice next time. Sirius twitched and Eddie punched him hard in the face with his left hand.

Sirius absorbed the blow and Eddie knew it had been a mistake, he should have just pulled the fucking trigger, he should have finished it instead of trying to be reasonable in front of a dead friend who didn't need impressing anymore. And he guessed Sirius was busy reading his mind, because the long pause had been a sign of weakness, and Sirius pounced on it. After all, he was a killer. He knew indecision when he saw it, and he knew Eddie didn't have the balls to pull the trigger, and that's what he counted on.

Everything dropped out of real-time and into slow motion as Sirius knocked aside Eddie's gun as though it wasn't there. It bounced off the corner of Mick's desk and landed near the waste paper basket, and in its place pointing at Eddie's left eye, was his own gun.

There was no reaction time for Eddie, he put conscious thought on standby, and a subconscious force took control over the levers and buttons inside Eddie's mind. Eddie ducked as Sirius fired and for a brief moment he felt the heat of the shockwave pass by within an inch of his ear, felt red-hot particles of spent exhaust singe his skin, and heard the massive boom of the bullet leaving the muzzle.

Eddie lunged and caught Sirius around the chest, forcing him backwards into Mick's desk. The gun went off again, and Eddie screwed his eyes tight shut and kept on pushing forward with all the strength in his legs and crushed tight with all the strength in his arms. There was no screaming, only the grunting sounds of exertion. Sirius swung around, managed to get his back to Eddie's front and he turned with Eddie clinging to his back like a tortoise shell, and heaved. Eddie's feet left the ground and Sirius fell back against the wall, crushing him.

But Eddie didn't let go. He held on with his left arm and brought his right hand forward, furiously, frantically searching out Sirius's face. Sirius whipped his head back and smashed Eddie's nose. The pain was blinding and for a moment it almost cancelled Eddie's autopilot, and that would have been the end.

Eddie found Sirius's chin. Then he found Sirius's throat and he grabbed it. He tightened his grip on the windpipe. Sirius bucked, threw an elbow into Eddie's abdomen, whipped his head back and forth trying to free Eddie's grip. And then moved against the desk, trying to throw Eddie off, but Eddie clung on, sinking his fingers into the fleshy part. The noise of air grating through Sirius's constricted throat gave him added strength, and he renewed his grip, tightened his fingers.

Sirius began thrashing about. He hoisted the gun over his right shoulder. Eddie saw it coming and ducked left as Sirius pulled the trigger. That momentary lapse caused Eddie's fingers to slacken and Sirius hooked his own fingers into Eddie's and began pulling his hand away from his throat. Eddie punched Sirius in the temple hard enough to make him stumble. Eddie yanked him backwards, crushing his throat again as he pulled him off balance. Sirius staggered, this time brought the gun around his hip and fired upward. The sound was enormous and for a second, Eddie stopped. His eyes, not screwed shut anymore, widened as he felt something change inside.

Sirius was off balance now and they both fell to the ground by Mick's feet. Eddie moved his head aside as they fell and butted Sirius's head into the floor.

And then it all stopped.

The only sound was the rain against the window. That, and Eddie's rapid breathing. He felt hot, and shaky, nauseous. Sirius's eyes were closed and Eddie removed his fingers from his throat. They were covered in blood.

He slid aside, freed himself and then sat against the far wall, panting. He held up his right hand, the one that had been embedded in Sirius's throat, and the wet fingers shook hard enough to spray blood into his lap. He looked across to Sirius, a big man with broad muscular shoulders, a man who didn't really have a neck to speak of, just a head and then a body; but somehow Eddie had found his throat, and there was nothing short of a bloody mess there now, a slow rivulet of blood trickling down and dripping onto the carpet.

And beyond him was Mick's computer. It too was silent now, not even a cooling fan running, no bright lights blinking. Eddie wondered if Mick had sent the email yet, or whether he was still too busy composing his story. He could see the USB ports from here, and in the uppermost one was a stub of the memory stick they had rescued from Henry Deacon's watchtower. The smashed remains of it lay smeared across the floor at the computer's base.

Chapter Eighty-One

Friday 26th June

"Kill the sirens," Benson said. "Should be up here on the left somewhere."

Two hundred yards later, it was; one left kink in the road and the sign for the farm appeared. The traffic officer braked hard and then steered onto the track. Benson reached over and cut the blue lights, and the driver shut off the car lights too.

"What's the plan?" he asked.

"I haven't got a plan," Benson said. Sirius had offered Eddie to Benson, which meant *he* wanted Mick; and if he wanted Mick, it meant he wanted whatever Mick had against him or his boss – whoever that may be. And if Eddie was there, what would Sirius do to him? Benson wanted Eddie badly. "Making it up as I go along."

There was a silver car parked on a narrow lane to their right, between the trunks of two trees, and what Benson assumed to be Sirius's car parked just ahead, its interior light glowing, no one inside it. The officer brought his car to a halt a few yards behind it.

"Want me to come in with you or what?"

"Fucking right I do."

"Well then, you tell me what's going on."

Benson looked across, and saw the officer's no-compromise look. "There's a bad guy, probably armed, who works for the government. I want him; he's up for murder, government man or not. Inside are two other men, one a journalist who hasn't done anything wrong, and the other is a renegade CSI who is on a Rule Three for murder. He's armed too."

"Fuck me."

Benson climbed out of the car and into the rain, and so did the traffic officer, checking his weapon, water running from the black peak of his cap.

"So, what do you want me—"

"I don't fucking know!" It was a shout, but muffled between clenched teeth, and further drowned out by the rain. "Catch the bad guys, I guess."

"I feel uncomfortable about this."

"So stay here and polish your car, you fucking wimp." Benson ran through the rain and the dancing puddles towards the cottage.

Chapter Eighty-Two

Friday 26th June

– One –

Eddie's eyes floated to the floor by Sirius. There was a thick red smear between Sirius's part of the floor and his own part. And there was pain too, in his right side just below his ribs. Eddie wiped his fingers across the carpet until they were almost clean of Sirius's blood, then found the source of pain under his shirt. Fresh warm blood coated his fingers.

"Fucking great," he whispered.

The pain came on in slow rhythmical throbs that steadily increased in intensity. He wondered how much damage there was; he'd seen enough gunshot wounds to know that most of them, if not treated quickly, could prove fatal, and those that weren't fatal incapacitated the victim extensively. But here, in the middle of nowhere, only an air ambulance could get to him quickly enough. And the odds of anything flying in this weather were zero.

He'd been shot in the leg last year and the bullet had nicked his femoral artery. He would have bled to death if the police officer hadn't parted Eddie's legs and stood on his inner thigh just below his balls. It had stopped him bleeding out.

And then guilt turned his watering eyes back to Mick, staring at his motionless back, at the lack of breathing, the lack of fidgeting. Mick was like a piece of furniture now. And he felt a great wash of sadness. All Mick had wanted to do was get the story into print, all he ever wanted to be was the best he could be, and now he was a piece of fucking furniture.

Poor Mick.

Had the story made it through to the newspaper?

Eddie held his breath and tried to stand. The pain in his right side was excruciating, but he didn't scream this time, made himself stay silent except for a hiss through clenched teeth, and slowly he staggered to Mick's desk looking for his mobile phone. He could feel the blood oozing down his leg, soaking into his jeans and gradually cooling.

Mick had told him to keep the phones switched off so the police couldn't triangulate their signal and pin a location on them; but they were well past that now. He found Mick's phone under a jotter, switched it on and waited for it to find a signal and scroll through its starting-up procedure. Seeing all the blood across Sirius's neck and face, as though a wild animal had ripped his throat out, made him retch. But the phone drew his attention: two messages.

One was from someone called Rochester asking if he was okay, sent three hours ago. Eddie was puzzled at the name then remembered Rochester was Mick's boss, the editor. The second message was from a Suzanne Child, sent an hour ago, and asking if he would mind her accessing his database.

Mick selected Rochester and pressed call. It rang five or six times before it was answered, "Mick?"

"No."

"Who is this? Where's Mick?"

"Mick's dead."

There was a pause. "Who is this?"

"My name's Eddie Collins, I'm a friend of his."

– Two –

"Beautiful, isn't it?"

Ros, heart hammering in her chest, eyed the man. He was very short, maybe five-seven, but heavy, somewhere around sixteen stone. He was bald except for a narrow band of blonde hair that ran around the back of his head from ear to ear like a letter C that had fallen over. He wore crescent-shaped glasses perched on the end of his large nose. He was smiling at her. "It is," she said, "very."

"How much is it?" Chris asked.

"Ah," the man pointed a finger at the ceiling, "that all depends."

He wore smart shoes. And a gold-coloured waistcoat.

"On what?"

"You've admired the other paintings by the same artist, and you've seen the price of them. Now," he whispered, "how much are you in love with *The Nymph*?"

"Beg your pardon?" Ros asked.

"*The Nymph*; how much do you love that painting?"

"You want us to make you an offer?"

"I do, yes."

"It's not even finished."

"Never will be. The artist is dead, unfortunately. But I like to think that detail adds a little something to the picture; it adds, as if one were needed, a talking point. But crucially, it adds an air of mystery too. You will spend hours, as have I, wondering how he would have finished it."

He shuffled back to where the smaller paintings were, to where light was better. "Look at it from here," he said. "This is the spot from which I admire it the most."

For the first time, Ros was able to take note of his snooker player's waistcoat. And she could see the shimmering golden threads.

"Come, come," he said, "stand and fall in love." The little man turned Chris abruptly, but with Ros he took a little more care and turned her slowly, almost as though he were smelling her perfume, as though he were scrutinising her.

She turned, but before she had her back to him, she noticed in the golden threads up at the very top of the waistcoat, a smear. Chocolate or even gravy hastily wiped away, but its remnants remained visible only to an eye that searched for it.

"How much do you love it?"

"I couldn't afford to love it as much as I'd like," Chris said.

The little man laughed. "I understand perfectly." Behind their back, he stopped smiling. "I have one more thing to show you. Follow me."

– Three –

"I need to get access to his informants."

Rochester sat behind his desk, contemplation on his face. He stared up at Suzanne, then nodded. "Okay, get into his database," she had already turned away, "and check his emails while you're there." She nodded and closed the door, and Rochester resumed his earlier musing, thinking not only of Mick's whereabouts and his safety – he hadn't heard from him since Thursday morning – but also of the story he was working on, the one he promised was an exclusive, the one that went right to the top of government. Of course he still had plenty of material to use, Mick had seen to it that Henry's taped "confessions" were available to him, but there was more; he had insinuated there was much more, and Rochester knew Mick wasn't lying this time. He had a certain enthusiasm in his voice he hadn't heard in years.

And then Rochester's mobile phone rang. It startled him out of his daydream, and read the screen: *Mick Lyndon*. "Mick?"

"No."

"Who is this?" he asked. "Where's Mick?" Rochester stood; ready to march out into the office to be at Mick's station.

"Mick's dead."

Rochester's fingertips touched his desk. "Who is this?"

"My name's Eddie Collins, I'm a friend of his."

Rochester tried to recall the name, but he was coming up blank. "Are you at his desk?"

"What, no I'm… How did he die, what happened to him?"

"He was shot. Ever heard the name Sirius?"

Rochester eyes widened; oh yes, he'd heard *that* name before. "Sirius shot him? Are you serious? Why, what happened?"

"Have a look at Mick's emails, see if anything reached you."

Rochester somehow made it out into the office; the noise of people talking and of photocopiers and printers whirring didn't exist; all he heard was this man called Eddie Collins breathing fast, as though he was under some kind of duress, "On my way," he said. "Are you okay, Mr Collins?"

"I've been shot too, don't know how bad it is."

"Well—"

"Hurry up, Rochester."

"Yes, yes." He approached Mick's desk where Suzanne looked up at him, saw the shock in her eyes, and wondered if he looked *that* bad. But Suzanne wasn't shocked at the look in Rochester's eyes, she was beckoning him over quickly. Rochester stared at the screen. "Oh my God," he whispered.

"What's there?"

"Erm, it's linked to an audio file. It's a transcript of an audio file." He scrolled down the screen. "Mick's put a story together around it."

"Is that everything?"

"I'm not sure, hold on."

"Hurry, Rochester."

"There's a crossword puzzle," he looked up at Suzanne. "I don't know what to make of it—"

"Decipher it and print it. Print it all."

"I can't just—"

"You have to! There's fucking people dying out here. Fucking idiots—"

Rochester was about to reply, when he heard a sharp crack over the phone and a cluster of noises as though the phone had been dropped.

Chapter Eighty-Three

Friday 26th June

Eddie dropped the phone on the desk, and looked around, searching for his gun. The front doorknob banged against the hallway wall. He heard the rain beating on the footpath outside the front door. He saw the gun over in the corner. Footsteps on the stairs. He walked towards the gun, cringing at the pain. He could hear the rain louder, could even hear it dripping from the clothes of whoever was walking up the stairs.

He reached the gun. He bent, clenching down on a scream, and grabbed it.

Someone was out on the landing, very close. He could hear their laboured breathing, could still hear water from their clothes or their hair dripping onto the carpet. It reminded him of the moss in the back yard of his flat. Eddie squeezed himself up against the wall and brought the gun up to chest height.

The breathing worsened, "Fuck me." Then Benson strode into the room, handgun down by his side, relaxed as though he thought the house was clear now. He walked over to Sirius, bent and took hold of his right hand. There was a deep injury just above the knuckles, healing, it appeared, but very slowly.

"Wondered when you'd show up," Eddie said.

Benson stopped dead. He stood up. He didn't look around, but Eddie saw him tense slightly. "Quite the serial killer now, Eddie."

"Drop your gun and kick it over here."

Benson dropped it, back-heeled it in Eddie's direction. "Don't think I've ever seen you sober."

"There goes another rib." Eddie nudged the gun across towards the skirting board, well out of the way. "Where're your friends?"

"On their way."

"Who did you arrive with?"

Benson said nothing.

"May as well tell me; don't want any nasty surprises. They make my finger twitch."

"A traffic officer drove me."

"He round the back?"

Benson nodded.

"When he comes inside, tell him to go wait in the car, and when the rest get here, tell them the same. Okay?"

"You know what they used to say in the old Westerns? You'll never make it out of here alive," Benson laughed and turned. His eyes immediately found the blood smeared against the wall behind Eddie. "Maybe sooner than I originally thought though. Shame, I wanted to kill you myself."

"Take your coat off."

"Fuck off."

"I'm on a Rule Three, Benson. You're talking to a dead man."

Benson shrugged out of his jacket and let it fall to the floor. It thudded, the cuffs poking out of the inside pocket. "Now what, you want me to get down to my Y-fronts?"

"Put a pair of handcuffs on. I see you brought plenty."

Benson ignored the ones in his jacket; instead he removed some from a small leather pouch on his belt, slipped them on his wrists and stared as if waiting for another order.

Eddie stared too, but at the spare cuffs. "You were going to arrest him, weren't you," he nodded at Sirius.

"He still alive?"

Eddie shrugged, "Haven't heard him breathing, but check for a pulse if it'll make you happy."

"I'm not fussed. If he's not dead yet, he soon will be; quite hard to live without a throat I should think."

"Why?"

"Why what?"

"Why aren't you bothered that he's dead?"

"None of your fucking business. Now hurry up and die, Collins, so I can get out of here."

"You got anything against Mick Lyndon?"

"Is that Mick Lyndon?" He nodded towards the man lying half on the desk and half in the chair.

"That is Mick Lyndon. Not guilty of any crimes whatsoever."

"Then I have nothing against him."

"That twat shot him dead," Eddie whispered.

"That twat shot Lincoln Farrier a week ago."

"Mick found something out about the government, and he'd found out who ordered Lincoln Farrier's murder."

"Figures."

"That it, '*figures*'?"

Benson shrugged.

"You people look everywhere but in the right fucking places. Innocent people die because you fail to do your job properly."

Benson stared at him. "This the final speech before you expire?"

Eddie brought the gun up. He saw Benson's smile waver. He pointed the gun at Benson's head; there were maybe three or four yards between them. He pulled the trigger.

Chapter Eighty-Four

Friday 26th June

– One –

Benson jumped, banged his head against the wall. "You dumb *fuck*!" he screamed. "Why did you do that!"

Eddie stared at him, amazed at how loud that was. The bullet hole was a foot away from Benson's ear, and a cloud of plaster dust rose into the air as lumps of it hit the carpet.

"Any idea how many bullets this thing holds?" Eddie asked.

"Go fuck yourself!"

The front door banged against the wall again, and then a voice shouted up the stairs, "Boss? Boss, you okay?"

Benson closed his eyes, shook his head. Eddie stared at him, gun still pointed at his head. "Fine." Benson called down the stairs, "Go sit in the car and play with yourself. And when the others get here, tell them to stand by."

The front door closed, and the rain grew muffled again.

"You put me on a Rule Three for killing Stuart."

"Taylor put you on a Rule Three, and it was provisional."

"You can't do that, don't you see? It's like you put that lad Christian Ledger on a Rule Three before we even finished the scene. I am innocent, and that kid is innocent too."

Benson said nothing.

"Doesn't that bother you? It might look good for the stats and the little competition you guys have with each other, but it's wrong. Not only have you accused the wrong men, you've left the way clear for two real murderers to go about their business again. And that's just the two I know of, there's probably dozens more."

"You're guilty. He's guilty."

"And you don't know all the facts."

"Look, look, Collins. You're slowly – too slowly – bleeding to death, and all we're doing is batting shit at each other from across a room with two dead men in it. This is getting us nowhere. I believe you and the lad are guilty, you're going down, both of you."

"How about if I could offer you some evidence to prove my innocence?"

Benson shrugged again. "Too late," he laughed, "I mean look around, this place is like a butcher's shop, and you're the one holding the fucking gun."

"That's my point *exactly!* You don't look beyond the obvious, you blindly accept whatever is presented to you; you need to see the whole picture, and that is precisely why forensic science is there."

"Fuck off; I've been doing this job for twenty years."

"Doing it wrong, obviously."

"Like I said, fuck off."

"Oh by the way, I forgot to mention: we're being recorded right now."

Benson snapped his head up then. "What?"

"I was on the phone to *The Yorkshire Echo* as you arrived. The line's still open. Say hello."

"Lying bastard."

Eddie laughed, shaking his head. "Really, it's true." And then he took a breath, winced at the pain and said, "I have a proposition."

"I don't do deals with murderers."

"Good, so you'll deal with me. This gun killed Stuart in the CSI office."

"Yes, your gun."

"No, Henry Deacon's gun. He's already admitted to it—"

"Henry Deacon is dead."

"I know—"

"And you killed—"

"Will you shut up!" Eddie flinched as the wound opened up. "And before you say anything else that falls into the category of utter bollocks, let me tell you that he," he nodded at Sirius, "killed Henry Deacon, and *that* is implied on tape. And I couldn't have killed Henry Deacon because the bastard was already dead when I found him!"

"Fuck—"

"By about four hours. And you can check that with your man, Taylor. Jeffery did the scene, and he's no dummy, he'll have worked it out. And this is Henry Deacon's gun. I found it at Deacon's place and I took it—"

"Why?"

Eddie was silent for a minute. "I don't know why. My hand brushed it as I was feeling under a wardrobe, and I grabbed it, brought it out."

"So why not leave it behind?"

"Because by then it had my DNA on it."

"So?" Benson shrugged, "If you're innocent—"

"Bollocks. No one dare use that old saying anymore."

"…you have nothing to worry about."

"Take your cuffs off."

Benson shut up then. "How can I?"

"I'm not stupid, Benson. Take them off."

Benson slid one hand out of the metal loop, wriggled the key out of the leather pouch and unclipped the ratchet from the other wrist.

"Here," Eddie threw Deacon's gun across the room.

It landed with a thump at Benson's feet, and Benson just looked at him with narrowed eyes. "Why?"

"The only way to prove my innocence to you is to give you his gun. Have the remaining bullets examined for DNA, and you'll find out that Henry Deacon loaded it. It was his weapon; I found it at his house after he used it on Stuart."

"Proves fuck all. It might be his weapon, and he may have loaded it, but you could still have shot Stuart with it."

"*Now* you're bothered about proof! I went to his house on Thursday around midnight, Stuart was killed and the office set alight twenty-four hours before that. Prick."

Benson stared at Eddie, mind lost in thought.

Eddie pulled the memory stick from his jeans pocket, waved it at Benson. "While you're thinking about that, you can have a think about what's on here."

"Why? What *is* on there?"

"Confirmation of my innocence, confirmation that Henry Deacon and that bastard over there did everything that you've been running around arresting the wrong people for. Wait till it hits the headlines, then we'll see who has an appointment with a Home Office bullet."

Benson picked up his coat. Then he walked across the room and took Eddie by the shoulders, spun him round and with his fingertips, pulled up Eddie's shirt.

Eddie squirmed. "How bad is it?"

"Looks like someone held a circular saw on your back." Then Benson let the shirt drop and dug a knuckle into the wound. Eddie screamed and Benson moved close to his ear. "Ever point a gun at me again, you'd better not miss."

– Two –

Chris sat on the shiny wooden floor, staring at the wall full of Christian Ledger's paintings. He stared at them for some time, but his eyes wouldn't quite focus on them; he saw straight through them, aware of their existence but unable to comprehend them.

On the floor at his side, the screen of his radio lit up again, and a voice came out of the speaker. He looked down at it. And then he tried to pick it up but couldn't. The thumb on his right hand was missing. There was a large tear-shaped space where it should have been. The tear shape ran almost the full length of his forearm, and he could see the remains of tendons in there among all the blood, and some white string-like things that he assumed to be nerves.

He had held out his hand in a defensive gesture and the bespectacled man's knife took it clean off.

In his lap was a puddle of blood.

A flood of piercing blue lights lit up the inside of the shop, glancing from the crystals in the chandeliers to make wonderful patterns on the walls and ceiling. The bell over the door tinkled and suddenly, the shop was full of police.

Chris began to cry. "I killed him," he sobbed.

DI Taylor knelt by him. "Ros. Where is she? Is she okay?"

"He stabbed her. She's alive but hurry. In the back room."

Chapter Eighty-Five

Monday 29th June

– One –

Eddie was out of hospital at nine o'clock on Monday morning. The doctor had said the bullet, which had raked out a six-inch long trench of skin and burnt the surrounding tissue, had missed his kidney by a little over three-quarters of an inch. It had suffered some harsh bruising however, and he could expect to pass blood for the next few weeks.

Being in one of the better interview rooms in Holbeck Police Station was the first confirmation Eddie had that everything was going to be alright. The second confirmation was the coffee in a proper mug.

The third confirmation was when Benson knocked and walked in with Taylor; maybe he had tagged along as some kind of moral support. Maybe he was there to remove any smugness or gloating from one Eddie Collins. He need not have worried on that score, there was no *smug* and no *gloat* to be seen anywhere.

"Eddie." Taylor held out his hand and Eddie reached up, winced, and shook.

"Eddie." Benson did likewise, though it must have been difficult for him; the last remaining confirmation that all was well and good. Eddie shook, and the two officers sat down opposite him.

"We sent Henry's gun off to the lab for overnight analysis," Taylor said.

"And?"

Benson cleared his throat. "As you said, the remaining bullets had Henry Deacon's DNA on them."

"Am I now off the Rule Three for killing Stuart?"

"All charges against you have been removed. And I owe you an apology."

Eddie could see those words coming out of Benson's mouth with bits of flesh and blood sticking to them as though they had barbs on them. It must have been painful. But still he wouldn't gloat because that would not be the right thing to do, ever. "Thank you."

"And you were right about Christian Ledger."

"About him not killing Alice?" And not once did Eddie even think of saying "I told you so".

Benson nodded. "We found who the prints at her scene belonged to." He then surprised Eddie by standing up and heading for the door. He turned. "I am genuinely sorry," he said. Then he opened the door and left.

When the door closed, Eddie looked at Taylor, confused. "I never expected that from him."

"When he said that '*we*' found out whose prints were on the cash and easel, what he should have said was that Ros found them."

"Oh wow," Eddie smiled wide. But then he stopped smiling. Taylor was not smiling. "Why aren't you smiling?"

– Two –

Eddie spent the rest of the morning in the station. He was knotted up with news of Ros. And then he'd spent until well after lunch in the posh interview room with Taylor, and then with Jeffery, but all the time he spent in there, his eyes were wet. He went through a box of tissues, and two whole boxes of regret and a crate of self-pity.

Jeffery wouldn't let him go and see her. "She's in a bad way," he said. "Maybe visit her tomorrow, eh."

He didn't mean to be rude, but he just got up and let himself out, Jeffery looking on, wondering what he'd done to offend him.

– Three –

Just as Eddie was knocking on his own door, Christian Ledger was leaving Yorkshire altogether. He had hired a van, and had very carefully strapped all his recovered paintings into the cargo area. In boxes tethered to the sides were his old easel, some boxes with tubes of paint inside, his brushes and palette knives and his palette too. He was heading south, towards Devon, and a rather splendid studio house on the coast.

In his pocket was a cheque that would see him alright for years to come, and in a carrier bag in a box in the back, was more cash than he had ever seen before, a generous interim payment from Her Majesty's Government.

In another four hours he would approach Sedgemoor services and this time, he would drive right on by without so much as a second glance.

– Four –

Eddie's smile drifted away.

She was taking a shower, that's all, or she was, you know, otherwise indisposed. He cleared his throat, rehearsed the lines over in his mind again. *Hey, listen, I brought you some flowers, Jilly. They're just a little token to say I know I've been a prick these last few months, but I'm good again now, and if ever you need me…*

"Where the fuck is she?" he whispered.

He knocked again, louder, listened at the door.

Eddie walked around the back of the house, and like the front, the curtains were still closed and everything was locked up tight as a drum.

He began to get worried. He trotted back around the front of the house, cringing at the pain in his back, and feeling small tingling sensations developing in the pit of his stomach. He banged on the door, peered in through the letterbox. "Oh come on, fuck's sake!"

It took him thirteen kicks to break through it. He found her in bed.

There was a small trail of reddish mucus leaking from her nose. She was very pale and her lips were tinged an awful blue colour. The tablet bottles were arranged neatly on the bedside table; the note and the pen she'd used to write it with were alongside.

It seemed as though she had taken a bath, blow-dried her hair, even put on a little make-up, then sat down to write the note in a cool and calm way, taken the tablets and climbed into bed, pulling the quilt up around her shoulders just like she always used to.

The note said, *'Eddie, I still love you very much, and I always have. Forgive me please, but I just can't live without my Sam. Jilly x x x'*

The Yorkshire Echo. 29th June

Our saviour is a murderer

By Michael Lyndon

SIR GEORGE DEACON was the stoutest proponent for turning Britain into a nation of law-abiding and decent citizens who respected each other's privacy, property and lives; a nation that believed in fairness and equality.

This reporter met with Henry Deacon shortly before he was murdered at his home in Leeds. And what Henry Deacon passed on to me caused his death.

He told me that his father, Sir George Deacon, would soon have him killed for being an embarrassment to him. In a shocking hour-long interview, Henry Deacon revealed exactly how callous his father was, and what he was prepared to do to gain power as one of Great Britain's top government officials, in charge, ironically of the Justice Ministry. Once he had that power, Sir George Deacon intended to keep it – at any cost.

I have a transcript of a secretly recorded conversation made by Henry, between Sir George Deacon and his bodyguard who goes by the name Sirius, [but whose real name was Brian Thornton – Ed]. The plan was hatched even before the GBIP came to power, indeed it was a plan that was supposed to help them get to power, and instigate the implementation of the new Criminal Justice Reform Act – known commonly as The Rules.

The plan was simple: murder the then Shadow Minister of Justice, Roger King, outside his home in Kensington. Sirius was instructed to use a handgun and at point-blank range, as close to his front door as possible, "to gain maximum effect and cause maximum outrage".

The next year, GBIP swept to victory riding on a swell of public fervour and enthusiasm for The Rules, which became law not long afterwards.

King was seen as the weak link in the proposed justice system overhaul, and killing two birds with one stone, by making his death abhorrent to the public who already despised gun crime, ensured Deacon's promotion to Minister of Justice.

But Sir George Deacon's criminal activity did not end there; indeed, it was just the beginning.

Part of Henry Deacon's package of information directly links Deacon Snr and Sirius to the senseless murder of Lincoln Farrier. This has subsequently been confirmed by forensic analysis of a police-only fingerprint and DNA database.

Sirius teamed up with Henry under instruction from Sir George to destroy the Jaguar motor car that was responsible for killing two people in Wakefield on the same day, an act that had the potential to cause embarrassment to Sir George.

Abducting a youth to cover Henry's car in his own trace evidence failed, so too did their efforts to kill the youth.

The Jaguar was then recovered by West Yorkshire Police and forensically examined, leading Sirius and Henry to burn down the police building that stored that evidence.

Fortunately that effort also failed, but during the attempt, a member of West Yorkshire Police forensic staff was shot dead.

All information has been passed to the police to aid their investigations, but I am able to confirm that several other cases of murder and attempted murder by Deacon and his subordinates are also being investigated.

The ministry was also criticised by many as putting pressure on law enforcement agencies to bring swift justice to alleged miscreants at the expense of the truth.

This man created a monster when he devised The Rules, and indeed he has put the public faith in them in utmost jeopardy; Howard League for Penal Reform is but one organisation crying out for their removal.

We hope that Deacon Snr is served with a fate befitting his new title: murderer. After all, if you want to kill serious crime, you have to kill serious criminals.

The Yorkshire Echo. 29th June

Death of a hero

By Suzanne Child

MICK LYNDON was shot dead in his home in West Yorkshire.

He died while sending this newspaper information given to him by Henry Deacon, and more he had found as a result of coded messages left to him after Henry Deacon passed away. Part of the information Mick was passing along was hidden inside an encoded crossword puzzle by Henry Deacon.

This newspaper deems it correct to pass on to the Great British public just how scared Henry Deacon was of his father, and to illustrate the lengths he went to in order to make sure the story got to the right person – Mick Lyndon, who gave his life for his work.

We will miss you, Mick.

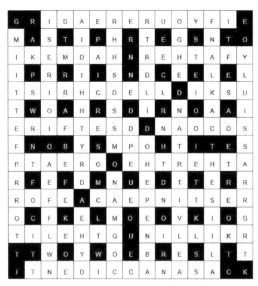

Inside the black boxes were hidden directions given to Mick by Henry Deacon so that he could find the incriminating recording already written about on the headline page. We have kept them blank because that location is now the subject of forensic investigation.

If you look at the white boxes however, reading from right to left, top to bottom, you will see Henry Deacon's admissions of guilt and acts of which he suspected his father. Here they are, laid out below:

IF YOURE READING THIS MY FATHER HAD ME KILLED

*SIRIUS KILLED ******* (Blanked out to protect identity)*

I SHOT SOCO AND SET FIRE

STOP MY FATHER THE GREAT PRETENDER

REST IN PEACE FORGIVE ME FOR KILLING LITTLE BOY WAS AN ACCIDENT

Epilogue

The fight had been valiant, had been like watching a modern-day enactment of David and Goliath, he supposed. But they were all against him; even Sterling Young snubbed him, had distanced himself wonderfully. And Deacon supposed he couldn't blame the man. But the speed of his ostracism had still been something of a shock.

They had stripped him of his title. And that was a sad thing. How he had loved to hear people refer to him as *sir*.

Deacon looked from one person to the next, and he didn't recognise any of them. This made him ever more confused and for a moment, he shook his head as though trying to clear away the rubble inside and see the reasons for his actions. But the rubble remained and the once proud and often pompous Mr George Deacon was guided into a wheelchair.

The wheelchair buzzed along the brightly lit concrete corridor. They were somewhere beneath Park Lane between the Bridewell and the courthouse. And next to the courthouse, was the affectionately named slaughterhouse. Deacon could feel the intensity of his heart beat increasing, despite the drugs they had given him to keep him well.

When they had first suggested it to him, he had laughed. "You want to keep me well in order that you may execute me?" he had asked. With straight faces, they had nodded. It was like the Geneva Convention: thou shalt not stab thine enemy with a rusty bayonet, lest he catch blood poisoning.

The little wheelchair buzzed, and the entourage – three in front and three behind – clopped along on the grey-painted concrete floors, but he thought that he could still hear them. The crowd, chanting above him outside the court and slaughterhouse, unaware, perhaps, that he was only a few yards beneath their feet.

His surroundings changed without his knowledge. He was in a white room. The walls were white, the ceiling was white and the shining floor was white. There were no windows, he noticed. *How sad,* he thought.

The air smelled minty but with a hint of lavender, very soothing. He felt quite tired and wondered if Henry would be home soon. It would be good to share a nice cup of tea with him before bedtime. He missed Henry, wherever he had gone, perhaps he was playing in the old quarry again. Deacon smiled. He loved Henry, he was a splendid boy.

In front of him a red lamp lit up and Deacon instinctively lifted his head a fraction – not more, because it was somehow restricted – and peered at it. Then he heard a whoosh, a sort of burst of air pressure, and then

* * *

It took eight months and six days for Sterling Young's government to fold and leave office. George Deacon's conduct had been the catalyst for what turned into the most intensive period of investigations into a British government ever conducted. Though never proven, questions were asked about Deacon's involvement with a certain Terence Bowman, the Victoria Subway gunman.

People looked back to the beginning of GBIP's rise to popularity, and it coincided with Bowman's crime. Deacon had cleared the path into the Justice Ministry by killing his predecessor, King. And he invoked a national backlash against gun crime by employing Bowman. GBIP had cruised into Downing Street, and The Rules began claiming lives.

The last life it claimed was Mr George Deacon's.

Author's Note

I write crime thrillers, and have done since 1996, the same time I became a CSI here in Yorkshire. All of my books are set in or around our biggest city of Leeds. I don't write formulaic crime fiction; each one is hand-crafted to give you a flavour of what CSIs encounter in real life. Every book is rich with forensic insight to enhance your enjoyment.

Get in touch.

For more information, or to sign up for my Reader's Club, visit www.andrewbarrett.co.uk. I'd be delighted to hear your comments on Facebook (and so would Eddie Collins) and Twitter. Email me and say hello: andrew@andrewbarrett.co.uk

You can make a big difference.

Did you enjoy this book? I hope you did. Honest reviews of my books help bring them to the attention of other readers. So if you've enjoyed this book I would be very grateful if you could spend just five minutes leaving a short review.

Reader's Club Download Offer

GET A **FREE** BEST-SELLER AND A **FREE** SHORT STORY.

Building a relationship with my readers is one of the best things about writing. I occasionally send newsletters with details of new releases, special offers, and other news.

Sign up to the <u>Reader's Club</u> at <u>www.andrewbarrett.co.uk</u>, and I'll send you these **free** goodies as a thank you:

The Third Rule, the first book in the Eddie Collins series – a 500-page best-seller.

The Lift – a first person short story. Climb inside Eddie's head and see life as he does.

Subject to change without notice

<u>Did you enjoy **The Third Rule**? Want to know what's next?</u>

Buy **Black by Rose** to find out who put a gun to Eddie's head!

  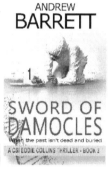

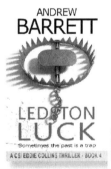 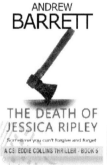 

Try a CSI Eddie Collins short story or a novella. Read them from behind the couch!

 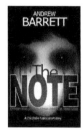 

Have you tried the SOCO Roger Conniston trilogy?

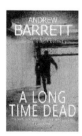  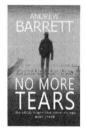

How about a stand-alone psychological thriller that will leave you shocked?

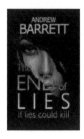

Thanks!

There's a long list of people to thank for helping to pull this book, and all of my books, into something that reads like it was written by someone who knew what they were doing. Among them is my amazing wife, Sarah, who makes sure I get the time to write in the first place. There can't be too many people who accept "I want to think of things" as a valid excuse to avoid life for a while - but it seems to work!

To Kath Middleton, and Alison Birch from re:Written, a huge thank you for making sure the first draft wasn't the final draft - you will always be the first people to read my books, and consequently always the first to point and laugh at my errors. It's because of you that this book has turned out so well, and it's because of me that you had so much work to do to get it there.

Thanks also to my Facebook friends in the UK Crime Book Club, my Andrew Barrett page, and my Exclusive Readers Group for their constant encouragement - who knew readers could be so assertive, demanding... and kind.

The Third Rule

is dedicated to my second dad, Bruce Jowitt; a man I admire very much.

© Copyright 2019

Printed in Great Britain
by Amazon

76700005R00305